Sean Cassidy

Claire Davis is the author of *Winter Range,* winner of the Pacific Northwest Booksellers Award and the Mountains and Plains Booksellers Award for Fiction in 2001. Her short fiction has been featured in *The Pushcart Prize* anthology and *Best American Short Stories.* She lives in Lewiston, Idaho, where she teaches writing at Lewis-Clark State College.

Also by Claire Davis

Winter Range

Claire Davis

Season of the Snake

Picador
St. Martin's Press
New York

www.picadorusa.com

Picador® is a U.S. registered trademark and is used by St. Martin's Press under license from Pan Books Limited.

For information on Picador Reading Group Guides, as well as ordering, please contact Picador.
Phone: 646-307-5629
Fax: 212-253-9627
E-mail: readinggroupguides@picadorusa.com

Grateful acknowledgment is made for permission to reprint the following: From *Reign of Snakes* by Robert Wrigley, copyright © 1999 by Robert Wrigley. Used by permission of Penguin, a division of Penguin Group (USA), Inc.

Library of Congress Cataloging-in-Publication Data

Davis, Claire, 1949–
    Season of the snake : a novel / Claire Davis.
      p. cm.
    ISBN 0-312-42564-3
    EAN 978-0-312-42564-7
    1. Married women–Fiction. 2. School principals–Fiction. 3. Remarried people–Fiction. 4. Herpetologists–Fiction. 5. Secrecy–Fiction. 6. Sisters–Fiction. 7. Idaho–Fiction. I. Title.

PS3554.A933414S43   2005
813'.6–dc22   2004056483

First published in the United States by St. Martin's Press

First Picador Edition: March 2006

10 9 8 7 6 5 4 3 2 1

To my sister, Mary Wolfgram,
for her unwavering faith and love

To Kim Barnes
sister in heart and letters

And to my son, Brian Wroblewski,
as always

Acknowledgments

I want to thank Margo Maresca, good friend, fellow horsewoman, and driving force of nature—now you can stop asking, "Is it done yet?" Thanks to friends, and fellow artists, Ellen Vieth and Ray Esparsen, for the downtime at the studio. I also want to offer my thanks to poet Bob Wrigley for his support and his friendship. My thanks, as always, to David Long, mentor and friend, who had the patience to listen to entire chapters over the phone. Thanks to Dr. Betsy VanClief and Dr. Marika Botha, for introducing me to the canyon. My thanks to Dr. Tom Urquhart, for his help with reference material, and his anecdotal stories that were too good to pass up. Thanks also go to Dr. Keegan Schmidt, for his delightful lectures on the geology of Hells Canyon, and to the LCSC Geology Club—thanks for the boat rides, folks. My thanks for the support and friendship of fellow faculty at Lewis-Clark State College, in particular: Dr. Bernice Harris, Division Chair; and Dr. Dene Thomas, President of Lewis-Clark State College. And to the people of the Lewiston/Clarkston Valley, who have made this amazing valley home; although I've used some of the names of buildings and streets in the valley, you can breathe easy, folks—none of the characters, or events related to the characters, is real.

A text that was of significant help in referencing the history and geology of Hells Canyon was *Snake River in Hells Canyon*, by Johnny Carrey, Cort Conley, and Ace Barton (Backeddy Books, 1979).

In referencing anecdotal stories and folk tales, two particular texts were of note: *Rattlesnakes*, by J. Frank Dobie (Castle Books, 1962) and *Rattlesnakes: Their Habits, Life Histories and Influence on Mankind* by Laurence M. Klauber (University of California Press, 1982).

Season of the Snake

Prologue

I t is a plague, a hatch of a hundred years rising up out of the swamp-land tributaries of the Mississippi River. A dry storm, a kinetic crosswind of insects—mayflies—pulpy bodies thick and long as a child's finger, bearing great glassine wings and trailing twin streamers from the base of tapered tails. They form a clot in the air three miles wide and a hundred feet deep that stretches from this small town of Trempaleau through Onalaska and LaCrosse and beyond. The air is a ferment: water, mud, a humus of greens and rot, a fishy Mississippi backbite. It is Wisconsin, the upper Mississippi, the river green and pitchy as it courses through a broad veldt of marshlands, around and over a string of tree-tufted islands, or channels below outcrops of limestone and tree-lined bluffs. It is evening on the cusp of summer.

The streets are mostly emptied, the summer play of children cut short. There are the brave few who run errands, dash between car and store or home. Or the three teen boys escaping TV reruns and earnest parents, who band together to wander the fleshy swarm, pretending to eat them, or pull them out of their noses; who scuffle down the street and shovel the insects into mailboxes, pack them like shotgun pellets into the tailpipes of parked cars. By the end of the evening, their hooded sweatshirts and sagging jeans are armored in bugs. But the majority of people huddle in homes and turn televisions louder. For them, it is just another storm to weather through. Every few hours, they will shake themselves loose from sofas or recliners and rise on stiff legs to peer out the windows, where they will stand, wagging their heads at the sight, already tallying up the hours and expense to clean the mess. Some few of them, while staring at the peculiar blur of streetlamps—the yellow light that is the congregate color of the hatch, and the ocean of movement, a million and more bodies channeled in currents and countercurrents, a whirlpool, an ebb—will imagine what it would be like to step into that atmosphere, but they turn their backs instead and trundle off to bed to sleep and dream, not understanding why, of drowning.

Dogs refuse to go out, planting feet at the door, turning tail on the sleeping porches, where the insects pummel the screens in a complicated hail or slip in under the door to tremble in tangled husks on the wicker furniture. Outside, the glutted birds have lumbered back to their roosts, while the neighborhood cats, hours past the initial playful swats and the first tasty bits, are desperate to escape the great weight of insects latching onto fur, bristling down cat backs and fluttering in ears and eyes, so that even the calmest and fattest of them have gone feral, attacking one another, or biting the air, or their own coated backs and limbs.

The night is thick with the slaughter; the insects clog the gutters, pile deep in window wells, blow across the lawns in drifts of carcasses. The streets are greased with them, and where the asphalt has slumped under years of traffic and the boggy heat, the husks fill the grooves, so that tires grip and spin even at the slowest speeds.

Nance and her husband, Joe, who have never lived through such a hatch, who have, in fact, consigned such things to the Old Testament or the odd calamities of Third World countries, find themselves driving the five miles to Onalaska, creeping along with what little traffic there is. It's worse than any fog—a common-enough hazard in this place—the air gone animate.

"I can't go any faster," Joe says.

"I'm not asking," Nance replies.

"You're thinking it."

She frowns, but his attention is focused on the the blizzard of insects pelting the windshield, piling inches deep in the gutter between windshield and hood—he has had to stop twice to clear them out. The inside of the car smells of their small meat frying on the manifold. His hands are white on the steering wheel, his back rigid. They have learned not to use the windshield wiper, some of the streaky goo still resined onto the blades. She wants to tell him, Take your time. She's sure her sister's safe now, in the hospital. Having survived this latest, and the worst yet.

She sighs, pats her cropped dark hair in place. She's trying to find some calm, something to center herself on, what with the phone call from their father—her sister beaten again, another *bad* man—and then the slick roads. They are driving blind through this rain of insects, the glittering, sticky pastiche of wings on the hood and road illuminated each time a car drifts by on the left.

They try music. Turn it off. Conversation falls mute under the concussion of flies. In Onalaska, they drive past the dozen or so mom-and-pop motels, the inns and courts, pink and green tubes of neon muted beneath the crush of bodies that droop in swags or hang pendent in fleshy stalactites.

They park in the hospital lot, jog to the emergency entrance with jackets held up over their heads. Nance feels the small creatures lighting on her hands, hears the little percussions against the denim. The sidewalk crunches beneath her feet.

They slip through the hospital's sliding doors and the cloud drafts in with them. When Nance steps onto the linoleum, her soles thick with gumbo, she sees the tracks of those who have gone before her. She shrugs an apology to a janitor pushing a long-handled mop back and forth across the mess, but the man gives no quarter, scowling at the mess they've brought in. She moves on, shaking her jacket of insects, sweeping them off her legs and arms, casting them from her fingers like lesser jewels.

They're directed two floors up, where her sister's been admitted for the evening. Under the banks of fluorescent, everyone looks shell-shocked. Not just the usual emergency room gothic, it's more pervasive: a strangeness about the eyes, fidgety hands.

Outside her sister's door, Nance prepares herself. *How bad this time?* As if Joe has read her mind, he takes her hand, squeezes it, says, "It'll be fine." She sets her shoulders and strides in. She manages to balance concern with calm, even when she sees the shaved square on Meredith's scalp, the stitched skin. That's what she has the most trouble with—the redness of the scalp, the way it puckers, like lips sewn shut.

Meredith passes a hand over the side of her head, tugging a long shank of hair over the wound, like a privacy curtain. "It's not that bad, Sis," she says. "Hey, Joe." She smiles, extends a hand, and he takes it.

He thumbs the medical bracelet. "Nice," he says. "Cost much?"

"This is not funny," Nance says. She gives her sister a too-hard hug, surprised, as she always is, at how solid her sister feels, even here, floating and insubstantial against the white hospital sheets, her face curiously rouged. Nance touches the skin.

Meredith winces. "Rug burns."

Nance's finger lifts away. "That son of a bitch—"

"Is in jail. For the night at least." She looks around. "Me too, I guess."

Joe shakes his head. "Food's better there." He pulls up a chair, seats himself.

"You would know?"

"Little Sister, it would surprise you—the things I know."

"Where's Pop?" Nance asks.

"I sent him for coffee. You know how he can be."

Nance knows: their father's inability to cope on a daily level with crisis, as when their mother struggled with cancer, her subsequent death. It wasn't that he fell apart, exactly. Rather, he became strangely . . . ineffective, though he managed to work every day, bring home a paycheck. Still, in the smallest, most necessary ways, he grew incompetent: tying shoes, cooking meals, doing laundry. The business of living. Long months after their mother had passed away from the cancer, they would stumble across bills—a phone bill, say, tucked in the bottom of the sock drawer, or the electric bill in a book on the shelf. "I meant to pay that," he'd say, or, as an explanation, "I had it in my hand, and then it simply wasn't there anymore," and he'd shrug and walk away. They'd learned to make do, the girls, which mostly meant Nance, twelve at the time and the older of the two, who'd become the housekeeper, the accountant, and mother to Meredith.

Meredith fingers the remote on her bed, and it hums into place behind her back. "I can go home tomorrow."

"Home?"

Meredith nods. "As in *home*. With Dad."

"He know yet?"

"Thought I'd let you tell him."

Nance shrugs. "He'll be relieved. We all will. Christ, Sis. How many times—"

Joe stands. "I'll just go check on your dad. He's probably touring the maternity ward." He hands Nance into the emptied chair, leans down and kisses her on the cheek. He whispers in her ear, "*Be nice. She's been hurt enough,*" then plucks a mayfly from Nance's hair, gently puts it in her hand. And then he's strolling out the door, while Nance wishes she, too, could skip this next part, turn away as easily as he has.

Out in the corridor, there's the dinging of a pager and a soft voice calling for doctor so-and-so. A nurse leads an old man past the door; he looks in at the sisters—a long, wobbling stare—then shuffle-walks onward, an IV on wheels dogging his heels.

"They still out there?" Meredith asks. "The bugs."

Nance nods, looking at the insect in her hand. The mayflies of the insect order Ephemeroptera, meaning "lasting but a day." The adult *Hexagenia*. Winged. Soft-bodied and elongated. She glances over at the window. "This is probably the worst of it. This evening. These will be dead by morning, and the hatch'll taper off over the next few days." She knows this because she researched it that morning, when the hatch began. Fascinating, these odd bits about the natural world. She's just finished her undergraduate work, with a major in biology, and is considering a graduate degree. Perhaps teach the sciences, as their dad has done all his working life. Though she's not sure she has the patience to work with children. She holds the insect closer, studies its many-jointed body, the short inconspicuous bristles that are its antennae. The large head with its prominent eyes. Its wings: triangulate, membranous, a delicate crosshatch of veins. "They're mating, you know. They only live a few hours."

Meredith shakes her head, a quirky grin on her lips. "Figures." She raises a hand to her scalp, fingering the sutures. When she puts the hand back into her lap, she stares into it. "I fucking knew, Sis. From early on this morning, I just *knew* this was going to happen. Dex was edgy. On his feet and jumpy, moving from room to room. Like he was looking for someone to take on."

Nance nods.

Meredith looks over at the window, where mayflies speckle the glass like pale ghosts. "And then those goddamned bugs come up from the river. Like the fight he's been looking for, except there's no one to swing at. It was crazy. I look out in the backyard, and there he is . . . stumbling around, throwing punches."

"Drunk."

Meredith shakes her head. "Damnedest sight. Damned fool."

Nance bites her lip, sighs.

"Hey, you got something to say here, just jump on in." Meredith snugs the sheets higher.

"So why didn't you leave? When you could?"

Meredith looks at Nance, but her expression is blank, as if she hasn't heard the question correctly, or as if Nance hasn't asked the correct question, but Nance is tired of second-guessing. They have a history of this.

"You think I asked for it?" Meredith says.

"Christ," Nance says. "You said yourself, you expected it. You saw this coming. So what do you do? Sit around and wait for it. What am I supposed to make of that?"

"Whatever you goddamn please," Meredith says.

Nance hunches forward in the chair. "You know, every time this shit happens, we end up having this same argument, whether it's at some bar, or a motel, or at Dad's house. Only now it's the hospital. So what's next? The morgue? Don't you look at me that way. You're not the only one being hurt by this. Your life's a string of wrecks, and frankly, I'm sick of picking up the pieces."

"Yeah, so who asked you to. Or maybe you're one of those people who like to come gawk at the latest pileup, so you can feel that much smarter."

Nance shakes her head. She wants to say, Grow up. Get a life, and stop fucking with mine. But it's all been said before, any number of times, and then she's relieved of the exercise when their father enters, followed by Joe.

She rises, gives her dad a quick peck on the cheek, and offers him the chair, but he waves it off. Instead, he arranges coffees and creamers on the hospital tray, pulls out a pocketful of crackers, as if it's a party. Nance is taken by how slight her father's become, how stooped. Surely he shouldn't look this ... old? He's only in his sixties, after all. Perhaps Meredith's at the heart of that, as well.

Nance crosses to the window. The mayfly's still in her hand, and she places the small creature on the sill. Below, the hospital parking lot is transformed by the luminous cloud rolling under the mercury lamps. All that frenzy. A genuine, damned orgy. She wonders what it's like, the abbreviated life of hours, with all your body given over to that one thing, the consummate consummation—a craving like none she's ever understood, the body honed to its most efficient end, so that even the mouth parts are nonfunctioning, fused in service to that greater appetite.

She changes focus and sees the whites of the bed and her sister's hospital gown reflected against the dark pane, how harshly angular her sister seems. She is struck again by how *diminished* her sister appears, and suddenly Nance's own life seems embarrassingly blessed: a happy marriage, her home, her school and work toward a career. Everything falling in place so *effortlessly* that it feels sometimes suspiciously ordained rather than earned. Not that she hasn't worked for it with school, and the day-to-day business of marriage. But wasn't it always Nance whom people had the highest hopes for? Teachers. Friends. Her own father: "I can always count on little Nance here. Such practical feet to stand on." Perhaps that's the thing that sets her apart from her sister? A disposition toward discipline. For surely it's not just a matter of luck—a coincidence of place and events and people. She's willing to concede there's some of that, but she also believes in a greater level of self-determination: a willingness to apply yourself, to be aware, to direct your own life.

But of the two of them, what set her so solidly on this safer path? What determined her practical nature? Being the firstborn? Necessity? The luck of the draw?

The thought startles her, and she is surprised by a fluttering in her chest, a rattle of fear she attributes to the smells of the hospital, to the rain of insects outside, and to her sister's pain. She is moved to compassion for Meredith, a softening of her anger.

She looks at the scene below the window. Traffic is creeping down the side streets, and where the bridge spans a side channel on the river, the yellow lights of city trucks perforate the dark. They are plowing the bridge, and she can imagine the spent bugs scraped off the pavement, the *beep beep* as the trucks lift their blades, back up, and then push forward again. She glances over her shoulder at her sister sipping coffee through lips bruised and sutured. Nance shakes her head, looks back out at the night, at the bridge where the plows scoop up the dead. She imagines the congregate weight. Pictures the wake of bugs spilling off the side of the bridge. A charnal rain. The thick skin forming on the river. The savage feeding of fish.

It's a bit of a shock, these bugs, here one day and gone the next—all but the carcasses, which are already beginning to give off a fishy stench. There's the drone of streetsweepers, and some few people revving up leaf blowers or mulching mowers. They'll work diligently throughout the day, ridding themselves of this short-lived affliction, though for long months afterward they'll come upon the remains of mayflies in the bottom of laundry baskets, between sidewalk cracks. Frying in lamp globes, or mashed between the cushions of lawn furniture.

For now, the worst of it is brushed aside, piled into mounds, bagged as garbage, or scooped into trucks and hauled away. Up and down the streets, home owners turn garden hoses on vinyl siding and windows, and trust a good rain to do the rest. Nance and Joe have shoveled out their window wells, and raked the drifts out from under the boxwood hedge. Five black lawn bags sit full on the grass. Joe jokes, calls them body bags.

The rain gutters are next. Joe's teetering atop the ladder, snaking a hose down a rainspout, feeling it jam, and shoving it down, forcing it in deep and deeper. Nance doesn't necessarily trust his judgment on these matters, but she holds her tongue and feeds him line.

"That's it," she says.

He gives her a thumbs-up. "Turn it on."

"I'm holding the ladder."

He looks down over his shoulder. "Then you'll have to let go, won't you." He gives her a crooked smile.

"You really—"

"Just turn it on."

She wonders about his safety, perched as he is atop the final step, and the uneven footing beneath the ladder's feet. He's got a red kerchief knotted around his head. He looks like a pirate with a foot on the plank.

"Nance?"

"I'm going," she says, lets go with one hand, then another. She steps back and studies the ladder, then hurries over to the outdoor spigot.

"Well? You gonna turn it on, or what?"

"I did."

He looks over and down at her, his eyes rolling. "Turn it all the way."

"I don't think—"

"Nance." His voice grates. His knees wobble below the cut of his shorts. "Just do it."

She sighs. She turns the knob hard to the right, hears the gush, the spit and snort of water traveling up the hose, up and over and down into the packed chute. She already knows what will happen—the water hitting the wall of debris, then shooting back up, erupting in a geyser from the narrow mouth atop the roof, a Vesuvius of filth: blackened leaf marl, bug husks, twigs, last year's maple seeds, cottonwood fluff—all of it gone to rot and stink. And, yes, Joe's a direct hit. Nance has only the briefest moment to gloat before she understands the next step in the sequence, the way his body rocks backward, hand grabbing air, the ladder teetering, as in a cartoon, with a slow-motion tip and fall, and Joe holding the air for that brief instant before falling, as well.

Only he doesn't–fall.

He's swinging from the roof, hanging by one arm, one hand around the hose, the far end of which, firmly wedged somewhere down the length of rainspout, has become a lifeline. The geyser cut off by the crimp.

Nance loses it, drops to her knees laughing, and then he's lowering himself, sliding down the blackly greased rubber. Nance is bundled on the lawn, arms around her sides and laughing, saying, "Oh my God. Oh my God."

He drops the last feet, stands and wipes his hands down the shorts wet and dark with the remains of mayflies, as are his legs and chest and arms, his head and the kerchief, which he takes off and shakes out. Nance is still laughing. The ugly fountain has started up again, dirt spewing out of the gutter head, leaving a black streak down the white siding.

"You think this is funny?" he asks.

She nods. She's on her knees and taking deep breaths.

He looks at himself, at her, and then he's crossing the lawn to where she's kneeling. Slings her up under an arm.

She's surprised by the suddenness of his action, the physicality, the awkward angle at which she hangs at his side. It hurts, bunched this way against his bony hip. When she understands what he intends, she's peeling at his fingers and hollering, "Don't you dare, don't you–"

But of course he does. Holds her under the filthy spout, getting wetter and dirtier himself, and when at last he drops her in the muddy grass, and she looks up at him, he's grinning, like the young boy she first knew him as, and it quickens something in her. Starts her grappling with his knees. She is a small, compact woman, surprisingly strong, and she's laughing, and tugging at his legs and then his shorts, so that his hands are kept busy holding on to them, at risk of losing his drawers out here on the lawn, in plain sight.

"Cut it out," he's saying. "Cut it out."

She goes at it harder, and then he's on his knees next to her, and they're still getting drenched, and then he has his hand on her breast, on the shirt gone slippery, and he's kissing her. And perhaps it's the momentum of the drop, the narrow escape from the fall. Perhaps it's the release of tension Nance feels as well, from his close call, or her sister's release from the hospital. Or, just as likely, a combination of both, along with the odd circumstance of mayflies, their great littering orgy, that has Nance and Joe in a struggle gone intensely sexual, and then Joe's up on his feet and pulling her after him. She just has time to break away and turn off the hose before following him up the stairs and through the back door and down the short hallway to their room, where they spend the next long while stripping down, lifting the leaf marl from armpits, the windowpane wings of flies from behind an ear, or stuck glassy to their backs. And each touch growing fiercer, until they are making love on the floor, atop the shamble of clothes, and finding the taste of each other is salt and earth.

It's late afternoon by the time they get back on track, cleaned up and garden tools in hand, but throughout the remainder of their workday, there are those quick looks over the shoulder at each other, Nance's soft sighs, and the sudden bursts of energy from Joe that remind them, and then one or the other will smile, or breathe a little quicker, anticipating the evening stretched ahead, or, for that matter, the lazy days of summer that have just begun.

In the days ahead, Nance will most often think of these few hours. That quiet complacency of the afternoon, the feel of skin where her husband has touched her. The way he teases her after making love: *"Next time, I bet I can do better than that,"* and *"Didn't you used to ride horses?"* and *"Sweet Jesus, but you are one fine woman."* She remembers the denseness of her lips. Her limbs insubstantial. It's these moments that she will play over and over, as well—the way she closes her eyes and breathes deeply, smells the rift of newly turned soil on the garden trowel in her hands. The smell of river water, and bridal wreath blooming against the fence. The sweet-sour smell of sex that even the shower afterward does not absolutely obliterate. And beneath it all the not-yet-unpleasant ferment of insects. She will hone these moments. This quiet time, the lull afterward, the calm anticipation of just another evening together.

This is before the phone call. The one from her father, saying: "Meredith's gone to the apartment to get some things. I'm not sure she should have done that." And Nance's conviction, even as she reassures her father to the contrary, that something bad is coming.

After a hesitation in which she questions her need to step in, she turns to her husband.

He's in the bedroom, slipping into his jogging clothes: shoes, shorts, and T-shirt. He slings the Walkman around his neck. "Call her up."

"There's no answer."

"Well, she's probably left already." He looks up. "Don't you think?"

Nance shakes her head. "I don't know. Maybe . . ."

"You worry too much."

She stands with her hands on her hips, resolute.

"I'm going to have to go over there, aren't I?" He leans in, gives her a peck on the top of her head. When he steps away, he asks, "What's the chances we let her figure it out on her own?"

Nance is moving now, brushing past him. "Fine," she says. "Never mind. I'll just drive over myself."

Joe snatches her arm, holds on. "I didn't say I wouldn't." He's shaking his head. "I'll go, all right?" He pulls her into his arms. "Tell you what. I'll go, but you gotta cook *and* do dishes tonight."

"Blackmail?"

"You betcha."

"Deal."

He laughs, buffs her cheek with a kiss. "See ya, Babe."

"Joe? You be careful."

"Always." He grins. At the door, he turns back one more time. "And none of those one-pot meals, you hear? Two, three courses. Lots of *greasy* pots and pans. I want the pleasure of seeing you dressed in an apron and up to your arms in a hot, sloppy tub of dishes."

"It's the rubber gloves, isn't it?"

"Oh baby," he says, and then he's out the door, Walkman strapped over his ears.

Early evening. A Saturday. Lawns are emptying, the last of the cleaning done for the day. People are drifting into houses where they turn on the first lights. He likes to jog this time of evening down tree-lined streets that are plumb and true. These are comfortable blocks of middle-income housing. Lots of young couples with the start of families in mind. It's the south end of town, one of the older sections, with a gentrified air and es-tablished trees, its respectfully aging bungalows—Craftsman-era homes with open room plans and built-ins: bookcases, window seats, timbered ceilings, hardwood floors.

He passes the elementary school, a long, rambling one-story building with a playground bound in cyclone fence, the same fence he used to hang on as a young kid, stuck in the school yard and longing to be out there in the larger world. He'd been a curious child, impatient with be-ing young. Perhaps some part of him, even then, sensing the urgency of this business of living.

He runs a little faster, blowing through his mouth with each exhala-tion. At the park entrance, he turns in between the twin columns of lan-nonstone. The asphalt is patched with shadow, the air he passes through pearling with the late-afternoon light. The path narrows, wanders be-tween shaggy arborvitae and wilted stands of iris. He jogs by the willow-lined lagoon. Swans lived here when he was younger, but now there're only a few mallards skimming the jewelweed. He passes the old boat-house where, back in the park's heyday, they used to rent out rowboats of a Sunday afternoon. As he jogs past the concrete porch, a covey of mourning doves startles up with a whistling *whew whew whew*. He's coming into the farthest portion of the park, where the path forks. Asphalt wanders right. To the left is a dirt path, a service road ground into the grass. He swings down the packed dirt. Here are the service buildings, park vehicles, rigs on blocks, engines in repair. Mounds of mulch and dirt, the slash from the flowering crabs, the remains of an oak felled by lightning. Here the trees are more densely leaved, the older oaks inter-rupted by stands of hawthorne and wild rose, the thatch of poison ivy that will never fully die. He wants to hurry his pace. It's dimmer be-neath the heavy wood, though the upper canopy seems brighter for the shadowed deeps, and so he runs with his face turned up to where a sil-ver light lattices the limbs, torches the green in a cool fire. Birds flit through the branches. There is birdcall, the buzz of flies, the ground be-neath his feet resonating like a drum, though he hears none of this with the Walkman filling his ears.

This is the way he is running: face turned up, arms pumping, knees lifting, his breath in small sounds like *ah, ah, ah, ah*. He is singing rhythm, a syncopated beat that nearly trips him up, so that he laughs when he stumbles. Picture this: the young man running through the woods, the dappled light—flash, shadow, flash. The end of the park an-other quarter-mile jog, just the other side of that wall of trees.

This is when the young boys catch up. They have come at him from behind, a hard sprint out of the trees. Out of the doldrums they've stewed in for most of the day. The vapid looks they give one another. Their fretting impotence. Three teenage boys stalled in the tracks of a world that won't stop long enough to let them jump aboard. Three rea-sonably well-to-do young men who can't squander their days fast enough, who can't locate the blame for a parent too strict or tolerant, for days too cold, nights too hot, for the girls who won't give it up, and the friends who fuck them over.

It's just a game—tagging along behind this guy. Another mild distrac-tion, like the baseball bat the one young man has stolen. The one that swings in his hands even as he's running. A game. Nothing more serious than the detergent they poured into the park fountain, or the late-night phone calls to random numbers. The bugs they packed into tailpipes the night before. They're just entertaining themselves. A bit of fun. Keeping that one stride behind, so that the guy, clueless, doesn't even notice them there. And the kid with the bat raises it and swings. Strike one, the aluminum splices the air behind the jogger's back. Strike two. The kid's almost upon him—the jogging guy—and he's lifting his knees high and higher in imitation. He's enjoying how goofy-looking he must be, and he's glancing back over at the other two, who are grinning now, pumping their legs and arms in imitation, as well. High and higher. Egging him on. Yelling, *outa the park.* And the boy, running on the heels of the man, suspended on the edge of a moment that will forever alter him, the young boy grips the bat tight, takes a deep breath.

He swings.

Book I

Ah, but it was something to have at least a choice of nightmares.

—*Heart of Darkness*, Joseph Conrad

Chapter One

O n the valley floor, the morning fog rises, a slow unveiling of trees, homes, and hills banked like cooling coals on three sides. The clean hills—an ascent of a thousand feet and more—limned in a woolly nap of cloud. The valley floor is T-boned by two rivers, and bunched about the banks on either side of the greater river are the small towns of Lewiston and Clarkston. On an inlet of this larger body of water, the Snake River, is Swallow's Nest Marina. A boat launch. A dip in the road, a bit of park, and a parking lot abutting the single boat ramp and floating dock. The dock planks are patchy with damp, and while the captain ferries equipment into the aluminum jet boat, Nance oversees how it is stowed. She does a rapid count of boxes, and fusses in her pocket searching for her list. It's not a thing she routinely does, make lists. *And this is why. Just another thing to lose.* She looks over at Ned, a tall brown-haired man standing at the back of the craft. Her husband. Sometimes it startles Nance, even now, to realize he is connected to her, or perhaps, more accurately, it is that she's surprised by the way her life has turned around again. Ned's standing with a foot hiked up on the back bench, and he's staring down into the water, where a school of blunt-headed carp mosey about on the stony bed.

"Ned? Did I give my list to you?"

He looks over his shoulder. "You don't do lists."

"I did this time."

He picks through a pocket, shakes his head.

"How about the other one." She points to his chest.

He pats his suit coat. "You don't make lists," he says again.

She plants a fist on her hip, looks up over the boat rail, up the dock. There are still boxes to be on-loaded, foodstuff mostly. The camping gear's stowed, the jugs of water. Down the shoreline where the cotton-woods crowd, her sister Meredith's turning something over in the sand with the toe of a shoe. Nance watches. It's been years since she's seen her sister, and she hadn't anticipated seeing Meredith for several more. But there she is, and now Nance is trying to understand how she feels about it.

Meredith squats on her heels, head bent, brown hair fanning over cheeks. She picks up a stick and prods whatever it is at her feet. And then she's snapping to a stand and backing away. Her nose wrinkles and she's rubbing the tip of her shoe clean in the sand.

Nance sighs. Some things never change, she thinks. She looks over at her husband. "I know I made one. . . ." She pats the back pocket in her jeans, pulls out a folded piece of paper.

Ned's rubbing the back of his neck with a hand; he grins. "Getting scary, Nance." He walks over, lifts the list clear, glances at it. "You really got all this?"

She looks around. "It's that or eat what we catch."

"Now that's an intriguing idea." He makes a face. "Still, it's only nine days and two women. You've got enough here for two weeks and a full crew."

"We'll be hungry," she says. "And hey, I have an idea—*you* could join us." Though she knows he has a genuine phobia about her work with snakes. "You could just stay at the camp, hang out. Relax."

He shakes his head. "I have work, too, Nance. Responsibilities."

Nance nods. It's part of what she finds so reassuring about Ned. She turns her face up. "Can't talk you into taking just one day off? Come along for the ride, and return with Pete."

He rests his chin on the top of her head. "I'm hardly dressed for a river trip. Some other time, okay?"

"Another time," she agrees, though it's always and never another time. She sighs. "Anyway, you're probably looking forward to being rid of me. You get to hog the bed–"

"Tell you what." He gives her a kiss on the forehead. "I'll make a point of missing you every evening." He glances at his watch.

Nance raises her face, and he kisses her–a long, sweet kiss that's mildly embarrassing in front of the captain and especially her sister. But when they finish, Nance sees Meredith's back is turned. The captain has the last box stowed.

"Looks like we're a go," she says, and walks Ned to the boat's edge. "Take care. Remember to eat." She tucks a finger in his waistband. "I'll see you in nine days."

He smiles. "I'll see *you* in my dreams." He rolls his eyes in a mock swoon.

She's pleased with the play, but she also feels a bit ridiculous to be so apparently in love with her own husband. Her sister's settling into the back of the boat, and the captain's waiting on Nance to pull the lines. She reaches for them, and Ned bends over, squeezes her hand.

"You be safe now, you hear?" he says. "I don't know what I'd do without you."

He looks so sincerely worried that Nance finds herself wanting to smooth the crease between his brows. At the same time, she feels strangely gratified to be this needed. It was such a long dry spell after Joe's death–seven years–first of grief, then a blessed numbness in which she neither needed nor wished to be needed by anyone else. Even now, she's surprised by how alive she's come to feel again during these three years of marriage to Ned.

"I'll be fine," she says, "as always."

He steps back, looks over Nance's head, and waves to Meredith. "Enjoy," he says, but there's a bite to his voice. He hands Nance the line, then strides up dock, frees the bowline, and tosses it to the captain.

The boat idles into the lagoon, and when Nance looks again, Ned has disappeared into the fog layering the upper lot. The mist holds to a ceiling just above their heads, and though the first light of the sun halos low in the atmosphere, for now, the three in the boat move into that corridor between cloud and water, pressing toward the river, where a great blue heron stands, its scissored head turning. The bird bounds upward, wings wading the air, legs trailing like an afterthought.

The jet boat swings into the main channel. It has a hull of lightweight aluminum, a canvas top, and Plexiglas windows: a riverboat designed by local boatwrights to navigate the rapids and shallows—the mouth of Hells Canyon. Nance tucks spare sweatshirts under the bucket seat. The captain, Pete Everwine, is a man in his early forties, features already blunted and rubbed to bedrock. Under the noise of the engine he's humming a tune as off-kilter and out of pitch as only a jet engine will allow. Nance glances at Meredith sitting on the bench seat in the boat's open back.

It'll be a three-hour bucketing ride up the Snake River. This journey has become for her just part of the job, getting where she needs to be—the depths of Hells Canyon, where she's conducting field research on the den attrition rates of rattlesnakes. They clear the park boundaries on the Clarkston, Washington, side. Across the way, on the opposite shore, is Lewiston, Idaho, where she's lived this past five years. Together, the two cities comprise the Lewiston-Clarkston Valley, with a population of roughly sixty thousand—large by Western standards. At a steady thirty-five miles per hour, they're cruising the slack-water pool created by the downriver dams of the Snake.

The Snake River. Boundary separating three states within an easy drive of the valley: Washington, Idaho, and Oregon. Ahead of them, the deepest gorge in North America, formed in a geological violence that uncoiled in increments mostly discernible only to the eye of God. From the Lewiston basin, a young 17 million years in age, they'll travel roughly 200 to 300 million geologic years up canyon.

They jet by the dipping beds of the Atlas quarry, where the floods that shaped the valley basin, the Missoula flood—600 million cubic feet per minute—and the subsequent Bonneville flood—18 million cubic feet per minute—are marked in two narrow lines of clay, one darker than the other. Sandwiched in the deposit is a lighter hash mark of volcanic ash from the Mount Mazuma eruption, a mere 7,500 years ago.

A cluster of cliffside homes reel away along the waterline and rise in staggered rows up the hillside. On the Idaho side, the Elks Club—roughly a two-hundred-foot climb. The building sits at the head of a landslide, a rubble of rock and dirt spearheading from the foot of the building and ending over the river road, where it forms an upstart archipelago on which a legion of yellow Cats and backhoes hum and worry like dim-witted bees. Erected in the sixties, the building sits on a sliding bed of alluvial clay, a kind of peanut butter and jelly composition that withstood the local geologist's gloomy predictions for thirty-odd years. Until this year, when after a spate of heavy rains and thaws, and under the additional weight of country club, irrigated golf course, a crosshatch of roads and subdivisions, it was discovered the hillside had been oozing out from beneath all along. The great pocket stopped just short of the club house, which stood like a grudge on the last ten feet of ground. An imprudent monstrosity with its darkly paneled walls, its many elk heads, and its shag-carpeted remains. *Serves it right*, Nance thinks.

They boat past Swallows Nest, a chunk of basalt angled out of the greening hills like the prow of a landlocked steamer, barnacled with the mudded nests of swallows. The banks are noisy with the birds, *such busy-bodies*, and some few dip and skitter across the river's surface like skipping stones, snatching up early insect hatches.

It's late March, and the water's a muddy mix of silt and early snowmelt. The peaks of the Blue Mountains, the Seven Devils, Waha, the Wallowas, and the Gospel Humps are snowcapped, weeks away from the major melt, by which time she'll already be safely home.

Twenty miles upriver, they pass Hellers Bar, with its small community of Rogersburg. It's the dead end of civilization: a clutch of homes, church, bar, minimart and gas pump. Here the real journey begins. Everwine throttles through the chop where the Grand Ronde converges. The hills are softer here, and broader, a green overlay of grass on a 200-million-year-old anomalous deposit of limestone.

Nance thinks to tell Meredith all this, but her sister's head is turned, so that what is visible is her brown hair rubber-banded into a roll like a fist at the back of her neck. Nance *is* pleased to see her, but she's also suspect of Meredith's overwhelming need to reconnect. Wonders *What's behind it?* Suddenly, night before last, she shows up on Nance's front stoop, 1,800 miles from their family home, where she lives, along the Mississippi, in LaCrosse, Wisconsin.

At the back of the boat, Meredith looks smaller, as people tend to against the backdrop of a mountain, or so much sky—a thing Nance has noticed since moving west, how humbling the landscape can be, how a wrong step, say, or a turn in the weather can set your perspective in order, or realign you in the food chain. But she also knows there's something about Meredith that has always provoked protection. At five five, she's taller than Nance, but less steady somehow. A thinly planed woman, a little underfed, with a square face and eyes deeply set. At thirty, she's younger than Nance by three years. Not a woman you'd call beautiful, no, but attractive. Enough to have been through one husband in a short six months at age eighteen, and any number of less than desirable men friends since, most of whom Nance has forgotten or never met in the first place.

She suspects another candidate's just been scratched off. For why else would Meredith show up, unannounced, tight-lipped and looking . . . snake-bit.

Everwine lines up with the channel markers, a line-of-sight course, and he swings the craft up and over the rollers, bores a parallel line to the white-capped curve, and guns it so that the back fishtails into the calm at the end. In the slower flow, he throttles down to root through a paper bag at his feet, from which he frees a thermos. Nance pours him a cup of coffee. "How about your sister?" he shouts. The captain's clearly on his way to smitten, and Nance, knowing the kind of man Meredith attracts, finds herself suddenly suspicious of his life outside of river guide.

Nance hands a cup of coffee to Meredith, then returns to the fore with a cup for herself. She takes a careful sip and her teeth ache with the heat, pain needling up behind her eyes, so that she blinks once and then again.

She loves her sister. Always has. Even during the worst of it. But *damned awkward.* She thinks about Ned's reaction when, over breakfast, he was informed of Meredith's unannounced late-night arrival. "Well, it's too late to do anything about it now," he said. "You'll have to take her with you."

"Ned, this is work, not a picnic."

He held up the slab of bread he was buttering, the blunt knife probing.

"I think you missed a spot," she said.

He smiled. His winsome smile. No other word for it, really. Ned. Gray eyes like washed stone. Charismatic, but effortless. A careless charm. On the downside: The way he butters bread. His horror of her career. His dislike of anything in the "great outdoors." His reticence about himself. "Maybe you don't want to know"—his boyish smile. "Maybe I'm just trying to spare you the worst." Her feeling that, for as well as she believes she knows him, there's something withheld, some knowledge exclusively in his keeping.

She'd meant to tell him that it would be difficult having Meredith up canyon. She'd get in the way. It wouldn't be safe. But she knew he'd scoff. "Right, but handling rattlesnakes is?" And truthfully, Nance knew it was up to her to do the right thing. Meredith was *her* sister, after all.

She'd meant to say this and more, but he was already off into the other room, as involved as he intended to be and as quickly absolved of dealing with the nettlesome sister-in-law.

They're entering a stretch of river where the orientation of the rocks changes, the canyon formation becoming part of an island arc system—volcanic islands akin to the Aleutians, drifted on plates into the continent, jammed into the great shelf of land that was to become North America. Here the canyon deepens, the river becomes chop, and then a series of broad watery steps that is Wild Goose Rapids. Meredith's hanging on two-handed to the back rail of the boat. In the calm afterward, she moves forward, face flushed, looking for more.

The morning sun breaks over the rim, limns the boat's ripples with a brittle light. Nance relaxes, lets Everwine describe the history of the place, the flight of the Nez Perce and Chief Joseph down this corridor. How the tribe crossed the Snake near the Imnaha River's confluence during the height of spring flooding. The women, the children. The horses.

The water's a hazy blue along the rock wall and bars of sand finger into drop-offs. They are moving and not moving. It's a dizzying sensation, stepping in time with the river without being taken in by it, for Nance knows that this river, with its one thousand miles of riverbed covering four states and its twenty-six dams, harbors in its depths sunken steamers, rafts, canoes, and dories. Entire forests—the effluent of a thousand spring melts—the bones of trees stirring in the hydraulics, and a stew of animals: elk and deer, coyote, cattle, horse, sheep, the numberless fish, the swallowed hatches of midge and gnat and salmon fly.

People, as well: the boating accidents, the suicides, the centuries-old murders. Nance stares into the water, half-believing she might see the thing she's always suspected—that larger world that moves beneath, the underside of daylight, the thing we write off to ill chance, bad luck, or circumstances. But there's only the drone of the engine.

The deeper they travel, the cooler it gets, and Nance hands a hooded sweatshirt to Meredith. "Put it on under your coat," she says.

Meredith stiffens at the suggestion but then bundles up.

Everwine combs his fingers through his graying hair. "You a snake wrangler like your sister?" When Meredith laughs, he says, "Rest of the family's normal, huh?"

"Everwine, who's paying for this trip?" Nance asks.

He turns to Meredith. "So. You come to visit and she takes you to the snakes." He shakes his head, turns to Nance. "I ever tell you 'bout my friend got chased by a snake once."

Meredith shifts in her seat. Nance rolls her eyes.

"No. Really. Hunk—"

"Hunk?" Meredith asks.

Pete nods. "Hunk Rabay, he's climbing the banks of the Clearwater, and this snake comes flying out of the rocks—"

"Flying," Meredith says.

Nance smiles. "Technical term."

He nods. "In a manner of speaking. It comes out, slithering and striking—"

"Slithering and striking," Nance says.

Everwine purses his lips. "Whose story is this anyway? This snake's hot on his heels, and Hunk races up the hillside, but when he gets to the top, the snake's *already* there. Waiting."

"How steep was the hill?" Meredith asks.

"How *slow* was this guy?" Nance asks.

Everwine shakes his head. "You two make a habit of ganging up on the unsuspecting?"

"It doesn't work as well if we serve notice," Nance says.

Everwine sniffs, swipes his nose with the side of a hand. "Well, I'm just telling you like it was told me. And that reminds me of another. One old-timer upriver saw two snakes choke down a shoat once."

Nance closes her eyes, keeps quiet. Really, she loves these tales.

"Said it was late summer when he saw these two big rattlers dancing up on their haunches, swaying back and forth. Twisting around each other, then they'd unwind and do it again."

Everwine tools the boat around a wedge of sandbars. "Well, this young shoat comes stumbling up on these two snakes. Now if it'd been a sizable sow or boar, it might have had a good feed—the big ones'll do that, you know, clear your property of snakes. But this little shoat . . ."

Everwine's hand cups, sways back and forth—a mock cobra that Nance doesn't bother to correct.

"Mesmerized," he says, and snaps his fingers. "The snakes strike him right in the face. Double dose. Pig seizes up, drops dead, and they start in on him."

Meredith's leaning in toward the older man. It's clear to Nance that Meredith is just as charmed by Pete. Nance sighs. *Same old, same old.*

"One snake's working on the head, the other on the—pardon the expression—ass end. Takes them the better part of a day to work their way across that pig, until they meet in the middle."

Meredith sits back.

Pete smiles. "End of the day, those snakes are trying to slip a jaw up on each other." He winks at Meredith. "Like thumb wrestling. You know, get the advantage. All through the night, they keep at it. By morning, they're pretty pooped.

"But one of them has slipped a corner of his jaw over the other's head, got a good purchase on an eye, and proceeds to devour the rest, as well. This here's the *interesting* part. He said you could see the outline of the snake inside still eating its way down the pig, while the one on top was eating him."

"Good grief," Meredith says. "Two meals for the price of one."

"Would have worked out that way, except the snake on top was the smaller of the two. Didn't have room for it all, and he set there a full day or two trying to digest that mess. Then a coyote comes along and has himself one heck of a meal."

Nance grins, leans her forehead against the window. It's one of the better ones.

They pass the confluence of the Salmon and the Snake rivers. The canyon walls are steep slabs, with undercuts where the water pools cold and black. Moss slicks the waterline, but above this the rock's abraded, a braille of flood and retreat. "Listen," he says, and cuts the engine. It takes a while for the thrum to quit in their ears, and at first it's the slap of the water against the hull, and then the smaller lick of water at stone. And then a hollow plocking—a tiny percolating that is the feeding of small fish. Down the canyon walls, the sun sheds a watery light on the lichens: rust and greens, blue and gold. A kingfisher skims through the gorge, and somewhere ahead another birdcall bells down the stone corridor.

"What ya think?" he asks Meredith.

She's staring upriver. "I had no idea it could be so . . ." Her hands fuss a moment, then open and release.

Satisfaction spreads across Everwine's face, her pleasure becoming his accomplishment.

Nance holds her breath. Beneath her feet, the craft ripples.

The first thing Ned looks for when he drives up to his school is the corner office that has become a second home. He parks on a side street, locks the car, and pockets the key. He's a little late—seeing Nance off on her trip upriver—and as he's usually prompt, he's sure the staff's concerned. He strides down the wide hallway. Along with the smell of waxed floors is that of coffee heating in the lounge. He greets the group that is nursing their first cups. His mug is prominently positioned on the shelf above the pot. He pours, adds cream, takes a sip, and lets out a long satisfying *aaah,* which gets the teachers laughing. He passes through the school office, where Cate Spencer, a long-legged red-haired woman in her forties, is seated behind the front counter. Glasses perched on her nose, she's studying the growing list of reported absences.

"Morning, Cate," he says. "How's it look?"

"Flu," she says, holding the list with two fingers, as if it is contagious.

There's a line of teachers waiting, and some bleary-eyed few have tissues wadded in their hands.

"Have Mattie issue a health bulletin," he says. Mattie being the school nurse, and the bulletin one they all know by heart: Wash hands, cover mouths when coughing, and don't share drinks. A standing joke among the teachers and staff, a timeless but futile gesture against the unwashed masses of K through six.

"Anything urgent?" he asks.

Cate stretches, and he notices a small button has popped open on her sweater. He studies the stack of messages.

"Not bad," he says as he shuffles through them. "I'll be in my office." He crosses to the door with PRINCIPAL'S OFFICE etched on frosted glass.

He sets the memos on his desk, turns to the window and unlatches it. The lead sash weights drop in their tracks as he lifts the frame. He enjoys this time, before the children arrive, before the ring of class bells, these few moments when he stands in front of the opened window, surveying the playground with its swing sets and monkey bars, suspension rope and sandbox, the soccer goals and basketball hoops. The rinky-dink T-ball diamond.

He's square on his feet, with hands clasped behind his back. The first cars are pulling up. On some mornings, he goes down to the cafeteria to take breakfast with these early arrivals, sitting in the small chairs, knees up around his elbows, teasing the little ones awake. It endears him to his faculty. He believes it keeps the cook staff honest.

Two elderly men in Day-Glo orange vests are at the crosswalk, their handheld stop signs propped against lawn chairs. In a half hour or so, the children will arrive in small droves. On the first and last week of school, he stands outside the door, making the children feel welcome. Letting them know who he is—their principal, and for the brief hours of the school day, a father to them.

He studies the street. There are the familiar cars, and a couple he doesn't recognize: a new canary yellow Volkswagen Beetle, a two-tone red-and-gray pickup truck—a Ford Ranger. There's also a delivery truck, and two men are wrestling a washer or dryer down a ramp, at the base of which is a woman with a roundhouse look about her—arms crossed over her chest—a look that suggests she'd like an excuse. Any excuse.

He's interrupted by a soft clearing of the throat. It's Cate. When he turns, she says, "Thought you might want to review the schedule for to-day's assembly."

He sees it's the fire chief today, and his dog, Sparky. Ned sighs. Hard to believe the aged dog's still on tour. Last year, incontinent or senile, Sparky lifted his leg onstage. The kids howled, and some of the youngest leaped from their seats, shouting, "*He peed! He peed!*" To give the chief credit, he took it in stride, told them, "*That's how Sparky puts out fires!*" The older kids snickered, while the younger ones' eyes grew round and solemn.

After the presentation, they moved to the school yard, where a fire truck waited with suited firemen and hose at the ready. Quite effective. But Ned couldn't help wondering if some of those littlest weren't expecting a battalion of dogs ready to lift their legs on command.

He spends the next minutes preparing his introduction. When he glances up again, it's only fifteen minutes before the first bell, and now he can hear the shouts and quarrels of children on the playground.

Ned swivels his chair, looks out over the street, and he picks his feet up, hooks his heels on the sill, and braces his hands behind his head. Down the streets, small groups of kids forge byzantine paths between houses, around trees and shrubs, and across the lawns.

It's going to be a fair spring day, and he briefly thinks about his wife on the river and feels a quick pang like a tic in his chest, an anxiousness in his lower back that he attributes to his already missing her. An echo of the rootlessness, the risk of a life lived without her. For he's come to appreciate his life with this woman. Rock-steady, his Nance. No-nonsense. He admires this most, how she keeps his life, *their lives* on track. He looks around his office, feels confident. Comfortable with his own presence, his job, his place in the community, his responsibilities. And he earnestly believes that without Nance, none of it would be real, that what success he'd achieved would be illusory. Understands it's she who keeps him here, who holds him as surely in this chair and office as in their bed at night, who lights their rambling two-story house with her voice and step.

He thinks of her on the river. Imagines he can feel her drawing farther away, and the stitch that ravels his life pulled thin and thinner. What if something goes wrong. He thinks of the sister, the risk she poses. He should have shrugged off the suit coat for a day, gone upriver. *One day. Little enough to ask.* What's here that couldn't wait? But then his phone rings, and on the other end of the line, the food distributor says something about substituting ham for hot dogs. "It's not a recall, you understand. But we don't want to risk it," he says, and then "Thanks." When Ned hangs up, he rocks forward and out of his chair.

He's noticed the Ranger is still out there, and that a group of kids have approached the pickup. *Probably nothing.* But he doesn't really believe that, and so he leaves the office. He wings a smile at Cate, tells her he'll be right back.

He jogs down the hallway and out the side door. On the playground, he smiles, pats a few children on the head or shoulders. Then he's out the fence and crossing the street. He wonders what the fellow's using for bait. Because that's what it's about. He knows the type.

The sounds of the school yard fall to a buzz. The morning sun is pinched between the broad-leafed catalpa trees, and when a breeze sorts through the canopy, a prickling light falls over the asphalt. The truck has a cap over the bed, and the canopy windows are a smoky amber.

He feels buoyant, balanced on the balls of his feet. It's as if a trip switch has been flipped, the charge zapping the length of his frame and snapping in his brain—electric. He takes a deep breath and circles the truck.

The guy's maybe seventeen or eighteen, dressed in jeans, dark T-shirt, and work boots. He has black hair, is gangly-armed, and Ned guesses long-legged, though the young man's squatting, so it's difficult to say.

He's offering something to a little girl. A coin, the chocolate kind wrapped in gold foil. A number of the others have them, as well.

Yes, Ned thinks. *I knew it.* "Can I help you?" he says, and walks up behind the young man. "I'm Ned Able." He nods toward the school. "The principal of Jefferson Elementary."

The children startle. A few of the smallest reach for his hand, saying, "Mr. Able, Mr. Able."

The young man rises. In one hand the gold coin, and under the other hand is the young girl's shoulder. "No," he says. "I don't need no help."

Ned asks the children to show him the candy coins. They hand them over, and he admires the chocolates, tells the children he'll hang on to them until after school. "Much too early in the morning for candy," he says. He waves them on their way. "Go on now. You don't want to be late." From across the street comes the brassy ring of the school bell, and the kids shout and run to where the crossing guards stand watching at a distance.

All that's left is Ned and the young man with a firm grip on the little girl's shoulder. Ned bends toward the girl. "What's your name?" he asks.

She's wide-eyed. Her lips are tucked between her teeth. Though there are no tears, her nose is running. She sniffs.

The young man pulls the end of his T-shirt out, swipes her face clean. "Her name's Harriet," he says, but doesn't look up.

Ned studies the young man, the wet spot on his shirt falling back into place over his stomach.

"Is that your name?" Ned asks the girl, keeping his eyes on the young man. "Harriet?"

She nods.

"She's my sister," the boy says, fretting with a cowlick at the back of his head.

Ned wonders if the boy's telling the truth. Suspects he is. He feels that brief exhilaration leaving, and in its place is a kind of nervous energy, a fraying at the edges, so that his hand taps against his thigh, a three-three galloping beat, while the other hand opens and closes as if working out a cramp.

"This your brother?" he asks the girl. She's staring off at the school yard, a slicked thumb in her mouth. She nods.

Ned turns back to the boy. "You understand how careful I have to be?"

No answer.

"You have any identification?"

From his back pocket, the boy fishes out a wallet—a pancake of leather with a few dollars, a picture ID. A sealed condom slips from a side pocket and falls to the grass. The boy blushes and ducks down to snatch it up, tucks it into the wallet. He hands over his driver's license.

The picture's recent, the license not nearly so worn as the packaged condom. "Cameron . . . How do you pronounce this?"

"Thebault. *Thee*—ball—t," the kid says.

Ned nods, but when he hands back the license, he feels the gold coins in his pocket. He pulls one out, flips it over.

"What's with the candy?"

The kid huffs, swipes the back of his hand under his nose. He nudges the wallet into his pocket. "It was just a dumb idea, I guess. Harriet's shy. Don't make friends so easy, so I thought this'd help."

"You're buying her friends."

The boy shrugs. "Didn't think it would hurt to try."

Ned goes down to one knee in front of the little girl. He picks up her free hand. When he stands, he steers her toward the crossing guards. "Say good-bye to your big brother," he says. "It's time for school."

With the little girl gone, Ned turns back to the young man.

The boy looks away, starts edging toward the curb.

Ned reaches across the distance and takes his wrist. His grip is firm, and he draws the young man close. He places his other hand on the back of the kid's neck. He can see the pinched look that comes into the boy's eyes.

He feels that tightening in his back again, and he wants to press harder. Knows how the thumb and forefinger placed just so starts the hammers going. But then he catches something in the boy's eyes, and he sees it as the boy must, and as the neighbors must see it from kitchen windows as they finish off the dregs of their coffee cups, and he's thinking, What the fuck are you doing? He sees the distress in the boy's face—not understanding what he's done to bring this on. *Just trying to help his little sister*, Ned eases up on the pressure. *A little too hard, too quick maybe. But understandable. In defense of the kids, after all. It was just common sense.* He shakes his head. *Which this guy clearly doesn't have.* He lets go of the boy's neck.

The kid stands there as if paralyzed.

Ned looks away and then back. "Hey listen, you understand, right? I'm a lot like you. A big brother of sorts, or, better yet, a father, say, for *all* these children. So I gotta be careful. I see someone out here giving the kids candy . . ."

He smiles at the boy, claps him on the back. "But hey, you meant well. You're a good brother, to worry about your sister that way."

The boy finally moves, stumbles off the curb and into the street. He's rubbing the back of his neck and shoulder. "Yeah, well. I gotta go now."

Ned walks toward the front of the truck, and as the boy climbs into the driver's seat, Ned leans into the open window. He drops the gold coins onto the passenger seat. "You probably don't want to do this sort of thing again, though. Right? People get the wrong idea." He raps on the door as the trucks pulls forward, and backs away with a wave.

Nance sits in a camp chair by the fire. Meredith's at the river's edge, scouring the plates, cups, and Dutch oven. Nance had cooked: garlic chicken, with potatoes, onion, and beans, nothing fancy. She's half-drowsing, eyes closed, listening to the rapids downriver, and the clinking of dishes.

They'd arrived in time to set up the tent and cots, check and stow equipment, collect firewood, make everything ready for the onset of the early dark this deep in the canyon. Everwine helped, off-loading boxes.

"Be sure to set up high," he said, as if Nance wouldn't already know. "They'll be letting water out of the dam later." He lingered, settling boxes one place before moving them a few feet higher up the beach. He offered to help with the tent, asked what they were having for dinner. For a moment, Nance thought he was going to suggest staying the night, but once camp was readied and the excuses ran out, he shuffled back to the boat, where he stood in the shallows. "I'll be back in nine days." In an unusual gesture, he stuck his right hand out, and when Nance took it in her own, he shook it, held on to it, and said, "Right here. You can count on that."

She cocked her head to a side. "I never thought otherwise, Pete."

"Yeah, well, but if you want me sooner, I could do that. . . . You got the radio?" He looked up at the campground, where in the sinking light the bright red of the tent faded like a blossom wilting on the beach.

She waited him out.

He paused, chewed his lower lip. He tugged the restraining line free from a snag on the beach. "Well, good luck. I guess." He paused, looked down the river, then up with a sigh. "I don't know what it is you think those snakes'll tell you, but who'm I to say it won't be the one thing we need to hear?" He studied the rope coiled in his hand, waited a beat. "Worse comes to worst"—he gave a dry laugh—"I guess it wouldn't be the first snake's led us down the path." He touched his forehead in a two-fingered salute. "You give your sister a nice visit." And then he left.

She has nine days to get the numbers on den populations. Collect samples. She'd hoped to have more time just to wander about, observe the area with a closer eye, let it sink into the quiet of her mind, where it would steep like a good tea over the next several weeks, over the long hours marooned over her computer, or slogging through the routine of home.

But now there's Meredith, and Nance admits she's got her reservations about having her sister here. Meredith. Impulsive, high-strung. Though that had first become obvious when their mother's cancer made itself apparent, and Meredith began to waste to shadow alongside her. Amid all the horror of their mother's cancer treatments—particularly brutal and almost always fatal in those days—they spared the time to take

Meredith to doctors, who proclaimed her a "nervous child." Those were hard days—their mother wasting with cancer, and alongside her Meredith, her face and ribs hollowed, wrist bones like door knockers at the ends of her starved arms. They'd finally shipped her off to relatives in Rhode Island, where they hoped she might recover apart from their mother. Their mother died a short two months later, and Nance always wondered if Meredith ever really forgave them for not letting her just fade away, as well.

Nance opens her eyes, zips the fleece liner closed on her jacket. The temperature has dropped from the low fifties of midday to what she guesses now is the low forties. Another couple hours, it'll be near freezing, but by then they'll be in a tent and in sleeping bags.

She watches her sister tidy up, and feels a genuine pleasure in seeing her familiar face, her gestures unchanged.

"It's nice to have you here," Nance says, trying the idea out.

Meredith crosses to Nance, leans down, and hugs her. Where their cheeks meet is grit from sand. She smells of dish soap and bleach, and river. "Hey, I'm glad to be here." She pulls a camp chair next to Nance's. "It's been," she says, and kicks her feet out before her, "lonely at home. Without Dad."

Nance hugs her arms over her chest. The fire crackles and an ember sparks into the dark.

"Five in the morning rolls around, and no smell of coffee," Meredith says.

Nance nods. Thinks of her father, the old blue terry-cloth robe he'd wear around the house in the morning. Coffee his first chore. It'd been a year since he'd passed. "Hard to think of the house without him."

Meredith turns toward her sister. "I did a little painting, rearranged things." She ducks her head.

Nance thinks of the first year after Joe's death, how she found it necessary to sell the chest they'd bought on a trip to Maine, the four-poster bed. She sold some things, gave the rest away, dismantled their history object by object just to keep ahead of the grief, and when even that proved insufficient, all that was left was to run.

Meredith picks up a stick and rolls a log to its side and the coals flare. She lifts the stick and watches the tip glow. "A new family moved in next door with two young girls, who look to be every bit the trouble we were."

Nance laughs. "Remember what old man Cassidy used to call us?" She imitates the man's voice, his palsied fist. *"'Terrorists.'"*

Meredith smiles. "We mostly were. Remember the time you glued me to the bedroom floor?"

"How you exaggerate." Nance crosses a foot over her knee and loosens her bootlaces. "It was just your hair." She looks up. "And you asked for it."

"I was *sleeping*." Meredith shakes the smoking end of the stick at her sister.

"In the middle of the bedroom floor and my scrapbook project." She lifts the stick away, douses the ember in sand. "Don't hurt yourself," she says, and hands the snuffed stick back. "The way I remember it—there was all this glue. So much glue . . . so little time."

"See? You're still enjoying it. It was wicked."

"You're just jealous I thought of it first."

"You always set such high standards."

The wind checks, shifts, and the smoke drifts upslope. Nance looks at the clear slice of sky overhead. The moon will be up soon. She hears Meredith's chair creak, and her sister is lifting another log onto the fire. She closes her eyes. "How *did* it feel? To be glued to the floor?"

Meredith flips the hood on her coat over her head.

Nance remembers her sister had gone still, pinned like a bug under glass, and then she'd roused herself, arms pushing up from the floor with a slow, fierce determination. To this day, Nance remembers clearest the sound of hair tearing.

"I remember," Meredith says, "you cutting me free with this huge pair of scissors."

"You looked scalped afterward."

"Not half as bad as the haircut you gave yourself. Poor Mama. Both daughters shorn like sheep."

Down canyon, an owl calls. The patter of the downriver rapids ebbs and swells. They sit with boots braced against the warmed stones, watching the fire pit, where sap whistles on a green log. Nance touches her sister's hand, nods toward the high east escarpment, where the first pale firings of moonlight touch the summit, a pale penumbra of light that spreads like hoar frost, until, at the lip of rock and sky and at the heart of the glowing, the moon brims upward, spilling into the narrow black. Then the clear blue light infuses the facing cliffs, kindles the tops of pines, flushes the shadows deep and deeper, like hound and hare. The moon is near full.

It's Meredith who speaks. "You cut your hair so I wouldn't be alone." She fingers the pins that hold her hair now. Her voice quiets. "How I loved you for that."

Nance rocks back in her seat.

Who would have predicted that? That her little sister would make heroic an act intended not as kindness but, rather, as a penance, reparation. Out of guilt? *In part, but that's not the real reason, is it?* So why? As a sign—her own scarlet letter—a warning to herself against the ease of cruelty, and the pleasure that could be had of it.

"Don't make more of it than it was, Meredith." Nance locks her hands in her lap. The fir snag on the beach is bleached with light, like a bone of the giants that swam these canyons under long-ago seas. Nance sighs. This is old business between them: what they hold each other responsible for. What blames they cannot shirk. She believes she already knows why Meredith's here, and so she has little-enough reason to ask, except that she wants to hear it out loud, from her sister. *Surprise me, give me a reason that's reasonable.* "Why'd you come, Sis?"

Meredith shifts deeper into her chair.

Nance bundles her hands under her jacket. It's getting colder, and they'll need to turn in soon. *You really want to get into this? Now? Ruin the one good day together in how many years?* "Well, pardon me"—she sighs—"but you come out here, all of a sudden, unannounced, and looking like shit."

"Always the tactful one." Meredith laughs, a sound like the hull of a boat on sand. She glances at her sister, then away, as if the sight of her sister pains her.

Nance waits.

"I needed a little distance, okay?"

1,800 miles. Nance remains quiet, chin resting on her chest. She settles the heel of a boot on a log and knocks it into the coals. Sparks fountain up and fall away like a bright rain in the wind, all but the few that land about Meredith's chair, and Meredith swats at them.

Nance sees one ember land on Meredith's sweatshirt, the cap of her shoulder. It winks out. Nance doesn't move, and then she smells the smoldering cloth, and something fiercely sweeter. *Scorched hair.* Nance pushes herself from the chair, swivels toward her sister with a hand raised to strike the ember away, but Meredith is already launching herself out of her chair, and then she's on her feet and facing Nance, her hands raised to ward off a blow, or strike one herself.

"Christ, Sis," Nance says, snatching an arm. "Hold still. You're on fire." She pinches the ember off the shoulder, flicks it to the sand. She lifts her sister's hair away with one hand and slaps the smoldering cloth with the other.

Meredith pushes her hand away. She peels off the shirt instead, feels the top of her shoulder with a hand. Pats her hair.

"You're not burned, are you?"

"My hair?" she asks, fingering the loose strands over her cheek.

"Still there." There's a faint fraying of ends where the spark landed; the smell's already dissipated. Nance picks the sweatshirt up, shakes it out. She fingers the small scorch mark and hands it back. "I think it's safe enough now."

Nance walks to the far side of the pit. She thinks about how Meredith reacted. Ready to take a blow? Or take it on?

"Did he hit you?" Nance asks, and then, "Why do you do this?"

"It's not something I do," Meredith says.

Nance shakes her head.

Meredith slips the sweatshirt back over her head. "Can we just sit and talk?"

Nance has already turned away. She moves over to the fire, stirs the coals with a long stick. Another loser, a dreamer, a brute. Another bully like Meredith's old boyfriend Dexter—the one who sent her to the hospital. She can still see him in the tight jeans and T-shirt, barrel chest and slim hips. It's a birthday party—her sister's—and he's playing host. Such a jokey, charming kind of guy at the evening's start, it's easy to see how a person could be attracted to him, but by the end of the night, he's slung across a lawn chair, his handsome face gone blunt and stupid. His arms are ropy with liquor, and he's loud: "Come 'ere. Bring that bir'day presen' o'er here." And Meredith? Where's she? Done apologizing for his behavior. "He's not really like this." Done with trying to maintain for the both of them. She's on the far side of the lawn, getting drunk herself.

And of course there's Joe. Holding Meredith's forehead while she vomits into the shrubs. Telling her, "It's all right. Just get it all out." Two, three weeks later, he will be dead.

She closes her eyes, hears the rapids in the bend downriver, the wind in the bunch grass, the fire sizzling. Nance wonders when her sister's going to figure it out. Nance opens her eyes, sees Meredith hasn't moved.

"What do you want from me? I mean, what can I possibly do for you now?" Nance spreads her hands, looks around the canyon floor, but she doesn't mean anything that specific. Rather, she means in this greater place, the West, this time, this new life, in which she has a career and home and husband. In which she has buried her first life, and with it her responsibilities toward Meredith.

A quiet settles over Meredith. "I thought we could start over."

Nance steps back.

"I mean, before Mom died," Meredith says, closing the distance, "it *was* different then, wasn't it? We liked each other. Didn't we?"

Nance remembers those earlier days. The rivalry, the teasing, and, yes, friendship, as well. She nods.

Meredith smiles. "I thought I remembered that, too."

Nance isn't sure where to go with this. Something in her wants their closeness back, but she also knows to be wary of it. She looks over at Meredith. "We have nine days, Sis. I've got a lot of work to do in a very short time, but I do want this to be a good time for us." Nance puts her hand on the place where the ember scorched her sister's shirt. She rubs the cloth, fingers the ash as she lifts her hand away. She turns toward the fire pit, picks up the fire shovel, and scoops sand on top. "You should get some sleep. I'll be in soon. I just want to make sure the fire's out."

Meredith stands at her shoulder, then steps away. Shortly after, Nance hears her moving about inside the tent, the zipper slide on a sleeping bag. She scoops more sand onto the fire, digs it into the ash and embers. When she raises a hand over the pit, there's minimal heat, but she picks up a bucket and carries it down to the river. She's always enjoyed these small tasks, the everyday matters, like buttoning down the campsite: fire out, foodstuff sealed and stored well away from the tent, firewood readied for the next day.

She squats at the river's edge, the bucket swinging in her hands. The water is a dark slide next to her, a ripple of black in the sand. She fills the bucket with water, then cups her hands and dips them into the river, rinses her face. *Snowmelt.* She can smell the brittle scent, and her skin fires. She looks back at the tent, where her sister is settling in, and at the hill rising dark behind it. She stands staring at it a long while, until she feels the footing beneath her feet go soft, and moves to one side just as the small shelf of sand slides into the current. She watches the river awhile longer, then lifts the bucket away and, turning, strides up the beach.

The day has sped by. This surprises Ned, considering how early he'd risen to see Nance and her sister off. But the rest of the day has been so busy that he's hardly had time to think of Nance. Until he gets home and hears his steps on the hardwood floor echoing in a way they never seem to when she's around. In their bedroom, he changes from work clothes into dungarees, a T-shirt, and jogging shoes. Walking through the house, he thinks about grabbing something to eat. An apple, say. A cold beer to chase it down. But then he's stepping out onto the wide front porch overlooking his yard. Too early for mowing, too late for pruning. It's that in-between season. He thinks about cleaning out the garage.

It's then he sees Chuck Hame—his neighbor two houses down—drive up with a new box spring and mattress roped into the back of his pickup. Ned watches the man park the vehicle and step out to stand idly at the side of his truck. He looks like a man cursed and blessed by this old labor of bringing home the goods. Chuck stares up and down the block, then over at his house, as if judging how best he might negotiate the wobbling weight of the mattress and the stiff bulk of the box spring by himself.

Ned shouts across the space of yards, "Hey, Chuck, you look like a man in need of help."

A cockeyed grin settles on Chuck's face. "You got that right."

Ned crosses the distance in long strides. At the side of the truck, Chuck extends a hand and Ned grasps it in both of his.

"Man, you're a good neighbor. The best, Ned." He looks up at the bulk looming over them. "Store said they'd deliver these and take away the old ones, but that wouldn't be until after the weekend, and Bitsy, well, she just couldn't bear another three nights . . ."

Ned's nodding. *And you couldn't bear another three nights of Bitsy.* But he cuts off the unkind thoughts. "Hey, you got to keep the women happy." He gives the man a wink. "And it's no big deal—I got everything you need for a job like this. Strong back and a weak mind."

It takes them over half an hour to move the new set upstairs and the old set into the back of the truck. At the end of which time, Chuck stands slumped against the back quarter panel. "I don't know what I'd have done without you." He pats the old mattress. "I'll just drive this off to the dump. You know what time they close? No? Well, hey, I'd offer you a beer. . . ." He looks skyward, at the small bunching of clouds.

"Hey, don't worry about it, Chuck." Ned's already stepping away. "I still got stuff to do. Good to see you," he says, waving a farewell, but Chuck's already moving toward the front of his truck.

Back in his yard, Ned no longer has the energy to tackle the garage. He looks at his house, the blank face of it. He thinks about Chuck and his wife Bitsy, the pair of them in their new bed this evening. Wonders if they'll break it in right. His own wife bedded in a flimsy tent, on a cot. Next to her sister, which, he has to admit, he finds intriguing. The two women. He enters the house, turning on lights as he moves through. He wants it bright. He turns on the TV for noise. It's his first night alone. He spends the early hours between dinner and TV, and the next several moving from chair to sofa to chair. When he can't put it off any longer, he makes his way up the flight of stairs, leaving the downstairs brightly lighted. He spends a long while in the bathroom, though he does not look in the mirror. An old bugaboo—*never know what you'll see coming up behind you.*

When he steps into his bedroom, he turns on the dresser lamps, both of them, as well as the floor lamp in the corner of the room. When he sees the bed he wonders if Chuck and Bitsy are doing it. Right now. He thinks about their old mattress, the intimate way in which it leaned into his body as he carried it, how it pressed against the side of his face. He thinks about stripping off the sheets, the cotton pad, and when they hauled it, mottled and pulpy from years of use, into daylight, how the dark continents of their sex life floated in stains on a satin finish: sweat, cum, piss, blood.

He stands at the foot of his own bed. There's a tightness in his back that he recognizes, and he rubs a hand down the lower lumbar, down to where his tailbone fishes into his body. The tension eases, and he leans nearer the bed. He runs a finger over the neatly made cover, pushes deeper, as if to feel the layers beneath. He pulls aside the spread, lets the blankets fall. Looks at the pinstriped sheets, the conviction of the corners. He unwraps them, sloughs the sheet to the floor. Then he lifts the fitted sheet clear and stands a long while looking at the pad, its bleached whiteness. He peels it down, like a glove from a hand, or like panties from a big-hipped woman. He studies the exposed mattress, with its quilted puckers, the splotches here and there, still few, still faint, but as good a record as any he can imagine of their short history together. Standing here, he feels like a voyeur, a backyard observer to his own intimate life. He thinks of the neighbor's mattress, the private history paraded out onto the back of a truck and hauled to the Dumpster, where crows will pull threads from its seams and the coyotes will leave their own dark stains. He sits and looks over at the window across the way, the glare of the floor lamp reflected in the dark pane, the stripped bed and the shape that is himself. He eases himself off the bed and crosses the room to the window, where he pulls the shade, as if there might be someone out there who would see.

Chapter Two

The den is in a side canyon halfway up the hill, a rigorous walk through wheat grass, horehound, teasel, and cocklebur. It's a scramble over talus and across a short slope of scree, through gooseberry, wood rose, and sumac, black raspberry and hackberry trees. The opening's in an old mine carved out by the European prospectors at the end of the 1800s. From the entrance, she's prized a number of good-sized boulders—*Just like rolling the stone away from the tomb*—and buttressed it with wooden joists. It's a good hunched-over twenty-yard walk before it opens into the wider cavern below, blasted and picked to fifteen feet in diameter, high enough for her to stand erect at the far end.

The walls are pocketed with copper—blue-green in lamplight—or brilliant with pyrite concentrations, and coated with webs like spun sugar, from which great dollops of spiders and egg sacks depend. There's the occasional niche picked deeper. Several smaller tunnels branch off, large enough to crawl into, but cinching tighter down their length until they end. Years back, she'd explored one, something she's not likely to repeat except in dreams, and then she finds herself caught as she was back then, nose snubbed against the wall, with the deeps of the mountain closed around her. Then that old horror hits again, her body snugged in the rock, her hips and elbows suddenly too large, and realizing how easily her clothing can hang her up, how suffocating too deep a breath becomes, and then she's prying herself free, inching backward, pressing back and back, keeping herself from panic by way of reason, the only defense she's ever trusted—*if she'd made it in, she'll make it out*—reasoning her way through the long, slow push from the tight stone womb, reaquainted with the thing we are blessed enough to forget in our lives, what a true and utter terror birth is.

The floor of the main chamber is a composite: sediment, rock, sand. And, of course, there are the snakes—a little over two hundred by her count. The number up slightly from the two previous years. Her chief interest? The Western Rattlers. One of the three subspecies: the Northern Pacific rattlesnake, *Crotalus viridus oreganus*. Some of the locals claim there used to be pygmy rattlers. If so, Nance thinks they are gone now.

She sits on a small camp stool, feet booted, legs gaitered in leather, packing up specimens: skin samples, fecal matter, bits of bone. She works in lantern light, the air articulate with the smells of dung, rodent and bat—musky and dense—the soured oil of snake, the dirt, the sweet smell of decay. Nearly one-third of the wintering snakes will not survive, and a number of these dead she has bagged. Her breath moistens her cheeks and eyelashes. She checks tags and drops the bags into a box, wondering what Meredith is up to. Her sister has taken to striking out from camp, keeping out of Nance's way, returning late afternoon to empty her pockets: bits of colored glass worn smooth in the river; a spoon; the skull of a shrew; worm-bored driftwood, river teeth and burls; a hummingbird nest, small as a thumb.

She's surprised at how amiable her sister's been, how accommodating. Keeping clear, and out of trouble. Letting Nance get on with her work. Meredith even managed to harvest some miner's lettuce for fresh greens, a dish of berries one night for dessert. All in all, it's been a pleasure to have her here. Makes Nance aware of how much she's missed family.

She looks up from a Ziploc bag, returns her gaze to the floor littered with snakes. Gopher snakes, otherwise known as bull snakes, ringnecks, garter, and, of course, the rattlers.

She feels strangely comforted by the utter physicality of the creatures. They are strung nose to tail, and tail to tail, and side by side, across one another, or wrapped in a number of great fleshy balls—two of them the goodly size of pie pumpkins, for while snakes are by nature solitary in summer months, when circumstances accommodate it, such as these, they gather together for warmth in the cold hold of winter. A disturbing sight for most people, this tangling of too much flesh. Sometimes the balls shift, a slight squeezing or a slow spilling over, as though the creatures breathe or dream together, and in the last two days, by mid-afternoon, the balls of snakes have started showing more movement, a tentative loosening.

Nance picks up her hook, eases it between two snakes, and plies them apart as gently as the sections of an orange. She pins the smaller of the two and grasps it by the head with her fingers, lifts it into her lap. She studies the spade-shaped head, the eyes, the vertical pupils just razor slices. Is it sleep? She wonders. Really? Not as we know it. She wants to believe they have some respite in dreams over the long, cold months. There are the pits—characteristic of vipers—which sense infrared, and these, combined with sight, are the means by which they judge the size and scope of enemy or prey, and, of course, the delicate nostrils—not that they smell with them—and below that the slim notch in the front of the upper lip from which the forked tongue flickers, tasting the air, transferring odor particles to the roof of the mouth, to the duct openings on the olfactory chamber and Jacobson's organ. What it must be like to see the intangible, to read the heat, and taste smell, like signatures in the air. Perhaps to see the world in ways more accurate than our own. All in all, as well prepared as an animal might be for the difficulties and hazards of a life condemned to its belly: *"You alone of all animals will have to eat dust as long as you live."*

She runs a finger down the spine. The skin dry, a dusky brown-and-tan color, the inscrutable blotches. She places her palm beneath, and its creamy underside lifts in a long, slow wave as her hand travels the length, pausing at the vent. A male, this one, with the slightly thicker portion just before the rattle, the hemipenes, a double-headed penis kept tucked away. She studies the tail, the parchment rattles—button tip long gone. *Such a handsome lad.*

Not that she loves the beasts as some of her fellow herps do, having

come to this specialty by chance rather than choice, her first love am-
phibians, actually. Still, over the years she has developed a curiosity
about them that will not let go, a kind of cold passion about their lives.
But her heart still lugs in her chest when she handles them; the hairs on
the back of her arms lift as if an electric charge passes through the
snakes' skin. *"I will make you and woman hate each other, her offspring and yours
will always be enemies."*

She arranges it over the canvas field jacket blanketing her lap, then
palpates a small section of the snake's top side, finds the beaded ridge
where the implant nests—a tiny microchip inserted last year. A pilot program. A sampling of snakes to determine which rattlers return to the
den, a means to track what area they traverse in the time between.

The animal in her lap starts stirring, warming from her own body
heat. She looks about at the nestling snakes, the ovoid balls, a crosshatch
of flesh, still motionless with the cold.

"Hello?" a voice calls down the long shaft behind her.

"Meredith? Stay there," she says, though she never once believes her
sister will have the courage to venture down the tunnel. "I'm just finishing. I'll be up shortly."

Nance lifts the snake, sees the pupil has widened, tongue peeking out,
the body muscling. This is when accidents happen. Work done, distracted. Now's when you have to take care. You didn't want to give them
the leverage they need to strike. She stands, leans over, swings the snake
gently away from her, and releases. It falls to the floor and flexes into a
loose coil, at a safe distance. It looks as if it means to rattle, but after long
moments, it sidles alongside a knot of snakes and folds into their comfort.

Nance hitches the box to a rope and pulley. "Meredith?" she calls.
"I'm going to send a box up. Unhook it, and send the line back down,
okay?"

"I'm coming."

Nance sits back on her heels, startled. "No. Stay there." Nance hears
the impatience in her voice. She takes a deep breath. "Sis?"

"Yeah?"

"Stay there."

"Why?"

"Because I'm asking you to."

She can hear Meredith's broad sigh.

Nance looks around. The snakes are quiet. Even the one she stirred up has settled back into the knot of sleeping serpents. Why shouldn't Meredith come?

Because Meredith isn't dressed for it. Because she's an amateur where amateurs have no business.

"You hate snakes," Nance says.

"I'm not *fond* of them, no." Meredith's voice is amplified by the length of the shaft, and Nance remembers the old voice tube that wove through the walls of their family house. How they loved pressing their mouths to it, like a small ear trumpet, and shouting down from second floor to first, or howling scary noises into it in the evenings, *awhoooo*.

Nance starts the box up the tunnel, pulling back and back on the line until she hears "Got it." The tension at the end of the rope loosens. There's a stirring at the tunnel entrance. Nance leans into the opening. She hears her sister worming her way down the narrow chute, sighs. *She never would listen*. She moves aside the collections and steps over with the lantern in time to see Meredith's grinning face.

Meredith rubs her nose with a closed hand, hands her the box with the other hand. "Something in here smells."

"Stinks. It stinks. You smell. Stay close. The snakes are just over there." Nance waves a hand over her shoulder.

Meredith steps onto the cavern floor.

Nance picks up the lantern. She thinks she sees movement in the general body of the den, but knows it's just her nerves, the general anxiety Meredith always seems to provoke. She hates that. Those moments when the world becomes shifty with imagination, when that thing she trusts most, good sense and senses, becomes unreliable. How did you defend yourself in a world like that? "Sometimes being brave's all you got." It was what her mother used to say when Nance was very young. "You might as well practice now."

Meredith is wiping her cheek with a sleeve. "Everwine's here.

Thought you'd want to know. Pulled in about forty minutes ago." She dusts off her shoulders, sleeves. "Hell of a hike up here."

Nance picks a clot of spider eggs from her sister's hair. "He's not due until tomorrow."

Meredith nods. "He says there's a front moving in. Big storm. We don't get out today, he says we might not get out by river anytime soon." Meredith looks around. "Oh," she says, tucks her arms and legs closer.

Nance had planned today for loose ends, tomorrow to break camp, but the equipment is mostly packed. Meredith can help carry it down. With Everwine's help, they could be out by late afternoon. She shakes her head. "Well, that's a surprise—a day early, but not so bad."

Nance lofts the lantern, swings it in a slow circle about the room, a jumble of flesh and scales, shadows and light. The thick columns of basalt on the far wall jump forward, the stone wrapped in webs, and in the cracks and crevices the small holes that riddle the walls, passageways into small and smaller worlds. Nance looks over her shoulder to where Meredith has pressed herself against the wall. "You okay, Mer?"

Meredith stares back, her face looking nipped in lamplight.

Nance puts a hand on her sister's arm and feels how rigid it is. "Hey, they're sleeping," she says. She swings the lantern back toward the floor.

"They're moving," Meredith says.

"No," Nance says, and pats her hand. "It's just the lantern light and shadows."

Nance looks away but keeps Meredith's hand in her own. She wants to say, You only get what you ask for, but she sees how her sister's face is opening, how willing she is to trust, and Nance feels betrayed again by that old streak of cruelty, wonders why, of all the attributes we possess, it's mostly the worst that persevere? Is it just her? A thing about siblings? Or is it that Meredith is still the easiest target in the world. Hadn't she just been thinking what a pleasure it was to have her sister here? To find family again. "You ready for the climb back?"

Meredith nods.

"Go out, unhook the stuff I send up. It'll only take a moment." She puts a hand on the back of her sister's head, guides it below the rock of the tunnel entrance. "Keep your head down, and keep climbing," Nance says, watching as the boot soles disappear into the dark. It's another moment or two before she hears her shout, and she knows what Meredith's feeling: the reemergence into the world, those first bright moments of sunlight.

The bar has about it a sameness that Ned's always found comforting: smell of smoke and spilled beer, the corner pinball machine, with its lights muted under the piling dust, the punched tin ceiling painted flat black, and, in a far corner, in the direction of the bathrooms, where at some time in the distant past the plumbing went to ruin, cobwebs bearding the exposed pipes. An air of age, a thickness of gut, a limpness like the one concealed in the drooping drawers of old men. The linoleum floor is a checkerboard: oxblood and ivory. The back bar, stocked in whiskey and flavored crèmes, is a sawed-off relic from the abandoned Episcopal church, and on rainy nights it's still redolent of myrrh and frankincense. The room's murky with shadows, and even the odd pockets of light are filtered through the husks of bugs in the overhead fixtures. Eight bar stools, four booths, three tables. He prefers a stool, as there's nothing more remarkable than a guy alone in a booth. The bartender pours drinks and ousts drunks and doesn't ask questions beyond "What do you want?" and "Another?"

Ned orders a whiskey neat, rolls the glass between his hands, keeps his head averted from his nearest stool mate, listens instead to the handful of patrons: "How you doing?" "Could use some rain." "Your boy get that job?" Or the couple in the corner booth, who just sit quietly across from each other. It's this odd mix that Ned relishes most.

Ned drinks deeply, chases the whiskey home with water. He glances down at his plaid flannel shirt, khaki pants, looks in the mirror at his hair, combed close, not too short, not too long. A buttoned-down look. Nothing to raise eyebrows. Nobody you'd particularly remember having seen the next day. He looks like someone who belongs.

Not that he does this regularly. He generally stays home when Nance is gone, and while most husbands savor time apart from their spouses, spend it with friends, or take to the strips and bars, it's a pleasure he knows he can not afford to allow himself. After all, he has his place in the community to think about. An appearance to maintain, and, along with that, the respect of his students and their parents.

A woman settles onto the stool next to him, and he keeps his eyes on his hands. Says sure when the barkeep asks if he'd like another, takes a sip of the drink, and then, only then, does he glance her way, gives her a quick nod before settling back into his own space, fully aware of her interest.

And why not? He's good-looking enough. Not that he's handsome, but in the past he's always counted that as an asset, for he looks vulnerable . . . attainable. In the right light, the break in the line of his nose is interesting. His bones are regular, and his teeth are clean and capped. He's been told he has a boyish charm, a quality he's been alternately pleased with and distrustful of.

In the mirror, he sees her eyes flicker. There. There again. Checking him out. A little thrill of pleasure in that, but a bite of guilt, as well. He pivots on the bar stool so that his back is to her. He congratulates himself. Feels a little steadier, a little stronger. Just because he's here, it doesn't have to really mean anything. He's simply having an evening to himself. Enjoying a little time away from the house—a house where of late the rooms seemed to have grown closer, walls crowding in, windows blank as a stare. How else to account for that feeling, while exiting a room, or climbing the stairs to the second floor, like a screw in the small of his back winding tight and tighter, that compulsion to run, to take the stairs two at a time, to snatch himself clear of the closeted rooms, even the house itself, its yard and watchful street.

He blames it on the stress of his job, his wife's absence.

When he swings back toward the woman, her elbow is propped on the bar, and she's stirring her drink with a shish kebab of fruit: pineapple, orange, cherry. What little drink there is is blue.

It isn't as if this has to go anywhere.

"Could you pass me the matches?" he asks.

She looks over her shoulder to see if he's speaking to someone else, and turns back red-cheeked. She hands him a book and the ashtray it's sitting on.

He pockets the matches. "It's not that I smoke anymore." He shakes his head, sees that she's mildly intrigued. "But I miss having matches on me. Know what I mean?"

"Yes," she says. "I know exactly what you mean. Everybody used to have them, didn't they?"

He nods. "Absolutely. You come here often?"

She shakes her head. "Just once in awhile. You?"

"First time. But with my wife gone . . ." he says.

She looks up, a startled rise to her eyebrows. "I'm sorry," she says. "I'm sorry to hear that."

He smiles. "No. Not *gone*. She's away, on business."

She looks confused at first, almost disappointed. "Well then, I guess I'm not sorry," she says. She lifts the dripping stick, plucks off a chunk of pineapple with her teeth, chews it. She is plump and young. Mid-twenties. Her hair is passionately streaked blond, a snarl of loopy curls done badly with rat comb and lacquer. Burgeoning beauticians. All of them. It is what makes the women so pitiable, young and old—these narrow towns with yellowed mirrors and swaybacked streets.

He stares at her hair, has an impulse to lay his hand on it, feel his way through the tangle like a blind man. He clears his throat, looks down at his drink.

"I mean, I don't usually do this," he says. "Go to bars." He shakes his head. "But I just needed to get out. The place gets so goddamned big when she's gone. You know what I mean? Like I'm lost in my own living room."

She smiles sadly, nodding, her shoulder inching toward him, and his body responds, shoulder mirroring hers, chin tilting, the same nervous pressing of fingertips against the bar top. Not that it's deliberate or even contemplated; it might as easily be a reflex, like a hammer tap to the knee, or the flinch from a heated coil, a reflex developed over long years, practicing a walk, an inflection, until it becomes as natural as brushing his teeth, as picking his way through the day. Conscious or not, the true genius is in the way it works on others at a wholly intuitive level, so that they recognize something of themselves, a vague recollection or fading echo, a comforting familiarity they confuse with trust.

"You must love her a lot," she says.

She's smiling now, her hands relaxed on the Formica top. The cuticle on her index finger looks fevered, a bit of crusted blood under the nail, and he pictures her sitting alone at night, watching television, picking at her nails, and just as surely he know this is a young woman for whom rooms are always overlarge, who longs for, above all things, a man who will fill them for her.

"My bet," he says, "is that your boyfriend feels the same way when you're gone."

She laughs, a hitching giggling schoolgirl sound. "I don't have a boyfriend," she says. "Oh, I did, but he wouldn't ever think like that."

"So you broke off with him. Good for you," he says, and touches his fingertips to the back of her hand, once, gently, and as quickly moves his hand away. A paternal gesture. A kindness no one would suspect, and he feels that fussing, that fidgeting again at the base of his spine, that thing rooting about in his stomach, and he shifts on the bar stool so that he might put one foot on the floor. Like in one of those old films, he thinks, in the love scenes where there's always one foot on the floor. A guarantee of safety.

Ned sits back, widening the space between himself and the young girl, telling himself he shouldn't have come, when what he really wants is to lean closer, like a father, say, put a kindly hand on her shoulder, whisper to her what manner of monsters might fill the rooms of little girls like herself. Open her eyes, open her to any number of possibilities. But all he says is, "Got to make a quick trip." And then he's off the stool and making his way across the floor.

In the men's room, he closes the door, drops the hook into the eye, and turns into the tight space. There's the one-seater with its streak of rust like a tongue pending from the rim, and around the toilet base, where the linoleum buckles up, a mange of dust and hair sprouts from the seams. His stomach cramps. He can hear it knocking in there, like an engine ticking awake. He drops his pants and settles onto the stool, knees knobbed under his hands, and he grabs on as his bowel spasms and his breathing goes shallow. Across from him, on the wall, is this month's full-size poster of a long-legged woman in a bikini straddling a beer keg. She has lips like inflatable rafts, and pointy tits, and where her legs scissor open, someone has tacked a bit of well-rubbed shag rug, orange, where her crotch would be. The pain passes, and he reaches across the small distance, fingers the patch of carpet. There's a gurgling in his gut again, and he breaks into a sweat as his bowel torques; he emits a great vacuous fart and grabs the patch of rug as his intestines squeeze and he doubles over, so that his chin hits his knees, and when his eyes open again, it is because the pain has passed.

He waits for another spasm, and when none comes, he relaxes some, his breathing deepening, and then he sees from the corner of his eye a small shape flat against the floorboard. For a moment, he thinks he's missed the toilet, thinks that the thing inside him that runs his gut with sharp little claws has escaped at last and taken shape right there on the floor next to him. But then he sees it for what it is, a mouse. A deer mouse, gray and anonymous in the sour air: farts, piss, and disinfectant, the dog shit someone came in with on their heels. Ned eases his foot over and the mouse doesn't move, its pelt shining against the pitted floor, its front paws pink and hairless and much, much too human looking. Then he sees how one side of its head has been flattened against the tile. A dead mouse.

Ned leans over, his ass lifting from the toilet seat, a cooling draft on his backside. He settles his toe against the mouse, gives it a little nudge, then draws the ball of his foot back, and the little package rolls beneath the sole of his shoe. He picks up the mouse by its tail and cups it in the other palm. He looks it over. Some drunk's stumbling step, or the intentional boot? He fingers the limp head. Either way, it's a sorry thing, a sad reminder of our place in the greater scheme of things. He drops the mouse, toes it into the corner. Stands, lifts his pants, and turns to study the toilet bowl, half-expecting to see the bloody tripe suspended in there, but, as always, it's empty. A knot of air and nothing more. He pisses in the bowl, flushes the toilet, and watches the foamy spume swirl down and down and away. When he turns to the sink, he comes face-to-face with the smiling bare-breasted poster woman. He sits back down and towels off his shoe, contemplating the space, the pornography scrawled on the walls, the bruise of mold on the plaster around the sink pipes, the small creature dead in the corner. He lifts the tiny package of meat again, a crusty bit of red, a tuft of fur, the flattened head. A moment of inspiration, and he makes quick work of it. When he's done, he washes his hands, soaps and rinses, then soaps and rinses a second time. He towels them dry, thinking about the sad young woman sitting at the bar. He looks up into the mirror. Composed, he checks his zipper.

When he steps back into the room, he keeps to the far side, pays his bill, lifts his jacket from the coatrack, and walks out. It is chilly, and he flips up the collar on his jacket, pulls it close about his neck. Colder up here than in the valley. Atypical weather, even for the prairie. Might snow yet.

He unlocks his car, settles his long frame into the bucket seat. He turns on the engine, the heater as well, though it blows cold and a sprinkling of ice crystals float down about him from the defroster. He leans his head back, tries to loosen his spine. He wipes a clear circle on the inside of the windshield, the single arc light over the parking lot haloed with mist. Besides his car, there are four pickups, a stock truck, two cars, all American-made. The sign over the door is in bright pink neon letters: THE FLAMING O. He drapes his wrist over the steering wheel, hums a monotone under his breath, and contemplates the long road home, the chain of small towns between—Ferdinand, Winchester, Cottonwood, Culdesac, Lapwai—and feels that old inexplicable mix of thrill and fear, so that he breathes deeply to calm himself, cracks the window for a dose of cold air. Nothing has changed. He's still Ned, someone you could respect: husband, principal, good neighbor. Just an average guy at an average bar, in need of a moment's escape.

When he feels steadier, he pulls out of the gravel lot and onto the highway. Already the thing at the hollow of his back feels smaller, that urgent pressure releasing like game sprung from a trap. He slips in one of Nance's CDs, some blues—a little Muddy Waters. Already he's forgetting the small bar behind him, with its tableful of wasted young men exchanging pointless jokes, the mousy woman fading with each milepost. By the time he's driven the length of the prairie and come to that point where the land falls away in abrupt side canyons, where high wooden railroad trestles, some of the last of their kind, span the blackened gaps, the evening will have become a thing of no particular consequence, a dimming recollection, and upon waking in the morning, he will struggle to recall what he'd done with the evening, and in the first light of morning, turning his pockets out for the laundry, he'll find that small patch of shag carpet and puzzle over it long moments before finally letting it slip from his fingers into the bucketed garbage bag. For now, he cruises past the tallow light of farmhouses glowing from pockets in the piney windbreaks, and across the sleeping face of the wide plateau, and as the car winks through the vanishing miles, already the bar with its closeted bathroom and its life-size pinup girl will have been chased deep into forgetting, along with the trampled mouse newly tacked to her crotch.

Chapter Three

T hey surprise him by coming home a night early, Nance bearing the usual load of dead snakes and specimens to pack in the downstairs freezer, where they will stay until she can move them to campus. And what a curious thing that is—to open it late at night and look in through the frosted windows of plastic bags at stiff ropes of flesh, eyes frozen opaque, or the hard pellets of digested stomach bits.

She smells of campfire, of ash and river water, and beneath it all is a spice of sweat. She's still dressed in warm jeans and flannel. He's at her elbow, handing her specimen packets from the Styrofoam coolers, scores of Baggies tagged and penned in her tidy script.

"Did you two have a good time?" he asks.

She's stacking bags, patting them in place with gloved hands. She glances over with a distracted look, then nods. "Oh," she says, "a little sticky at first. Sisters, you know." She blows on her gloved fingers, holds out a hand for more packets. "Meredith spent the time exploring. I was busy in den . . ."

The freezer air mists her clothing, her hair, and as it streams off, it carries a scent of something darker from the folds of her cuffs, or from beneath the curls of hair at her neck, behind her ears: a musk, both tangy and sweet. A scent that he almost calls familiar, but at the same time makes him inexplicably anxious.

"Evening, we sat by the campfire and talked." She pauses. "And mostly it was good." Her mouth opens, closes, and she glances into the chest at the bags of frozen snake parts and falls silent.

He waits for her to ask about his week, but she won't, caught up as she is in her work. He thinks of his last few nights of freedom. The trips to the small town bars, the diner counters, the women he sat next to. He turns away so that she won't see the way his hands want to stray, reminds himself he has nothing to feel guilty about. No need to offer anything other than honest silence. "I had a quiet week," he says.

She turns toward the chest with a hand on her hip, then dips back into the freezer. She pushes a packet to the side. "So you had a good time?" she asks. "Miss me?" She looks over and touches a gloved hand to his cheek.

He flinches and raises a hand to deflect hers. He can see the surprise in her eyes. His hand softens around hers; he leans in and cups his other hand over it. "Brrr," he says. "Pretty nippy."

She laughs, looking at her fingers. "I'd forgotten."

"We'll have to warm them up later." He pats them before releasing.

"Do you think?" Her lip catches between her teeth. "Might be a bit awkward. Meredith in the next room and all."

"She'll sleep. She has to sometime." He reaches over and peels a hair from her sweater. "When's she leaving?"

Nance cocks her head. "What do you two have against each other?"

He picks up one of the last packets, hands it to her. "A case of bad chemistry?" He slips a hand around her waist, gives it a squeeze before releasing. "Hey, I'm trying. Honest. But you have to admit, Meredith's a strange bird," he says, and, as if she agrees, Nance says nothing, but shuffles the last packet into the freezer and closes the lid.

Back upstairs, they find Meredith has already showered and dressed. She's toweling her hair dry. He offers to cook, and Meredith suggests she could help, though he can see her reluctance; he steps near her, lifts an onion from the hanging basket. "You must be tired," he says. "It must have been a long week for you."

She moves casually away.

He looks over at Nance, sees she's watching, and so shrugs his shoulders. He turns back to Meredith, noticing the way she keeps a savvy distance, close enough to be polite, space enough to make a statement. "Tell you what," he says. "You two relax. Let me do what I'm best at."

"That being?" Meredith asks.

It startles him—her suddenly addressing him so directly, the way she rises on the balls of her feet. A fighter's stance.

He smiles. "Being good to my women."

Nance rolls her eyes and laughs, but he notices the flinch in her sister's eyes.

When they go upstairs, he is left alone in the kitchen. He thumbs the utensil drawer open, slips out the chef's knife and lays it across a finger. He taps the handle so that the blade teeters on his knuckle, and overhead, as their steps cross the ceiling, he counts them. He sets down the knife and flexes his fingers. Then he retrieves the chopping board, peels the onion, the cloves of garlic. He lays aside sprigs of parsley, rosemary, slaps the pork chops down—thick-slabbed and pink—trims the fat from each, handling the knife with proficiency. He keeps them keen-edged. In the interim years—his solitary years—he's become a good cook. Finds a real pleasure in the absorption of these small tasks. The mild distraction, a relief from the rest of his day. And, of course, there is always the reward of appetite. With the pork chops trimmed, cleaned, and patted dry, he dips them in an egg wash and breads them. When they're ready for the oven, he sets on a pot of herbed rice, steams new asparagus. A lemon butter sauce on the side. He hums random notes under his breath.

When at last the table is set and the women have seated themselves, he serves the meal with a towel draped over his arm, understanding that there are few things women love more than to see a man make a fool of himself, or believe in more completely. He suggests grace. He bows his head, gives thanks for food, for family. Asks that Meredith's visit be blessed and her return home safe. At the end, he sees how Nance has softened.

Through the first course, there's little speech, but as their hunger blunts, the two women begin recalling their trip. Ned asks Meredith what she thought of the den.

She looks up, her expression almost amiable. "Not so horrid in hind-sight."

"Great. Yet another convert." He puts his hands up. "I'm surrounded."

"I'd hardly call myself a convert."

"But at least *she's* willing to try," Nance says, grinning at her husband.

"She," he says, points his butter knife at his heart, "can't imagine why I don't care to wallow alongside her in the pit."

"What an idea." Nance carves into a chop, spears a chunk, and studies it. "Did we wallow?" she asks. Bites the meat, chews, and swallows. "Actually, the closest I ever came to wallowing in snakes was in graduate school. My prof used to bring them in in a milk can. Those old-fashioned metal ones?" She holds a hand above the floor. "This tall, and about yea around."

Meredith nods. "I know the ones."

"He'd bring the cans in, open them up, and turn them over. I mean, they were packed to the top. Rattlers flopping out onto the floor, hissing like rain on hot asphalt. We were fresh grad students, just off the bus." She shakes her head. "You should have seen the leaping and shouting. And that old man? He says, 'Put these away, will you?' and walks out." She laughs. "Never looked back."

"What did *you* do?" Meredith asks.

"Grabbed a snake hook and put them away. Safer than letting them roam around a whole lot longer, and it weeded out the weak of heart." She looks down at her plate and smiles. "Which was, I believe, his reasoning all along. By midsemester, those who stayed had the routine down. As second-year students, we knew better than to be around when he came back from field trips."

"I'd have bailed," Meredith says. "One look at those snakes in the den . . . God, I was scared."

"You got over it." Nance reaches over, touches the back of her sister's wrist. "And being scared's not unreasonable in a viper pit."

Ned sets the knife on its side across the plate, leans back in his seat. "You ever afraid, Nance?"

She pauses. "When a snake coils or rattles, the hairs on the backs of my arms and neck still rise." She lifts a spear of asparagus, nibbles the tip. "For the most part, you can overcome the fear, control the level of risk by being prepared, by knowing your subject."

"Know your enemy," Ned says.

"No. You have to know the nature of snakes." Nance points her fork at him. "See, that's where people always get in a muddle. It's not *the enemy*. It's just a snake . . . doing what snakes do, which is really little enough."

From the sideboard, the dishes gleam in the candlelight, and then across the tabletop and around the dishes and under the rims of the cups, small shadows dart as the furnace cuts in with a hum and a warm draft moves through the room. Nance sighs, takes a sip of coffee, and settles it back on the saucer.

"If you need to speak in terms of the enemy, think human first. Not the poor snake."

Ned sees a look pass between the sisters, a current deeper than what he is privy to, and that's a thing he can not conceive of—being that well known. He feels that familiar anxiety pecking at him: back tightening, legs beginning to vibrate. They finish dinner, the conversation only taking one dangerous turn before winding down, and then the women offer to clean, and he lets them. "Think I'll go for a walk," he says, but the sisters are already absorbed in clearing the table.

He crosses the living room, steps over the clutter of equipment, and hefts a jacket from the closet. On the front porch, he settles onto the top step. He shrugs his shoulders high, lifts the collar about his neck, and closes the jacket over his chest.

Someone calls from down the street. A whistle. A shout. A door banging shut. He leans back and the wooden porch step creaks. He supposes he could have stayed and wedged his way into their conversations. But standing out in the clear, cold air, he realizes now how much he needed to escape: the commotion, the chatter, the new camaraderie that has sprung up between them. The way they orbit the house and each other, independent of his needs. Especially Meredith, who can be in the same room, standing at his elbow or across the dinner table, and never touch him. Who manages to be there and not be there. As if he has an unseen contagion.

He thinks of the tag end of dinner, how they lingered over a cup of coffee and Bailey's. They were talking of how, on the river, the coyotes' barking had wakened them in the night, and they'd opened the tent to watch the moonlight on the river, and stayed on for starlight after moonset, and then Meredith had set her fork aside and said, "I could love this place. I see now why you stay." And Nance had said, "You should move out here. I mean, what have you got back there anymore? Dad's gone. You're alone." Then they'd gone on drinking their coffee as if nothing had happened. Though all through the dregs of dinner he could sense change, and he could think of two, maybe three other times in his life, with Tina, or as a kid with his parents, say, when he'd felt the forces of a moment conspiring to change him and the course of his life in just this way. He realizes the two of them are, even now, coming to a decision without him.

He rocks forward on the stoop, puts his elbows on his knees, and looks down the length of the street—houses battened down, doors shut, yard gates locked, even lamplight confined to the backs of drapes. The temperature's actually rising, a warm breeze wincing through the trees. A big front's blowing in, rain or sleet by morning, and more forecast during the week. The remains of a newspaper flap down the sidewalk and across lawns, rustle from where they've snagged on bushes and fences, while overhead the sycamore's bare branches knock like a knacker's mallet.

Across the street, old man Turnbull's house gleams through a lattice of hawthorne and vines. Cats caterwaul from his yard, and Ned can hear the convening howls moving down the alleys, from neighboring yards and streets.

The man keeps cats. Fifty, maybe sixty, or more? Though he hardly *keeps* them, except by the loosest means: dishes of food seeded here and there in his yard. On his porches, crockery and plastic tubs filled to spilling, stoking the feral population. It's a squall of animals, their musk pooling in hollows and underbrush, all pheromones and lust assembled in the odd corners of the night, the air so pitched with piss and blood that it carries a kind of resonating charge, an olfactory hum fine as the ring of a tuning fork. An extravagance of cats, humped together, snubbed crotch to rump, and howling under the glazy light of moon, and he imagines the besotted old sod standing with his face pressed to the window. Under cloud cover or the bright moonlight, listening to the electric screams and watching the congress of animals. *His own private glory hole.*

He pushes away from the stoop and, standing, leans into the wind that snatches at his hair, at his jacket collar. He jogs down the stairs, steps off onto the sidewalk. He cuts the street on a diagonal, and on the far side, under the bare-limbed trees, he stands a moment, looking at the overly bright lights of his house. He can not see the business that goes on in there–the industrious women already filling the washing machine, cleaning the counters. All the ordinary tasks of ordinary life, which is, he believes, the thing he's coveted for himself.

He moves on to the end of the block, where he turns right at the corner and slows. There is about him a sense of things shifting as quickly as the weather, an old, old excitement. He walks past the tidy homes around the Normal School, now a small four-year state college. This is the older, gentrified section of town, and he strolls with his hands bunched in his pockets, glancing into windows, where he believes all the ordinary people live their uncomplicated lives: nothing mattering more than the next television program, the next meal. Walls riddled with family portraits, gewgaws on knickknack shelves.

He walks down the next two blocks at a brisk pace. The school yard is closed and locked; the empty swings stir in the wind. He walks up to the main entrance and, fishing in his pocket, lifts out a key. He opens the door and steps in. An overhead light is on in the entry, and he supposes it's Orval Jeffords or Kenny Nelson, doing some late-night maintenance. He claps the door shut behind him, and down the hallway he sees someone. It's Nelson, squinting. "Oh, it's you, Mr. Able. You're here late."

Ned gives a small wave. "Just can't seem to stay away."

Nelson leans on a mop. "Well, I don't suppose that's as sorry as those of us who never get away in the first place."

"My heart bleeds for you, Ken."

"Yeah, yeah. Well, tell you what, don't do it on the floor I just cleaned."

"Night, Ken."

Nelson touches two fingers to his forehead, then disappears back into a classroom with the mop, and Ned moves down the corridor to the end of the hall. He unlocks the door, crosses through the secretary's space, checking for memos. In his office, he sits at the desk, a small banker's light on the side table all the illumination he needs. He crosses his feet under the desk and knits his hands behind his head. It feels good. His own house suddenly grown overfull.

Who'd have thought? He feels that little nervous jump in his head, his mouth dries, and he squeezes his eyes shut.

When he opens them again, it's to the solace of books arranged by title and category: administrative texts, teaching texts. File cabinets stacked, locked, and labeled. The budget tight but workable. His teachers win awards; his programs bring in grants. *His* children, for that is how he sees them, are safe.

He turns on his computer, pulls up the school logs, scans Web sites, chat rooms, notes some of the searches the children have done for school projects. With all the security devices, with all the checks and balances on the ways the world can enter his school, there is always the avenue you haven't prepared for. Contrary to what people think, it is not a whole new dangerous world out there; it's merely a lot more convenient.

He pauses, looks over the top of the screen at the wall with its certificates, diplomas, commendations, and recognitions. He has a sudden vision of himself as a good man doing the good work, keeping back what ranges out there: child pornographers, pedophiles.

Scum. For this is a thing he has learned painfully—that behavior has boundaries. Lines you draw between what's available and what isn't.

And while some lines are not always as clear as others, or have some flexibility under the right circumstances, on *these grounds* he is close to righteous. He leans back in his chair. Feels comforted and generous. Forgiven and forgiving.

He recalls dinner, the conversation about fear, fear being one of those things that holds his attention absolutely. A thing he's frankly never considered when he thinks of his wife: scientist, outdoors woman.

Snake handler.

Maybe she's learned it from the snakes—the way she looks people in the eyes, steady and long. The first time she turned it on him, it had taken all the resolve he had to keep from flinching, and even now, when he can return it gaze for gaze, still his hand will swipe down a pant leg at an imagined itch, or tug at some part of his face, or rub the back of his neck as if something's there, fussing at him.

Thinking of home, that brightly lighted, anxious commotion, he closes the windows on his computer, shuts it down, and sits quietly while the drive whirs to a stop. He turns off the small lamp.

When he lets himself out, he locks the office doors. His jogging shoes chirp on the clean linoleum, and as he pauses in the thin red light of the emergency exit, he can hear no one else—Nelson having moved into the other wing perhaps, or gone home. He walks past trophy cases full of soccer and baseball and volleyball trinkets. Past the small auditorium with its dollhouse seats and stage. School banners drape from the walls, maroon-and-white felt pennons with the Jefferson School Chipmunks rampant. It's an old building and smells of wood and plaster, paper, glue, chalk dust, and marker pens. Old latrines with white ceramic tiles dosed weekly with disinfectants. The teachers' lounge with its innumerable pots of boiled coffee and weak-kneed herbal teas, its microwave with the spattered remains of last week's lunches.

He steps out the main doors, locks them, then strides away. It's good to be on the move. He cuts through the mechanic's parking lot, then crosses the street, where he steps through the wrought-iron arches of the old city cemetery grounds. To the right is a small stone mausoleum, but he keeps to the narrow asphalt road that forms the trunk of a cross intersecting the lawns, an area three blocks square. Most of the markers are plain stones sunk level with the grass—a level playing field—the odd stone angels, lambs, or crosses standing white, like solitary players against the dark. He wanders into the oldest section, past the headstone that reads DAN BOOTH's WIFE—just so everyone will know that what was buried there was first and foremost property, and only second a woman, and by obvious omission an Indian. He's strolling now, feeling no less comfortable with the dead than with his own company, savoring the long blocks ahead, and though the clouds have formed a thick bunker over the moon, he does not hurry. This is the rainy season, but he's come to an accommodation with the rain, as everyone here does. No umbrellas. No rain slickers or galoshes for this tough little town and its people, a lot of old-timers—ranching and farming retirees. The descendants of pioneers, holdovers of an older West, and a little rain wasn't going to hurt them. You get wet. You dry off. End of story.

He circumnavigates the burial plots, winding in and out among the stones, his footsteps an intaglio in the moist grass. At the street, he files out the stone entrance and walks down the middle of the road. Two blocks over, he angles across the college parking lot and into the alley that is a narrow gravel tract between dated one-car garages and carports with cement pads that hold boats, campers, snowmobiles, and, at one place, a horse trailer still rank with manure. He walks down the center hump, and a small terrier savages a yard fence with his bright teeth, his high yaps jumping in a chain reaction over whole blocks, igniting baleful howls and yips from half a dozen unseen dogs. He moves on, outpacing the noise.

A good half mile from home, he spots a light shining in a small window at the rear corner of a house. He leans against the weathered picket fence, staring down the wide corridor between the house and the next yard. The light at the corner is dim as a suggestion. He eases the gate latch up and stands a moment with it open, like an invitation in hand, before stepping through.

The wind tugs at his jacket. He keeps to the shadow of the privet brush lining the yard's length, listens for the rasp of a chained dog, or a sudden voice. His chest tightens, ribs a caliper to the hammering in his heart. In the far back of the yard, he steps out of the shadow, moving obliquely to the thin column of light that escapes the narrow window. Shade drawn. There's a good four or five inches where the shade does not close. The first drops of rain spark off his forehead and hands. He stands close enough to see most of the room, but well enough back so that he doesn't have to stoop. He stands quietly, until he is just another fragment of the yard's dark.

There's that old pleasurable stirring and he tries to breathe deeply, but the constriction moves up his throat as a woman moves into view, and the rain comes on now, the first ponderous drops that clot down the back of his coat.

It's a bedroom lit by the amber glow of twin dresser lamps. Against one wall is a full-size bed battened in quilts, and the walls are papered in a frenetic hopscotch of birdsfoot violets that will never evoke sleep, and he wonders at the choice, unaware it has been chosen because it was cheap, unaware that she'd wearied of it a short six months after hanging it. But he can not know this about her—nor that she covers the dresser tops with linen runners laundered twice monthly, and scattered over them are the odd boxes full of costume jewelry she hasn't felt the need to wear these last five years. She moves between closet and dressers, readying for bed.

She bends for her slippers, then, sitting on the side of the bed, slides her breasts out of the bra, scratching at the line creased beneath her breasts. Truth is, it would never occur to her to look for someone here, in the dark of her yard, considering herself long the other side of any man's desire, with her simple looks and the homely spread of back and buttocks developed from a taste for late-night candies and sugared drinks. A woman with two children grown and gone. A woman whose short string of husbands found other pleasures long ago.

She'd be the first to admit she might miss a man in her life, might even imagine one of those short-lived loves coming back to take up his side of the bed again. But to be partnered in the dark. With a stranger. This she would not conceive of.

Oh, she might *believe* such things happen in the world, but she would not understand it. Certainly not the randomness of it. Nor could she know that shape, size, age, or even sex isn't what matters. None of it, finally, making a difference—man, woman, or both, because, and this would be fully outside of her comprehension, the pleasure is not in the *thing* seen but in the *act* of seeing. Having to do with what runs on rodent feet up his back, the shiver of anticipation. The possibility that roots about in the hub of his brain. The *unimaginable*. And in those moments, he sees himself watching, as if from a distance, sees himself framed against the side of the house, just a thin wall away from the person in the room. Privy to his or her most secret parts, their obsessions and predilections. *Like a thief. A confessor.* How could she know? How could she begin to imagine that even as he watches in the rain and wind, and lightning flickers in the distance, he promises it will be this one time only and never again, and even as one side of him contemplates the comfort of that assurance, another creeps in from that other part of himself and ponders just how he could have gone on so long without it. Without even this. *This smallest of transgressions, surely.*

Chapter Four

N ance studies the computer screen. She's in her home office, a converted spare room just off the living room. The room's crowded with bookshelves, books, file boxes, a stack of paper a foot high next to the desk bristling with stick-'em notes. Disorder? Absolutely. But chaos? Not yet.

She scans Everwine's story as she's typed it into the computer. The serpents feeding on the shoat, and then on each other. The image not unlike the myth of the worm Oroborous—the serpent coiled at the center of the earth, feeding endlessly on his own tail and, in his struggle to feed, turning the world with him. There were other parallel myths as well, for even as Everwine's snakes doomed the shoat and each other in turn, it is the coyote, that old trickster, that finally carries away their life in his belly.

She's spent the day compiling and transferring data onto the computer. In a separate file she's typed in Everwine's story along with the 223 other odd tales she's recorded in the years she's been here. The usual sort: the snake that sucks the cow dry, the snake that removes its fangs while courting. The rattle of snakes worn about the neck to cure fits and convulsions. Need rain? Put a rattler on its back.

And there were the long, convoluted stories of death. The father struck by a rattler dies, and years later, his sons—each successively wearing his father's boots—mysteriously die. Until one bright mortician discovers a fang still buried in the leather of the boot. And then there's the addendum where the mortician takes out the fang, buries it. Except his dog digs it up, and he dies, as well.

Or the one where a cowboy mistakes frozen snakes for fence posts and pounds them in. Come spring, the snakes thaw and tow miles of barbed wire behind them. Or the cowboy who ties down his saddle pack with what he thinks is a rope—rattler thaws out, bites the man, and rides the horse home.

She yawns and turns off the computer, feels pleasantly fatigued. There's always a bit of a letdown after a field trip. She thinks of her sister, who called late that afternoon to say she was safely home in Wisconsin. What was it she said? "It's snowed here. A lot. The house smells like a shut-in. I miss you."

Nance takes another sip of tea. The real revelation for Nance this day has been in discovering how much she misses Meredith, as well. In fact, just thinking about her brings on a sudden tenderness, like a wound she hadn't known was being inflicted.

With cup in hand, she walks over to the window. She lifts the blind and looks out, presses her forehead to the pane to feel the soft blows of rain against glass. Outside is a smear of light and night and water. It's been raining off and on for a week: downpours, drizzle, mist, and mizzle. Though flooding is not new to Nance, in this place of desert landscape, it's a surprise.

She thinks about the day before, the last day of Meredith's vacation, their drive upriver in Nance's '84 Dodge Ram—a noisome clunking rig with heavy-duty suspension, a granny gear that ground its way into place. The river moved in slow rollers, a broad elastic band of water, mud, and debris, and from within the river came a deep knocking—boulders, some of them the size of small cars, tumbling down the river bottom, as well as the sound of lesser rocks colliding, the punctuated cracks like snapping bones. Wave on wave, they passed through, like earth-bound asteroids journeying through the valley on a watery belt.

She turned up the Cloverland grade, and in the hairpin turns they could see the river growing smaller, the hue deepening to a husky red. On the ridge top, the sky blew open before them, high and wide and gray with a scut of clouds. They were on the spine of Hells Canyon, with drops of a thousand feet and more. Nance idled onto a pullout and they stepped out.

They stood well back on the road, holding hands, as they had done as children, and then Meredith let go, took a step forward, another.

"Meredith," Nance said, her tone cautionary.

"Yeah, yeah," she said. She toed closer to the edge. The wind was fierce, and Meredith opened her arms, so that it set her back on her heels.

"Okay, Sis. That's enough," Nance yelled.

And then Meredith was standing on the tips of her toes, her arms out, jacket ballooning, and she was leaning into the wind, as if she might lift right there. Take flight. Or fall.

"Jesus," Nance shouted.

Meredith bobbled, the gusts hitting her, her upper body suspended over the gulf of canyon. "This is so cool," she shouted.

And then Nance couldn't take it anymore. She stepped forward, snatching Meredith by the back of the jacket, and there was an instant when Meredith pitched forward, and Nance thought her sister was going to shrug out of the thin shell, slip free, and fall the thousand and more feet, and in that moment, her sister's face turned to her with a look of resignation—as if she'd believed Nance would push her over the edge.

Meredith rocked forward, then, dropping on her heels, stumbled backward into her sister, laughing. "Damn, girl, you can let go the chokehold." She spun in her sister's arm, pulling the jacket free, wrapped both arms around Nance's shoulders. "What'd you think? I was going to jump?"

Nance felt like stone. "I thought you might fall."

"Not a chance." Meredith laughed, slapped her sister on the back, then jogged back to the truck.

In the truck, Nance started up the racketing engine and the heater. She was shaking. She swung the vents open.

Meredith threaded her fingers through her hair. "What a rush."

Meredith reached over, hugged her sister again. "Hey, I'm sorry if I scared you, Sis. Really. I didn't mean to. Honest."

Nance settled against the bench seat, rested an elbow on the door frame. *You never do.*

Meredith closed her eyes, ran her hands up and over her forehead, over her wet hair. "You happy, Nance? Out here?" When she opened her eyes again, she looked at Nance. "I worried about you, you know. I worried you couldn't be happy again. After Joe."

The cab smelled of wet wool and of shampooed hair faintly muddied with rain. Nance looked out the side window, startled again by the green hills, the first blush of color on the buck brush. Were the hills already greening upriver, around the den? *Surely I would have noticed.*

Nance shook her head, looked over at Meredith. "Ned's a *good* man, Mer. Give him a chance."

Nance rouses from the memory. She lifts her head from the office window, the rain battering the glass harder. What was it her sister had answered? "I do try. Honestly. But he makes me feel . . . anxious."

She picks up her cup from the bookshelf and smiles down at the snake. "Hey, Ramone," she says. It's a Western Rattler, forty-five inches from head to button. A beautiful specimen. Taxidermied. Not the usual coiled serpent striking. Nor the disembodied rattles and heads embedded in acrylic paperweights: *Don't tread on me!* Or the latest trend in rearview mirror art, swinging on the end of leather straps and alligator clips, the preserved heads topped in miniature Stetsons, wearing spectacles, mustaches, and beards, or glued-on braids with Indian headdresses.

No. This is the rattler as it was for the better part of its days. Just going about business. She'd found it in a taxidermy shop, where it had been nailed to the pine paneling in a vertical crawl up the wall. Maybe that's what touched her—its unending climb up the wall, a reptilian Sisyphus if she'd ever seen one. Silly, this errant sympathy for a long-dead snake, and not something she'd admit to. But she bought it, made it a home on the flat of the bookcase. Her friend Bob, a poet in the English Department, took one look and named it Ramone. How could she argue with that?

With a little conditioning, the snake's colors have reemerged. An elegant creature. She stoops to eye level. Sometimes, late of a night, in the dark of the room or with only the computer screen to illuminate it, Ramone comes alive, the eyes bright and fluid, scales waxy and flexing.

Ned hates it. "It's too real," he says. Once asked her if she couldn't take it back to her office at the university. But she won't. Somehow the thought of it in her closed school office, no real home, would seem like abandonment.

She walks into the living room. "Ned?" she calls. In the kitchen, she turns on the heat under the kettle. She tidies the counters, and at the first hint of a whistle, she's already lifting the pot from the coils, pouring the water into her rinsed mug.

She steeps the tea bag for a count of ten—hardly tea at all, her father would have said. Spoons in sugar and stirs. The clock over the stove reads 10:00 and Ned has been gone for a good hour now. "Just going to the store. I forgot coffee. Might as well pick up a few other things. . . . No, it can't wait until tomorrow."

She takes her tea upstairs to their room, thinking perhaps Ned has slipped in and that he's under the covers. She imagines it, his hair already tousled, his face falling into lines like stress fractures, which make him look so much older sleeping than awake. He's a fitful sleeper. And though he claims never to remember, it's clear he does dream, and they are of little consolation.

She sips tea and walks about the room with its four-poster bed, the ecru crocheted bedcovers—her grandmother's handiwork—and the marble-topped dressers Ned picked out, though she's not fond of them, the cool stone surfaces resembling too closely the dissecting tables at work. She opens one of his drawers, the carefully folded clothes meticulously ordered. She lifts out a sweater, amazed, as she always is, at how his clothing doesn't look lived in. She folds it back onto the stack of reds, and feels oddly guilty, as if prying.

The first time they met had been at Fred Melton's new home. Fred, a botanist, had invited the new principal at his son's school to the open house. She remembers Fred steering her by the elbow right up to the chair where Ned was sitting. What was her first impression? Just this very thing perhaps, the creases in his pants, the impeccable taste, the got-it-together look, that put her off momentarily.

Until he'd stood to meet her. His hands warm, dry. His handshake firm but kind. His hair, a ruddy brown, kindled in the late-afternoon light. The way his eyes took her in. They way he looked at her—a way she hadn't been looked at for so very long. It had surprised her to discover how much she'd missed the attention of a man. The warm regard of his eyes.

They'd spoken a bit, drifted apart as new people arrived, but kept finding their way back to each other throughout the course of the evening. Amazing, really, how comfortable she'd felt with him. They had such similar habits and tastes. Her favorite foods were his. He thought her jokes funny. He was alone, and new to the area. His parents dead these several years. No other family that he knew of.

For days afterward, they'd come upon each other: while shopping at the grocery store, or at the gas station, or strolling the levee. It was companionable. She found herself looking forward to seeing him, to his calling her, and time alone now only emphasized how ready she was for change. She was eager for conversation over dinner. She liked having again someone whose step fell in alongside hers. Some one person she could anticipate walking through the door. She discovered she was tired of being alone, if not lonely.

And when it became sexual, if it wasn't as it had been with Joe—that kind of frolicking and intensely joyous sexuality—she understood that was a thing of youth. Of first loves. And there were compensations to this more mature sexuality. The accomplished lover. A deliciously considered lovemaking. He brought to bed a kind of precision. Finally, it seemed to Nance, their pairing was something other than fate. It was . . . gravitational. They were married four months later in a small ceremony down at the courthouse. No attendants beyond their witnesses, Fred Melton and his wife. There was a handful of rice tossed outside the courthouse steps, followed by a quiet dinner for two. Perhaps remarkably unremarkable for a wedding, but it was what they'd both wanted.

She looks down into the neat piles of clothes. Impeccable. Feels the urge to put a finger in and stir it up a bit. Instead, she nudges the drawer shut with a knee and strolls out of the room.

She moves into the guest room, where she sets the cup on the bedside table and begins to strip the bed. She shrugs the pillowcases off, and a fragrance—lily of the valley—wafts up. It's the scent she has paired with her sister since they were girls. A will-o'-the-wisp, "now you smell it, now you don't" kind of fragrance that Nance could never own, as *she* is more likely to smell of formaldehyde, rubbing alcohol, or snake musk, and has long ago given up hope of smelling of anything better than de-odorizing soaps. She lifts a strand of her hair to her nose, sniffs. Even now, after all these days away from the lab and preserving jars, she's certain it lingers in her hair, on her hands. A kind of slow embalmment. How many men would be as understanding of that as Ned?

Nance bundles the sheets, carries them in an awkward wad to the laundry chute, and, plucking the small door open, wedges them down the narrow opening. She thinks of Meredith's fascination with the laundry chute in their childhood home—"It's a hole in the house," she'd say, as if that suggested a structural fault, an imminent collapse that would take them all. It was the first thing Meredith did after their mother's death: nailed it shut.

Ned strolls the aisles of the Albertson's Store. It has taken three tries to find a shopping cart that doesn't bump or lock wheels. He leans his elbow on the cart and scopes out the sales: a can of cashews, cereal, coffee. This time of night, the store's nearly empty. Alternate banks of lights have been turned off in the name of conservation. In the dim lighting, the store—with its pimpled bag boys, its aging checkout clerks, its boxed goods and cans—even the produce, has about it a kind of rosy bloom, and all the bruised and blemished flesh becomes a shadow, a mishap of lighting. He balances an orange in one hand and flaps open a plastic sack with the other. He drops six into the bag, chooses the thinnest-skinned fruits.

From across the aisle, he catches quick glimpses of a woman, and when the opportunity presents itself, he studies the sandy hair falling in tight ripples down her upper back, the cropped wool jacket, or the knee-length skirt creased at the crotch, the run up one black stocking, *the bright ladder of skin beneath.* A thin woman, but not small, for as she bends over to pick through the apples, her flattened rump is broad, and he finds the mannish spread of her shoulders exciting. When she moves on, he follows with the ease of a practiced shopper, sorting through sales, ignoring impulse items. He skips two aisles, circles back. Overhead, an orchestral "Fly Me to the Moon" plays out of the store's sound system. From the dairy case, he can see her at the meat counter, deliberating. Two packages in hand. He imagines them choice cuts. Cradled in fat and plumply red.

His limbs feel weighted, a kind of pleasurable thickening, a slight dizziness, like the blowsy release of a mild drunk. He reaches behind the rows of waxed milk cartons, and the cool air shivers up his arms. And then she is rolling her cart over to the butter and cheeses. He wanders to where she stands, and when he reaches into the refrigerated case with its waxy globes of Gouda, he can sense her at his back, and he wants to touch her. Nothing dramatic. Just an awkward collision. A flutter against the ribs, *did he just do that?*— a finger at the small of her back—*surely not*—or an abrupt turn to reach across for the Muenster—*oh, excuse me.*

She selects a square of baby Swiss, and when she moves on, he lingers.

It's a game. No harm to it. He just *happens* to be here. Although sometimes he'll make it a little more interesting. Speak to her, say, or, best of all, should she notice, he'll look over her head, or away to keep her guessing. Let her know he's not really interested. And he's not, he tells himself; it's a game. A pleasurable diversion from lamb chops and celery.

But he does commit them to memory, the women, for later. This one: the tiny mole that crowns one ear, the blunt-tipped fingers, square palms, and ropy arms. The gape in her blouse and the pale slit of skin—*that almost certainly rosies up when she's excited,* eyes an indifferent blue. Her narrow lips purse in a perfect O.

He follows the length of half an aisle, scanning the salad dressings. He stops at the condiments: jars of caper berries, and Manzanita olives—he has a fondness for the darkly pitted fruits, their oily bite. He should pick up some feta cheese for a late-night antipasti. Nance would like that. He holds the jar in his hand, the small orbs bobbing in their ocher fluid, and for a moment, just a blink of his eyelid, there's a charge in his head like static, and it seems as if he is in some darker, crowded place, with dirt pooling at his feet. Someone's breath is on the back of his head, his neck, and then he's in the store again, with the jar still in his hands. He's already forgotten what it is he thought he saw, but his stomach's gone as small and hard as those fruits and bobbing in its own juices. He breathes through his nose and a cold sweat beads his forehead. He sets the olives in the cart. He wipes his forehead with a sleeve, and as the sickness subsides, he's orienting himself, focusing on the shelves with their bright bites of red maraschino cherries, the pale wands of pickled asparagus, and plump artichoke hearts. He turns, his hands locked onto the cart handle, and wonders where Nance has wandered off to, and then remembers he's come alone. There's that familiar ache blooming in his gut. When the spasm lessens, Ned dusts a hand down one pant leg, checks that his shirt is tucked in, pats the back of his neck, and moves on.

He checks out before she does, exchanges pleasantries with the woman at the register. She's a parent to one of his children: "Oh yes, Victor. Victor Kriss. Fine, fine, doing fine." Then he trundles his groceries out to the car, where he sits in the dark, waiting.

She steps into the cold air, clutching her jacket closed. A young bagger rolls her loaded cart into the lot, white apron flopping loosely between his legs. He packs her groceries into the trunk. She says something, and he ducks his head and nods, angles his arm out and to the right, his hand skipping over the parked cars and then stopping to point where Ned is parked. Ned flattens against the seat, heart lubbing a long moment before the finger moves on. She nods and unlocks her car door, slips into the driver's seat as the young boy bumps the cart back up the sidewalk and into the store.

The second-floor lights are on. He thinks Nance is at the window, then sees he is mistaken. He pulls into the dark one-car garage, built back in the days when that was still practical. He closes his eyes. He wonders what time it is but can not muster the energy to turn on the light to check his watch. He looks over at the plastic bags slumped on the seat. Small pickings. He threads his hand through the handles and swings his legs out.

The garage smells of gas, and oil, and cedar. It's musky with mouse droppings and the piss of cats that stalk the mice. Glancing across the way, he can see his neighbors have gone to bed. Up and down the street, the houses are dark. Many of them are unlocked. Not exactly careless. Clueless, perhaps, for believing that there was no need for such measures here, as if this place were outside the times we live in, and that locks were only for long vacations.

The night air is damp and bitter with the mill's residue. When he looks up, he sees the overcast is thinning and that the moon has already gone down. He lets himself in, locks the door behind him. In the kitchen, he doesn't turn on the lights, but opens the refrigerator, the lone bulb bright enough for the small circle he works in.

He can hear Nance upstairs. He sorts out the small pile of goods: one for the pantry, two for the fridge, another for the bathroom. He thinks of the woman with the split up her panty hose, the ribbon of flesh. His hands fall to his side and he closes his eyes.

There's the wink of streetlights, red brake lights, the green of traffic signals. The long, tedious chase up Thain grade. *Is it a chase if the one being pursued doesn't know?* The back of her head silhouetted in his high beams.

Wal-Mart scrolls past, its big dumb smiley face leering over the valley, and next to that Outlet Groceries, and Hastings, and the local hardware store that's been here for two generations, now all but doomed by the arrival of the upstart Home Depot just a mile down the hill.

Let a car slip in between, then another. Like at the grocery store—now you're here, now you aren't. She turns into the gas station, canopied lights glaring over four banks of pumps. He keeps on for a half block, and pulls into the used-furniture store's empty parking lot. Points the nose of his car streetward. Settles back. Believes even at this distance he can see the band of white up the back of her leg, the shine of her crimped hair. He imagines the feel of it in his hand. He thinks about cutting it.

She gets back in the car, and he follows at a distance down dark side streets in an area of town known as the Orchards. The clutter of yards is haphazardly lit in rounds of yard lights or in pale squares cast from windows. Her headlights sweep the narrow road and the fence line, where a Roman-nosed horse droops in sleep, a leg cocked beneath him. She slows. He passes as she turns into a driveway. He looks over his shoulder, orients himself. Motors on. Headlights off. He stops.

When he hears footsteps coming down the stairs and rounding the corner, he opens his eyes and sees the pale face again, that perfect O on her mouth. He wonders how she's come to be *here* but as quickly understands it is Nance, his wife, and imagines himself as she must see him, stooped over in the light of the fridge, the white-skinned bags emptied at his feet.

"Ned, are you all right?"

The question surprises him, but he recovers. "Stomach," he says.

And then she's leaning over him, fitting her hand around an elbow. "Here . . . here, sit a moment," and she leads him to a kitchen chair. She shuffles through the dark cabinets and he hears cans sliding on the shelves, and the rustle of paper, and then she's standing next to him and a small square of crackers appears on the table. "Try some of these." She moves toward the light switch.

"No," he says. "Please." He waves a limp hand, thinks of that anxious knot in his lower back. The headache in the store, the sudden dizziness. "No lights."

She sits beside him, her hand fretting with his hair, briefly touching his hand, his arm. "I was worried," she says. "You were gone so long. I couldn't imagine . . ."

He nods, smiles. "Not your average fun shopping trip," he says.

"Managed not to embarrass myself too badly, though." And it's become, for him, a possible truth: a case of the flu, a bad night at the grocery store. The rest of it he shrugs aside. After all, nothing of real account happened. He smiles wanly. "I'll be better now."

Chapter Five

N ance sits in a corner booth at the Ramrod, a small diner with walls the color of browned butter and decorated with maroon Naugahyde booths and cowboy art: branding irons, bits and spurs, the usual Remington reproductions. Her favorite: the large black-and-white poster of John Wayne. There's counter seating, but Nance hasn't sat at one since she was a kid, when she and Meredith would linger at the Woolworth's counter, sipping cokes on Saturday afternoons. She watches her sister work the tables. Meredith's been living in Lewiston a month now, having moved some few of her belongings out while listing their old home with a rental agency. "You were right," she'd said. "I didn't have a thing back there to stay for. And the more I thought about my visit out here, the more I knew it was what I needed. A whole new start."

The locals frequent the Ramrod for its down-home food, its aspiration to be nothing more than what it's been for the last fifty-odd years: consistent, clean. The best coleslaw in the valley. Meredith's already won them over, and is even now charming the elderly Dutch, who buddies up to the end of the counter every noon with his oxygen tank and pack of Camels. She gives him a clean ashtray.

Nance studies the menu, opts for krab salad and ice tea. A group of women sit in the large corner booth in riding pants and half chaps. Their talk is of horses. For Nance, *horseback* means fieldwork in the hills with pack animals during a week of ninety-plus-degree days, the seams of her body wet with sweat and chafing. She has that to look forward to—trekking up canyon with a small group of grad students, tracking snakes from the den. Jerry Mathes will be topside in a truck on the Oregon side, while Brenda Volk will do the Washington side. In the fall, Nance will compare the data, work up the baseline stats for future studies: territories, range of travel, variations in movement in relation to habitat and seasons.

The waitress, Gaylene, a young woman with lips oversized in pink lipstick, brings her salad and delivers the check to the table across from Nance, where a woman sits with a toddler. Gaylene offers a sucker to the child. Toys, crayons, food, and a drizzle of milk form a pastiche on the tabletop and floor. The mother picks up the check; for a moment, Nance could swear the woman's planning to bolt. But no, she opens a canvas tote bag, fishes out a checkbook, and starts ladling in toys, along with unopened packets of bread sticks and crackers.

The child has crammed the sucker, wrapper and all, into her mouth and is slurping happily as she's hauled out of her chair by an arm. She plants her feet and skids past Nance, and as their eyes meet, Nance wonders what it would be like to have a child. If Joe had lived long enough?

She picks out a chunk of krab, wonders briefly what it's made of. Of course, nothing said she couldn't still have children. Thirty-three is hardly old. But at forty-four, Ned's used to a life without them. He's made that clear enough. The rabbity look that came to his eyes when she mentioned it. "Kids? I got kids all day long. And they don't cost us a thing."

It's understandable, she supposes. He's been so long without commitments in general. Until their marriage. She looks out the window, over the gravel parking lot, where a dust devil is chucking debris into truck beds and open car windows. The mother is stowing the tote bag into the backseat, where she has also belted the toddler into a child seat, and it's all done with an economy of movement that implies time whittled down to its smallest increments. So, how do you balance a career and children? Ned had brought that point up as well: "Kids and snakes. That's a likely combination."

"Hey, Sis."

Nance turns to see her sister has scooted into the seat next to her. "Should you be doing this?"

Meredith smiles. She slips a piece of lettuce from the plate into her mouth and chews. "They think I'm the cat's meow."

A phrase Nance hasn't heard since her father was alive: *Your mother was the cat's meow.* She's struck with a wave of nostalgia, which is happening more and more often with Meredith here.

"Anyway," Meredith says. "I just wanted to give you a little hug." She does, and then she's slipping out of the chair. "You dining alone?"

Nance shrugs her shoulders. "Looks like it."

"Stood up, huh?"

But Nance prefers to think Ned has run into something unexpected, or has forgotten, rather than entertain the idea he doesn't want to see her. Not a thing she would have even considered a month, two months ago. She glances out the window for the car with the mother and child, but there is only a space between cars, the suggestion of wheel treads in the gravel. When she looks up, Meredith is studying her.

"You really have been, haven't you? Stood up."

Before she has to admit as much, the diner door opens and Ned enters. He eases past the counter seating, narrowly misses the oxygen tank parked next to the counter, smiles at the old man, says: "How's it going?" He bends to hear the old man's reply. He laughs, says something, and then the old man's coughing and laughing, too.

Behind him, Everwine enters the restaurant, and Nance has a moment's confusion, but he quickly sees it's not her he's here for, as his gaze searches out Meredith.

Ned brushes past Meredith, and Nance watches as her sister steps back, a hand brushing at the spot on her thigh where they grazed. Nance looks away, smiles over at Everwine, who's coming up the aisle. "Hey, Pete, good to see you."

He salutes with a finger to his hair, which is neatly combed, though the crease where the ball cap usually sits may be permanent. "Hey, didn't expect to see you two," he says.

Ned slides into the seat facing Nance, stretches back, and studies Pete with a look that's at first indifferent, then interested. "Join us?"

Everwine calls over his shoulder to Meredith, "Cup of coffee, ma'am," and seats himself. "How's snakes?"

He grins up at Meredith as she sets his cup down, along with cream and sugar. Meredith blushes.

"Three more weeks. You ready?" Nance asks Pete. It's the first scheduled trip of the summer.

He nods. "Got the guide and pack animals reserved up above Imnaha. Then by boat to the den site, then Waterspout, and . . . ?"

"And then we'll see."

Ned's looking about. "So this is where your sister works. Is she planning on making a living, or what?" He picks up the menu, glances at it. "Waitressing. You don't make a living without tips." He shakes his head. "Best tip she'll get here is to work somewhere else." He turns back to the menu. "Nothing but cowboys."

Nance feels Everwine shifting uncomfortably next to her. She hopes Meredith hasn't overheard, but she's across the way, chatting with a couple of the old-timers. One of them throws his head back and guffaws, and the woman next to him slaps his arm. A couple of the men wear double-rivet jeans and the wide red logger's suspenders. They're the ranchers and farmers—faces tan up to their pale foreheads, like a browse line, where cowboy hats or baseball caps usually sit. The women are in tight jeans, or loose dresses and sensible shoes. A number of the jackets slung on the chair backs are lettered with Potlatch—a paper mill, and the valley's largest employer. Most of the patrons know one another. It's social club as much as eatery. Lots of elderly, and many of those coming in each day at the same hour.

Nance clears her throat, says, "She likes it here." She doesn't mention how content Meredith seems, living in this valley and working at the small café. "Like another world," she's told Nance.

Of course Meredith would love this. Nance tries to imagine being jovial every workday. Decides she's probably better suited to the pit.

The rest of Everwine's visit is small talk, and when he leaves, he stops briefly to speak with Meredith. Nance looks across the table and sees that Ned's watching her.

"Started without me?" He looks at her half-finished salad.

"You were late," she says. "I thought you'd forgotten."

He studies the menu. "What's good?" he asks. And so she understands he's not about to explain.

"Did I get the time wrong?" she presses.

He closes the menu. Gaylene's approaching with order pad in hand. He orders a Reuben, a Coke, and fries. He hands back his menu, tells her what a nice necklace she's wearing, and for that, his order will come more quickly. Nance thinks about trying one more time to get an answer but finds she's lost her appetite for that as well as the krab. She sets it to the side, wipes her lips with a napkin. "How's work?"

In an unexpected gesture, he reaches under the table and squeezes her knee. "Soon as school's over, how about you and me go on a little trip? Spokane maybe? We'll get a nice room at the Ridpath. Dinner at Fugazzi's. Or on to Seattle to take in a little nightlife. Some jazz."

She can hardly believe he's saying this. "Ned. I've got the field trip in three weeks. I'm knee-deep in planning, lining up students, equipment, supplies."

He looks surprised, and this she can't imagine, not with all the preparation already under way, the conversation with Everwine just moments ago. She wonders where Ned's been, and yes, he's been gone a lot lately— two-, three-hour trips, errands, the late afternoons and nights at work. Anyone other than Ned, she'd wonder about infidelity. But not Ned. She thinks about the notes he scribbles out, leaves tucked in one of her shoes, or a book, or tacked on the bathroom mirror. Just to say "Hi, I was thinking about you." Or "Love you." No, this new distraction is nothing to worry about. It's just the end of a school year, she tells herself, always a busy time. *"No rest for the wicked"*—their old joke, meaning administrators.

His head is cocked to one side. "Of course," he says, "of course. The field trip. Can't be forgetting that. How long? Couple, three weeks." He hums a few random bars, a thing he does when upset, a habit she's always thought curious.

Gaylene has hustled over with his pop and a basket of fries. "This'll hold you, till the sandwich comes."

When she leaves, Nance turns her hands palms up. "Listen, Ned, I'm sorry."

He waves his hand; a french fry dangles from his fingers. "No problem," he says, and eats the fry.

She tries to read his mood, but he's turned to the empty table behind them, from which he lifts a ketchup bottle.

"You know I have to do this," she says.

He's tapping the bottom of the bottle over the basket and ketchup comes out–*blat*–in a thick red wad. "Oh, Christ," he says, looks up and grins. "Oh well. It's the best part anyway. Hey, I understand, absolutely." He swipes a couple french fries through the ketchup. "You gotta count them *snakes*." He eats the fries, wipes his mouth.

"Where did this come from?" she asks.

He looks up, pauses, in hand a french fry tipped in red. "What?" He pops it in his mouth.

They pass the next several minutes elbows close to their sides, glances abbreviated. There's a ripple of movement in his jaw, a clenching, and she understands he is angry. She's about to speak, when Gaylene interrupts to set the sandwich in front of him. He lowers his head over the plate, inhaling. He asks the young woman, "What's the way to a man's heart?"

She looks confused a moment, then says, "Through his stomach?"

"Wrong," he says. "Apron strings. Breaks a man in half to see a woman in an apron."

Gaylene blushes, her hand flickering over the small apron tied around her waist.

Nance watches how he leans toward the woman, even as he slices into his sandwich, lifts the forkful to his nose, and looks at her. "Heavenly," he says.

Nance clears her throat, embarrassed, but his attention's on Gaylene, who's moving off, and Nance is left staring at a point somewhere over Ned's shoulder, at the sad cowboy gear on the wall, for that's how she sees it now–a depressing reminder of better times.

What's happened to us? But of course she doesn't ask this. Knows, in fact, how far out of the way she will go to avoid asking, or risking a scene. Preferring to keep pent up whatever's between them, until one or the other of them finds some easier way around it. Or better yet, *Given enough time, it'll sort itself out*—her dad's favorite—which generally meant it would be forgotten.

She looks out the window at the parking lot. In the bed of a purple pickup, an enormous rottweiler sits with his head braced on the tailgate, eyes riveted on the restaurant windows, as if he's looking in. Staring right at her. It's the dog du jour of this valley, and because of its brute size and questionable temperament, it's a breed that most often appeals to the people least capable of handling it. Just another loaded gun shoved in a drawer. Or left loose in the back of a pickup. Though this one looks friendly enough. There's a sticker on the chrome bumper: BORN TO HOWL. She can almost hear the baleful sound, the tuneful junkyard solo.

She shifts in her seat and catches the waitress's attention. "I'd like the check, please."

There's a look of surprise on Ned's face. "You're not leaving," he says. He reaches across and touches the back of her hand. Her first reaction is to pull away, but the look on his face is so genuine, so guileless. She lets her hand rest under his, and is surprised by how grateful she is for the touch.

Gaylene's just standing by the table; then her hand fusses with the ponytail and she turns to the next table to ask after their meal.

Ned's hand withdraws with a pat and then he's cutting the Reuben into manageable chunks and spearing them into his mouth. "It's been a rough one," he says. "This morning, I have two parents in a fight over last week's soccer game. I'm at my desk, when I hear shouting outside. So I get up and look, and there's two grown men street side, hollering at each other. Their kids are at it, too, swinging backpacks at each other."

Nance nods. She's attentive now, and feeling stung by her own petty jealousy.

"By the time I'm on the playground, they've moved the fight to the gate, and the kids are pulling at each other's jackets. So I show up, and those kids stop pretty damn quick." He looks up at Nance, his chest lifting, fork stabbing the air between them. "By now, the entire school yard's watching, and the two men are going at it, bumping chests. The whole nine yards. I tell Marsha to get the kids inside. It's not even eight in the morning. Can you imagine?"

He takes another bite. Chews a while, then shakes his head. "Kids are still arriving. Coming early to play on the playground. You know, that's one of my favorite sights in the morning?" He cocks his head up at Nance.

She's reminded of what first drew her to him: how genuine he was, how close to his emotions, how unafraid to admit to something like loving the sight of children in the morning. She shakes her head. *One of his favorite sights. I should have known,* she thinks, and wonders why she never asks him about such things.

"But this morning, they gotta see this? Two grown men fighting? Anyway, by now Gene Lange's there, third-grade teacher. Small guy, muscles about the size of the bags under my eyes." He grins at Nance. "But a real trooper. He asks if I need help.

"One father's looking pretty sheepish, clearly wants a way out. But the other's a belligerent son of a bitch. A bully.

"So I suggest we take it out of the view of the children. Suggest they think what a bad example it sets.

"The one dad's backing down the sidewalk, hands up, like he's surrendering, saying, 'You're right. Hey, I'm sorry, man.' " Ned takes a sip of water, sits back, and then picks up another bite of sandwich.

"But the other?" Nance prompts.

Ned nods. "He's all for a good show. I can just imagine what it must be like to be his kid—acting down to his father's expectations. The old man's trying to chest-butt *me* now. Asks who I think I am. Lange's backing away, says, 'I'll call the police.' "

"Good for him," Nance says.

Ned looks up, startled. "You think I couldn't handle it? You think I'm afraid of some loudmouthed, beer-gut bully?" He sets the slice of sandwich down. "Hey, I'm no easy mark in a park."

It takes a while to sink in. Then Nance pushes back in her seat, her hands flattened on the table. The man at the next table peels out some bills from his wallet, leaves them scattered across the table, and walks away. From the kitchen comes the sound of fat sizzling, the fleshy aroma of potatoes flashed in heat. The smell of cigarettes from the smoking section—just the other side of the single room. *No easy mark in a park.*

Ned's checking his lap for bits of kraut. There's a trace of grease around his lips. When he finally looks back up, he seems surprised. "Something wrong?" he asks, and shakes his head. "Anyway, I tell the guy I'm the principal, say if he takes another goddamned step, I'll have him in jail, and his kid kicked out of school. Well, that calmed the guy right down. He left on his own." Ned dabs his lips with the napkin, stretches back in his seat, his shirt rising from the belt around his waist. "Good sandwich," he says, patting his stomach.

Nance shifts in the seat. She looks back out the window to where the truck waits in the sun with the patient dog, his muzzle still braced on the tailgate. She notes the solemn slope of his head, the sorrowful eyes. Her impulse is to stand and leave. Walk through the maze of tables and out the door. She wishes she could take up station next to the dog, pull his head into her lap and console him, warn him about the peril of a jog in a park, or of early mornings in a school yard. Of having lunch with someone you love.

Ned's staring at Nance's empty place setting. "You want a little ice cream, maybe? Some bread pudding?"

She shakes her head.

He sits back. "Are you angry at me for something?" He pats his lips, puts his napkin on the table.

She shakes her head again. "No easy mark in a park? Like Joe? Is that what you mean?" Nance isn't wavering this time. Not making excuses for him, or backing down. She's angry. It was . . . *what*? Inexcusable. Cruel.

Ned pushes back in his chair, his hands braced against the table edge. "Christ, Nance, I tell you something about *my* day, and do you care? No.

You get all freaked-out." He looks around the room, as if expecting agreement from another quarter. He turns back toward her. His head wags with a wounded kind of movement. "Are we done with this lunch?" he asks, his voice pained and the look on his face weary. He waits a long moment, then stands, and the chair scrapes on the tile. He settles it back under the table and walks away.

She watches as he strides up the aisle, past the counter, and out the door. The waitress Gaylene looks after him, then over her shoulder to where Nance still sits.

Nance takes a deep breath, studies the table: a tussle of plates, wilted lettuce, kraut, crumbs. She slips a purse strap over a shoulder, settles the bag under her elbow. She straightens her back, and as she turns, she sees Meredith at the cash register.

Nance walks up there, writes a check.

"Food okay?" Meredith asks.

Nance nods.

"Service?" Meredith rolls her eyes toward Gaylene. "Attentive?"

Across the parking lot, Ned is settling behind the wheel of his Forester. It's clear he doesn't mean to wait, and perhaps that's just as well.

Her sister takes the check, eyeballs the tip. "Feeling generous?" she says.

"Let it go, Sis." Through the glass door, Nance watches him back out of his parking space. She turns back to the counter as he pulls onto Thain, hears the chirp of tires on asphalt in a juvenile gesture that's unlike him. *So what else is new?* Nance looks up at her sister, shrugs.

Meredith takes a dollar out of the tip, presses it back on the counter. "We don't want to encourage her." She smiles, flashing teeth.

At Meredith's back, past the order window, is the kitchen, painted a muddle of yellow and green, a light patina of grease over the stove, where a middle-aged man dodges between flaming pans and smoking grill; a cook's hat limp as a cabbage leaf rides his head. At the prep counter is a young boy, and he's chopping root vegetables roughly the same size as his fingers. He has a distracted look in his eyes. A radio is playing a country rehash of "Wild Horses," and it's clear the music has become as much white noise as the other constants: fans, conversation, the sizzle of hamburgers and deep fat.

"You okay, Sis?" Meredith asks.

Nance waves the question off, turns toward the door. When she steps out into the light of sun on white gravel, she feels strangely calm. She crosses the lot to her car, sees where the jerk of Ned's tires scratched in the gravel. She should feel upset, she realizes, but there's the used-car lot next door with its bright rows of cars, the dazzle of chrome and buffed windshields. She stalls at the side of her truck, hand on the door, snagged by the sound of the colored flags snapping in the breeze, by the sight of a small cluster of red, white, and blue helium balloons dimpling in the first real heat of summer.

Ned brings flowers. She'll be charmed by the cliché, think it affection-ately clumsy and typical of a man, if unusual for him—their relationship having so rarely warranted an apology. He rings the doorbell as a stranger might. A suitor.

She's in jeans and T-shirt, a dust cloth in one hand. "Flowers," she says.

He ducks his head. "This is the part where I apologize for being such a jerk, this noon, today, yesterday. These past few weeks. Tomorrow."

She stands there solemn, for a long moment, the dust cloth wringing in her hands. And then there's an ease in the tension in her jaw. She sighs, smiles. "I think I should get this on film."

"I think you should accept my humble apology."

"I'm out of practice."

"You weren't going to hear me say that." He extends the flowers wrapped in paper and ribbon. "We're wilting," he says, and, "They're roses."

She's smiling, but doesn't budge from the doorway. "Cost a lot?"

"Only if they don't work," he says.

She lifts the bouquet from his hands. Steps aside.

When he enters the house, he sees she's spent the day cleaning. He's encouraged, and snugs an arm around her waist. "House looks great," he says. He gives her waist a squeeze and follows her into the kitchen.

He calls for pizza while she arranges the flowers in a vase—yellow roses tipped in crimson. She lights candles on either side of the counter, and he pulls a couple of cold beers from the fridge, puts some Coltrane on the stereo.

It's pleasant. An almost festive evening, and after dinner they take their beers out onto the back lawn, where they settle into lawn chairs. It's nearly eight o'clock and the sun's still above the rim of the hills. To the east, white plumes stream out of Potlatch's stack, piling high and higher in counterfeit thunderheads.

"This used to be one of my dad's favorite things to do of a summer evening," Nance says. "Sit in the backyard at sunset. 'Watching the world close up for the night'—that's what he called it. One night, I argued that the world didn't close up, the sun just moved on. I was a testy child."

"No."

"Yes." She nods. Nance sips her beer, settles it back on the grass next to her chair. "Unlike my sister." She belches, ducks her head, and smiles. "Excuse me," she says, "that was the evil in me coming out. Fact is, I've always envied Meredith. For being so like my father."

"And you? Are you like your mother?" he asks.

She shrugs. "I never paid enough attention to know. We were pretty young, and mostly I was out playing, or getting into scrapes with Meredith. And then Mom was sick, and next thing I knew she was dead." Nance scoots down in the chair.

"Dad taught science at the high school, so I guess I'm most like him in that, but—" She looks down at her feet, shakes her head. "Well, for a man of science, he loved the things that confound science—the questions that'll never be resolved. He loved the unknown. Called it his 'only defense against a life reduced to facts.' He used to say, 'Without mystery, life is a beer without the head.'" Nance takes a hefty swallow. "He should have been a mystic."

"So why'd he go into science?" Ned asks.

Beer trickles down Nance's chin. She catches it with the back of her hand. "Well, that's just one of those mysteries, isn't it." She laughs softly, lowers a leg over the side of the chair.

"Well, you look more like your mom's pictures than your sister does."

"Do I? Dad always said he saw Mom in both of us: in my eyes, and in Meredith's chin. Tangible things, like he wanted us to look in the mirror and *see* her."

She finishes the last swallow, drops the empty to the grass. "Your turn. Tell me about yourself. Only this time, you can't be tight-lipped. I'm going to ply you with beer, get you falling-down-spilling-your-guts drunk. Which is to say, I'll get us another." She catapults herself from the lawn chair and jogs to the house. The door bangs behind her, and he tips his head back. The last of the sun's light is clamped between the hills and the dark platter of clouds. He closes his eyes, and behind his lids, his eyes chase as in dreams.

Next thing he knows, Nance is slipping a cold beer into his hands, kissing him on the lips. "I missed the sunset," she says.

He nods. "We both did."

She drags her lawn chair closer. "Okay. You can start now."

"There's little to tell," he says. "Pretty boring stuff. I was a geeky kid . . . skinny legs—"

She nods. "Bookish. Lousy at sports, and the neighborhood kids didn't much like you. I've heard that one. . . ."

He shrugs his shoulders. "I warned you."

"Your parents," she says, "I wish I could have met them." She leans forward on the chair, touches his arm. "I wish you had more family. Someone to connect with. Hard to imagine such a solitary life—single child. No uncles or aunts. No cousins."

He shrugs. "Hey, you don't miss what you don't know."

Nance shakes her head. "Tell me about your parents."

"My parents."

"You had them. I've seen the pictures—all two dozen," she says. "You on the pony, your mom next to you. The one with your dad in the car?"

It's interesting that of all the photos in his album, she's picked out those two. Not the other odd dozen. Two photos—two fairly unremarkable bits of his mostly unremarkable history. What's left of it; what wasn't lost, or thrown away, or embellished. "Well, then you know."

Nance laughs. "I know you made a sad-looking cowboy, but your mom was pretty handsome."

He tilts his head back on the chair. "She was small, like you, but with a big laugh. You could tell her a joke, and she'd throw back her head, hold her lips tight, and just when you'd think nothing was going to happen, she'd bust out. 'Hah, hah, hah,'" he mimics. He shakes his head. He looks down, flexes his fingers. "I got her hands."

He grins. "Enough?"

"Hardly. How about your dad?"

"Just your everyday dad," he says. "Kept a small garden, grew more cucumbers than you could bear to eat." He imagines this man with hands that are square, compact, adept. The fingers cunning. The scene shifts and it's a machine shop with a lathe, and Ned can smell the burn of steel shavings, and he thinks it darkly romantic somehow, the dirt and burn. And maybe it's a garage, for there is also the smell of gasoline on this man's unlovely hands, and an oil rag bulging from the back pocket of his coveralls. The concrete floor is stained with dribbles of oil.

He corrects the image. "He was a fastidious man," he says, "patient and practical." He sees a button-down shirt, sleeves rolled to elbows, fingernails pared, the beds clean. He puts himself in the picture, a young boy of six, standing in the far corner of some sweet-smelling shop—a well-lit, airy shop—the clean duff of wood shavings rising about his ankles. *Neil,* the man says, *get over here.*

Ned shakes his head. "What?" he asks.

"Was he large?" Nance asks.

"Medium. Absolutely unremarkable," he says, and a scar comes to mind, a sickle-shaped fold of skin that trails across a shoulder and inside the upper arm, like a harrow in that tender place. "Light-haired," and that's true enough, but then he adds, "thinning at the crown. Like a monk," he says, and sees the pink scalp as if he's looking down at it. The mole just right of the center.

"Great. I love bald men," Nance says. She reaches over, and fingers a lock of hair behind his ear. "What did he do for work?"

Nothing comes to mind but the sound of an instrument. "He played accordion."

"He was a musician?"

"No," Ned says. "For amusement, polkas, scherzos, sappy Italian love songs." But it's his mother, and it's her long fingers on the banks of buttons, the short bed of ivory keys that Ned sees. She's sitting on an old horsehair sofa, hunched over the pleated squeeze box, playing. . . . *You like this one, Neil?*

"I think," Nance says, "I could have fallen for your dad."

Yes. Ned nods. "He was that kind of guy." He looks to where the hills have flattened in the indigo light. "He was a salesman." He sees the wide spatulate hands again. Ned feels nailed to the chair. "Cars," he says. "He sold cars," and this is too close for Ned, and so he pushes himself from the chair and strides to the far side of the lawn, where the grass ends and the hill falls away in a hash of brambles and stunted shrubs and weeds.

Looking out across the valley, on the river, he can see the lights of a tug trolling westward. At the blunt prow is a train of barges, two wide and three deep. Boxcars filled with wheat are stacked high on the flat decks. The tug's passing beneath the ironwork of the raised railroad trestle. Ned says over his shoulder, "He was a reader." He can see the books, and the magazines with their blowups, and glossy foldouts, littered about the house—in the bathroom, under the sofa, the chairs, in the closet of his bedroom. *Lookie here, boy.*

He turns back toward Nance. "He had dreams. He should have waited to marry."

Nance's head is down; she's picking at the label on the beer bottle. She looks up, across the distance. "Is that why you waited so long?"

He's startled by the question. "No," he says. "I waited for you."

She rests her head back on the lawn chair, looks up at the stars. "First roses, now flattery. If I didn't know you so well"—she rolls her head to look at him—"I'd think you were trying to get into my pants."

"Imagine that," he says. He recrosses the lawn to stand at her side. "So, what are my chances?"

She shakes her head and laughs—a liquid sound in the dark—and he wonders if she isn't mildly drunk.

She says, "Not bad, but it's *so* beautiful out here." She winks. "And *dark.*"

The idea thrills and upsets him. There's the cover of shrubs to the west, where the street winds down the grade. To the north is the open view of the valley, and midway down the tangled slope is the alley and their garage. To the east, separating them from their neighbor's yard, is a fence, and the only true egress is the narrow walkway, a dark corridor along that side of the house, leading to the street. He tips her face to his with a finger under her chin. Kisses her on the lips. When he draws back, he says, "I vote we go in the house, throw open all the windows in the bedroom, strew rose petals over the bed, and tear it up without any Peeping Toms."

She snorts. "Peeping Toms. Where do you come up with these things?"

"Well, if you really *need* to know—" He flutters his eyebrows like Groucho Marx.

She throws her hands up. "No, no. If it's got to be a bed of rose petals, I can put up with it." She rolls to the far side of the lounge chair, plants her feet. When she stands, she sways a bit. "I'm a little drunk," she says.

He steadies her up the stairs with a hand in the hollow of her back. By the time they get to the room, the rose petals are long forgotten.

He has no difficulty achieving an erection. Never does. That's not it. For even though he finds familiarity blunts the appetite, he has his ways around this problem. He makes it a game: Do this; try this, then that. With Nance, he takes his time. He searches out those tender areas: behind the knee, in the crook of the elbow, the top of the eyelid. The earlobe. That small bite of skin between thumb and forefinger, the hollow on the inside of the thigh. He studies her responses—the way her skin flushes, say, how long she holds her breath. It's nothing extraordinary really, nothing any ordinary couple might not do.

What's remarkable, finally, is his stamina. He has all the stamina he will ever need with her or any woman. *Staying power is not the problem.*

She makes a small noise, and he echoes the sound and then another, until each of her sounds becomes his, and what she takes into herself, he takes, too, and when he brings her to the edge, he feels himself on the cusp, as well. She shouts, and he shouts, "Yes," and "Yes," and when she shudders beneath him, he *wants* to empty himself into her, wills himself to release, to let go. But cannot. And so he goes where he needs to, and it's no longer with her, or this room, or even this time, and some of the things he imagines, he's even done.

It's then that he finishes, cries out, and collapses at her side in the dark. After a long moment, she nuzzles into him, and he says, "I love you." He means it. For who's to say this isn't what love is, or what it feels like? After all, he's careful of her feelings. Careful not to hurt her. Shouldn't that count for something?

In fact, for the better part of his life, hasn't he mostly been a careful man?

Nance wakes in the dark. The alarm clock with its bright digital numbers reads 12:30. She is burrowed under the covers, a pillow under her head and another bundled against her breast. She reaches over, feels the empty space. She looks at the clock again. Her body feels thick and warmly connected to the bed.

She thinks about getting up to see if Ned is downstairs, but then she closes her eyes and is about to drift on, when she rouses again. "Ned?" she asks. She pushes up on an elbow. "Ned?" Her eyes adjust to the dark and she sees his silhouette in a chair by the window.

She thinks perhaps he's fallen asleep sitting upright, facing the window, overlooking the yard. "You awake?" she asks softly.

He looks at her, over his shoulder, though he still doesn't answer, and it reminds her of how her mother would sleepwalk some nights, eyes open but unfocused, right into their room to draw back the covers and feel their foreheads and pat their cheeks. She would say, "Eat your peanut butter," or "Don't forget to run," and never remember a thing the next day. As far as any of them knew, it was the only sleepwalking routine she had—check up on the kids. She remembers then how Meredith, just a bird of a girl, would wake and, in the dim glow of the night-light, rise rumpled and sleepy from bed to lead their mother by the hand back through the dark of the house to her own room. "She might get lost," Meredith would say. Funny, she'd forgotten about that. How tender and fiercely protective Meredith could be. As for herself, Nance only remembers how her mother's appearance would frighten her, and how resentful she would be at first, being wakened like that. But then, oh how they would laugh about it the next day. What was it their father used to say? "World's only time-and-a-half mother."

"Ned? It's late," she says.

The chair creaks. He moves to the bed, settles himself on top of the blankets. "Did you have a nice evening?"

She stretches, says, "Um-hum. How about you?"

He sits with his back against the headboard, his hand flat in the space between them.

"Are you okay?" She sits up in the bed, plumps the pillows behind her back. "Are you upset about something?"

"No, no," he says, but she hears an edginess in his voice that suggests otherwise.

She turns on her side, places her palm on his chest. His heart's beating as if he's been running. "What's wrong?"

He puts a hand over hers. "I worry, that's all." He fidgets atop the sheets.

She has the impression he's trying to say something. She can hear the intake of breath, almost feel the way words take shape in his mouth, and then there's silence. What could be so difficult to say, or ask?

He finally says, "You going up canyon and all."

She sighs. "Is that all? I'll be fine."

He pats her hand, removes it from his chest. "Yes. You'll do fine."

One foot rubs up and down the other shin and then stills. "You enjoy it, don't you? All those trips upriver. By yourself."

"Ned, you know you're more than welcome–"

He laughs softly. "No, I'm just saying you like being alone. Don't you."

She raises her knees, wraps her arms around them. "I don't know," she says. "I don't mind being alone. I'm so busy up there, I hardly think of it."

He stands, walks over to the closet. Opens the door in the dark. She hears the chime of clothes hangers.

"Do you want the light?" she asks.

"No," he says. "I'll manage."

The pale light of his body extinguishes as he puts on a robe. She's always found this remarkable, how modest he is. The way he will clothe himself. Even when it's just the two of them. He pads out the door and into the bathroom. The bathroom door closes, and a light shines from under the crack. She can hear the long stream of his urinating, the flush of the toilet, the water running in the sink.

He returns smelling of soap and mint. He slips the robe over the back of the chair and sits on the side of the bed a long moment before lifting his legs in, sliding under the covers. He pulls her against him, spoons her into his body, the way he does each and every night they are together. "That feels better," he says.

She snuggles closer, knowing he has a hard time of it while she's gone, that he doesn't sleep well alone. "Ned?"

"Yes?"

"Am I being selfish? Leaving you like this for weeks at a time?"

"Yes," he says. "But it's okay." He strokes her cheek with a finger. "It's your work. It's not like you're running away."

She burrows closer, enjoying the feel of him against her back, the way his hands palm her breasts. He is a thoughtful lover. Remarkable really– how cued in with her he is, how attuned to what it is she wants.

"You're a good man, Ned. I'm lucky, aren't I?"

He kisses her neck. "Go to sleep, lucky girl."

She *is* tired, realizes she's still mildly tipsy. It will feel good just to drift off, but she struggles up one more time. "Ned?"

"Yes?"

"Will you be all right while I'm gone?"

His warm breath riffles through her hair. She can feel his forehead press against the nape of her neck. "I'll be fine," he says, and then: "Go to sleep."

These are the rituals he performs each night: snugs her close, tucks the blankets in—summer or winter—and lastly, as he is doing now, brings his breathing in step with hers. How that surprised her the first times he did it, that compliance of breath. She lies there, marveling, as she so often has, at how hard he works to fit himself into her life, and she wonders yet again why it is always him. Why it never occurs to her to go to such measures.

Chapter Six

The sisters sit on chairs tilted back against the house, feet propped on the porch rail. A pale moon rises, and because it's a mere two weeks from solstice, it rises in a sky that's still light well past the supper hour. Children on their second wind are readying for night games. A small group quibbles on the sidewalk, and an adult voice calls, "If you kids can't play nice . . ." The group breaks and runs for cover, laughing. Though Meredith's house is only ten blocks from Nance's, on this side of Normal Hill the residences have been portioned into studio apartments, or have slipped into a seediness from years of being let out to college students, or enlisted as subsidized housing. The yards have been ground to dirt; the Italian prunes have gone to the worms.

The apartment buildings across the street have a drug-house history in this valley. Acid and weed in the seventies. These days it's meta-amphetamines. From the second-floor corner, the sound of rap is so ramped, the better part of the block can hear it.

Nance settles her head back into clasped hands. "There are maybe five really unsavory blocks in this town, and you find one."

"I scoff at danger." Meredith takes a sip of lemonade laced with vodka, then settles the glass between her legs on the seat. "Think the lemonade needs more sugar?"

"That sound you hear? That's my lips puckering."

"So you think my neighborhood has character?"

"A number of them."

Meredith nods. "Two doors down, there's an old woman, wears high-water pants, a red all-weather coat, and those fuck-me boots so popular nine or ten years ago. Mornings, she goes to church, then to the grocer, where she buys a bag of day-old doughnuts, and then down to the levee to feed them to the marmots. Evenings, she sits on her porch, weather permitting." Meredith hitches a thumb over her left shoulder. "I say hi sometimes, but she makes it clear she's not interested in making new friends."

Nance looks over, sees someone hunched in a high-backed chair—a mop of gray hair, the concavity of chest and shoulders. Wonders what it's like to live a life aimed at such solitude. She thinks of her own work, the wide, empty hills. She hears Ned's voice: "You like being alone." But that's different. She tries to remember what it was like to be really alone. And then there's Ned's phone message: "Won't be home until late. Don't wait up." She thinks about the last several weeks, the way things have been off-again, on-again with him.

Like yesterday. A Sunday morning. How he'd fussed over breakfast. Played the clown, flipping flapjacks for her. Made plans for a drive up into the mountains. Then disappeared. There one minute, gone the next. She'd searched the house, the upper floors, the basement. Found him in the garage.

What she remembered clearest: the dim slant of light across the workbench and all the tools strung out in descending order and type: wrenches, pliers, hammers. He was holding a pipe wrench, a big-fisted tool with a handle the length of his forearm.

She'd felt strangely relieved. *What did you think? That he'd run off?* "Hey, you," she said softly. "Thought we were going for a drive."

He didn't answer.

She worked her way between the tight fit of car and wall. Stumbled over the hand mower, stepped over the empty gas can to stand just slightly to the back of him.

"You about done?" she asked.

She could hear the shallowness of his breathing, and there was a curious tension in his back, a pinched posture she didn't recognize, as if he were uncomfortable, or in pain, though his hand worked an oiled rag over the head of the wrench in a circular, clearly automatic gesture.

She touched his arm. "Hey, are you okay?"

He jerked, his back snapping. The wrench dropped, clattered on the floor, and his hand clamped into a fist in front of him.

He spun on his heel, and in the instant it had taken for him to turn, for his focus to hone in, she had the sense he was somewhere else, and that the fist he raised was not for her, but another threat. She stumbled back against the hood of the car, and then she saw the recognition coming to his face, and the fist he'd raised lodging in the air. It was a long moment and then he turned his face away, as if embarrassed, his fist opening to run a hand over his hair. He bent over and picked up the pipe wrench. "Goddamn it," he said. "Don't sneak up on me like that." He barely talked to her the rest of the afternoon, but that evening, he was shifting gears again. Offering to take her out for a nice dinner. A movie afterward.

She's roused back to the present and her sister's porch by the sound of a beer can being tossed to the pavement. A few young men have come down onto the street, sweaty and wringing the hair back from their heads. Most of them are dressed in oversized tank tops and low-rider shorts. Wanna-be gangsters in Idaho—a lost cause.

On the stoop, a girl prods an elbow into the ribs of a young man sitting next to her. He slaps her on the back of the head, then laughs, meaning to pass it off as playful, but the young girl backhands him in the chest, yells, "*Motherfucker.*" The other young men look on with interest and a few girls giggle, or turn away, annoyed. "Just fuck her and get it over with," someone calls.

Meredith is suddenly restless, swinging a foot up onto the banister, then off. She stands, moves over to the porch steps, where she seats herself. She nods toward the couple. "That's what it's all about. The part where they make up." She shakes her head. "Things get a little dull, a little old, you shake it up. A slap, a punch, a few tears. Whatever works."

Nance leans back. "Well, that's as bleak a view as I've heard in a while."

"Think so?"

More people are joining the party. A car pulls up and two middle-aged men climb out. They're in tight jeans, T-shirts with sleeves rucked up over their shoulders. A feral pair, with longish hair and steel-capped boot heels. They stop next to the couple. One of the men talks to the boy while the other, the taller and darker of the two, cups the back of the girl's head in his palm. Then the men move up the stairs and into the complex.

"Chicken hawks," Meredith says. "The men with the bankroll, stash in a pocket. Pretty heady, you know, when you're young—the attraction of those worldly, dangerous men."

"Where did you learn all this stuff?"

Meredith laughs. There's a droll turn to her voice. "I read a lot."

Nance's suddenly uncomfortable watching the stream of people in and out of the apartment house. She's wary of what she'll witness, what misfortune is about to happen. It's like picking through a stranger's pockets, not knowing what you'll pull out next.

A number of kids in their late teens are standing on the lawn, the sidewalk, the front stoop. One or two sit on the hoods of parked cars. The embers of cigarettes glow and dim, rise and fall through the air. A full beer drops onto the lawn and it splashes on the legs of some girls. A boy carries a speaker onto the balcony, and the music cranks louder.

The music turns to salsa, and some of the young girls across the street are stepping to it under the street lamp. One of them stumbles and catches her balance. Soon others are dancing. After a song or two, Meredith is tapping the porch step with her feet, and then she's on the sidewalk in front of her house. The glass of lemonade is pressed against the back of her neck. "Want to dance?" she asks. She's moved onto the small square of lawn, where she's toeing the grass.

Meredith's clearly comfortable with the music. Her movements seem to Nance strangely erotic, though not consciously provocative. There's no bump and grind, no overly enthusiastic hips as in the younger girls across the street—and one can forgive them that excess, because they are so young, and caught up in themselves, but already sensing that most of their lives will not be like this summer's evening under the streetlight and the admiring gaze of young men waiting in the shadows.

Meredith is simply pressing the pads of her feet into the grass, her weight shifting quietly from calf to thigh and hip. Her arms are out to either side, and in one hand, held by the tips of her fingers, is the glass of lemonade.

She doesn't look at the porch where Nance sits, but her free hand beckons. "Come on, Sis," she says. "Take off your shoes and dance with me."

Meredith's sandals are strewn like tipsy footprints on the sidewalk. Nance imagines her own broad-strapped practical footgear cast off into the grass. *Just for fun.* Dancing on the lawn with her sister. As if they were young. As if none of their past had come between them yet.

She's lowering her feet from the rail when she spots the men—"*Chicken hawks,*" *isn't that what Meredith called them?* One is studying the young girls. But the other, the darker, thinner, sharper-edged of the two, is turned toward this house, staring into this yard, where Meredith dances.

He watches for a time, then steps off the curb, slipping in and out of the pools of streetlight, and then up onto their curb. He's to the side of the spreading lilac, nearly concealed beneath its bushy canopy. He bends over to lean his arms down on the fence. His hands hang this side of the picket.

With all the din of the young people across the street and the music, it's a quiet thing happening here, and there's a curious tension about it— the silent man, the observer; and Meredith, of course, dancing; and Nance watching it all, trying to understand what it is that's happening, believing that by studying this she might discover what it is about Meredith that occasions disaster, just as when observing snakes she can learn how to avoid danger, or gain some measure of control. And so she watches, even as her sister is watched by this man in dark jeans and a shirt almost too white to bear in the dark.

The man's clearly interested, and Nance tries to see her sister as he must: the gray cotton-knit shorts and sleeveless T-shirt, the way they ride her body. There's a fine line of sweat—a single stroke down the length of spine—ending in an inverted triangle over her buttocks. A shine of skin at the ball of her shoulders. And there's her scent, that frangible bite of sweat.

The man stays on the other side of the fence, his arms in their fetters. "You like to dance?" he asks. His voice is moderate, pleasing.

Meredith steps into a turn to face him, doesn't stop dancing. Nance tips forward and the chair legs sound a soft thump. He glances at the porch. "Ah, another." He nods toward Nance but asks Meredith, "She as pretty?"

Meredith slows her steps, nods. "But . . ."

"Yes?"

"Smarter."

The man shrugs. "That's okay. I got a friend. He's pretty smart, too."

"And married," Nance says from where she's standing on the porch.

He throws his head back. Laughs. "It happens." He pauses. "Doesn't mean you can't dance now, does it? How about you?" he asks Meredith. He lifts his hands from the pickets, walks over to the gate, where he stands with his hand on the latch. "Married?"

She takes a sip of her drink.

"Well, I know you like to dance." He swings the gate open, steps through.

"I like to dance," she agrees.

"Alone?"

"I'm not alone," she says.

"Without men, then."

Meredith shrugs.

The music moves onto something slower. And then he's approaching, and she's not backing off. He lifts her free hand in his, and then they're dancing. Nance can see how Meredith keeps a clean distance, her shoulders plucked back, her chin up and ponytail bobbing. They turn once and then several more times on the lawn, and Nance thinks they look good together. Comfortable. As if they'd stepped into familiar arms. He leans into Meredith, his mouth moving at her ear, but she gently breaks loose, dances another step on her own, leaving the man with his hands at his sides.

Across the street, the other man calls, "Yo, Syd. Where'd ya go?" He has a hand over his eyes, as if shading them from the streetlight, and then he's crossing the street. There's a swagger to this one.

"You prefer it without men?" Syd asks, ignoring the friend who is aiming for the gate.

"I *prefer* to know the man," Meredith says.

Nance cues in on the inflection in her sister's voice: boredom, resignation. Something else. *Interest?*

"Name's Syd."

"So I heard."

The other man enters the yard, and Nance moves to the top of the steps.

He glances over at Meredith. "Cool," he says, then adds, "Fresh meat."

Meredith snorts. "Thought you said he was smart."

Syd shoots a hand out to the side and is wrapping an arm around his friend, a sort of playful tussling, which Nance suspects is not altogether fun. When the friend quiets, Syd says, "Hey, there's as many kinds of smart as stupid."

Meredith nods. "And all rolled into one. Isn't that interesting."

Syd laughs, and there's a painful grunt from the other. "This here is Lewis."

Lewis is rubbing his arm where Syd's fingers have dug in, and then something passes between them, for Lewis turns away to look at Nance standing on the porch steps. Nance thinks she can see his grin in the dark.

"And you are?" Syd asks Meredith.

"Having a fine evening on our own," Nance says. She hears a spurt of laughter from Meredith.

Syd turns toward Nance. "But the more's the merrier, right? I think we can do a little better than this."

"You and Lewis?" Meredith takes another sip.

"We got the stuff, baby." Lewis gives a sly nod.

Syd steps closer. He lifts the glass from Meredith's hand, ice chinking in the dark. He takes a sip. "Needs more booze to cut the sour."

Meredith holds her hand out for the drink.

Nance is fascinated by the way her little sister transforms. There's a boldness that Nance doesn't recognize. And something else she can't quite put a finger on.

Syd hands back the glass. She looks at it.

"There's a ready-made party across the street. You could get to know your neighbors."

Meredith looks over. "A little young for my taste."

Syd steps to a side. "Kids keep ya young. You never heard that?"

Lewis is bopping in place to the rap that's back on the speakers.

Syd glances over at Lewis. "Why don't you go sit over there?" He points to the porch steps at Nance's feet.

"No," Nance says and moves down a step. "I'd rather he didn't."

Lewis stops midstride. Shrugs, and says, "Whatever." He turns back toward the gate. "You coming, Syd, or what?"

Syd looks at Meredith. "How about it?"

Meredith looks up at the sky. "I'm thinking I'm just dandy where I am."

"Syd?" Lewis's tone is impatient.

Syd looks over at Meredith. "He doesn't have to play, you know."

Lewis is wagging his head as if he's been struck with a blunt object. "Hey, you said—"

"Lewis." Syd stops on the name as if it's a dead end.

The sound brings Lewis up short. He raises his hands, palms out. "Hey, yeah, fine. Well, you'll excuse me if I'm going back where there's a *real* fucking party." He dismisses the sisters with a wave. "There's more where this came from. Better," he says, and steps through the gate, starts across the street.

Syd turns back to Meredith. "Just that easy," he says.

But Meredith's stepping off the lawn and back onto the stairs. She smiles at her sister, mouths, *Don't worry.*

"Right," Nance says under her breath, backing up onto the porch.

Meredith sits on the top step. She stretches her legs out.

Syd walks to the steps, looks over his shoulder. "Damn, it's a hot one." He looks back at Meredith, points to the step. "You mind?" And then he's seating himself. "Thanks," he says. "Dancing I don't mind, but standing around like a fool was getting to me."

Meredith laughs.

Nance can hear how he's working his way closer to Meredith, and Nance is startled to find herself resenting not her sister's gullibility but his attention to her sister. He's clearly a practiced womanizer. Still, she finds herself wanting to have him look her way, as well. Just once. *Pretty heady, the attraction of these dangerous men.* She catches herself, wonders what it is she's doing on this porch, instead of being at home like every other married woman, snug in her own living room, with her husband crowding the sofa next to her. But that certainly isn't her life. Is it? Not with Ned. Even in the privacy of their home, over dinner, while watching television, or in the intimacy of their bedroom, she always feels some tiniest distance between them, a thing she's always written off as the difference in second marriages. A difference of maturity. A quality she's attributed to Ned being by nature a more private person. *What's the big deal?*

Syd eases back on an elbow. Looks over his shoulder and up at Meredith. "So how come I never seen you here before?"

Meredith touches the back of his head, and it's curiously reminiscent of the way he'd palmed the back of the young girl's head earlier. Nance feels a pit opening in her stomach.

But Meredith lifts her hand away and settles it in a loose fist at her side. She leans back. "Let's not even go there, okay? Let's cut the bullshit. Instead, how about something like: 'You look halfway decent in the dark. What say we get it on, and afterward I'll figure on whether it's worth another go-round or not.'"

Syd rocks back on the steps. Tilts his head so that he can see her better. He shrugs. "Hey, if you're game—"

Meredith interrupts: "And let's just say that maybe you're not the worst lay I've ever had, either."

"Jesus, Mer . . ." Nance says.

He grins. "Ah. So it's Mary."

Meredith waves it off. "And we both decide this ain't such a bad thing—you know? Like it could work for us." She points at herself. "I'm steady. I'm reasonably attractive, and I know the ropes. I won't be hitting on your friends, or getting into your stash when you're not around. I don't get sloppy drunk, but I know how to have a good time."

"I could fall in love," he says, grinning.

"And you"—she points at him—"are reasonably attractive. . . ."

He picks up the conversation. "I know how to keep a woman happy. And I wouldn't be getting into your stash when you're not around, either."

"I don't keep one."

"All the better," he says, leans back.

They sit quietly looking out over the street to where the party is kicking into gear. High-pitched laughter, and growling young men. There's the sound of broken glass, and a couple of the younger men dash down the street, spraying beer on the running girls.

"Hey, Sis," Meredith says. "You need anything?"

"Sisters, huh?"

Nance sighs. Lifts herself from the chair she'd retreated to, steps over to stand next to Meredith. "No," she says. "Not a thing." She starts to take a step down, but Meredith reaches up and clasps her fingers. Holds on. She gives a squeeze, then pulls Nance down to sit.

Meredith leans forward a bit, says to the man, "How about you? You need a drink or something?"

He nods. "A drink would be good."

She hands him the lemonade he'd sipped from. She hasn't touched it since.

"Could use a little more booze, don't you think?" he asks.

Meredith turns to Nance. "See?" she says. "That's the way it starts. You've got this dreamy thing going. Next thing you know, it's slipped a cog. He starts finding things wrong."

"Now hang on a minute—" he says.

"Like there's not enough booze in the drinks, or that color doesn't look good on you."

Nance pitches in. "He wants to go out; you don't—"

"He goes anyway. Finds himself a little entertainment," Meredith adds.

Syd sits forward. "Maybe you're reading this all wrong . . ."

The sisters look down at him. Nance nods at the house across the way. "She's younger. Always."

Meredith nods. "Fresh meat."

"Now, goddamn it, that was Lewis. Not me," Syd says. "And if we're playing this game—what about I come over some night and you got someone else on the steps? Some other guy, and you're saying, 'Oh no, sweetie,'"—he pipes his voice high—"'he just stopped by for directions.' But just let me *look* at another woman, and suddenly I'm the shithead."

There's a commotion in the street, and though it's difficult to make out the details, Nance sees some pushing and shoving going on, as if someone's trying to start or stop a fight. One of the young girls is yelling, *"You fucking asshole"* over and over. Lewis is at the center of it. Another young man is trying to grab hold of his jerking arms. The yelling intensifies, and porch lights start coming on down the street.

More insults, a period of quiet, and then another spurt of yelling just before the real fight. "I'll break your head, man. I'll break your fucking face." It's Lewis shouting at a slip of a boy. Two or three others are trying to winnow the kid clear, but Lewis is grabbing at them, as well.

More of the partygoers start gravitating toward the well opening in the center of the street, and Nance watches as they form a loose knot around the commotion. Lewis is throwing punches. They're mostly ponderous swings that would be comical if staged, but in the streetlight, in the combative energy of all the young men, his roundhouse swings seem as deliberate as a mower blade through grass. There's the sound of flesh connecting and then a grunt.

Nance thinks to rise, to call the police, but before she can say as much, a streaky blue light flashes on the apartment face and a squad car rounds the corner. She expects the group will splinter off now, but the knot tightens with a renewed energy, shuffling on its many legs closer to their yard, toward the gate left open with Lewis's departure, and then the group holds and sways just the other side of their picket fence, and there's a pulling at the edges, a fraying of the outer line, as police arrive and some of the girls start drawing the boys away. Upstairs, the remains of the partyers are at the windows. The music's off; someone's hustling the speaker back inside.

More cops are pulling up, and there's the crackle of police radios, a streak of lights over the dark trees, and the straggling crowd of youngsters. The cops move in, and on the edges they spot out one kid and another with flashlights, while more cops move in a wedge into the heart of the struggle. "Break it up. Break it up. What's going on here?"

Nance watches as Lewis is backed off at last and isolated by the bulk of two officers. It looks at first as if he's kissing the knuckles on his hand, and then Nance can see he's licking them. Licking the blood off. And she wonders if it's his, or the younger man's.

Syd's still sitting at the bottom of the stairs. He hasn't moved much beyond running fingers through his hair. Syd wags his head.

"Let me guess," Meredith says. "He's holding."

"Always."

It's clear the police have found it, because Lewis is spread-eagled at a squad, being cuffed and read his rights. He glances over into the yard, to the porch steps, where the three of them observe the scene, and Syd perches a little closer to the edge of the step, but then the cop is kicking Lewis's feet forward and pulling him upright in the same motion. Leads him to the open squad door, and bundles him inside.

It all happens quickly, the party resolving into the evening as young men and women drift away. Few are singled out for rides to the station. The squad with Lewis inside pulls into the apartment parking lot to turn around. They can see him in the backseat, a dark profile as the car motors past. Then just the red taillights and they're as quickly gone.

There's a slow intake of breath from the bottom step. "What an asshole," Syd says.

"Yeah," Nance says, "and my guess is that your friends will always be assholes."

He stiffens, then takes another deep breath, laughs softly. "Yeah, you're probably right." He looks at Meredith. "And your family will always poke its nose in where it don't belong."

She nods. "Absolutely."

They sit a moment longer, and then he's stretching his legs out, pushing down on his knees with his hands, and rising to his feet. He looks up and down the street. "Shit," he says, bending deep to stretch. "There ain't a new thing in this world, is there?" He straightens up.

"I don't know," Meredith says. "But we're already old business."

He nods. "Well, hey." He turns toward the two women.

"Good night," Meredith says.

He stands with the gate in his hand, steps through, and then he's striding down the street.

Ned's on the Clarkston side, walking the levee, an asphalt path that winds through the riverside parkway—a narrow belt of green that threads between the bluffs to the west and river on the east. People walk dogs here, or Rollerblade, or bike, or take leisurely strolls. In the daytime, children play here, but at night, except for the occasional couple, the late-night dog walkers, the insomniac, it's mostly empty. Lining the river are willows and burly blackberry bushes. Against the hillside, trees of heaven spindle skyward. In the riverside hollows, black locust cluster in groves, dangle fleshy blooms that sway like fragrant fruit in the night.

A half-moon hovers, the same moon his wife observes, though he does not know this. He doesn't think of Nance. Intentionally keeps her clear of his thoughts in an ordering of boundaries that's as sure as the river hedging him in on the east and the bluffs to the west. He likes to keep his home life separate. Safe, he believes, as long as the one doesn't impinge on the other, like that old saw: If a tree falls in the forest, and there's no one there to hear it . . .

He strolls the path, the narrow belt of green widening to a lawn with picnic tables, and off to the far side a cement blockhouse rest room. Riverside, the grass thins to sand like the pate of a balding man. There's a swimming beach roped in with a horseshoe of plastic buoys and chain. At the base of the hill is a ten-slot parking lot. The lot's empty.

Ned crosses the grass, keeping clear of the sprinklers. A gaggle of geese huddle at the sandy edge, and, as he passes, the ganders arc their necks and hiss. Goose turds populate the lawn like plump, moist worms.

He stands on the beach, staring downstream, where city lights reflect in a smear of orange and pink and green, then back to where the river is a black hollow with a narrow crack of light that is the moon's. Across the river, atop the levee, water cannons fire volleys in long white bursts, the sound of the water's *shoop shoop* carrying clear. A vee of geese honk overhead. He watches the way they turn and bank with the same dispassion that he observes the goose shit in the grass, or the plop of a fish in the shallows. He has no interest in animals, having exhausted his curiosity about them long ago, so that now they are just barely *there,* in the same way some people are less there than others. After a moment, center river, there is a splash as the geese slide to a landing, and a sound like mumbling, and then quiet.

He drops to a squat, rocks back on his heels, and sifts his fingers through the sand. He comes upon a flat stone, picks it up and couches it between thumb and forefinger. He remembers that as a boy he used to skip stones, and this takes him by surprise. There's never been much available to him from that time, just odd bits and pieces of memories, or a talent he stumbles onto—like discovering a pair of gloves that, strangely enough, fit.

It was a lake. Probably on the Washington Coast, though whether that is real or imagined, he can't say. A knob of land like a pointed finger stretching into the water. He recalls foothills, blue sky, and bright sunlight, though it must be cold, for he remembers gooseflesh on his young arms.

He tries to sharpen the image, but it's a split kind of seeing: blue sky, night, lake, river, a sprinkling of mica glinting in sand. He hears a man's voice, *Neil,* and when he looks back over his shoulder, he realizes it's in his head—a thirty-year-old echo—feels the flesh rising on his present-day arm. He lets his focus go soft, sees himself as a thin-legged kid sailing stones out over the water and counting, *One, two, three, four, five,* and then faster as the skips flatten, *six-seven-eig-ni-ten-leven-elve.* He's good. The stones leap; the water sparks beneath each hit. He tries to imagine why he's at the lake, pitching stones.

It's a picnic, he decides, and this he's more comfortable with—creating a past that's mostly never been. A picnic. Sees a car, a 1954 or '55, vaguely familiar, black-and-white Ford parked roadside. It's the car that's in the picture, the one and only picture he has of his father, and in it the man is a shape, small and indistinct in the driver's seat, arm crooked out the open window.

He shakes his head, imagines instead his mother stretched out on a blanket nearby. He sketches birds overhead, a few wisps of cloud. The grass a burnt shade of green, a red-and-yellow plaid blanket. And suddenly that's true—the blanket—it was red and yellow, and it was warm. Even in repose, his mother looks oddly regretful with her fingers locked beneath her head, legs crossed at the ankle. Next to her is the food, but all that's left is a paper sack leaking fruit rinds, bread crusts, and bones.

He lifts the stone to his lips, touches his tongue to it. He looks at the river's edge, where water trickles up onto sand. Thinks again of the memory. None of it real, he decides, except the act of skipping stones, and the figure of his mother with fingers locked beneath her head.

The fly walking her eye.

He stops, rises to his feet. That particular detail, he knows, belongs to some other time and place—a bedroom, maybe, bed linens stripped. The late-afternoon light blunted through drawn blinds. The sound of flies behind the blinds, skipping the glassy surface. And it's not his mother.

He settles the stone in his fingers, bends to a side, arm crooked at the elbow. He takes aim and side-arms the stone out over the river. It sinks after one faltering jump.

He finds another stone, and then another, and another, arranges them in a small cairn in the sand. When he's gathered what he can, he tries again. The next stone skips three times. He sails them out, his count jumping up, down, and up again.

The geese have moved downstream. With his last stone, he takes aim and lets fly, but the stone falls short. Still, a number of geese startle, their alarm rippling outward, wings laboring through the air with a *whop, whop, whop* that sends layer on layer of birds into flight.

He watches as they wing downriver, trailing a scold of honks. He dusts his hands off, but when he brushes at his pant legs, he has the feeling he's being watched. He half-expects again to hear that familiar haunting–*Neil*.

He almost doesn't see her, except for the hair, which is like a pale piece of moonlight broken free, floating unattached in all the shadows. She's in a cove of cottonwoods, perched on the top of a picnic table, her feet on the bench.

He walks the beach, looking for more stones. "Thought it was just me and the geese," he says.

She stirs. "I didn't mean to intrude," she says, and falls quiet.

He takes a step closer, sees her shoulders lift. He turns back toward the river, where all that's left of the moon's reflection are brittle bits in the center chop.

"Just pitching stones," he says. "Didn't mean to . . ." What was it he didn't mean to do here?

He turns the stone over. A light weight. Drops it back in the sand. "You wouldn't happen to have–"

"No." She cuts him short. Her arms flex as if she's ready to push herself off the table, plant her feet on the grass.

He backs up. "Ah, see, I have disturbed you," he says. He sees her pause, settle back onto the tabletop.

"No," she says, "you haven't." Her voice is graveled like the voices of women who have spent a lifetime shouting to be heard. She gathers something in one hand.

It's tough reading her in the dark. But she hasn't walked away, and although he doesn't mean to, he can't help but notice that at her back is a wall of blackberry bushes. What little light there is sifts down through the tree limbs and onto her. There's a settled quality about her body. Middle-aged, or nearly. Old enough to know better.

Her arm rises in the dark. He sees the pale hair lift away from her neck and fall back. Her attention's on the river.

Gutsy. He turns back to the sand, bends over and picks up another stone. It's cumbersome, but he throws it anyway, hears it hit the water once, twice, three times.

"I should have stopped while I was ahead," he says. "I haven't done this since I was a kid. You ever skip stones?"

"Not that I'd brag about," she says.

"To tell the truth, I hadn't remembered I could until just now. That ever happen to you?" He toes the sand. "Forget you know how to do something?" He's curious now, wondering if others have the same fragmented past. While there's no reason to believe this woman, this stranger, could provide any clearer understanding of his cobbled memories, he believes it's safe to ask precisely because she is a stranger.

"Like the way you never forget how to ride a bike," she says.

"Well, yes," he says, "except you don't know you ever owned a bike, or rode one, and then suddenly you're pedaling down the street."

He believes he has her answer in the silence that follows. He laughs to cover his own embarrassment. "Now I've done it. Gone and frightened you for sure."

"No, no," she says, but stands anyway.

"Chased you off," he says. He feels how close he is—it's just the two of them, the hill at her back, the empty road and parking lot. The cinder-block rest room with a door you bolt from the inside. One stall, a sink. And high up, a glass-brick window where hobo spiders spin funneled webs.

His legs feel jumpy, and he doesn't know what to do with his hands, so he puts them in his pockets. He glances across the wide stretch of river. He thinks about this woman, making herself . . . available. *Who does she think she is?*

He catches himself. Knows where this is going. Knows what he wants even before he's thought it. There's the taste of ash in his mouth. A pinching in his chest. He feels the impulse to cross the distance, the urging in the narrow of his back like a hand shoving. He takes a deep breath and another. And then he's turning away and stepping back onto the sand. He looks upriver to the Southway Bridge that's a white slash against the dark. He can see a flash of blue lights on the far side, heading up Bryden Canyon. He checks how he feels. His hands have steadied; his legs are still beneath him. He thinks about skipping more stones, or, better yet, heading home. He can think about Nance now, with this woman at his back. Considers this yet another indication, proof that all it takes to walk a fine line is balance. *And you're a genuine tightrope walker, aren't you?*

The woman's getting ready to leave, but that's of no consequence. He feels nearly paternal toward her. She steps forward, slaps her leg, and says something, and he turns to see what it is she wants. It's then that something under the picnic table shuffles loose and lumbers out into the open. It's enormous: a dog. Bullmastiff.

Ned stands absolutely still, wonders if it can smell the sweat that suddenly washes over him. The dog stretches, and as it pushes up onto its front legs, chest broadening, the mouth opens wide, and a sound that starts like a sliding yodel ends in a deep-chested bark, *harumphf.*

The woman steps forward, clips a leash to the dog's collar. "Have a nice evening," she says, then "Heel, Sweetie," and the dog butts its ribs into her hip, though it keeps Ned in view. "Enough," she says, and it's a rebuke, so that Ned wonders what he misses in the dark. What fine tension she feels in the leash, or in the hairs bristling against her leg. "Good luck with your stones," she says.

"Yes," he says, and suddenly he feels angry, cheated, robbed of something by the loose-limbed dog. By the casual way in which it snagged from him this one good deed. A deed of omission.

Two blocks from Meredith's, Nance still isn't sure where she wants to go. Just knows it's not home. They said good night, but the interplay with the men has left her restless. She drives past the elementary school, and she can't keep herself from looking for Ned's car, noticing that the corner office is dark. He's probably home, waiting. She slows. But if he isn't? *Don't wait up.* She turns toward downtown, heading for Main Street. It's a roughly mile-long one-way stretch that starts a block short

of the rivers' confluence and ends the other side of the old town shopping district, with its brick-faced buildings, the minimall of Morgan's Alley: deli, smoke shop, flower shop, bridal store, and Bojacks Broiler Pit,
with its painted fork-tailed demon beckoning beside the door. She idles
past the row of storefronts with windows plastered in UNFIT FOR HUMAN
HABITATION signs—fire damaged when the cornerstone Weisgerber
building burned down five years ago, one of a spate of arsons that has
leveled a number of downtown buildings over a ten-year period. The
town's history has always intrigued her, with its casual conflagrations. A
periodic violence that sweeps through the valley like an ill wind. The
string of rapes and abductions ten years ago. The serial murders. The
lone lunatic, meaning to dismember the devil in an apartment building
on Main Street, who beheaded the only man who ever befriended him.
She looks up at the apartment, where a blank bank of windows faces out
over the street.

At Fifth, she files into the ranks of teenagers cruising the short drag,
past the parking lots where they congregate in small cliques. There are
middle-aged men here as well, worming their way into the youthful
boredom. This is old business.

She continues on Main Street, while the youngsters opt for the loop
by way of D Street. This end of Main is used-car lots, used-appliance
stores, insurance offices, gas stations, the county courthouse and jail,
and the all-nighter's Anytime Café.

She turns up Twenty-first Street—Lewiston's strip of humble malls,
hotels, motels, bars, and cafés. Midway up the grade, she pulls into the
Red Lobster parking lot, slips the truck into neutral, and sets the parking
brake. The engine idles and she looks out over the sprawl of valley
lights. The crests of the far hills are black against a bale of stars. She
studies the restaurant, whose long row of picture windows faces the
dead-end view of a parking lot. Only the cook staff on cigarette breaks
and the twin Dumpsters have the panoramic view: the march of hills,
the spectacular sunsets. When the building went up, the locals shook
their heads. "Ass-backward," they said. Though there was speculation
that the design was intentional, meant to encourage a rapid turnover.

Nance crooks her arm out the window. She yawns. Rolls out of the parking lot, away from the restaurant's willfully blank set of eyes, and back down into the heat of the valley.

The blocks are quiet, and on Eighth where the sycamores steeple over the street she parks across from her house. She feels childish for staying out late. An act of spite. Her hands are crossed on the steering wheel, and she rests her forehead on the back of them. A light's on in the house. Ned's home. Asleep or not, he keeps at least one light on. She knows he does the same when she's gone: a hall light, or one in the study, the spare bedroom, the entire house, depending on his need. Curious, that need. It's not that he's afraid of the dark, but it's as if he can not bring himself to sleep without knowing that some small part of it is lit.

She's learned not to tease him about it.

There's a hollow in her stomach that she wants to ignore or blame on the sour lemonades, but she's struck again with the certainty that something's wrong. The wind's picking up—a shuffling of shadow and light on the street—and she rolls down the window. It's a dry wind that smells of dust rather than river, and in the wind's fitful gusts, she wonders if something larger is brewing to the west. Her trip begins in a couple days, and she starts listing what remains to be done. Stops herself.

So, okay, it isn't all Ned's fault; she has her own distractions. She opens the truck door, lets herself out. She's almost to the door before she sees him on the far side of the porch.

"Home early?" she asks. Can't help herself.

He doesn't answer.

She starts for the door.

"I couldn't sleep," he says. "Lay there, eyes shut and wide-awake. What do you think? A bad conscience?"

She pauses, her hand on the door. "How would I know?"

"Ah," he says, "you're angry. I almost don't recognize it. Isn't that strange? That we argue so seldomly. Do you think that's strange?"

She stands with her hand on the door. He's right. There's been little disagreement in their marriage until recently. Even when they did disagree, there was always a politeness about it.

"Most people would envy us that," she says, and thinks of the young couple across from her sister's house, their violence. *A slap, a punch . . . Whatever works for you, I guess.* Nance pulls the door open an inch, lets it fall closed.

"What is it you want, Ned?" She takes a deep breath, lets it out. "Because I'm at a loss here." She tugs a lock of hair back from her face, shucks it behind an ear. "And it's clear something's not right with us these days."

"Is it?" he asks. "It all feels such a muddle to me."

Facing her, he looks like a schoolboy, his hands prim in his lap, head tilting to one side. He appears smaller, as if his frame has sunken in on itself. She sees how vulnerable he is. Scolds herself, knowing how easily wounded he is. She's shamed. She looks down at her feet so righteously planted on the porch floorboards. "I only mean to say . . . you seem so absent these days. You're gone so much of the time and—"

"It's a busy time at school. Budget cuts. Lots of catch-up from last year. Planning the next."

"But even when you are home, it's like you're not here. I enter a room, you leave. I talk, and you don't hear me." She steps forward. "I'm worried, okay?"

"Well then, I'm sorry. I don't mean to worry you. Listen, I can be careless sometimes. I know that. Thoughtless." His hand floats up and then falls back into his lap. "But I do try."

She crosses the porch, perches on the railing next to where he sits in the far corner. The streetside light dapples his lap, his left hand, a patch over his chest. His face is a jigsaw of light and dark. The tip of one ear, a crescent moon.

"I try very hard." He doesn't look at her. "This," he says. "You, the house, my work. Everything. It's daunting, you know." He looks down the street. "Sometimes I hardly feel up to it. I feel unworthy of it all."

Unworthy. She doesn't know how to answer such a word. She leans forward, her elbows resting on her knees. "Well, it's not so very grand a house," she says. "And as for myself, I'm rather more odd, don't you think, than daunting? The snakes and all?"

He makes a sound, and she thinks he's laughing, though his head is down, and so she wonders if he isn't crying instead. She drops to her knees in front of him, takes his hands in hers, and when he looks up, his eyes are moist. She's confused, and then embarrassed by her own earlier distrust. "What say we go to bed?" she says. "We can duke it out in the morning. You know, determine who's worthy of whom?"

His hands are a deadweight. She presses them, gives a little squeeze. "Think you can sleep yet?"

And then he's stirring and he says, "Sure." At the door, he pauses and turns to her. "I do try. You don't know how hard I try."

She nods. When she steps over the threshold, he follows, and she hears the porch light click on behind them.

Book II

There are side canyon gullies, drywashes
and scumbled slides, half stone
half soil, and shed skins blow in them
like a snow of translucent leaves.

–"The Reign of Snakes," from *Reign of Snakes*, Robert Wrigley

It's Nance who finds the rattler. They're at a beach, China Bar, where they've set up camp. The mules, fed and watered, are hobbled un- der a brace of hackberry trees on the hillside, where the guide, Jeanette, a Nez Perce woman, dozes in the shade. The two graduate assistants, Peggy and Jody, are exploring an abandoned gold mine up on the hill—a short half-mile tunnel that has been picked and blasted out of rock.

Nance floats on her back in a small pond formed by a narrow inlet on the river. It's a semiprivate bath, the pool banked by hillside and rocks on the north and exposed beach on the south, so she remains clothed in shorts and tank top. The water is warmed by the basin of white sand and kept fresh with the influx from the river. It's a blue-green pool, deep- ening to amber where tannin leaches from a stump abutting the edge of the river. Everwine's craft is moored to the enormous stump.

Along with supplies, he's brought Meredith. Their involvement comes as no great surprise to Nance. The two of them are chatting by the camp- site. They sound companionable. *Maybe it'll be all right.* Truth is, she's anx- ious to discover Pete's the reasonably good man she believes he is. She really does wish the best for her sister. And on the selfish side? He's a skilled guide, and she knows how tough it would be to replace him.

Meredith and Pete are cooking tonight's meal, and Nance is more than happy to let them, and just lie here, letting the aches of five days on a mule's back soak loose.

She opens her eyes in the clear pool. A small trout flits back into the narrow channel to the river. She pushes herself down, until she's standing on the bottom. Sunlight ripples over her feet and legs and there are dark glints of pyrite about her toes. She releases a breath of air and it rises in a globe to disappear on the bright surface.

She hangs there a moment longer, enjoying the weightlessness. After a long day of baking in the heat of scrub-grass slopes and basalt walls, there's nothing like immersion—from the crown of her head to the nail beds on her toes.

She releases more air, a trail of bubbles bobbing upward, and then follows, pushing herself up along the rocky side of the pool. She breaks the surface with a gasp, one hand holding on to the rock wall while her other slicks back water and hair, and it's then that she sees it. Her hand stops in midmotion. She's eye-to-eye with a rattler. The snake pivots its head, tongue flicking, tail lifting. Because the snake is cooled by the shade of the rocks, its rattle is a lower pitch than the excited buzz of sun-warmed snakes. She slowly moves her hand from the ledge and dips back under, moves clear. But stays relatively close. For the eye interests her—like a milky blue pearl in its socket. The rattle stops, but Nance still hears the buzz of blood in her ears. She hangs in the water, a toehold on an underwater rock to steady herself, and watches.

Ecdysis: molting, shedding. The startling blue of its eye is merely the spectacle, a scale that covers the eye in the early stages. She hovers closer than common sense dictates. For this she also knows: It's a dangerous time, when the animal is ill-tempered, and even the most mild-mannered of snakes will strike with greater frequency.

But somehow, in the wild, it makes all the difference, seeing that eye—that liquid blue—floating, as it appears to, against the grays of rock and dusky sheath. In a matter of days, the scale will soften and clear and shortly thereafter, over another four or five days, the snake will shed its outer sheath intact, revealing the bright new coat of scales. She sinks down in the water, moves incrementally forward. She can see the small tearing that's begun on the supralabial and infralabial scales at the mouth's margin, and she watches as the snake sets to rubbing its head on the rock, starting at the tip of its lip and pressing back with a slow, even pressure. She can see also the internal movement, a kind of shrugging that loosens the aging corset.

Nance feels strangely privileged, and then a bit uncomfortable. It's the intimacy of the act, this baring of skin, and the vulnerability of it. She lets her head slip underwater again, paddles back another stroke, and resurfaces.

She's startled by this unease. As a scientist, it's what she does, after all: observes, records. The animal's hardly blind, with its sensory pits and the accurate, delicate tongue. How, she asks herself, is this any more invasive than the laboratory, inducing their anesthetized sleep, inserting the small radio chip beneath their ribs, deep in the coelom, or, for that matter, studying them hibernating in their den?

She wonders if this is one of her snakes. *Her* snakes. She's wary of such terms—their implication of possession—aware as she is of the dangers inherent in such arrogance: *our snakes, our land, our rivers.* Later on, she'll send Peggy down with the handheld telemetry receiver to check whether it is a snake from the den site and record the data.

She treads water a moment longer, moves toward the sand, where she sits in the shallows, keeping cool. She's staring at the rock where the snake labors on. She wonders if it's like an itch that needs to be scratched. The old sheath walls grown thick and keratinous with age, until the bottom-most cells begin to die—softening and dulling the appearance of the old sheath—and then liquefy, and it's then that the old sheath slips off, as easily as a sock from a foot, leaving the *Oberhauchen*— the bright new coat of many colors.

Does it feel like release? This slipping out of your skin. Like rebirth, all shining and new and of a piece.

She thinks of all the cast skins snagged on weeds, or lodged in rocky places. And of the million tiny exoskeletons of insects: grasshoppers still clutching the long-stemmed grasses, the mayfly's translucent ghost, or the sturdy caddis husks haunting riverbed stones. The piecemeal clutter: tiny glassine panes of termite and ant wings, antlers of deer and elk and ram.

Feathers. Numberless.

She imagines the sheer bulk of cells cast off by a single person in a lifetime. The congregate shedding of the world's population, animal and human, multiply it by tens of thousands of years—no, millions. This is the way worlds grow fat, she thinks, on the duff of sloughed skin.

Nance wraps her arms around her knees, rests her chin on a forearm. A mule brays from the hillside with a brassy hiccuping sound. She can hear the shuffle of dishes that Meredith and Everwine are setting out. She imagines Jeanette stirring from her nap, and Peggy and Jody scrambling down the hillside, hungry. Dirty. They'll want a swim. She'll warn them about the rattler, but they'll want to see it, of course.

She stretches back on the sand, and when she looks up, Meredith's come to fetch her.

"Dinner's nearly ready," she says. "Water feel good?"

"You can't imagine." Nance shows her sister the inside of her thigh, where the flesh is chafed. "Mules," she says.

"You have my sympathy," Meredith says. "Hey, 'sit okay with you? Me being here?"

Nance wraps an arm around her sister's shoulder, finds the solid feel of her reassuring. "It's a nice surprise."

"Pete meant to ask Ned along." Meredith slips off her sandals, slides her feet and legs into the water. "Oooh," she says. "Maybe a midnight dip?"

"Just stay this side." Nance points to the rock across the pool. "A rattler's curled up in there, shedding. Makes them *very* testy."

Meredith raises her eyebrow. "Do they swim?" she asks. "Snakes?"

Nance nods. "But he won't. He'll be busy scraping the hide off his back."

Meredith says, "Put him on a mule."

Nance throws her head back and laughs. She eases farther up onto the sand next to her sister to dry off. "Clearly, I forgot that snake skin on the saddle prevents chafing."

"You're kidding."

Nance nods. "An old folk tale. Like putting the powdered skin in your enemy's food or coffee, and in a few months he'll be filled with snakes."

"Lovely."

Nance leans back on her hands. A bead of water trickles down her back. "So Pete asked Ned to come?"

"He wasn't home. Pete said the house was dark and locked tight. Car was gone. Pete left phone messages, but he never got an answer."

"That's odd." Nance pushes the wet curls back from her forehead. "Hope everything's all right."

"I'm sure it's nothing," Meredith says, and pats her sister's hand. She lifts a foot out of the water, slips a sandal on. "If it was an emergency, he'd have called Pete. Or the Forest Service. He has the numbers."

Nance nods, lifts to her feet. "You're right. He's probably away on school business. A trip to Boise maybe."

"Yeah, that's probably it. You hungry?"

Nance nods, made aware of the empty pit in her stomach, the twisting that's going on in there. "Tell me it's ready," she says.

Ned checks the answering machine. Yet another message from Everwine: a weekend fishing trip upriver at Nance's camp. He riffles through the day's mail. The house is stuffy, and he moves through, opening windows, and although it's still light outside, he turns on lamps: living room, dining room, kitchen, stairwell. After which, he returns to the living room, where he stands looking about. He feels almost ghostly. Here and not here.

He turns on the TV for the sound, then walks over to the window. Outside, two young boys are riding bikes up and down the street, daring each other—no hands, eyes closed. They stop and talk. The smaller boy's clearly less willing to risk what's being planned. But then they're back on their bikes and headed toward the steep downhill grade. Ned presses his forehead to the warm glass and watches as the boys sail between potholes and bumps. He loses sight of them on the last quarter of the hill, but he knows the road, its high-banked left side and eroded shoulder, that last span of washboard ruts and pitches; he can almost feel the way their teeth jar in their heads, and the bicycle grips sting their palms. His own hand is pressed flat against the sill, and when he finally remembers to inhale, it is to the smells of the sun's heat rising off the wood, the slow-cooking dust. He lifts his hand, wipes it on his jeans, and turns away.

He wanders the kitchen. The refrigerator is gutted to a stick of butter; a carton of cottage cheese—lid bulging—which he pitches into the garbage; wilted celery stalks; peanut butter; jam; assorted condiments. He thinks about the freezer downstairs. The snake parts are long gone from atop their household meat, though he has trouble trusting the identical freezer bags, the contents indistinguishable through veils of frost. He chooses the peanut butter, but there's no bread, so he spreads it on crackers and calls it good.

He carries them on a plate into the living room, where he turns on the TV and settles into his favorite armchair. The news is on, and the pudgy-cheeked anchorman is teasing the coanchor, a slab-sided woman who smiles but keeps rapping papers into order on the desk.

There's a cutaway to a live-action report on an empty street. The usual accounts of auto accidents, a trucker who spilled his load, fender benders, a hit-and-run. A report on the third consecutive quarter of losses at the paper mill that won't finally close down. They finish with a feel-good segment—an old woman turning one hundred—complete with footage: the birthday cake, the woman blinking and buckled into a wheelchair, a party hat sliding over an ear.

He turns off the TV before the weather and sports. He finishes the last cracker, and when he sets the plate aside, he's feeling anxious in spite of the familiar room with its comfortable furniture, its braided rugs and well-hung pictures. Even the room lights in broad daylight fail to ease the pressure at the base of his spine, the prodding that will keep him awake and walking the empty rooms into the wee hours. It will be a difficult night. He can tell. He places his forehead in his hands, his elbows on his knees, and it feels as if the house has gone elastic, as malleable as the hours of the long night ahead, the house expanding in a shell over and around him, its silence like a surf in his ears.

He thinks of his school, his office—someone usually around, janitors at least. Or taking a drive up to Moscow, say, and having a few drinks at

CJ's, where Alice, the bartender, knows to keep her distance and pours a full shot. He grabs his keys, strolls out onto the porch, pauses to lock the door, then lets the screen door bounce shut behind him.

He moves with a curiously detached feeling, hears his feet striking the porch planks but doesn't feel it resonate up the balls of his feet. His knees are rising, arms swinging. It's as if his body's taken on a life of its own. *Just going along for the ride.*

The streets are empty, except for the odd car passing through. There's the oily smell of lighter fluid in the air from a backyard grill. He steps off the sidewalk and crosses the street, where he stands at the side of his car, fingering his keys. Something's niggling, some impression that only half-registers, a bit like déjà vu, though nothing that precise. He looks at the sun slanting over the houses, the angularity of the shadows, the way the trees, recovering from the day's heat, fidget with light.

It's a taste he can't name, or a name he can't put a face to. He stands at the opened car door, looking into the interior, but all he can see is a fly walking that narrow space between windshield and dashboard. It's a come-again, gone-again thing. As shifty as the wind. And then he understands it *is* the wind, for the breeze has turned, and suddenly he knows exactly what it is.

He looks across the roof of his car and up the short flight of stairs that leads to Turnbull's cottage, a trim little structure squandered in the heart of the weedy yard. He sniffs again, catches the edge, a peaty compost of aged piss and shit and rot.

He closes the car door. Takes the steps slowly. Halfway up, he turns and looks back at his house, at the half-light of lamps through the windows. It looks smaller from here, and far away—whole blocks away. He tells himself he doesn't have to do this. But that's just wishful thinking; he has as much say in this as he had in being born. He looks at the parked and empty cars, the sidewalks bare, the people indoors, or just gone, and even the birds have taken to other streets. He continues up the short flight of concrete stairs and pushes open the gate.

It is still early evening and the sun has not yet set, but the yard is a tangle that the slanting light doesn't penetrate. Ned sees cats insinuating themselves into the cover of blackberry, and barberry, and the weedy multifloras that crowd the yard's perimeters. The small patches of grass are knee-high and dried out, and strewn across the yard and into the branches of barberry and juniper and onto the dark ground beneath the lanky cedars are rolled copies of the local *Money Saver*. The mailbox next to the gate is full, and Ned sifts through it. "Jack Turnbull" is on the letters and Ned remembers his neighbor's full name for the first time in— what, years. So used is he to thinking of him as old man Turnbull, and so removed has the old man been from the usual conversational commerce of the neighborhood. Of habit, Ned picks out the bills and arranges them atop the junk mail, carries the bundle in one hand as he makes his way to the front door.

The blinds are drawn. No hint of lights inside. Door's locked. He walks around the house. There are no rolled newspapers back here, just empty bowls of all shapes and sizes. And nearer the house, scattered bits of insulation like soiled cotton candy dot the ground from where cats have rooted into the crawl space under the house, and he imagines them in that narrow place, breeding and squabbling and raising their kits.

He's never been in the yard before, and the air's so dense with the stench of rut and fecal matter and urine that he nearly chokes. There are eyes everywhere, and the space is hot with their attention as cats wander out of bushes and rub themselves against his legs, or weave in and out on the path ahead. The noise of it: throaty purrs, yowls, cries, and mews. He can feel the friction, the charge that passes up his legs from their fur. It makes his skin crawl—their collective craving.

They keep coming. He's amazed. For all the evenings he's watched them passing through the neighborhoods and alleys, he never dreamed there were such numbers. He hurries, tripping over cats, and when he gains the back porch, they rise on hind legs to claw at the wooden door, the jamb, the porch rails. Their voices rise, and a fight breaks out, two cats, and then another, and Ned can feel the tension bred of hunger. He pushes at the back door, the hook and eye breaking loose, and as he opens it the stench is a wall he must move through. Some of the cats hiss and back away, while others hunker just short of the threshold.

He takes a deep breath, gathers his courage, and eases inside the enclosed back porch. He stands awhile, taking shallow breaths, trying to acclimate to the smell. It takes only a few breaths and the expected gag reflex before he holds a kerchief to his face and breathes through his mouth instead, though even then the air seems oily. Once he's recovered enough, he looks about. There are plastic garbage bags piled in a corner, and he pulls one open, sees it's old cat-food tins—tuna and chicken—the cans scoured clean. Stacks of newspapers and magazines, bundled in neat packs, line the inside wall. He navigates his way between them and finds himself in the kitchen.

There are only two cats here, and they are more suspicious of his presence, slinking off to the far corner or under a chair. Their bellies haven't shrunken like those of their brethren outside. In a pantry the size of a cook's galley, he finds a sizable bag of cat food spilled across the counter and floor. The shelves are stocked. Canned goods are sorted by vegetable or fruit, by size and color. There's an entire shelf dedicated to macaroni and cheese. The bottom shelf is dry goods: flour, sugar, rice, and several boxes of cereal—all of which are puffed or sugared. And more cat food, bags and bags and a few tins.

The drapes over the kitchen windows are blue-and-yellow checked, and an ironing board hangs on the wall. The sinks, countertops, and stove top—all meticulous. Ned opens the refrigerator. He'd envy the well-stocked shelves, but on closer inspection, the vegetables and fruits are past prime, and the quart of milk is clotted in the wax container. Center kitchen, there's a maple gateleg table and one chair. Overlooking it all, atop the refrigerator, is a religious statue of Mary in a blue-and-white robe, a gold sash about her waist, a serpent under her heel. A small vase filled with plastic violets sits in front of her.

Ned feels a little . . . let down. This place is not what he expected. The litter box is overfull, but Ned knows that's the least portion of the stink. He steps into a central hallway, from where he can see the living room off to one end, and a dining room, and, on the far side, a corridor, down which, he assumes, are the bedrooms, the bath.

The odor varies, a shallow pool in the living room. In the dining room, it's formidable. He lingers in the living room. Four cats nest on the couch, the cushions shaggy as mohair—thick with molt. The cats' narrow gazes follow as he passes through. He wonders if by now they've gotten used to the smell. Has it become just another fact of their existence?

He finds Turnbull in the second bedroom. At first glance it looks as if the corpse is moving, but of course it isn't; it's the flies. The room's blowsy with them. Ned finds his way into the bathroom, where he throws up bits of peanut butter and crackers. He flushes the toilet, wets the kerchief in the sink, and wipes sweat from his face. In the medicine cabinet, he finds a tube of toothpaste and puts a dab on his tongue. There's a small vial of camphorated oil, and he opens it, dabs it under his nose, the numbing camphor a welcome relief. When he feels stronger, he pockets the oil and returns to the bedroom. At first, he avoids the body, orbits the room instead. There's one chest, a highboy, and the drawers are mostly empty: underwear, socks, T-shirts, a pair of pajamas—price tag still on—the old man clearly fondest of sleeping in the altogether. On top of the chest is a jar filled with holy medals. There's a King James Bible and a smattering of holy cards. The closet is a narrow space with a short clothes bar: one suit, three shirts, two pressed pairs of pants. On the floor are dress shoes side by side, old-fashioned wing tips, brown and black.

There's a mission-style desk and chair next to the closet. Some books that Ned glances through: *The Ecstatic Heart: The Life of a Saint*; *The Jesuits: A History*; and a concordance. In the drawer is a journal of household accounts, along with a yellow pad, two ballpoint pens, and a pencil. Over the desk is a mirror, and Ned is startled by his reflection. How like a stranger he looks, out of context in this room. His brown hair thinner, his eyes a fainter gray than he remembers. He touches the mirror. At his side in the silvered glass is reflected a large black wooden cross with its pale Christ figure, and directly beneath that, the old man's headboard.

The body. Seen in the mirror, the body seems almost animated. The old man's head slumped on his chest, arms thrown back in a gesture of surprise, while the legs drape the side of the bed, feet knuckled over on the floor.

Ned pulls the chair away from the desk, turns it and himself to face the body, and sits down. From the bedside table he picks up a copy of *The Watchtower* to flag at the flies, and a string of black beads falls to the floor—a rosary—the old man curiously ecumenical.

The corpse is black with flies, and the gasses that swelled him early on have already deflated, and all the fat and subcutaneous matter have gone to jelly, seeped into the mattress or pooled onto the floor, where they dried to a gummy mess, and given enough time and dry heat would evaporate. The corpse is already in the process of reduction: a bundle of bones, meat gone to jerky, skin a shriveling casement.

He leans to a side, looks past the toes furred with flies. Under the bed are the usual dust balls, cat hair, the odd shoe and sock. That's all. No cats. It's a wonder that the old man was spared that final indignity. Probably by the stock of cat food in the pantry, or perhaps it was the coddled nature of the chosen few. Ned thinks of the avaricious howling of cats outside, the feral and semiferal. They'd have done a job on him.

He puts another dab of camphor under his nose.

"So, old man," he says, and sits back. "Tell me something I don't know."

The old man mumbles, though it's really the fumbling of flies Ned hears, but he doesn't care; he likes the idea of flies being the dead's mouthpiece.

Ned hums a bit, feels how steady his own heart is, feels the blood vibrating in his legs, his hands. "So," he says. "What's it like? The other side?" He cocks his head.

Waits.

Ned crosses his legs at the ankle and slumps down in the seat. He waves the journal in the air, a few flies spinning in the updraft. He stops, looks at *The Watchtower* a moment, then continues fanning. Who'd have thought it? Ned had him pegged for a screwball, but not of the religious persuasion. Wonders what good religion's done the old man now. He leans forward, speaks into the harvest of flies in the old man's ears. "Well, if it's mortification of the flesh you're into . . . I got to tell ya, ya got it down."

He sits a long moment, his foot tapping the floor. He opens the bedside table drawer, pulls out a cardboard box. There are pictures inside, most of them faded, worn at the edges, creased from handling.

He holds up an old-fashioned studio portrait of a man and woman and baby. He puts his forefinger on the baby. "This you?" he asks. The flies mumble on. He puts the photo back. There are a number of navy pictures, with what must be a young Turnbull at sea, swabbing the deck. He studies the other photos, picks out three more: a birthday party, a toddler playing with toys under a Christmas tree, a young woman with her skirt hiked up a leg, her foot on the running board of a dashing circa-forties coupe.

He sets the box back and closes the drawer. He fans the four pictures out in his hand, then eases them into his pocket.

He raps the corpse on a knee with the paper and a horde of flies rises, clots in a bottleneck over the body, then settles here and there, on a finger, lip, on the chest hairs, his nose. A few buzz Ned's shoes, but he loosely rolls the journal and swats them and they land on the floor, where they roll in buzzing circles. "Gotta go, old man."

Ned pushes himself out of the chair and walks over to the window. He lifts the shade from the side, and the view is a thatch of elderberry, the limbs laden with flowers still green and furled. What little light there was has faded. It's that pearly hour of the evening. He thinks of home across the street, with its well-lit rooms, and silence greater than that of this house, with its noise of flies. The room has sunk into a kind of gloaming, so that the white bedsheets seem remarkably bright, and the lone figure's a hole punched in the light.

He considers the corpse, grateful that the eyes are mostly gone, fallen into the head perhaps, or dried to small pips like raisins. He doesn't care to examine it any closer. It would require turning on a light. Many lights. And in this time and place, in these circumstances, he understands at a level wholly outside of reason that he's not ready for that.

When he leaves Turnbull's house, it's to cross back to his own. He works his way through the brightly lit rooms, to the upstairs with the stink of Turnbull still in his nose. It's on his skin and in his hair. He peels his clothes off, piles them on the bathroom floor, pulls out a plastic waste bag and seals them in it. Later, he'll throw the clothes in the laundry: soap, bleach, water hot as hell. For now, he steps into the shower and turns the tap. The stink feels like a slick on his skin, or an oily extrusion. He wants to scald it off, and when he steps under the steaming spray, he clamps his teeth on a scream. He steps back, moderates the heat to where he can bear it with gritted teeth, and when his body is flushed red and beyond stinging, he scrubs at it with soap. He shampoos his hair once and twice more, and then rinses off, and, before stepping out, turns the shower handle quickly to the left and stands beneath that cooling stream until it begins to burn in its own way.

He stands dripping in front of the sink with its stainless porcelain basin, the oval mirror above, and studies his face. He lifts a razor from the vanity. His hands are steady, but when he puts the blade to his jaw, he cannot see except for the cavities that are eyes and nose, the layer of bone, and the sinew and string that tie the bones together, and so he sets the razor down and seats himself on the closed toilet lid.

He sits that way a long while, his heels backed against the cold porcelain. It is a collusion of events. How else to explain Turnbull's death and his own knowledgeable nose? He feels yet again that circumstances are conspiring. He sees it in a moment of startling clarity, a burst of intuition that drives through him as cleanly as a spike, that this calm is not his life at all, but a moment between the events that set the parameters of his real life.

He is breathing through his mouth, as if he cannot take air in fast enough. He looks down and sees his arms, and thighs, and stomach still rouged with heat. When he rises, he walks into the bedroom and turns the lights off. He picks through his clothes by feel, and glancing in the dresser mirror, he is surprised to discover how his image seems more substantial than he feels. He dresses in the dark, then picks up the bag of soiled clothes from the bathroom floor. On his way out, he drops them in the garbage. Shoes and all.

It's a gibbous moon. One of those cloudless nights when the ample moon lays a wide stroke of light onto the canyon floor, fires the river's surface, and ignites the white sand beneath their feet. At the height of this moon, only those few brightest stars, or the odd planet, shine through.

Still in shorts and tank top, Nance is stretched out on her cot, lying atop the sleeping bag. The tents are set up, but no one will use them, for this is a night to sleep under the stars. A gentle snoring comes from a rise on the beach where Peggy and Jody have set up. Their guide, Jeanette, has bedded down near the horses. "Cats," she says.

Everwine's on the far side of the beach, fishing, his T-shirt ghostly against the dark grasses. Nance watches how his arm sweeps back and forward in a cast. There's a steady quiet, an unexpected patience as he stands in moonlight, waiting.

She used to fish with Joe for perch, bass, crappie, or her favorite, the pantry bluegills. She realizes she hasn't missed it until now. She wonders if Ned enjoys fishing. He likes to read, and, of course, there's his work and the infrequent evening of theater or music, or the even rarer social gathering of friends or colleagues—usually hers. Truthfully, even on those occasions when they do go out, she often has the feeling he's doing time, just waiting to be released.

Is there one thing in this world that he really, truly enjoys, or is passionate about? And if there is, why doesn't she know what it is?

Because she's always believed she would come to that knowledge eventually. That they would grow together. That she would get past his reticence.

So. In three years of marriage, what one thing can she say about Ned without reservation?

She shakes her head. What can she do about it now, but determine to do better. Encourage—no, insist that Ned be more open with her. She looks down the beach, where Meredith is sitting near Pete. She can hear them talking. She is surprised by the pleasure she has seeing Meredith happy and at ease. Thinks her sister may have at last come to a good place in her life. Then Meredith's standing, dusting sand from her legs. She strolls over to where she's set her cot next to Nance's.

Meredith sits on her cot, smiles. "Thought you'd be zoned-out already."

"I think I'm at that stage where I'm too tired to sleep."

Meredith wipes her feet before lifting them up onto the bedding. "I told Pete to wake me if he catches anything bigger than a chihuahua."

"So"—Nance eyes the cot arrangement—"no hanky-panky between you?"

Meredith laughs. It's a word their father would use after they checked in on dates: "No hanky-panky, was there?" he'd ask.

Meredith crooks her arms about her knees. "A chaste kiss now and then."

"Chaste," Nance says, rolling over on her back but keeping her head turned toward her sister.

The two sisters smile, and Nance flops her feet clear of the warm bag. Soon enough the air will grow chill and she'll wriggle down into the bag, but for now she loves the looseness of her limbs and the way the breeze moves over and around her, as if she's floating in the currents.

"He's got something," Nance says, and Everwine's stepping into the water. His arms rise and play forward and to one side. His knees are bent, but his back's straight. The torque on the rod's not the kinetic flight of a trout, or the terrier tugs of bass. No, this is the drag of a plow through earth. Pete plants his feet.

The struggle lasts a good while, but then he has the blunt-headed fish on a stringer and is raising it, dripping, before the women. "Can I catch 'em?" he says.

It's a good ten-pound catfish. "As beautiful as they come," Nance says.

Pete heads back down the beach toward the shallows, where he'll ease the fish into the water to swim the night at the end of its chain.

The sisters chat while waiting for the next strike, but then they fall silent, and after awhile Nance slips into half dreams as easily as conversation, unsuspecting of where one ends and the other begins, and suddenly Joe's with them, fishing, and because he's young yet and undamaged, some part of her knows it's a dream, while that other part doesn't care, means, in fact, to have sex with him one more time.

He's barefoot and bare-chested. How strange that she'd forgotten how beautiful he is. The river's altered. She knows this to be true, just as she knows none of it is true at all. It's wider and slower, like the lower Snake. He's wading in the shallows, and she's on the beach. "Hey, girlee, girl," he says, a favorite tease. "Hey, girlee, girl, come on in. Fishing's fine."

And then she's in the water, and they're both young, and even in her dream she can feel that sweet craving, thinks, *do it now, before I wake*, but he's stepping away, says, *"There's a snake,"* and yes, there is a snake swimming against the current, near her thigh, and when she looks down, she sees the electric blue of its eye, and when it strikes, the sound is like the crack of a baseball bat, and it startles her, upward, out of the dream, and though she lies a long moment with her eyes shut, hoping to fall back into that place where Joe is, it's too late. Her eyes open and it's full dark, and she feels cheated. And then she feels like a cheat. Yet again.

The moon has nearly traveled its arc and the near canyon walls are dark, the last of the light having receded to the hills across the river. The river itself is a dimmer coil within the canyon's pitchy hue, and she looks over and sees that Pete has settled in on the far side of the beach. The sound rouses her again, and she sits up and looks toward the river.

Large comes to mind.

For a brief moment, she wonders if this is not a dream within a dream, this thing rising out of the deeps, this form surfacing with the slapping largesse of a dolphin or small whale, rolling in the water, in the last of the moon's light.

"What is it?" Meredith asks, her head raised on an arm.

"Sturgeon," says Nance.

"Criminey. It must be enormous."

"Ten-footer, maybe."

"Pete should be fishing now," Meredith says.

"They're protected," Nance says. "Takes them almost twenty years to reach spawning size, and at that age they're still young pups by this canyon's standards." One of the largest surviving freshwater fish in the world. *Surviving*. "White sturgeon. There used to be green sturgeon, too, but they were finished off by the dams." Unable to journey to the sea anymore, or adapt as these had. "It's strictly catch and release. Look," she says, points to the slim dorsal fin and tail of the fish cutting a wake. The fish rolls onto its side with a heaving of flesh, a loud slap against water, and sinks.

"Oh," Meredith says. "Wait."

Nance laughs. "With any luck, it'll surface again."

It's a good five minutes before Meredith spots it, the body slicing through the water. They turn their pillows about to face the river, and watch side by side, on their stomachs, chins braced on hands, knees crooked and ankles crossed. Their feet bob over their backsides, swing in tandem.

Meredith's voice is low. "It's so . . . *otherworldly*," she says.

Nance launches in. "Imagine this: Right here, where we're camping, this canyon is about two hundred million years old. But we have fossil records of sturgeon that predate the canyon by about a hundred million years. That animal"—she taps a finger against the cot—"is about as *worldly* as it gets."

Meredith nods. "Okay. But imagine this: maybe it's not a sturgeon at all, but a creature shoveled together out of mud and stone and popped to the surface by some weary, beneficent deity who saw us dreaming away this perfectly amazing evening and said, *What the fuck . . .*"

"Gods don't say *fuck*," Nance says.

"Roughly translated," Meredith says. "Anyway, what are the chances of you and me and that three-hundred-million-year-old fish—"

"That's the fossil record, not the fish."

"Details. What're the chances of it all coming together on this one evening, this one hour? What are the chances of our waking to hear it?"

"Oh gee, Meredith, I don't know," Nance says, "it must be a miracle."

"Damn right," Meredith says.

Nance dangles an arm off the cot, runs her fingers through the sand.

She could argue the fine points, the deep pool and the habits of sturgeon, but at the rock bottom of science, she isn't adverse to a bit of the miraculous, though her father's term—*mystery*—seems less heretical.

It's harder to see the fish, as the moon has dipped down over the near hills, and the black of the canyon is deepening, lit only, as it now is, by starlight.

Which is no small thing. Nance taps her sister on the shoulder and points skyward. They both roll on their cots even as the sturgeon lolls in the water, rotating its creamy belly to the sky's light before sinking one last time to the river's bottom. The dale of sky is filled with the light of stars, and each star's an adamant fire in a congregate brilliance that has the women blinking, and silent, and questioning whether they still sleep to dream such life into the light that swarms overhead.

They are speechless for so long that Nance believes her sister has fallen asleep, but when she glances over, her sister's eyes are open.

"It wasn't the fish," Meredith says.

"What?"

"That woke me. You were talking in your sleep." She links her fingers behind her head, glances over at Nance. "It was mostly nonsense."

The sounds of the canyon filter in: crickets, frogs, the rustle of cheat grass where a small rodent, deer mouse or vole perhaps, journeys through. There's the lapping of water on the sand.

"I was dreaming of Joe. He was here. Fishing with us."

Meredith nods. "He'd have enjoyed this."

"It's usually Joe I dream of, and then I wake up, and not only do I lose Joe again but then I feel like I've cheated on Ned."

"There it is, that hyperactive conscience." Meredith tucks her arm up under her pillow, burrows in deeper. "You can't be accountable for dreams."

"But sometimes I worry that I don't love Ned enough. I mean, with him it's so different." She rolls her head to one side to better see Meredith. "He's so . . . reluctant to talk about himself; it's like pulling teeth."

"Unlike Joe," Meredith says, grinning.

Nance nods. "Joe. There wasn't a thing I didn't know about Joe, or didn't want to know." Nance looks up at the sky.

"So why'd you marry him? Ned?"

Nance shrugs. "I fell for him." She looks over at her sister. "*Most* people find him attractive. Charming. We get on well together. We have a lot in common, we're compatible. It all seemed so . . . natural. Safe."

Meredith lays her head on her hands. "Safe? Really." Meredith pushes the hair back from her face, stretches out on the cot. "Maybe it feels safe because you don't *have* to love him as well, because he's never asked that of you. Less risk. And maybe after losing first Mama and then Joe, that was just fine with you, too?"

Nance kicks a foot loose of the sleeping bag. Hangs it over the cot's edge.

"What's changed?" Meredith presses.

"I don't know." What is it she can't bring herself to say? That something in her household has changed. That lately everything smacks of secrets. She pushes the thought away. "Maybe I'm just feeling guilty. Would I spend this much time away from Joe?"

Meredith blows a small bug off her arm. "Apples and oranges. That was a different time. A different life. But Joe would be here with you if he could."

Nance laughs. "This is hardly what Ned enjoys. I can't imagine him sleeping under the open sky."

Meredith flops onto her back again. "Remind me not to fall in love with a man who won't sleep in the open." She pauses. "In the altogether."

"Any other conditions."

"He's got to be true, honest, brave, endearing, kind, hardworking, sensitive, and generous."

"Anything else?"

Meredith grins over at her sister.

"What?"

"He has to know a miracle when he sees one."

For the second time in one evening, Ned finds himself headed for his car, though this time, he doesn't catch a distracting whiff. He eases in behind the wheel and drives off. An aimless thirty minutes later, he's in the industrial end of town, the other side of the bridge, where between the trucking docks and the feedlots, warehouses, and processing plants are scattered blocks of residential houses, a warren of lean-tos, cars on blocks, Dumpster-slag piles. There are no yards here, just a series of battered fences separating this junk from that: three-legged chairs, appliances, moldering mattresses, the hulls of coaster wagons and truck beds, wheelchairs. There are doghouses gnawed to pulp, a rusted chain still attached, and the fat links on the far ends stretched so thin that you imagine the dogs there still, flesh gone to mulch, ribcages stitched with a ligament of weeds, skulls shining like backyard pearls.

Here there are the hard-timers, households double-bolted, windows draped in bedding or packed shut with insulation, and what few people you see about in the daylight hours are the elderly. Or the oddities—skittery hands and Old Testament eyes—adrift from the transient highways, the scamsters, the hard-luck cases, the heavily medicated, the painfully poor with their shared packs of children, the youngest of whom have about them the look of imminent roadkill. There's the six-room Nighty Night Motel, and Pepi's Italian-American. There's the Arbor Lounge, closed these past seven years, after its streak of parking-lot abductions, rapes, and murders.

It is the night side of the valley. The junk drawer. It's the other, other side of the tracks. Ned's kind of town. And in this bar, he's just another drifter. A risk in the offing.

In boots, jeans, and T-shirt, he sits at the far end of the bar with his back to the wall. In his fingers, a cigarette burns a worm of ash. A pool table with its scuffed and mended felt is to his right, and the players: a short, moonfaced man, his lids heavily suggestive of Down's, the other a young kid in checked flannel, his hair still wet from the shower. A tall man—a streak of lightning, with his zaggy frame, shock of white hair, and pale skin—buddies up to his moonfaced pal, sets their bankroll on the pool table.

The kid ponies up. He breaks, and it's a ball slammer; a solid drops. Ned can almost see the boy tallying his take.

The tall one has moved next to Ned. He crooks an elbow on the bar, snaps a nod, and raises his beer. It's a long pull, and when he lifts the bottle away, foam spills over his hand. He wipes the foam on the back of his britches. He looks over at the table as the kid misses his shot. He stares a long moment at his partner; his lips crook into a smile. "Hey, Wee Willie, you gonna play that table or yourself?"

Wee Willie has a hand in his pants. Ned almost expects him to say, *An' I take care of the rabbits?* But Wee Willie takes his hand out and bellies up to the table. When he makes his play, it's a two-bumper combination shot for the side pocket, and he pulls it off with a finesse that confounds the other player.

The tall man next to Ned shakes his head. "Sumbitch," he says, knowing the game's out, and this will be the short pickings of a long evening. He turns to Ned. "You see that?"

Ned hums a tuneless ditty, looks at the way Wee Willie is sizing up the table. Says, "Gifted."

"Gifted." The stranger agrees, shakes his head again. "Give him a stick in his hands or his pants and he knows what to do. But take him to the grocer's, tell him to pick sumpin'? It'll be his seat or his nose every time."

Ned pushes a twenty across the bar, signals two beers to the bartender, one for himself and the other for the tall man next to him. When they arrive, he turns to the man. "Name's Nate. And you must be George."

The tall man looks confused, but smiles. "Nah. That'd be someone else. Name's Doug, but I'll take that beer." He finishes his brew, plocks the empty down, picks up the fresh one.

"Hey, Willie," Doug calls out, "you want nuther?" Wee Willie nods, lines up another combination. Sinks two, moves on. There's nothing dim about him at the moment, the table light glossing the wide plate of forehead, and about the sloped eyes there's a solemn and curiously elegant patience.

"In pool, he is *purely* gifted." Doug threads his fingers through his white hair. "But tell him something easy, like just lie in the weeds awhile. Just to keep things interesting, you understand, 's not like we're pool sharks or nothing."

Doug's grin is wide and toothy, and he guzzles, finishes his beer, then tips Wee Willie's down his throat, as well. Clearly means to make the most of Ned's generosity. Ned pushes a ten from change forward, waves two fingers toward the barkeep, and fresh bottles line up. Ned looks over his shoulder to the dance floor, where a middle-aged couple are knocking knees to some Texas swing piece off the jukebox. The man's got a hand down the back pocket of his girl's jeans, and when she wags her ass, his hand wallows like a carp in the shallows. Tables ring the ten-foot dance floor, mostly empty, save for the odd man or pairs of women. At one table, an older woman swabs the inside of her mouth with a finger, and a shockingly pink upper plate of teeth rests on the Formica tabletop.

Doug's nattering on, and while Ned nods sympathetically, he watches Willie. Wonders how this pair found each other, the artful idiot and the idiot.

Willie's made short work of the flannel-shirted kid, who's sulking off to the far end of the room, embarrassed to be young, buff, and beaten by the likes of Wee Willie.

Doug scoops up the odd bills and change from Willie's dimpled hand. Pockets it. "This here's Nate," says Doug, and Willie looks over.

"Wanna play?" Willie asks, his words mildly thickened. There's an avid look in his eyes.

Ned shakes his head. "You're too good for me," he says.

Willie's eyes gloss over, and Ned wonders where it is he's gone, what world he sees with a focus as soft as his dumpling face. They spend the next half hour chasing beers with shots, and Doug's taking the fast slide. Willie sticks to beer. It's clear Doug mistrusts his luck enough to drink fast, and Ned keeps him lubed. Waits it out. Down a few seats, Ned hears, "Ask me, that woman needs slapped" and then another voice: "But no one's fucking asking, are they?" There's some jostling that turns rough, then knocks off just as quickly. Ned's attention wanders back. Doug has no end of stories, but Willie has turned his attention to women, nods and winks if he catches their eye, and when Willie leaves to go to the men's room, Ned asks Doug about him.

"Name's Willard somethin'r nuther Dempsey." Doug leans back, hooks a heel over the iron foot rail, nearly topples before steadying himself. "Like that old-timey prizefighter? But I give him the Wee Willie moniker." He pokes a thumb in his chest. Waits a beat.

"After Wee Willie Winkie," Ned says.

"Yeah. You got that, huh?" He eyes the small reservoir of beer and backwash in his bottle, waves it toward the rest room. "Though, truth is, the only thing wee about his winkie is the mind behind it."

Ned cocks an eyebrow at Doug.

"Shit, he ain't bashful about it." He takes down the last swallows of beer, looks at it wistfully. Ned hands him another. Doug salutes Ned. He takes a long pull and then smacks his lips on the tail end of a belch. "And I ain't bragging, but I can hold my own, you know."

"But why would you want to?" Ned asks. The joke goes over Doug's head, and Ned's nearly convinced Doug just might be the dimmer-witted of the pair. Though Doug is baggage. It's Wee Willie that Ned's interested in, that moonfaced babe with his pudgy hands, distant stare, and slack mouth.

By the tail of the evening, Doug's in a waking stupor, but Willie's still as alert as he's ever going to be in this lifetime. Ned helps Willie lead Doug out of the bar, and they stumble across the highway to the Nighty Night, where they deposit Doug in a room, and when Willie makes as if to stay, Ned sets out the bait. There are some women he knows. "You interested in women, Willie?"

"What about Doug?" Willie asks.

Ned pats Willie on the shoulder. "You're a good friend, Willie. You're a good friend." And Willie's nodding, a serious expression on his face.

"Doug's fine. Look at him," he says, and leads Willie to the bed. "Out for the count."

Willie laughs. "Out f'r the count."

"But you and me, Willie—"

"Out f'r the count."

"No, no." He shakes his head, leads Willie to the door by his hand. "Evening's just started—*I know this woman,* Willie."

Willie looks over his shoulder one last time, and then Ned steers him out into the dark.

"Good night, Doug," Ned whispers, putting a finger in front of his lips.

Willie nods with a swooping of his head. "G'night, Doug," he says. "Out f'r the count."

Fifteen minutes later, they're in a room just three doors from where Doug's passed out on the bed. In another hour, Doug will wake enough to stumble into the bathroom, where he'll fall into the bathtub and pass out on his back. In the morning, the cleaning crew will find him—still on his back, but dead, his mouth packed with a slurry of beer, whiskey, and the remains of a chili dog. But Ned has no way of knowing this. In fact, Doug's long gone from his mind, for his attention's on Willie. Willie and the woman they found wandering the bar's parking lot, looking for an open car where she might crash in a backseat, or, failing that, the back of a pickup. She was homeless—a sad thing, she said. And she was high, but not so much she couldn't see the potential. "Two to one?" she asked, and "Hey, I got scruples."

Which cost Ned an extra ten—thirty dollars and a room.

The two of them are on the bed, while Ned, still clothed, keeps to the armchair next to the window, where he has an unobstructed view. The woman is . . . unremarkable . . . on the early side of thirty, though it's hard to tell, her skin sallow and hair bleached yellow. She is fleshy in the way women are who live on a diet of plenty and starvation. Her love handles have draped, and her breasts and belly are sketched with shining scars in the aimless paths of snails. A birthmark, dark and large as a thumbprint, rides high on her left buttock, and each time she bears down on Willie, her small feet curl into ingenious fists.

But the greater weight of his fascination is on Willie. The child-man. His ass as broad and luminous as his face. The hairlessness of his body. The white and whiter skin of thighs, calves, only the bottoms of his feet purpled with the flush of excitement. After a short while, Ned tells the woman to turn about on the bed. To let Willie on top. For Ned wants it all.

What he notices is not the slippery in and out of conjoining flesh or the way Willie's winkie labors at a workaday pace; rather, he attends to the man's face, the liquid *unh, unh, unh,* Willie grunts through the slack-water pool gathering in his mouth. The jaw is locked in a forward thrust, so that small teeth picket his upper lip. His hair is wetly flattened back and the skin over his forehead is stretched tight as a bedsheet over the domed plate of bone.

Ned is breathing through his nose and there's a whistling as from a tiny squeeze box. And there is that familiar twisting at the base of his spine. He leans forward, elbows on his knees.

Willie's eyes are as dark as plucked almonds, his gaze directed somewhere over the top of Ned's head—to the window, maybe, with its drapes of palm fronds and blue ocean and kayaks that undulate across the pleated cloth. He chugs like a train in a noisy coupling.

He has stamina, a thing Ned had not expected, certainly not after that first untimely emission, barely unzipped. She'd shaken her head, turned to Ned, and said, "Price stays the same." But then Willie had gone on as if nothing had happened, stroking himself until he'd achieved another erection, and he's been going at it ever since with a workman-like rigor, a straightforward in and out—an economy of movement as stripped down as his mind. The act is cumbersome, and painfully banal, the pair overexposed under the glare of an overhead light that Ned insists on. For it is ugliness that most excites him, understanding absolutely that the act is best, by nature, base and degrading. Not the sanitized version you imbibe at home with a wife, or the airbrushed widescreen fantasy. No. He takes in the hairiness of the woman. The runnels of sweat and lines of grit. Pockets under arms, cracks between cheeks. The wet sounds like exaggerated kisses. Clown's farts. The sticky smells congealing in the room.

At his back, through the thin partition of wall, Ned hears the sounds of traffic just thirty feet from the door, and as the couple lumbers on, there's the hiss of air brakes, and the woman cranes her head back, her eyes opened in a doppelgänger moment, in which he sees her in the act, and yet another her, any number of other hers. The sounds of trucks and cars gearing up, the sound suddenly so immediate and dense that Ned believes he smells the stink of diesel, and oily drip pans, thinks for a moment it is the woman he smells, the lubricated engine of her body. While the man atop her, that carnal idiot, aimlessly pumps away. Ned spreads the drapes an inch, two, and sees the stream of lights trailing over the bridge. He cannot see the void beneath the steel girders, but knows it is there and that it is a river, black and deep as any pocket, and just as nasty.

Ned stands. He should not go there. He knows this. Though all the while he tells himself *no,* his hand is fidgeting in his pocket. He makes his way to where the linens have slumped onto the floor, and as he stands at the side of the bed, the woman looks up. She's clearly tired. Wants nothing more than to roll over and drift into sleep without the slogging about on top of her. She turns her head away, sighs.

Ned moves nearer. He's in the room and he's not. He sees the long zagged crack in the plaster over the headboard, the dime-store print of a seashore at sunset tilting from its nail, but he also sees shadows sketched in grass to the side of him, a bird bolting into a blue sky. There's the smell of dirt and shit, the dark stain that is always spreading in the dust, and he's bracing himself for the heat that will drive its way up his groin and into his backbone, where it will leap like an electric charge through his body, and he reaches forward, his hand connecting with the soft flesh that covers Willie's wing bones, and it brings Willie's head back with a snap.

So caught up has Willie been in his own labor, stoking the unexpected pleasure he's stumbled onto, that when Ned touches Willie, he turns his head and his face stirs, wakes to the present with a look of incomprehension—as if he doesn't know where he is. As if he's forgotten what it is he's doing, who he's doing it with.

He looks at Ned a long, confused moment, and there is something in what he sees that settles him back on his heels, separating himself from the woman. Something that makes him reach for the end of the blanket to cover himself modestly. He looks around. Perhaps to reorient himself to the here and now. Or perhaps he looks for Doug.

The woman's twisting under him, trying to free herself, as if she, too, has seen. She's been around long enough to know what's coming next, and she heaves Willie off her hips and scuttles to the far side of the bed, hits the floor at a run. She locks herself in the bathroom, but it's only a sad hook and eye, so she throws her body's weight against the door, and then keeps still. Means to make herself invisible. Forgettable. She covers her ears, but still she hears her mother's voice, as if one or the other of them were already dead: *You bring this on yourself. Like always.*

Chapter Eight

It's been two weeks. There was little about it in the paper. TRAGEDY IN LOCAL MOTEL. "In a pair of unrelated incidents . . . Man found dead of aspiration." A couple, just another homeless couple, who took up with the wrong company. Small column. Back page. Willie would be in the hospital for an indefinite stay. Ned imagines the moony face gone even dimmer, those plump hands on top of the sheets. Like an inflatable Wee Willie Winkie, complete with tubes and respirator. And the woman? Bolted before they could do much more than stitch her together. He carried the article around for days, transferring it from pocket to pocket like a half-forgotten token he kept stumbling on, until he put it safely away.

It's also been two weeks since finding Turnbull. Ned still wakes in the middle of the night believing he can smell the old man on his hands, on the web of skin between thumb and forefinger, or the fleshy pad of his palm, and he'll rise and wash again—but no one else had come across the old man since.

It's become a source of major interest. When watching TV in the living room, say, or sitting on the porch, he finds himself looking over there. Waiting for someone to stumble on the smell, or notice the old man's absence. The elderly Leona Rodeen, who lives next door to Turnbull, will come out to pick up a newspaper or gather the mail and pause a moment to snatch at a weed in her lawn, or scuff dirt off the sidewalk with the toe of a shoe. Then her face will orient like a hound on the next yard. She'll stand there quizzing the air, and Ned's sure she'll admit what it is she smells, that stink beyond the casual piss and dung that by now must be second nature. But all she does is wrinkle her nose and shake a fist before shuffling back into her tightly sealed house.

Down the street, there's Jake Murphy, a bear of a man, with his curly black beard and hair, his shambling gait, who plays trombone in the civic orchestra. Ned's watched him on his twice-weekly walk to rehearsal, instrument case in hand. Midblock, he'll start listing to the far side of the road, as if tacking into a fierce wind, to end up on the opposite sidewalk.

The neighborhood kids are brutally honest. "It stinks," they say. "Somebody pooped," they say, "in their pants." They shout at the house and run down the street. But the neighborhood men and women—friends and strangers—speed up, or duck their heads, or dodge to the far side of the street, or run for cars with air conditioners and windows sealed as tight as their minds.

It's like a hole in the neighborhood, a crack in the cement that everyone stumbles over but never falls into.

Sure it's ignorance. But who's to say it isn't *willful* ignorance, and that at some level, every mother's one of them knows what it is they're skirting. That small cottage with its well-kept rooms: Its prayer books and statues, its pauper's box of photographs, and its sacrificial cats are just artifacts in a tomb. The old man died utterly alone. Who of them wants to know that what waits in there waits for them?

Which is all right with Ned, for he finds it comforting—the old man. His own little secret. A confidant. Truth is, he never found Turnbull this engaging in life. Has much, in fact, to thank the old corpse for.

He wonders if at a deeper level it hasn't affected the others. So that Jake blows a more lively trombone now, or the old woman next door trims the horny nails on her toes with a renewed ferocity these days.

The house has been shut tight and remains unvisited, though Ned did think to feed the cats. The indoor ones. Before leaving, he opened a new bag of food and kicked it over for them. The yard cats, he left to their own devices. Sometimes he can hear them squalling over there. Though many have wandered off to other handouts in other yards, and some few have probably gone the way of their former benefactor, still a dozen or so remain to hunt whatever mice or rats or birds they can and hobble about shriveled in the hips, inflicting endless injuries on one another.

It's been a liberating experience, all in all. A lesson he learned long ago, but then forgot. He's hard put to explain this, but it's as if he's turned a corner, made the step he's been teetering on for years. He doesn't just feel freer to indulge in a little pleasure; he feels compelled. There's really no harm in it, as long as he does nothing too risky, keeps to just a little something on the side. Granted: Willie was a bit much. Over the top, perhaps, but it was a freak occurrence. A matter of unfortunate timing, coming as it did on the heels of Turnbull. Ned just wasn't quite himself that night. Since then, he mostly takes his pleasure on the road, in the smaller communities—Colfax, Pullman, Pomeroy, and Dayton—though sometimes the larger cities provide what he wants—Walla Walla, Spokane, an overnight to Seattle, Tacoma, or Portland. He can't believe how hung up he's been on the trivial this past three years. He feels . . . renewed.

He thinks about the woman he met three nights ago in the small town of Orofino, a town as down on its luck as logging. It was in the Cosmos Club, the bar with the 1950s rocket fashioned from pink neon above the door. She was a moderately beefy woman, with a shelf of breast, and wide rib cage above narrowing buttocks and legs—an inverted triangle—a slow-moving load. She said she drove trucks. The big rigs. An eighteen-wheeler.

But you can't believe half what these people say, so he'd been skeptical. Until she took him out back where her rig was parked, diesel running, and escorted him up into the cab, the sleeping quarters with its white-carpeted floor and walls, its full-sized bed sporting baby blue sheets and velour blanket. The minibar and box fridge, the overhead cabinet with snap-in glasses, plates, washcloths, and towels. A small chest of clean clothes. A toolbox, flashlight, and fire extinguisher.

"You really are a truck driver," he said.

"I can handle a stick," she said, her smile showing an unfortunate gum line. But that didn't matter. She was clean, and competent.

And he didn't do a thing to her she didn't ask for.

One way or another.

Nothing in the paper. Tough trucker lady. She had a reputation to maintain. It would not behoove her to speak.

He wants to think about it, the things he did in the tight space of the truck cab. But Nance comes to mind instead. She'll be home in a matter of days. He fears she'll notice the difference in him, but then convinces himself she'll never really know what it is. It'll be like the neighbors who skirt the house across the street, moving in the force of its fragrant wake while never questioning the steps they took. In fact, he looks forward to her return; it's been almost three weeks, after all. He thinks of what he might buy her, a small gift to show his love.

For he does love her. He tells himself this and closes his eyes to test what he's feeling. There's a tenderness like a thin prickling under his eyelids, and his eyes moisten, and this reassures him. It is a thing he does from time to time—tests what he feels, though it's generally not so well defined, more a matter of testing whether or not he feels at all. As a child, he would practice tears, an odd thing for a child to do, certainly, but somehow comforting. He's discovered that women are gratified by tears, reassured to find a man whose heart lies as close to the skin as their own.

He rubs the back of his neck, and then his hand travels up to his hair and back down again, prodding at the knot that's forming there. It had been a tiresome day in meetings with the principals of the other elementary schools, as well as the junior high and high schools, discussing the recent budget cuts. The first time in the state's history that the state government included elementary through secondary education in budget cuts. All to protect a tax break given to industry the year before. And why not? Ned thinks—the path of least resistance, taking candy from the babies. It had been a devastating blow, hitting hardest those outlying rural communities least able to withstand it: forcing layoffs, the reduction of essential programs, school closures.

"This isn't just bare bones, folks," Franklin's principal, Rozee Schultz, had said. "We're gnawing the marrow."

And it was true. All of it. It was a disgrace. A black eye to the children he'd worked so hard to protect.

Just another thing to walk away from, he thinks, and by the end of the day he *is* weary of it, his colleagues' hopeless optimism, the fevered speeches, and so when he left the room for the afternoon break, he'd walked right out of the building and never stopped until he hit the sofa in his living room, where he put his feet up and stretched out. Slept until just an hour and a half ago, and since then he's been sitting here with a beer at his side, waiting for his pizza to be delivered and watching the neighbors steer a wide berth around the stinking dead.

The delivery boy, when he comes, could be eighteen or thirteen. He's dressed in oversized shorts and T-shirt, ball cap wrung down over his forehead. He's driving a teal-colored 93 Geo Metro: a banged-up two-door death trap with just enough room in the backseat for the stack of pizza boxes.

The boy smells of pepperoni and transmission fluid, and after he hands the box over, he swipes the back of his hand against his sagging shorts.

"That'll be," the boy says, looking at the slip, "nine ninety-three, please," and holds his hand out.

Ned cracks the lid of his pizza box. "Big night?" he asks.

The kid looks confused.

"Lots of deliveries? Car break down?"

The boy shrugs. "Somethin' the matter, mister?"

Ned takes out a ten and a single, offers it to the boy.

The boy takes the money. Twists his lip at the tip. "Wow. Gee, thanks, man," he says.

Ned knows he should just pass it off, but the pizza is cold and the beer is beginning to swagger in his stomach. He watches the boy hop the three lower steps to the sidewalk and fold his long frame into the car. Ned catches up and sets his pizza on the car's roof. He holds the boy's door open and leans in.

The kid is shrinking back toward the passenger side. "What, man? What d'ya want?"

Ned leans further in, looks into the backseat of the tinny vehicle, where boxes sit, pizzas wilting. "A little gratitude," he says. "The pizza is cold."

The kid's shaking his head. "Man, I don't—"

"And I give you a fucking tip, which you sure as hell don't deserve, because the pizza is cold."

"I didn't—"

"But you don't think it's enough, so you make a face and get smart with me."

The boy's hands are spread open. "Hey, I'm sorry, okay? Like I didn't mean to piss you off or nothing. It's been a bad night. You know what I mean?"

"Well, that's unfortunate." Ned wraps a fist over the ponytail that juts out of the boy's cap, and he pulls the kid's head back. "But your day just got worse, didn't it?" He leans in close. "Didn't it?"

The kid nods.

"And it didn't really have to. A little courtesy. Is that too much?"

The kid's hand is twisting at Ned's, trying to free his hair. "Listen, mister," he says. "Listen—"

But Ned's letting him go, has already lost interest. Ned's nose is picking up this new mix of smells from the car's interior: pizza, and booze, and carnal knowledge, and oil and transmission—a trail of fluid that ends somewhere under the car—and above it all is the distinctive tang from old Jack and his cats across the street.

He steps back, slams the door shut, and walks away. The kid's still apologizing as Ned walks past. The car pulls away with a chirping of tires, and the pizza flips off the roof and lands upside down on the hood of the car, then slides onto the road. The kid never stops.

But Ned doesn't give a rat's ass. He's headed back to his house, where he grabs his car keys, and when he steps back down the stairs, it's with a jaunty lift to his feet. He's humming. The night's about to begin.

He drives up the Lewiston Grade. At the top, he takes turns toward

Pullman, and just outside of Pullman he takes the turn off toward Spokane. Though he won't go quite that far.

Not tonight. He's thinking just enough distance for what he has in mind.

The woman tips back another whiskey, elbows like outriggers on the tabletop. Her chest is boyishly flat under the Spandex tank top, and her head, fattened with hair, floats on the stalk of neck. Her legs are crossed, so that a narrow foot dangles in a straight plane, toe touching the floor. There is about her a gnawed-upon look. A delicate disorder about the edges: cuffs frayed, nails splitting, the ends of her sentences trailing off. One hand frets, moving from the whiskey glass to her face and over the tip of an ear, nose, an eyebrow, to the back of her neck, or down a pant leg. Tugs at the belt crisscrossing her navel.

Such busy hands.

It's Friday night. There's a live band. The room's populated with people from the belt of small towns between Colfax and Spokane. The music is a campy mix of rockabilly and country—surprisingly good. The dance floor is a fifteen-foot square of inlaid wood battened in on three sides by tables and slick with spilled drinks and sweat, so that between sets a young man paces the floor, broadcasting grit from a burlap sack.

They don't dance, Ned and the woman, but keep to themselves at the far end of the room, nearest the latrines. A straight line to the back door. She's all the company he needs, and that's little enough.

If asked, she'd tell him she's never been good at conversation or the games people generally play in such situations. But she won't offer this or anything more than the few words he seems satisfied with—mostly yes, or an occasional no. Still, he seems kindly enough. Moderately attractive. The drinks keep coming, and though early on she wondered what it was he expected in exchange, she could have told him he didn't need to go this far. She's perfectly willing to do her part. Thankful as she is to be rescued from the crew she'd tagged along with this evening, her coworkers at the canning plant. A clutch of oddly large women who have long since left the bar without a backward glance, as if she were their pound of flesh to be shed.

By now, she's fairly tanked on the drinks he's bought, which is just rosy. She's almost got the smell of peas out of her head, and only rarely now will she find her fingers sorting across the table, searching out the nightshade, the hard little green look-alikes that find their way onto the endless belts of peas. Her job, her particular talent at the plant being a fierce focus paired to the frenetic activity of skinny fingers. She thinks of the portly matrons who man the upper belts, and the river of peas slipping through plump digits.

Even with her prodigious metabolism, the internal engine with its outsized hunger that she has spent a lifetime appeasing, her small body cannot keep up with the sheer number of drinks she's consumed, and the glass slips in her hands, drops to the tabletop, splashes whiskey up the flat of her arms and around an elbow.

She looks bewildered, says, "I am dead drunk." In the foreground of the spinning room is his face, smiling.

"No," he says, his voice slowed through water, "not that far gone, surely."

She nods. "I gotta . . ."

"Go home?" he asks. "I'll take you."

She laughs, slumps down. "I got no legs."

He stands, *tsk-tsks*, and eases his hands under her arms to lift her away from the table. Her ribs feel plucked beneath the thin skin, and his hand sinks into the pocket of her armpit. He swings her arm over his shoulder, and then she's standing, with his hand supporting her. He leaves a modest tip, checks that nothing's left behind, and then they're walking an ambling line past the bar and along the back wall toward the door.

The music is crashing on. The stage is hopping with lights—blue and red and white—the dance floor jammed with couples, a quake of hands in the air, but he will catch this only as an afterimage, long after this night has concluded, and then he won't give it any more detail than what he's grasped in quick, careful glances: the table of retirees, the birthday girl at the bar slumping into her celebratory drinks, the farm boys with grange caps and home-clipper haircuts, the married couples flirting with the spouses of friends. The usual small-town, small-life high jinks. And then he's walking out the door with this woman draped under his arm, past the row of pictures on the wall of past bar parties—the deliberate, smiling faces, ghoulish in overexposed frames, shot after Polaroid shot pinned to the wall.

In the dark, Ned guides the small woman over to the car, packs her giggling into the passenger seat, and belts her in. When he pulls away, the doors lock, and the woman's head lolls on her neck. She belches. Dozes off. Never tells him where home is, but that's not where he's inclined to take her anyway, so when he pulls onto the highway, it's open country he heads for. He hums the long road into the dark, and when he comes to the small dirt lane, he turns off the headlamps, the shine of the moon all the light he needs.

The woman snores, a thin line of spittle slung from her lips. In a few minutes, he will wake her, for he very much wants her awake.

He parks the car far from the highway, and the only building in sight is a barn that has buckled onto one side, roof sloping into the dirt, door to the haymow bowed open in a perpetual exhalation. He lowers the window on his side. Listens. Lets the hum and clutter in his head fall away along with the sounds of the faraway bar and the highway, until all he hears is the wind in wheat, the distant yip of a coyote, the shallow breathing of the woman.

He rolls the window up. When he rouses her, it's with a slap. Gentle first. To one cheek, and the other, and another slap, and each increasing in intensity and frequency until her eyes open and her head rocks against the seat and her hands flutter in the dark like moths against the glass, against his arms, his chest. Her mumbles turn to yells. And then he's telling her, "Shut up," and pulling her out of the car. He drags her by a wrist into the field, into the hip-high fields of green, the bristling beds of winter wheat, her heels a harrow in the dirt.

She's crying, and she throws up, but none of this deters him—not her pleading or silence, and certainly not the blood. For as he sees it, this is what it is all about. The way her eyes shine wide and white, the quiver in her thighs, a vibration as subtle as a tuning fork, the bowing in her back against his knee.

He aims for the humpbacked barn, a castoff in the field, like the carapace of an enormous beetle, and he enters through the old hay door, double-wide and sagging. He holds her on the threshold until the black-on-black becomes grays and blues, and the gapped slats in the far wall slowly fill with stars. Then he brings her beneath the worm-bored loft, plowing a wedge through the wood duff, the dirt, the bedding hay rimed in mold. Center floor, the building's sole pack rat watches a long moment before hurrying back to its hoard of trinkets.

They stumble-dance in a tight circle, packing the bedding beneath their feet, and in his hands her ribs expand and compress, the folds of her flesh as pliable as her sighs. She has come to that place where she hands it over, as in a bad dream, or a cautionary tale. A place where she bends to save from breaking, where she visits, a partial observer to what will inevitably follow.

He rapes her. For that is what it is and what it's meant to be. With hand, and cock, and the odd implements he finds hung on the walls of the barn, he rapes her. Dragging her—from stall to aisle, to deep in the tack shed, and the hay mow's matted heart—he takes her again and again in ways that will keep her absolutely there. For the long haul.

Until it comes to that point he has yet to cross, when he has expended all the energy he has to spare, then he will pause awhile to deliberate, and in that restorative quiet, he will hold her as if she were his true love, as if all the pain were a mistake, a thing he can woo her past.

Hidden in the barn, in the keep falling to peat and dirt, a husk of timbers, a rot the wind sorts through as easily as the tines of the hay rake at his back, he will sit among the remnants of scythe, and shears, a handful of discs scattered like coins in the dark. He will hold her as a person holds himself against the blow he knows will fall. Against that birdish thing beneath his ribs, that rises and quickens in his throat—a distant kin to sobbing. And he will stroke the cheek where a tooth has slivered through, kiss the meat that was lip. He will finger the broken ribs and pat closed the torn places. And when he's got her quiet, when he sees a softening about the brow, or a drooping in the lid, as in paralysis—a thing he will interpret as gratitude—then and only then will he put his lips to her ears to whisper of things darker than this night's work. And then he will offer her respite, if all she will do is name some one thing he hasn't imagined yet. Knowing she will fail.

The canyon walls waver, and the leaves of hackberry and mountain mahagony curl with the fierce summer heat. Nance sweats under the floppy cap, runs the kerchief tenderly over her sunburned face. Summer has hit full force in the weeks she's been up canyon, and so she's doubly grateful it's time to return home. She looks at her well-baked arms, finds herself fantasizing about air conditioning. Though it's not just the heat that signals the change, for the farther downriver they travel, the more congested it is. Tourists. Which might explain Pete, sullen, tight-lipped, and tightfisted at the captain's wheel, spinning an endless string of complaints. Pete cuts the engine, reducing the wake for yet another group of rafters strung out in four large rubber rafts, trailed by the outfitter's rig: tents, cooking supplies, food staples, and the sealed plastic buckets that serve as chemical toilets. Two young men row the company raft with a bored nonchalance, tipping their hats to Pete, but he's focused on the tourists, hats slouched on heads, shoulders and noses peeling. In the center raft, a young woman is throwing up into the water while a young man pats her on the back.

A small group of kayaks paddle in and out among the rafts. Farther down, a school of one-man rafts drift at the pace of ambitious carp, all of which has Pete alternately edging forward and backing off. Added to the mix is the parade of tour boats on the half hour—the largest of them, forty-two-foot jet boats with twin Cummins diesels—their captains choking down the engines to squeeze past floaters where the waterways narrow.

Which has Pete telling Nance about an altercation last week. "You should have seen it," he says. "Hell, it's some dumb jerk in a raft, angry over God knows what . . . Anyway, he pulls his pants down, moons a jet boat, only it's BJ, and while BJ, being a pretty easygoing guy, wouldn't normally take offense, this time his sister's kids are with him, and so he brings the boat around and butt-ends into the raft. Rams the dumb son of a bitch, knocks his ass clear into the water.

"BJ never looks back, doesn't see that the guy's still got his pants around his knees and can barely keep afloat, even with a life vest.

"The guy hits the rapids, and we all think he's a goner, except Pete Fong's downriver, and he snatches the cracker out of the current and into his own boat. Takes him down to Lewiston, where he drops the guy off at the hospital to be checked out.

"Best part?" he asks. "That night, the local news does a feature on limiting jet-boat access up canyon. And there's that dumb son-of-a-bitching, sad-assed rafter on-camera, blinking in the lights like some trophy fish being held up as a prime example of how jet boats can save lives." Pete shakes his head.

Nance snorts, but she knows it's all unfunny. Every summer, the canyon was transformed under a pestilence of tour boats, fishing boats, rafters, and kayakers. The boon of tourist industry, both blessing and curse that kept the locals divided against one another, and within themselves, as well. For even as they mourned their loss of solitude, the privacy integral to who they are as westerners, they'd also come to accept the inevitability of this New West industry, took it on with a pioneer fervor, meaning to get what was to be got.

"Where were you when all this came down?" she asks, remembering how, when the park system decided to regulate the number of jet boats in the canyon, the boaters, Everwine included, had staged blockades at the confluence of the Snake and Clearwater, held rallies, printed signs, fired off letters to editors, and took up a whole new grudge against the Goddamnenvironmentalists just about the time the spotted owl had started to lose its sting.

"Well out of it," he says. "I was with your sister." There's a curious resonance in his voice. The lines about his eyes deepen as he squints downriver.

She sighs. Moves next to him. Eases the flip-flops from her feet and crosses a leg. "All right," she says, "tell me. What's up?"

She doesn't think he's going to answer, but then he slows the boat, steers with a wrist through the calms.

"Well, we've been seeing each other, your sister and me. A lot. Getting on fine, I'm thinking. And then, all of a sudden, the other night Meredith says she should leave. Just like that, she says, 'I'd better go back home.' To *Wisconsin*, of all places."

The river reels them downstream. At the waterline are enormous slabs of rock stepped like oversized staircases. The stones are blackened, blunted with volcanic heat, and buffed to a soft gloss by a patina of iron and manganese, "river pudding," the locals call it.

"Says it's got nothing to do with me." He looks over at Nance. "Hell it don't. That's the kinda shit people say when they don't want to tell you the truth, ain't it?"

Nance is disappointed, but isn't it what she's been expecting? She wants to comfort him, tell him it *is* the truth. It has nothing to do with him.

"You could talk to her," he says.

"That's not my place."

"Funny. I thought she was your sister."

Nance locks her arms over her chest. She could say she's been sister and more than sister since their mother's death. Hasn't she put in enough time?

But it's never been easy. She remembers when Meredith was fifteen. A trip to an emergency room with walls the color of bile, and fluorescent tubes buzzing overhead.

The doctor held an empty prescription bottle under Nance's nose. "She could have killed herself with these," he said. As if that wasn't obvious.

"Where're your parents? Who's taking care of you girls."

Meredith lay on the bed, looking as if she'd been reduced to bone and gristle. She rolled open her eyes, said to the doctor, "Lay off, asshole," and attempted a smile at Nance.

Nance still can't fully account for her reaction. She snatched the empty bottle out of his hands and threw it at Meredith, the plastic cylinder landing with a laughable *plock* against her sister's chest. Hardly indicative of the anger, the relief, Nance felt. For what—yet another close call? Meredith taking it to the extreme, and then managing to rise yet again from the nearly dead. Center stage. Her smile. *Lay off, asshole.*

Nance squeezes her eyes closed, leans her head back. "Meredith pretty much does what she means to. You can get in her way, but it won't stop her." She wants to tell him about how Meredith finally gave up trying it by her own hand, gave it over to a procession of men instead.

She wants to tell him about good intentions and the unintentional damage it can bring on. She wants to tell him about Joe. How she sent him to his death in the name of her sister. She'd tell Pete how with every good intention she asked him—no, insisted he check on Meredith. *I'm going to have to go over there, aren't I?* There are enough dangers in this world without taking on Meredith.

A flotilla of rafts come bumping out of the Salmon River into the confluence, and Pete steers a course around them. The shadow of an osprey strides over the bright water, and Nance glances up. It's an elegant bird, with a wing span of six to eight feet. As it passes out of the glare, she sees in its talons a fish swimming the air. She half-hopes the fish will swim free, but then the bird banks toward the hillside and turns back. Nance looks over her shoulder, thinks she can see its mate high in the air behind them.

You could talk to her. Not that much to ask.

She's torn between the dregs of her old anger and a newly discovered regret. Does *she* want to lose Meredith? She thinks of the many times she's come close to losing her sister in the past, all those years of Meredith's self-destructive impulses, the string of violent men.

But isn't it different this time, with Meredith making the effort? Coming back on her own power. She thinks about the night they camped out, when they watched the sturgeon rising, and she confessed her concerns about Ned. Not something she would have considered doing a year, two years ago even.

She studies her hands. When she looks up, Pete's eyes flit back to the river. "Okay," she says. "But if she's made up her mind . . ."

Pete flashes a smile, and for a good part of the remaining trip, he's whistling through his teeth, probably making plans for the rest of his life. They pass through the stretch of canyon that is the last stronghold of summer cabins on the canyon's doorstep, a dozen or so homes built on stilts.

Here, Jet Skis join the procession of downriver boats and several party boats. A hot-red jet boat blasts by, the scream of its engine slicing down the canyon, adding to the noise of a shore party's amplified music, the drone of fishing boat engines, the yells of floaters and kayakers. In the instant the boat passes, Nance sees the mute screams of the two young women, the look of shaky bravado on the pilot's face.

Pete's yelling, and she figures it's some obscenity aimed at the idiocy of jet boats fueled by testosterone, or their heedless hedonism, but she can't hear him for the din. She points to her ears and shakes her head. He leans in and shouts, "When?"

It takes a moment before she realizes he's talking about Meredith. She shouts back, "Later. Maybe tonight. We'll see."

He wants more. A promise extracted. Quick action. A guarantee. But she's got her own life to attend to first. There's unpacking. Specimens to be stored. Nearly a month of dirty laundry. An entire household to put in order.

It takes Nance half a day to get most of the camping items stored, equipment inventoried. By late afternoon, she's catching her wind on the front porch. When she arrived home, she found a note on the hall table: "Welcome home. Call me when you get in. Love u." There was a vase of flowers and a small gift-wrapped box. A sign saying HANDS OFF! She shook it gently, then set it down.

She called Ned's office, but he was out. When she next thinks of calling, it's already midafternoon, and she knows he'll be coming home soon anyway.

She has a glass of ice water and a slice of watermelon from the fridge, which has recently been stocked: the vegetable compartment full, milk fresh, the half melon still wrapped. It surprised her, knowing how, when alone, he tended to let things like eating slide.

She sits on the top step, melon wedge held over her lap, a paper towel draping her legs. The melon is sweet and wet and laden with seeds, which she drops into a pile on the paper towel. A quick gust of wind lifts the drooping leaves on the sycamores, jumbles shadows across the sidewalk. This is what she's doing when she smells it—pulling back her hair, watermelon juice trickling down her other arm and onto the paper towel with its little pile of seeds.

She has been home less than a day.

She sets the melon aside. Walks across the street. When she looks into the yard, she sees the newspapers fallen against the bushes, finds the mailbox full; she stands a long moment with her hand on the gate before turning away. Back home, she makes a phone call.

It takes the police eight minutes. One squad car shows, and then two more, and by the end there are five parked up and down the street, blue lights rotating. The neighborhood kids are dashing about, or circling in and out on bikes and skateboards, while the adults watch from behind curtains, on front steps, or from the small knot collecting on the street in front of Nance's house. She's in Turnbull's yard, answering questions.

Says, "I don't know. I was gone for three weeks. I just smelled it and *knew.*"

When they ask her how, she credits her acquaintance with the dead, her work in the field, in the dens of snakes. Anatomy labs. "I'm a scientist," she says. "It smelled like roadkill. Only large. Very large." And thickly sweet. She remembers one other time she has smelled it, but does not tell them about that.

"Did you know the man who lived here?"

"Mr. Turnbull? Sure. Enough to say hi."

A cop comes out of the back door. The skin about his mouth and around his eyes is white, nearly luminous in the twilight of the overgrown yard. He stumbles, and a cat zips out from behind him. "Will somebody do something about these *fucking cats?*" he yells.

The cop talking to Nance ducks his head. "It's his first," he says. Nance waits while he goes back over his notes. "You didn't go in?"

Nance shakes her head.

"Not at all?"

"No. Why would I?"

"No reason," he says. "Just that . . ." He waves it off. "Anybody who might have? Who'd have a reason? A son or daughter, say, someone who might have come to visit?"

"Far as I know, all he had in the world were the cats."

The cop excuses himself, asks her to wait while he speaks with others, who have just come out of the house.

Nance steps nearer the rose hedge. She wishes she could just fade away, disappear right back onto her own front porch. She hears bits and pieces: "chair" and "a visitor," and something about cat food, and "mail on the kitchen table." And she comes to understand that she was not the first. Someone else has been in the house.

There's the sound of laughter from inside, and the young cop looks over his shoulder with a sudden furious expression. "Fucking Moyers. How was I supposed to know?" He takes his cap off, wipes a kerchief around the inside band. The group moves away, all except for the one who interviewed Nance. He scans the yard, and when he spots her, he walks over.

"We got your number . . . if we need anything else. If you think of someone that might be able to help with . . ." He waves a hand at the yard and the house.

She tries not to think about old Turnbull, or the state his house must be in. *What a nightmare.* How many more animals are in there? "And the cats?" she asks.

"I'll get the animal guy out tomorrow latest. We'll close the house up until we find family, or the courts figure it out. Depending on what the coroner says, we might be back, but my guess is the old guy just gave it up. Natural causes." He steers her out of the yard with a hand on her arm. It's clear he's already onto other business.

She looks across the street, where the neighbors are waiting. And then she glances up the porch stairs, to the top step, where the water-melon rind and the bit of paper wilt on the stoop, and then her heart jumps a little, for in the shade of the overhang she can see Ned.

The neighbors cut her a path as she nears, and a few step forward.

"No funny business, was there?" Leona asks.

It takes a moment to register. "No," Nance says. "It looks like natural causes."

Leona's head is butting up and down. She's wearing an apron that hops from the palsied fist she keeps in a pocket. "They gonna take care of them cats?"

Nance nods. Relief moves through the group. She regrets that what little pity or grief she and they might have felt for their neighbor's death is subsumed by the weight of all these cats: their noise, their furtive presence, their relentless stink over the years.

When she finally breaks free and joins Ned on the porch, he hugs her, says, "That's a sorry welcome home."

She rests against his chest, grateful for his arms, and he's leading her into the house, away from the neighbors and squad cars.

Late that evening, they eat a light supper that Ned prepares. Though Nance mostly picks at it, apologizes for having no appetite. After dinner, they move to the backyard, where they sit on lawn chairs in the first of the evening's breezes, a fortunate wind that blows from the west, a clean, airy sweep of the beleaguered neighborhood. Ned hands Nance the gift-wrapped box, inside of which is a pin—a small silver lizard with eyes of bright blue lapis. She thinks of the shedding snake, this being so like the blue of its eyes. She holds the pin in her palm. "It's lovely," she says.

He waves it off. "I saw it in the jeweler's window downtown. A fortunate whim, considering. That couldn't have been easy over there."

She's slumped in the lounge chair, the lower part of her body dipped in the shade of a weedy cedar, but her torso, her upper arms, and her hair are glazed with late-summer light, the same amber blush that limns the hills across the valley. Her hair is held back from her face in plain barrettes, and the brown of her hair seems all the darker for the burning highlights, a few tendrils uncoiling like fiddlehead ferns. She's smiling at the pin in her hands.

He's trying to read what it is she feels. Remembers his own experience with the old man. How it felt walking out of the house on the heels of revelation. He's pleased it was Nance who discovered the body. They have this in common. Though he should have expected as much. It took her what? Half a day? One good whiff?

"Hard to believe none of us noticed," he says.

She's plucking at her blouse and threading the broach's needle through the cloth. She stops, her head tipped down and cocked to one side to admire it. "What?" she asks.

"Turnbull. You'd think we would have noticed." He's wondering how much she saw.

"You know, I thought so, too, at first, but then I thought, *Why would they?*" She looks up with concern. "Are you blaming yourself?" She leans forward. "Don't. Really. It has stunk over there forever. People get used to it. It stinks, and they think, what else is new? Guess it takes the oddball like me to ferret out one bad odor from another."

He commiserates with the great care she took to shower, to powder her body, even perfume her hair. Though this he also knows—that the rank sweetness will bind itself to her strongest in imagination.

He leans back. "So what did he look like? The old man? His house?"

She wrinkles her nose, and when she looks at him, he sees he's misstepped. There's a narrowing about her eyes, little more than a blink, and his heart's a fierce kick in the chest, and he feels a curious mix of fear and pride and the nervous anticipation of being found out. But he sees that instant of suspicion is quickly gone. He glances out over the valley, composes himself.

She's speaking again. "I didn't go in. I came home and called the police."

She pauses, and there's another moment of distress. He can read it in the way her eyebrows peak, by the wrinkle in that tender bite of flesh above the nose.

His face mirrors hers. "Yes?" he asks. "Something wrong?" He's tender, consoling, and he means it. At the moment, he feels bad for her.

"Well"—her hand searches down the side of her chair, plucks a tuft of grass—"the police think someone else discovered the body first." She lifts a handful of the green to her nose, crushes the blades in hand, and inhales.

He waits, and after awhile she tips her hand over, watches the grass fall. He'd almost accuse her of playing with him. Then he wonders if she's telling the truth—if she didn't go in there after all. Can't believe she didn't. *To go right up to the steps, and turn back?*

"Why do they think that?" he asks.

She shrugs. "I couldn't hear much, but it had something to do with the mail. Can we not talk about this anymore?" she asks. "Can we discuss something else? Something absolutely everyday boring?"

He sees it then: how wrong he's been. Knows that she did not step through that door. She's an innocent. Though, most certainly, acquainted with the means and smells of death, an innocent nevertheless. He breathes deeply, feels relief and comfort, but vastly sad. And then, in an act of genuine generosity, he says, "Tell me about your snakes."

It's two in the morning. No reason to believe Meredith will be awake, but here Nance is anyway, parking in front of her sister's place. She can't explain what brings her here, but she knows she can't lie in bed awake while Ned so soundly sleeps. Nor can she bear to wake him. He's been so kind. Even to the point of putting her to bed early. "You must be exhausted. All those weeks sleeping on the ground." Later, he joined her, but with no demands. "Just sleep. You've been through too much."

For which she's grateful. She couldn't stand being touched or having him inside her with that smell still in her head. She had, in fact, fallen off to sleep quickly. Hardly remembered putting her head to the pillow. She'd slept right up until about an hour ago, when she'd roused out of a nasty dream.

She shuts off the engine, rolls the window down. She does not want to think about the dream, but it's there: Turnbull's corpse under her bed. Ridiculous, of course, but she'd been hard put to lower her feet over the side of the bed—as if the corpse might be there, reanimate itself, and reach out and grab her—all her childhood bogeyman fears awakened.

She looks at Meredith's house. Her hands are locked on the top of the steering wheel, and she rests her forehead on them. The window on her side is open, and crickets are singing in the curbside grass. There's a bitter bite in the air, residue from the mill operations. She unbuckles the seat belt.

She walks up to the house, steps over to the big bay window, and tries to peer in. She crosses to the screen door and opens it. Knocks on the thick wood of the front door, her knuckles stinging. She hasn't the heart to ring the rude buzzer. Instead, she jumps down from the porch, and in the side yard, on tiptoe beneath her sister's bedroom window, she reaches up and raps on the glass. She raps until an eye peeks through the blinds.

Nance curls her fingers in a small wave. The slats drop and then the window's being tugged open, and her sister's head pokes out, the blinds draping the back of her head and neck.

"The dam broke," Meredith says.

"What?"

"Tell me the dam broke and I'm in danger of drowning." She yawns. Nance shakes her head. "Guess again."

"The town's on fire, and it's headed this way." Meredith rubs a hand over her face, the skin elastic. She stares over Nance's shoulder to the houses beyond. "What time is it?"

Nance settles back onto her heels, glances at her wrist, realizes she's not wearing a watch. She shrugs. "Late?"

Meredith looks into the room behind her. "Early's more like it. It's two in the morning." She holds a hand up, palm out; sleep lines crease the inside of her arm. "Let me guess. . . . You can't sleep."

Nance stretches up, crosses her arms on the sill. "Damn but you're smart. How do you do that?"

Meredith snaps her fingers, but they don't work. She leans down, pats Nance's arm. "*It's the genes.* So, you want to come in through the window or the door?"

Nance offers her arms. "Pull me up?"

"Tell you what. Come to the door and I'll hand you a ladder."

Nance smiles and walks around to the front of the house. When Meredith appears, she's configuring a silk kimono over her chest; her hair's tousled and she's barefoot on the wood floor.

"Hey there," she says. "Welcome home." She hugs Nance and steps aside.

"Hey there, yourself," Nance says, and follows her to the kitchen, where Nance seats herself at a vintage diner table. She admires the chrome legs and bright yellow Formica top, the matching chairs. The kitchen's been recently painted: butter yellow walls, white woodwork. The cabinet doors have been removed and a set of plain white dinner-ware lines the shelves. It all looks crisp and fresh, and Meredith oddly settled, for someone readying to leave.

Meredith's belted the robe about her, a plum-colored silk with a flock of embroidered cranes winging across her back. "Tea?" she asks, setting a pot of water on. "Sleepytime?"

"Black," Nance says.

"Good choice." Meredith pads over to the refrigerator, opens the door, and hauls out a box.

"Girl Scout cookies?" Nance asks.

Meredith snorts, pours a handful onto a plate. "That old lady down the street, the one who doesn't make friends—"

"You made friends."

"She gave me a dozen boxes. Keeps them in her freezer. Seems she's been buying them for years." Meredith sets the plate on the table. Her shoulders slump and her hands turn up in a gesture of despair. "All shortbread."

"I like the mint ones." Nance picks a cookie up, places it between her teeth, chews slowly.

Meredith disappears into the bathroom, and Nance can hear water running in the sink. The tea water boils, and Nance gets up to pour it in the pot. Sinks the silver ball of tea leaves into the water. When Meredith returns, her hair is combed, face washed. Nance pours the tea. Spoons chink as each sister stirs in sugar. It's a comfortable silence, a sip of tea, a bite of cookie, another sip. When the plate is nearly emptied, Nance tells Meredith about Turnbull and then about her dream.

"Well, just hearing about it's enough to keep me up the night." Meredith goes to the fridge, takes out the box of cookies, and plops it on the table. "Sustenance."

Nance nods. "I couldn't bring myself to wake Ned. He's been so kind. He made dinner. Bought me a welcome home gift, a pin."

Meredith frowns. Looks away.

Nance swallows her irritation. "What?"

Meredith shakes her head. "Nothing," she says. "Same old."

Nance wants to press, but what the hell; she's hardly up to an argument. Not tonight. Not on the heels of today. "So okay. Let's talk about you instead, then. Pete tells me you want to leave. Did something happen? Did Pete hurt you?" Nance lifts the pot and pours herself another cup.

Meredith laughs. "Good grief, no. That man couldn't hurt anything." She taps her sister on the arm with a finger. "He's a good man."

Nance feels relieved, but it leaves her wondering. "So then what's the problem? I thought you liked it here. You've got Pete pulling his hair out, thinking it's something he's done."

"Really?" Meredith's elbow is cocked on the table and she leans on the arm, chin sunk into palm. Her eyes brighten and her free hand snugs the robe over her legs.

"So are you? Leaving?"

Meredith's eyes shift right, focus on Nance. "I'd been thinking I might." Meredith reaches for the teapot and refills her cup.

Nance looks at her sister over her cup. "So what's the bad news." She tries to keep her gaze on Meredith, but she glances at the stove instead, at the clock on the wall above it. "It's not trouble, is it? Not another man?"

Meredith's head lowers, and when she raises her eyes to Nance's face, Nance wants to look somewhere else, avoid what's coming, but that's not her way.

Meredith's tone is level. "If I could take back my tea and cookies, I would." She picks up the box and pitches it out of reach onto the counter.

Nance looks down at her lap where her hands have folded across one another. This is Meredith when most deeply hurt—quiet, cold, and utterly calm. It's something Nance has witnessed before, though not often. First time she saw it? Meredith's first day back home, after their mother's death. Eight years old, and she'd looked as if she were brittle with age. She'd walked through all the rooms of the house, reacquainting herself, relearning the shape of a home and life inexplicably altered in her absence.

Meredith had stood holding the door of her mother's closet open on all the space inside. The row of empty hangers like ghosts lined up on the clothes bar. The significance of it had hit Nance, as well. *Even the clothes are gone.* And oh, the panic Nance had felt at that moment, when she'd looked over her shoulder at their father, only to see him standing there, hands at his side, his face as emptied as the closet. As removed from them by grief as Meredith had been removed from the house. They stood there silent a long while, until it felt to Nance as if she were the only one with substance left. In that quick glimpse, she understood she had lost not just one parent but both.

Finally, Nance had stepped forward. Lifted her sister's hand from the door and closed it. Meredith looked at her a long moment, said, "I could have helped," and then turned her back and walked away. She'd refused to speak to Nance or their father for weeks.

At the time of their mother's illness, it had seemed the right thing to do—send Meredith away—but now Nance wonders if there weren't depths to Meredith that none of them knew about. Or maybe they'd just lacked the courage to trust.

She looks at her sister. Thinks of the thing that's been on her mind since early afternoon.

"When I came back for Dad's funeral?" Nance says.

Meredith sits stiff-backed in the chair. Her arms lock over her chest.

"At the cemetery, after the service? You were still in the chapel with relatives, and I thought I'd just wander over to the crypt where Mom was. I walked down the aisles, past all those marble slabs with names on them. I thought they looked like rows of drawers, imagined all the dead neatly tucked inside. And then I came to the one with Mom's name, and now Dad's name, too.

"The workers had broken the seal." And she can still picture the neat edge around the marble front, remembers the cool air drifting out from within. "I figured that later they'd open it up and slip Dad in next to Mom. It all seemed so"–her hand fidgets in the air–"clean. Comforting. Know what I mean? I had this picture of them together again. Side by side. Like a marriage bed." She looks at her sister.

Meredith tugs the robe over her chest where it has crimped open.

"But then I stepped closer, and there was this whiff of air coming from the cut in the seal, and there was this smell . . . and then a fly crawled out . . ."

Meredith's arms loosen; her hands lower.

Nance is thinking of the smell. Unmistakable. And the fly squeezing up out of that crack, stopping on the marble slab to clean its legs and wings before lifting into the air. Buzzing her, spinning in her face. It had tried to land on her, and Nance had been driven back and back. "All I could think of was what Mom had become in there. And that that fly had been in with her–on her." Nance looks down into the cup, at the dregs of tea. "Though that can't have been the case, can it? She was closed in a casket."

Meredith rests an arm on the table. "You never told me."

"I left right after. Didn't want to think, let alone talk about it. You know, it was like I'd seen something personal and deeply . . . hurtful. Something a child, no matter what age, was not meant to know of a parent. I kept picking at myself–the whole day–my flesh crawling. It felt as if that fly had made itself to home on my skin."

Nance turns to Meredith. "And that's how, this afternoon, when I got a whiff of that stench, I *knew* what was in that house."

Meredith reaches over and retrieves the box of cookies. "Here," she says, offering it to Nance. "Take them."

Nance lifts the box away, pours a handful onto the plate.

Meredith pushes back from the table. "No way in hell I'm going to sleep after that." She puts fresh water on to boil, then stands with her back against the stove, one foot crossed over the other, a hand on her hip. "But you understand this doesn't excuse what you said?"

Nance nods. "Didn't mean it to. I guess I wanted to put it in context."

"That you were still upset. Said what you normally wouldn't?"

Nance nods again.

"So . . . what you normally wouldn't say is the truth. You'd clean it up." Meredith's head tips to one side. "So it wouldn't stink so frightfully."

Nance winces.

"And what the hell," Meredith says. "I must look like an overnight conversion. Sister comes west for a new start. Yeah, right." Her voice trails off. The kettle ticks with heat. She steps to a side. "Why would you trust it?" The kettle whistles and she pours water into the small pot, settles the lid back over. She carries it to the table and sets it between them.

"The truth," Meredith says.

She looks weary, her lids heavy, hair combed but still disordered. A cowlick prickles at the crown of her head, the way Nance still remembers Meredith waking with it as a child. Nance remembers how sometimes, in the car, or at a restaurant, she would spot the belligerent tuft and spit on the palm of her hand and press it to her sister's young head. Trying to restrain that wildness with a lick of spittle.

"The truth?" Nance urges.

Meredith takes a deep breath. "Well, I got to thinking, What if I have come all this way just to screw up again in your backyard?

"These last weeks, with you gone and Pete busy, the bars around here began to look pretty good. Music. People dancing. Everybody having a good time. A few drinks. A little flirting. I even drove to this cow-boy bar outside of town." She shrugs. "What could it hurt?"

"What did you do?" Nance asks, not sure she wants to know.

"Went in, came back out. How do they stand that music?"

There's the sound of the clock over the stove tapping away the seconds, and the creak of wood that is the house settling into the night. Meredith leans over and opens the window, so that a breeze fills the kitchen with the smell of dew on grass. Meredith's looking outside, her hand holding on to the window frame. "Why am I so goddamned afraid to be alone, Sis?" She looks over her shoulder at Nance.

Nance shakes her head. "I felt the same way, after I lost Joe. I thought then I'd just as soon bury myself." She shrugs. "But here I am." She ducks her head, gives her sister a crooked smile. "Nothing says you'll always be alone."

Meredith's smiling. "We'll see."

"So. You going to stay?"

"Yup," she says. "Right where I am. Me and the old lady down the street. Name's Belle," says Meredith.

"Imagine that," says Nance. She moistens a finger, dips it in the crumbs on the plate. She looks over at Meredith, who's smiling.

Nance licks the crumbs from her finger.

Chapter Nine

S he packs the picnic basket while mulling over the phone call from her research assistant, Jerry Mathes. He's deep into Oregon. Has been following the snake he named Poker Joe—one of several that made it up onto the canyon rim. But unlike the others, Poker Joe kept going, traveling well over a hundred miles, and was, according to Jerry, "On his way to the coast, man." He'd been determined to follow Poker Joe "to the end of the road." Had to admire the man's resilience, his determination. Not always an easy task. Radio telemetry being tricky sometimes, as when the snakes hid and the signal bounced off rock shelves or from under outcroppings. She probably should have put a stop to his pursuit, but he'd been insistent. Had, in fact, taken it on, on his own time.

But today, the phone call: "A fucking eagle, Nance. I could not believe it. About broke my heart." And she could hear it was true for him. He'd make a great herp. Passionate about the work. Dedicated, absorbed, obsessive.

She tried telling him such things happen and that it wasn't such a bad way to go. But he would have none of it. "Joe was smarter than that. He shoulda known. I mean, I look up and there he was stretched out beneath that fucking eagle. Flying. West. Like he was just going to the ocean after all, Nance. To the ocean."

She shakes her head, brings herself back to task. The summer has all but slipped away these past several weeks, while she was logging data on her computer, or checking figures with her assistants on long weekend trips upriver. So this was to be a day away from work. A day of play. Time with family.

She layers the goodies. Enough for three. A jar of chilled peaches next to a bottle of wine. A tin of smoked oysters. A nice crusty bread. And cheeses: baby Swiss, Gouda, Havarti. A jar of Kalamata olives. Grilled flaked salmon. Two containers of three-bean salad, the other a pasta salad. Then there's the real treat—three freshly baked fruit *galettes*, a delicate pastry wrapped around huckleberry, or apricot or raspberry, that she picked up early this morning from Sage Bakery.

The back of Ned's vehicle is packed with blankets and towels, snorkels and fins. The old woman across the street watches from her front lawn, her back turned on Turnbull's house like a grudge. Nance can't help wonder if Leona's resentment is because the old man died, or that he didn't take the stink with him. She pushes the unkind thoughts away and waves. "Good-bye, Leona. We're going swimming," she shouts.

Leona smiles, gives a slow parade wave that suggests a past Nance never would have imagined. "You have a good time," she says. "Be careful."

When Nance pulls up to Meredith's place, her sister's on the curb in swimsuit and sarong; a floppy straw hat slumps over her shoulders. At her feet are soda, bottled water, and a half round of watermelon.

"Are we set, or what?" she asks, and plumps the drinks and melon into the cooler next to the picnic basket in the trunk.

Nance rubs her hands together. "That water is going to feel *so* good."

It's eleven o'clock in the morning and already the temperature's well into the eighties. Cool compared to the last two weeks of record heat—triple digits in the valley. At the peak, 117 degrees in downtown Lewiston. During which time Nance holed up in her air-conditioned home office, hedged in between boxes of field notes and her computer, with only Ramone for company. She'd typed in banks and banks of data.

She's always amazed at what little was known about the lives of snakes for so many thousands of years. What reclusive, shy lives. And that, over so short a period of time as, say, forty years, a base of knowledge could broaden so dramatically—the advent of radio telemetry in the sixties, then the computer, and especially improvements in surgical implantation having made much of the private lives of snakes public.

"Just a minute," Meredith says, "I have something for you." She dashes back to her house, comes out with a package under one arm and under the other an inflated pool toy. It's a snake—a good eight feet in length. A pair of oversized sunglasses are on its nose."

Nance is laughing when Meredith hands it to her.

"Just what I've always wanted. How did you know?" Nance says.

Meredith shrugs, tweaks the snake's tail. It rattles. "I saw it. It spoke to me." She pulls a package out from under her arm. "This one's mine. Thought I'd wait to blow it up, though."

Nance reaches, but Meredith holds it at arm's length.

"What is it?"

Meredith twitches her eyebrows. "It's a surprise."

"Any more?" Nance asks.

Meredith tips the hat back off her head, loosens the string about her neck. "Nope." She settles herself into the passenger seat.

Nance eases the inflated snake in through the rear window, tucks its head behind the seat.

They drive Prospect to the riverside Kiwanis Park, where Ned's putting in an appearance. "Baby shower," she explains to Meredith. "One of his staff." Nance turns the car into the parking lot, and the two women wait, windows open, arms draped over the warm metal. "He's supposed to be here by now." Nance checks her watch. "I probably should have gone with him?"

Meredith slips on a solemn look. "Your wifely duty."

They wait another beat before Nance asks, "Where is he?" She opens the door, steps out, and Meredith follows. Together, they stride across bright lawns. The dike rises in a long twenty-foot-high swell of grass and shrub and trees. Small lagoons have been dredged on the lee side, and pedestrian paths wind among them.

They walk between blackberry hedges and emerge on a path circumnavigating the main lagoon. All about the pond are children perched on the banks like waterfowl. They're tossing bread crumbs to a mix of wild and domestic birds that live here year-round.

Ned's on the far side. Nance waves, but he doesn't see her. Nor does he seem to notice the toddler who's crying just feet away, or the young mother who dashes down to the pond's edge and snatches the child by the arm.

He's focused on a commotion in the water. But there's so much sunlight glancing off the surface, it's just a jumble of color and movement. Meredith hangs back while Nance steps forward. She overhears comments, the odd remarks from mothers: "Never you mind what they're doing," and "It's nature, honey, like on TV?" and "Oh my." And then Nance sees what has the young mothers embarrassed and has gotten Ned's undivided attention. The mallards are mating.

Only it's not that polite, is it.

There are five or six males. One female. She looks like a bit of rag, some wilted roughage from the muddy bottom. Her head and neck've been plucked by beaks, bloodied by their attraction. The heavier males pile on, mounting her, or scrabbling at her sides, driving her under as they flounder about, striking at her, at one another, wings clipping the air with a snap like sheets on a line. The dun feathers drift in sodden clumps on the water, or snag in the rushes along the bank.

Nance is no novice to nature and spends little more than a quick glance. No, it's Ned who has her attention—the breeze riffling through his hair, the sunlight bald on his smiling face—and what she sees in his face—his eyes wide with a kind of happy recognition, as when you come across a familiar face in a crowd.

The female resurfaces. Though she is bobbing like a cork at high tide, she's struggling back toward the shore while the repleted and discouraged males waddle a short distance away to preen.

Nance has the impulse to walk away. Wishes she had arrived just minutes later, after the fact, the day ahead feeling strangely soiled. But these thoughts are quashed, for she's already questioning what it was she saw in his face, and then she feels a stab of disloyalty, which turns into impatience for her own pedestrian reaction and of those around her.

She moves up beside him. "Ned?"

He turns, blinking. His hands, unknit, fall loosely at his side.

"Hey there," he says. "I missed you." He plants a kiss on her forehead. Squeezes her hands in his. They are dry and cool.

She looks for Meredith, but her sister's nowhere to be seen. They walk back to the car, and he tells her of the expectant mother's surprise and pleasure. Meredith's already in the backseat of the car, her hands locked over her knees, bare feet resting on the inflated snake's head. She gives Ned a brisk nod.

They drive on the Washington side, heading up the river road, where the beaches are small but numerous. They pass Asotin and the outlying farms, the hay fields knee-high in a bloom of timothy. They pass the Arabian horse farm with its immaculate paddocks, its stabling that looks like a Kentucky bluegrass estate dropped whole onto the unlikely fields of sage. The horses, grays and sorrels, dash up a weedy slope. The Snake River courses behind them, and its surface is a drowned palette of shaggy riverside trees, green rush, and yellowing willow, the browned glaze of hillside grasses.

Five miles past Asotin, they park on a roadside pullout. It's a beach of their own—a narrow spit of upriver rock acting as a breakwater has fashioned a bowl in the shoreline, a broad shelf of sandy beach. It's here they set up: chairs, blanket, cooler, and picnic basket. Meredith inflates her pool toy, a giant toad, whose legs scissor neatly about her waist. She reclines her arms across its back, floats a lazy twenty-foot circle on the river's eddy.

Nance nicknames it Bufo. "For the genus *Bufo*; of the family Bufonidae; order Anuran; species *boreas;* subspecies, *boreas*; *B. boreas boreas*—the boreal toad. More commonly known as the western toad." She breathes deeply at the end of the awkward mouthful.

Meredith dips a handful of water, pours it over her head. "As usual. I pick a toad named Bufo." Meredith wipes her face. "Though I believe I've been with worse."

Nance has wound her snake under her arms and around her back. She's paddling in the slow vortex, rattling the tail off and on.

"So what's yours called?"

"Philbert."

"Let me guess," Meredith says. "Of the genus *Philbert,* family Philbertus, order of the Royal Garter Snake, species–"

"Nope." Nance rests her chin on the snake's broad back. She's in lightweight cargo shorts, a tank top, and sports bra. She can see Ned reclining on the blanket in the shade. "He just looks like a Philbert." She lowers her face into the clear water. A school of minnows, sides bright as pyrite, wends through river weeds that have jimmied up through a jigsaw of rocks. She lowers her feet but can't touch bottom, so she pushes herself down, holding on to Philbert with the tips of her fingers, and she drifts that way, hands stretched overhead, swaying in the eddy's soft pull. She looks up at the bright surface, at the clumsy cut of the pretend snake, and thinks of how graceful in water the genuine snake is, the liquid wave of torso. Limbless locomotion. A silent glissando. A lateral undulation as fluid as the element itself, ripple within ripple.

She surfaces and grounds the inflatable snake on the beach. Then she takes another deep breath and ducks back under. She pushes downward. The water is cold on her eyes and she blinks. She pulls herself around a large boulder. There's a squawfish, corrects herself: northern pike minnow, recently renamed in one of many efforts to eradicate the more offensive terms of history.

It's an unlovely beast. A thick-bodied, stub-faced creature with a price posted on its head each spring by the Washington Wildlife Department, the cost of the fish's fatal fondness for salmon and steelhead smolts. This one hovers just above the river bottom as she approaches, then wallows away. She surfaces, flops on her back. The sky is a stainless blue, and she closes her eyes in the mixed pleasure of hot sun and cold river. She flips, does a slow side stroke toward the beach, where her sister is using Bufo as a beach chair of sorts while she spreads lotion on an arm. The smell of coconut ripens in the air. Ned's reclining on a blanket in the mahogany's shade. Nance can see his elbows bowed out behind his head, the knobs of his raised knees, and the long, thin shins, the reddening tops of his feet. He's already set the picnic lunch out on a cloth, knowing she'll be hungry after the swim, and she's reminded of how thoughtful he is. She squeezes her eyes shut, submerges with eyes closed, and hangs suspended, listening to the hum of the river. She thinks about the turn her life has taken, her career, her marriage to Ned, this new kinship with her sister. She feels pleasantly surprised. Wonders why she's been so worried lately. Looking at it this way, from the cool pool of the river, her life looks pretty damn good. When she surfaces again, she finds her footing in the sand and emerges onto the beach, wringing her hair with her hands.

They eat in the shade, fingering the knubby olives into their mouths and savoring the cheeses. They fork tender chunks of salmon onto crusty bread and wash it down with a large-bodied wine. They finish with thick slabs of watermelon wedged in their hands, seeds surrounding them like small beetles slumbering in the sand. Afterward, Meredith moves back into the sun with a book, and Ned turns onto his side to sleep. There's the drone of flies, and the slap of water against the shore, the punctuation of jet boats on the half hour. Sightseers in straw hats and loud shirts wave from the decks, and Nance finds it amusing that she's become local color for tourists.

She wades the shoreline, picking up stones, shells, an old fishing lure, which she drops into one of many pockets in her cargo shorts. One pocket's filled with monofilament, a snarl of fishing line, from which she's picked the bones of a bird. She wades in and out of water, river sandals gripping the rocky bed. She finds a western fence lizard, and she strips a slender willow branch and fashions some of the microfilament into a catch loop. The creature is clinging to the side of a boulder. Its head is turned toward her, legs crooked at the elbows, crouched for flight.

If she approaches it with her hands, the lizard will dash into the nearest crevice. But lower a loop over its head, and it will sit there until snared, and sure enough, she catches it in the noose and it flings itself forward onto hind legs and sways upright, toes jigging on the hot rock.

She pockets the small beast, eager to show her catch with its neat rows of spots along sides and back. Frightened, it has lightened to a pale dun from the near black it was while basking. She pulls the Velcro strap closed on her front pocket, pats its gently, and feels its weight as she walks, hears the diminutive scratch of claw on fabric.

Back at the picnic site, Ned has the basket packed and blanket rolled. The beach chairs are already stowed in the car's trunk. He's standing with his back against the tree. Meredith's nowhere to be seen.

Ned says, "She decided to hitch a ride back early."

Nance shakes her head. "Of all the stupid . . ." She plants her hands on hips, turns to Ned. "Did something happen? Between you two?"

Ned shrugs. "We talked; she left. Hey," he says, pushing away from the tree. "She's your sister. You tell me."

They walk the short slope to the car, and Ned has the inflated snake clamped under an arm. The long body drags, tail rattling, carving a track through the sand just ahead of Nance's steps. Nance carries the sagging Bufo, the air valve pinched open between her fingers. One of its bulging eyes falls inward, while the other continues to stare up at the blue sky over Nance's shoulder. She can't imagine what set her sister off. Meredith seemed happy enough to spend a day beachside with them.

Nance blames herself. She should have taken Meredith with her. Or stayed on the beach herself, read a book, or something. *You know they don't get on together. Now she's hitchhiking back to town with God knows who.* Nance thinks of the rapes she's read about in the paper. The assaults. She pushes the thoughts away, and with it the panic.

When they reach the car, she can't resist asking, "What did you talk about?"

Ned's trying to coil the inflated snake into the trunk, but the snake struggles, pushes out and over the trunk lip. Ned's hands drift up in frustration.

She pulls the toy out, settles it under her other arm while he slams the trunk shut. His face is tight and he's squinting into the afternoon sun. It's three o'clock. The peak of the day's heat is just coming on. Already Nance is wishing she was back in the river. She opens the car doors, and the air inside smells of baked upholstery and road dust frying atop the vinyl dashboard. She funnels the toys into the backseat and steps over to the passenger side. She looks back at the river, and it's then she remembers the tiny body in her pocket.

"Oh, Ned, just a minute," she says, and lifts out the lizard with a gentle nip of fingers. "Look," she says. But Ned's already settling into the driver's seat, impatient to be gone.

She ducks her head into the window. "I'll be right back," she says, and she dashes around the side of the car before he can complain, jogs down to the river. At a jumble of rocks, she lets the creature go. It scurries off her palm, but the feel of its feet—the scratch of claw and soft pads—stays with her well after it disappears.

Then she's bounding toward the waiting car and her husband, caught between anger and fear for Meredith. Hopes they'll find her along the way, even as she can't imagine what she'll say if they do.

What if the wrong person comes along? Out in the middle of nowhere, thirty miles from town. Canyon walls on one side and river on the other. No escape. Hell of a stunt. What can she be thinking?

Nance settles into the seat, buckles up. "What did you say to her?"

Ned pulls onto the road, the tires casting up a thin spray of grit. The back end of the car breaks loose on the gravel, slides to the side. His hands grip the wheel with a twisting forward motion. "So now it's what *I said to her*? Hey, she asked what I thought about the scene at the lagoon this morning, that's all."

Nance shifts in the seat. "Well, that can't be all. She's gone. What exactly did the *two* of you say?"

He shrugs. "We were just talking, and she brought it up. She was talking as if it were a rape or something. So I laughed. She looked at me like I was some kind of . . . creep. I told her she was being melodramatic."

They wind down the road, Nance keeping a watch for her sister. They pass a house where guinea fowl roam the lawns and gravel drive. They're ungainly birds, bulb-bodied and long-legged, but the ideal watch birds, with their eerie jungle cry. Snake-eaters.

She prompts Ned, "That hardly seems enough to get angry about."

He glances in the rearview mirror; then his eyes flit to the side mirror and back to the road ahead. "I don't know. I said a few other things—

mostly about seeing the world like it is. In the end, she said I was a typical fuckhead male." His smile goes no further than his teeth. "Or something like that."

Nance slides down, rests her fingers on her forehead, looks at the
river winding at their side. It was such a nice day. "She's had bad times
with men. . . ."

"And my guess is that it wasn't so great for them, either," he says. He
glances over at Nance, one hand warding her off. "Yeah, yeah. I know
you love your sister, and you'll go on seeing her through those rose-
tinted sunglasses no matter what, but I'll bet she gave as good as she got."

Nance is leaning against the door, arm out the window, hand gripping the side-view mirror. "If you'd seen the bruises–"

"On her or them?" he asks.

"Fuck you, Ned," she says, and is startled by her own anger. *Where did
that come from?* she wonders.

They cross the small bridge that is also a cattle guard, and the metal
rails stutter under the tires. Ned has both hands on the wheel. His breath
comes in long pulls, as if he's drawing air through a narrow straw. When
he speaks, his voice is quiet. "'Fuck you, Ned'? Well, isn't this a sudden
turnabout. First you lose your sister, and then your sense of humor."

"Right," Nance says. "That was a joke?"

"Hey," he says, "So shoot me for bad taste." He glances over at the
narrow shoulder of gravel and bunchgrass, its backdrop of teasel. Fallow
fields open as the river yaws off to the right, moving briefly from sight.
His gaze returns to the road.

"What is it you're so upset about?"

"She doesn't always make the best choices."

On the side of the road, a crow is hopping about, tethered to the asphalt. Clamped in the bird's beak is a snake, flattened and glommed
tight to the tarry surface. As they near, the bird drops the roadkill and
flaps off to the graveled shoulder to scold, its bright beak open on a
blade of a tongue. Nance's trying to identify the snake, but they're moving too fast. It's then that she understands Ned has said something.
"What?"

"I'm getting pretty tired of this," he repeats.

She's looking down the narrow road as it slices through Asotin, trying to see into the cars ahead, and down the sidewalks, the park with its queue of benches. "Tired of what?" she asks.

"She's a walking fly trap, and everybody around her gets caught up. Come on, Nance, count the years of collateral damage."

She thinks of Joe. Pushes that away, but not before she feels that familiar anger quickening, and she wonders if it will ever completely go away. She doesn't look at Ned. Understands he has no idea how close he's hit home. He doesn't know about Mer's connection to Joe's death. And why should he? No one does, except Nance.

Nance looks out the side window at the small waterside church, its flock of Canada geese on the lawn. "She's changed," Nance says. She knows how ridiculous this sounds, but having said it, discovers how much she wants to believe it.

Ned slows the car and his eyes flicker up and down the side streets of Asotin, as if finding the path as he goes. "Listen, it's not me I'm worried about. It's you, Nance." He waits a beat. "And *us*. I mean, look at us. Fighting. Ever since she came out–"

"No," Nance says. But she doesn't know how to counter this. Truth is, things *have* changed between them, and she has worried about Meredith's influence. But coming from Ned, it feels less an attack than . . . what?

"No," she repeats, then says, "You don't get to use her as an excuse for our problems."

"Well, there you go," he says. "Suddenly, we have *problems*." He's shaking his head. "Like we never had before, but God forbid I should put two and two together–" And then he's slowing and pulling over.

Nance looks away from him, and she sees Meredith standing roadside.

He reaches across the seat back, pops the door open. "You going to get in?"

Meredith's got a crooked grin on her face. The brim of her sunhat is limp with moisture and the crown looks blistered on her head. She shrugs and steps down into the car. It takes her a while to arrange herself. Then she looks up. "The last ride was in the back of an open pickup with two brats and a well-mannered cow dog."

Little is said on the ride home—the three of them content to let whatever happened end there, and when they drop Meredith off, she blows Nance a kiss before skipping up the stairs, towel and deflated swim toy tucked under one arm. Nance watches her as they pull away, has a sudden desire to follow her sister, get another side of the story, something that will somehow set the day straight.

The room is dark and the window across the way is open, so that what little breeze there is stirs the lacy curtains, and the light from the streetlamp shines in at an oblique angle. Ned's stretched out on the bed. His shins are mildly warm, but the tops of his feet are furious with heat. He might have cooled off in the water as Nance had suggested, but he's not a strong swimmer, and generally keeps to bodies of water that stay put— lakes, ponds, pools, and bathtubs.

He can hear Nance downstairs: the clatter of last-minute dishes being stacked in the dishwasher, the back door closing. He can hear the toilet flush, the water in the sink running. He runs his finger down his spine to the place where it seems a knot is permanently hobbled. He feels nothing beneath the skin. Just an elastic tension that comes and goes.

Of his argument with Meredith, he doesn't care to ponder long. Lets it slide off his back. *Like water off a fucking duck*. He does think of his contentious sister-in-law straddling the inflatable toad. The bulbous eyes between her thighs.

A tease. Who will always get what's coming to her.

He turns over onto his stomach when he hears Nance in the hallway. She stops outside the bedroom door. She's stalling. Their conversations over the late afternoon and early evening have been kept carefully courteous, and far afield from the business of Meredith. When Nance enters, she finds her way in the dark to the dresser, where she steps out of shorts and shirt. In bed, she lifts the thin cover over her legs.

The room slips into quiet, and even the breeze has let up for the moment, and a stillness saturates the room, so that no cars are heard motoring down streets, no planes droning in the heavens. Even the barking of dogs has seemed to cease, and the night is finely tuned down to the smallest deliberations: a drift of gnats, the powdered concussion of moths against streetlamps. Then the wind picks up, lifts the leaves on branches and the hairs on the back of the lone dog that barks to be let in. In this way, the night amplifies and mutes with an ordinariness that comforts, like breath.

Ned feels her body easing into slumber, and he asks, "You asleep?"

There's a rousing. The springs quietly complain. "No," she says. "Still awake, mostly."

He faces her on the pillow. He can see her struggling up out of that state of half sleep, eyes heavily lidded but liquid in the dark. Her face soft. She lets out a long breath, sets her hand on his hip.

He's not certain what it is that irritates him, if it's the ease with which she claims him, or the sudden heat of her hand on his already warm skin. He snuffs his impulse to swat at it. He lifts her hand to his lips and gives it a kiss instead. Asks, "You tired?" and sets her hand on the bed between them.

"I guess it was all that fresh air." She reaches over and lifts a curl from his forehead, rakes her nails through the fine hairs above his ear. "Too much down time on the blanket this afternoon?" she asks, yawning.

He feels that itching at the base of his spine and the familiar pressure budding behind his eyes, so that his free hand worms into the bedding under his pillow, and he finds it difficult to focus on where he is and who he's with. *Should that matter?* He breathes deeply, like a distance runner, concentrates on the bar of light from the window that bares his legs, the way it runs in a stripe up the wall and angles over the ceiling, then down onto the dark pool that is the dresser and the mirror with its hard coin of moon glimmering deep beneath its dim surface.

The ends of the curtain draft outside the house, flap on the clapboard walls. In the lee of the house, the shrubs hunker, while the rest of the yard bounds and swims with shadow and light, and the breeze bucks through the flower beds, the elderberry and lilac bushes, rises up into the catalpa tree, where the leaves commence a heavy clapping, and a cat cat-walking the branches drops to a sudden squat on his swaying perch. Above the canopy of roof and tree, a scud of clouds douse the moon. In the room, the mirror goes black.

Ned closes his eyes, breathes in the smell of grass and leaf, fresh linens, the smell of bar soap on skin, an undercurrent of sweat and salt, the faint musk of moist places. There's an edginess banked just beneath his skin, like an itch that wants scratching. His mouth is dry. He inclines his head.

"What is it you think you want?" he asks, the tenor of his voice unfamiliar in the context of this room.

She's startled. He can tell by the way her hand stops its careless petting, the fingers framed against his temple. He finds this delicious. Wonders why it's taken him so long to approach her in this way. And even as he does so, he's questioning, *Can you pull it off?*

"Because—" he traces her eyebrow with a finger—"I could probably oblige you." He moves his finger down the side of her nose and onto the dip of skin on her chin. Identical to the one he's noticed on her sister. Presses his finger there. "Something a little . . ."

"What?" she asks.

"A little more pleasurable."

He cuffs her upper arm with a hand, thumb stroking the soft underside. There's a ridge of muscle against the pad of his palm, and he smiles. She will not let on to concern, but he reads it anyway.

When he kisses her, he feels her body becoming more dense somehow, her movements slowing. He could turn on the lights. He likes to see it all, although the dark has its advantages—the mutable flesh, the imaginative possibilities.

He lifts up on an elbow, slips his hand out from under the pillow, moves it beneath and around her back, pulling her close while his other hand slides down to the club of bone in her wrist. He kisses her again.

It doesn't do to go too quickly.

He puts his knee between her leg, urges her open, and still he can sense a core of resistance—a begrudging acceptance, not dutiful, no, that's not Nance. But it's something.

He presses the length of himself down onto her. "You're not still upset?" he asks. He takes her breast in hand, cups the flesh.

She hesitates, and so he knows she is. He lowers himself, takes her into his mouth. He can feel her loosening, her joints unbuckling. He eases her arm out from behind her back and feels her sink deeper into relaxation.

He brings his leg up and spreads her with a knee, and he can hear the quick intake of breath, feel the way her back tightens. But he doesn't let up, doesn't let on, acts as if he doesn't hear, doesn't notice.

She says, "Maybe this isn't the best time—"

But his mouth's on hers with smallish pecks that begin to linger and then with a ferocity she's unaccustomed to from him. She can't speak, and at the end of a long kiss that leaves her feeling more suffocated than giddy, he catches her lip in his teeth and holds it there, and just before he lets go, there is that bite of pain. She lets out a small sound—as on the heel of a hurt already passing, a mishap, an accident—*did it happen, or no?*—but then he's tender and he's whispering, "sssh, ssh, I'm sorry. Did I hurt you?" and he's kissing that spot on her lip, and moving onto her cheek, the lids of her eyes, and he's clearly concerned with her comfort, her ease, taking it slowly, until she is liquid and languid beneath him and making those sounds he echoes—the pitch and timbre—pacing himself, and when she comes, though he cries out with her, he does not finish, but pulls himself clear and cups her hand in his.

When his hand moves to her back, it takes her hand with it, so that she is locked there, the arm crooked at a right angle, though she does not realize it yet. Then he captures her free hand in his own, knitting his fingers through hers, and plants it with his weight next to the pillow.

Nance is pinned, her body strapped down by his, and her hands—one pressed between the middle of her back and the bed, the other held in his hand. She's just coming up, out of her pleasure, a dreamy, sodden feeling, a limpness she's slow to rouse from. For he's an accomplished lover. And though she's beginning to feel something is not as it usually is, it's not as though she's actually nervous—he's her husband, after all— and it's not as if it's even painful, though there is a feeling of compression, a mild discomfort. A vague sense that things are out of kilter, like a familiar room in which you're suddenly stubbing your toe.

She turns her head and blinks, as if to wake for the second time this evening. "Ned," she says, "I'm pretty sore," and realizes she is feeling raw from the long bout of sex, though it's not what's got her saying "No." She's not sure what it is, why she wants nothing more than to be allowed to slip into sleep, free of the weight on her.

There's the sound of the blankets slipping to the floor, and the wind funneling through the open window. She's stirring, and it's a curious thing Ned feels beneath him, as though she is knitting muscle and sinew back together. Bones and flesh reconnecting to will. He straddles her as her hips rise, and at first he thinks it is to accommodate him, but he quickly realizes it is to slide him off. Clearly he's underestimated the strength of the woman—fit from her treks up canyon, this snake wrangler, this woman unhampered by drugs or alcohol—and so he slides to one side before he is thrown, but he reaches beneath, grabs her wrist, and flips her onto her stomach.

His hand's on the flat of her neck, so that the side of her face is pressed into the pillow, and he *knows* he can take her—in any way he pleases. He's already reaching between her legs with his free hand. His voice against her ear is strangely rough, and he's saying, "This what you want? This what you want?" and he's repeating it over and over, and somewhere in there he's forcing her arm higher up her back, hurting her genuinely now.

She's lodged between his legs, her hand hooked high behind her back, her back hollowed. She yells, *"No,"* and *"Stop."* Then again. But it doesn't let up—his hold. She can't believe this is happening, wonders what he can be thinking. Imagines the downstairs door open and this intruder slipping in in Ned's familiar place. His knee is wedged in the back of her thigh.

She tries bucking beneath him, but he quelches that with the point of his knee bearing into the meat of her thigh, and she tries rolling, but his weight is cunningly distributed.

When she goes utterly still, it's then he hears the breath hissing from between her teeth, catches the look in her eye, feels her skin glassy in his hands. He feels a chill, as if there's a door open somewhere in the house and a draft has spread over him, exposed as he is in the dark above her.

He sees she's assessing—judging the efficiency of his hold, its efficacy. The moment stretches longer, and he becomes aware that his cock has gone shy and small in a way that genuinely upsets him. His heart quickens, and the pressure behind his eyes is building again. A new kind of anxiety worms inside. *What if I've gone too far?* He thinks of the house like the story of this life unraveling—the rooms and doors and windows falling away.

It wasn't supposed to have happened. He's casting about for a way he can turn it around. He's fretting for a way to let her up without letting her go. He eases the pressure on the back of her neck, but Nance remains motionless.

For what has come to her is the occasion of snakebite. She's thinking survival. Of finding her way out with the least damage done. Though she no longer trusts the landscape of her home: the linens that tangle about her legs, or the dresser, its mirror with the solemn eye of moon staring out, the pillow slumping into the mattress. The man with his hold on the back of her neck.

She realizes that he has released her arm, and she draws it slowly back around. Feels a wicked stabbing in the shoulder.

"Hey," he says. Laughs a little. He strokes the back of her head, and while he's let go the handholds, his weight is still on her. She does not move, though she wants to escape to the far side of the room, the house, or somewhere outside, on the street.

"Hey," he says again. "You okay?" His voice is soft and recognizable, as if the other man has stepped aside and let her husband back in. She can feel him shifting off of her, and before he's clear, she's rolled out from beneath. Her thigh is aching where his knee fit, the circle about her arm, the back of her neck. She's on the edge of the bed, one foot on the floor. She's watching.

He raises a hand, palm open, but she snatches his wrist with a speed and strength that startles him. She has a lock on the wrist bones, the same grip she uses on the viper's head.

He laughs uneasily. "What?" The streetlight from the window shines over his back, his shoulder, and the crown of his head, so that his dark hair is a burnished halo. His shoulders slump. A world-weary posture. "Nance, Nance," he says, as if addressing a child.

She drops his hand and backs out of the room. She jogs down the narrow corridor, down the single flight of steps, pads barefooted through the house, half-expecting the sound of footsteps following. She feels her way in the dark to the downstairs bathroom, locks the door, and makes her way to the toilet, where she sits on the closed lid. She rubs her arm, feels the place in the back of her thigh where his knee ground. The first word that comes to mind: *skillful*. How easily she was disabled. She kneads the muscle, where pain is forging its way down her leg.

At the sink, she wets a washrag in cold water and holds it to her face. She does not look into the mirror above the sink to see how pale her face is, how newly deep her eyes are set. Instead, she stares at the red line around her wrist, like the old Indian burns they gave as children. She places her hand over it, measures his hold against her own.

Should she leave? If so, then where. She thinks of Meredith—who might best understand—but cannot imagine appearing on her little sister's doorstep with no more clothes than what she might find in the downstairs closet, or the laundry basket. No, be truthful. It's this hand print on her wrist. She looks at it, feels the heat rise to her cheeks, and then she's locking her hands on the porcelain sink basin. She bends over, breathes deeply. When she straightens back up, the anger's still there, as well as disbelief. But it's humiliation that is the surprise, the keen sense of shame she feels, so much so that she wants to hide her hands behind her back. *What did I do to deserve this?*

"Not one . . . goddamned . . . thing," she says, and snatches a plastic cup from the countertop and throws it, but it hits the wall with a sorry-sounding crack before rolling the length of the bathtub. This is not something she would have suspected—not of herself certainly—how automatic a reflex it is to shoulder the blame. After all, there has to be a reason, doesn't there?

It's a genuine surprise. Being on this side of it. She has a sudden image of Meredith in the heat of summer, wearing long-sleeved shirts and high-necked T-shirts. How easy, almost second nature, to assume the worse: "Why do you bring it on?" That has her sitting down on the edge of the tub. She lifts her hand and studies the red mark wrapped around her wrist. *So what really did happen?*

She runs her hand down the back of her leg, feels the soreness there. *This is what happened. This.* The back of her neck. Her wrist. *And this.* Runs her hand over each in turn, but by the end of the catalog, that other part of her is already summing it up: *a hill of beans.* She sits awhile longer. This is not a thing she would have expected, how quickly you lose your focus, how easily you become your own enemy. When at last she emerges from the bathroom, it is to a house still and dark. There's no sound above, and she imagines Ned sleeping as if this were any other night where she's wandered off to use the bathroom, or read a bit after sex. She finds the thought of his falling asleep nearly as disturbing as the violence. She crosses the central hall to stand at the bottom of the staircase. She remains there a long moment, letting her eyes adjust to the dark, and then she steps forward.

She climbs the stairs, and each creak of the floorboard bangs in her head. She knows this is not wise but feels compelled to see him. To see how much or little he is affected. She keeps to the far wall, moving down the long hallway, past the guest bedroom, and past the bathroom with its amber night-light—the small part of the dark he insists on keeping lighted even when she's home. There's only the soft pad of her footsteps on the wood floors. She stands at the threshold, letting her eyes adjust to the starlight coming through the window, and the darkness resolves into a chair and table below the window. The dresser across the way. The bed. There's the sweet-sour smell of sex. The rumpled bedcovers are still slumped onto the floor, and she can see the silhouette of his head against the pillow, the dim light of hair against the pillowcase. She steps in, her hands balled into fists. She's trying to keep her breathing quiet, but it feels as if she's run a marathon, as if she cannot get oxygen enough to keep legs under her.

She nears the bed, walking as if she needs to watch where she places each step. As if something lies in wait. When she reaches her side of the bed, she sees that he's turned on his side, facing away. The pounding of her heart in her ears quiets enough that she can hear his breathing. See the fall and rise of blankets. The careless way his foot has crooked out from under the sheets and hangs thickly off the side of the bed. She treads to his side of the bed and stands opposite. Studies the broad shelf of forehead, the narrowing around the nose, the way his mouth is caught slightly open as on a long *aaah*.

Appalling. How at rest he is.

She wants to shake him. She wants to strike him. To press his face into the pillow with a hand behind his neck, leverage his hand into his back. She wants *him* to know what it's like to feel his thigh wedged beneath her knee.

She wants—what?—to know what it felt like to be the one on top, an insight into what it was he gained in the struggle.

She stands, waiting for him to move, as people do in dreams, that anxious little kick, the curling at the back. Waits for him to sense her presence at the side of the bed and wake. She wants—what? An accounting. An explanation. The opportunity to face him, prepared. Standing on her feet. She tries to imagine shaking him awake, or just speaking his name, but knows she won't do this. Not now. Not tonight. *Why not?* Because it's not smart. Because she doesn't understand why it all happened. *Because you're scared.* Yes.

After a short while, she steps away, walks out of the room and down the stairs. She finds her way through the dark, her fingers skirting the edges of the side table in the downstairs hall, and the chair in the corner, the door frame, the kitchen threshold with the rag rug she's careful not to slip on. She crosses to the stove, turns on the stove-top light. She puts a pot of water on. Sets a cup and saucer on the table. Tries to steady her hands. She lays out a napkin and the box of tea, the bowl of sugar. There's comfort in this small act, the ritual of preparing the tea, laying out the table. She thinks of all the times she'd done this for her father and sister when they felt ill, or sad. How recently Meredith did it for her. She has a flash of memory—a cup of tea nested in her mother's hands, steam rising as if from her fingertips. "Careful now, sweetie. It's hot."

The kettle rattles on the burner. She empties it into the teapot. She will sit at the table throughout the long night, the water cooling in the pot, the cup of tea resting on the saucer, untasted. She plans to take what time she needs to think this through, to make it make sense, or determine what course of action to take. She should probably leave the house and find a motel room, but she knows she will not do that. Will not yield him that much ground, and so when the break of morning steeps the kitchen in its yellow light, she will be there, her back to the wall. Waiting.

Book III

Chapter Ten

N ance checks the gear in the back of the pickup but finds herself glancing at the house. Ned's finishing lunch in there, and she'd just as soon leave before having to engage in yet another exchange, when what is said is nothing more than she'd say to a stranger. They've settled into an uneasy distance this last week. Nance has moved into the guest bedroom. Locks the door at night.

Curiously enough, it's Ned who looks wounded. Ever since the morning after, when Nance had tried to face him down and he'd only looked confused. He hadn't a clue what she was talking about. In the following days, the perplexed look resolved into indifference, then disbelief. "Aren't you being a bit paranoid?" he'd asked.

As for the bruises ringing her arm and the back of her neck, the deep purpling on the back of one thigh, he was surprised. He conceded it might have happened, but he called it accidental. "So maybe I got a bit carried away. It's not like I *meant* to hurt you. Think about it: What exactly *did* happen? Nothing. Because the first time I try something besides missionary style, you act like I'm going to rape you. I thought you'd enjoy it. For Christ's sake, Nance, grow up. We're husband and wife." He snorted, shook his head.

After a few days of sparring, he turned attentive. Quick to notice if her coffee cup was empty. Took care to point out if her shoe had come untied: "Don't want you getting hurt out there." He was the man she'd always known him to be. Considerate. More so. Some days so much so that it had the feel of a veneer applied too thickly.

After a couple weeks of this, the pain's gone; the bruises have mostly yellowed, and even she's beginning to feel detached from the whole thing. Is it possible she did overreact? Though she's reluctant to come to that much accommodation yet.

She circles to the driver's side and settles in. When she pulls away, he's coming out onto the porch with briefcase in hand. Now that he's preparing for another school year, there's even less contact. She's grateful for that, thinking that given enough time and distance, it'll sort itself out, or make it clearer what she should do.

Nance heads toward Meredith's. Her sister called last night. "How about some hang time?" Even though today's work isn't conducive to Meredith tagging along, after the confusion and silence at home, Nance is grateful for the company.

Meredith's waiting on the sidewalk, dressed in sweatshirt, jeans, and leather boots. Nance lifts the door latch, raises a booted foot across the bench seat, and kicks open the catchy door. "Yo, Sis," she says.

They hug and then Meredith's strapping herself in. "Snakes, huh? Oh goody."

They drive east on Highway 12. The ride is filled with rumors about Meredith's fellows at the Ramrod: who's courting whom these days, and the empty space at the end of the counter where Dutch, the guy with the oxygen tank, used to sit. "He hadn't been feeling so well. When he didn't show up for his daily meal, the lunch crew called his neighbor.

"He found Dutch on the bathroom floor. Called an ambulance. Poor old guy had pneumonia." She braces a foot against the dashboard. "Cliff wants to put a little plaque on the back of the stool. You know, in memory of . . ."

"Sweet," Nance says.

Meredith nods. "It's what I like about this place. It's so personal."

Nance can't imagine. This is not the Lewiston or the West she knows—the sprawling hills, the rivers' relentless currents—the water and everything in it just passing through. Nance discovers she urgently wants to know how her sister sees things.

She crosses the metal bridge spanning a narrow section of the Clearwater. The sumac's scarlet against the dun-colored fescue. The site's above the small town of Lenore, which is comprised of a post office, a couple dozen homes, a community center across the highway, and an abandoned grain elevator that dominates the scene with its complex of rusting sheet-metal buildings, loading docks, and storage elevators, the sides of which have been whitewashed by pigeons.

The truck's rear end skitters on washboard as the two-lane road angles upward over the hillside, a steep grade rising to three hundred feet above the river. At the top is a fork, the road to the right drifting up and over the summit connecting the small feeder roads from the prairie towns above: Weippe, Pierce, Headquarters.

Nance takes the left fork. The road's a narrow ribbon following the hill in a series of hairpin turns. In some places Nance can overlook the weedy inches that separate road from air. She hugs the hill, though in some of the turns she believes she can see the front bumper swing out over the edge. She turns onto a driveway, a gut-wrenching cut beneath a crumbling bank of shale. It's the home of one of her colleagues, a sprawling one-story ranch-style house crowding an abbreviated lawn. The front of his home, with its wide deck, is perched on pylons, the footings blasted into bedrock.

Mike Johnson's an ornithologist. He's small, a sandy-haired, freckled man with thick-rimmed glasses and eyes that have an owlish look. He jogs over. He's wearing a sweater and vest, a red-and-white wool cap with the Canadian maple leaf jaunty on its side. Nance makes the introductions, and he invites them onto the deck overhanging the canyon, where there's a spotting scope sited on an osprey nest downriver. He gives each of them a look.

"They'll be leaving soon," he says. "The fledglings are in the air more than not. Next come the bald eagles." He rubs his hands together. Speaks briefly about the snow geese that migrate through. "So white," he says, "startling. And pelicans. You should see the pelicans." He's behind the scope again.

When Nance reminds him why she's here, he offers to point them to the site, but he won't go any closer than the road. Says, "I'm not good with snakes."

Nance grabs a pair of work gloves from the truck. From the truck bed she lifts out a snake hook and then a spade, which she hands to her sister.

They follow Mike back up the driveway. At the road, they strike off a short quarter mile west to Rattlesnake Point. He points at an abrupt cut in the hillside, where a wash of rock and gravel has been exposed. "Yesterday, that whole area was buzzing," he says. "I swear."

Nance looks up the slope. Then she turns away, studies the long trek down to where the river courses. Across the river and the highway is Angel Ridge—heavily timbered, in sharp contrast to the treeless slopes this side of the river. When she asks about this, he shrugs, claims, "I'm not good with geology, either." He pats her awkwardly on the back and sets out for home.

Meredith's watching his retreat. She shakes her head. "Well, is that the oddest little man, or what?"

Nance is on one knee, double-knotting her bootlace. She looks up at her sister. "Actually, I've always thought that for an ornithologist, Mike's pretty normal."

"From the point of view of a person who's into snakes, maybe."

Nance tucks the hook under an arm. It's a broad spit of land that wedges out from the summit in long, slight declines, with recently built houses potted here and there. A number of barns, as well. A few head of horses, or sheep, or goats are corralled in dry lots.

Nance steps up onto the hillside. "You stay here," she says, regretting she hadn't suggested Meredith accompany Mike back.

Meredith has her own ideas. "Oh, come on, Sis. I'll be careful," she says. "I'm wearing boots." She hikes up her jeans to show a pair of heavily tooled bright yellow leather cowboy boots, stack-heeled.

Nance shakes her head. "You'll scare 'em to death. Or break an ankle."

"No way. I've danced in these babies. Sort of. Hey, if it gets hairy, you say so and I'll freeze, or leave, or whatever." She hefts the spade. "I'll carry the shovel."

Nance looks over at her sister, says, "Fine, have it your way. But pay attention. These are not snakes in den. These are going to den, possibly a good number of them. And they'll be scattered about in the grass, and aggressive. Some will be bearing their young—they're oviparous, and bear live young—and the little ones, while harder to see, are just as dangerous as the big ones. So don't be poking at any cute babies. Snakes can strike at a distance of about half their length"—she starts walking away—"which isn't always easy to judge when they're coiled. And though the bite's not usually fatal, it's extraordinarily painful. Takes a hell of a long time to recover. It'll swell the skin so fast that your flesh will split, and it'll turn red, then black—lots of necrophotic material—but with good care . . ."

Meredith's hanging back, says, "Maybe you're right, and I should just stay here."

Nance nods. "Good choice," she says, and starts climbing. The slope steepens for a span of a hundred-odd feet. Soon Nance is feeling the effects of her month of office work. She's keeping a keen eye for snakes, but the higher she goes, the deeper the grasses. If it is a den site, there might be any number of them around the perimeter. Though she doubts it's as Mike claims—the whole hillside buzzing. People tend to exaggerate when it comes to snakes. She unzips her jacket, loosens the collar.

She checks over her shoulder, sees Meredith by the roadside, leaning on the shovel. Meredith waves, shouts, but Nance can't hear, and then Meredith points to the shovel, lifts her hands in a shrug.

Nance waves it off. Just as well. If there were any real numbers, she'd hold off digging. This is a touchy time of year—cool evenings, days still warming to hot by midafternoon. She wasn't just giving Meredith a line. The snakes would be aggressive.

Overhead, turkey vultures loop in loose convergent circles. On the ground, two of the birds pick at something. She cuts a diagonal toward the birds, fishing the tall grasses with her hook, as a blind person will do with a cane. There are rustlings, though it's hard to say what it is that moves through, snake or vole, mouse or wind. She's listening for the rattle, but knows they don't always signal their presence. She's booted and geared up, but it's a different thing altogether when you take it to the den.

The vultures are plucking at a carcass, and long strips of flesh string from their horny beaks. It's a reeking brew, and for a short moment it reminds her of Turnbull and the great stink of his death. She shakes her head, brings her attention back to what's at hand.

The birds on the ground spread their wings and hiss but then back off as she approaches. Some rags of hide are still attached, enough so that at first she wonders if it's a coyote that's been baited, but it's too small, and then she sees the leather collar. A dog. Short and compact, maybe fifteen inches at the shoulder. What tufts of hair that remain are white and brown. She picks up a bit of wiry fluff.

She levers the snake hook under the carcass, and beneath is a carpet of beetles. The dog's jaws are locked on what's left of a snake, though most of the reptile and a goodly amount of the dog have been peeled away by birds and bugs. She can almost reconstruct what happened. The unlucky dog nosed up the snake. For the dog, it was a great game, dashing in and around. And the snake coiling and striking, missing, but keeping to the distinctive S coil used in striking, and moving backward through the tall grasses. The dog following, its nose probing. Until the dog lingered once too often with its nose, or left its neck broadside to the snake, and the snake struck. So fast. The proverbial lightning in a bottle. She wonders how long they struggled.

She gets down on a knee, slips a gloved finger into what remains of the dog's jaws, and sees the snake's vertebrae capped over an incisor, neat as a ring on a finger. The dog caught it too far down its spine. It probably would have released the snake, except it found itself locked on. She imagines the snake's head whipping back, its fangs sinking into the soft muzzle or flap of neck. How the dog must have yelped in surprise, or struggled to break free even as the toxins coursed into its system.

She turns what's left of the dog's head, sees a sizable chunk of snake trailing out the far side of the mouth. She measures a knuckle against the bone. Fairly big.

The grounded vultures are hopping from leg to leg, peevish and pecking at one another. She'll leave them to it, knows they'll do a neat job, right down to the bone, and what bone is left will be calcium for the mice. Have to admire the efficiency of nature. An assembly of flies is gathering, and Nance waves them off, dusts off her knees, and heads toward the slice in the side of the hill.

She's a close twenty feet from the cut when she hears the first buzz—a smallish rattler tucked deep in the grass. She checks it out, snake hook in front of her, and the small creature coils around its base like a caduceus before winding off and away. She sidesteps its path. Within ten feet of the cut, she feels the mass before she sees it, nothing tangible. Rather, it's an intuition developed over the years. She sees at the foot of the cliff a couple dozen snakes winding about one another. The air itself seems agitated with activity, as if they bleed off a kind of charge, an ozone of their own making. She's easing her way forward when the rattles start, one and another, a trip-hammer buzz from snake to snake, until there's a drone of rattles, and she hears what her colleague has described. Sees more now, pocketed here and there in the grass. The hairs on the back of her neck lift, as well as the small hairs on her arms. She rubs the fine hairs down.

It's not a central den like the one up in Hells Canyon, though she hadn't really expected that. Central dens are rare here. Back in the Midwest, in the cut limestone caves, yes, but not here, not in this place of basalt and granite. Here the standard is snakes hunkering down in solitary burrows, alongside ground squirrels and field mice.

The cut is a mix of dirt, clay, and stone rubble, numerous small holes pockmarking the softer dirt. She tries to estimate the length of catch fence she'll need. She'll have to get permission to set it up this winter, more net than fence, string it the length of the cut. Come spring, when the snakes reemerge, they'll be trapped, easy pickings. They'll do implants, then return them for study, map their travels, chart attrition rates. She'll need more assistants. It's a convenient spot. Ideal. She thinks about the time involved, setting it up.

And, as happens so often of late, she's suddenly picturing Ned again, the way he seizes her hand, nips it behind her back, and, with a knee to her groin, flips her over. The ease with which he puts her down. Her cheeks heat as she remembers the feel of her arm hooked behind her back, her face ground into the pillow. His hand clamped behind her neck.

She shakes her head. It won't do to be thinking of this now. She needs to stay focused. When she looks up, she sees Meredith has approached, no more than thirty feet away.

"Stop," she shouts.

"I've got the shovel."

"Goddamn it, Meredith. Stand still," Nance screams. "Don't move."

"I'm fine."

Nance steps forward, sees the belligerence on her sister's face, the way she holds the shovel out in the air before her, like a damned banner. What comes to mind is the small dog with its teeth locked on the snake, and even as Nance is thinking this, she sees the snake, though for a moment it looks more like a coil of rope, a large twist of stick, but then it's as if she's stepping on a live power line, the way its back cracks against the sole of her boot, and the animal uncoils and strikes. Fast and, conversely, slow, so that she believes she sees it all, the way the jaw flexes open, the fangs already lowering, and she barely has time to breathe, and then she feels the impact against her calf, a hit like a dull punch, and then the snake is free and drawing back and back.

"Shit," Nance says. "Oh shit."

She doesn't move. She's waiting for the pain. Like a wasp sting. Only larger. Much larger. She's been here before. Once, in the laboratory, a mishap, a quick bite to the soft skin between thumb and forefinger. Then it was a snake that had been recently milked, and so she was able to draw most of it out, and suffered little more than pain, and little enough tissue death, and a waxy scar that still itches sometimes. But she has no idea how much venom this one's delivered. It's a big snake, and maybe it's so wide in the belly because it's fed recently. She earnestly hopes so, for then there'd be less venom to deliver into her leg. She's standing there, waiting for the pain to hit, when she hears her sister's voice.

"Nance? Nance? Something wrong?"

"I've been bit," she says, realizes her voice is a whisper. "Nothing," she says louder. "Stay there."

"Something is wrong. I can tell." Meredith's voice is rising.

Nance drops to a knee. She's all thumbs, unstrapping the canvas gaiter. She's feeling flushed, her heart squeezing. Maybe there's a tingling in her leg? Or maybe she's been lucky, a dry strike, a miss. She calculates the drive to the nearby town of Orofino, with its healthy stock of antivenom.

She's thinking about the toxins—unlike the neurotoxic venoms that attack the central nervous system, the rattler's works through the vasculary system, a hemotoxin composed of digestive enzymes: proteases, cholinesterases, ribonucleases, hylayuronidase, this last a spreading factor that increases absorption through connective tissues. The hemorrhagins—enzymes that break down tissue proteins and promote the breakdown of the key structural components of connective tissues—finally causing the collapse of cell metabolism. The limb swells; the skin blackens and blisters. Grotesque and painful, yes. Shock. Gangrene sometimes, usually from the incorrect use of tourniquets. The loss of a limb or digit is not uncommon. And always the risk of tetanus, secondary infections.

"Nance, Nance, answer me."

Nance raises an arm, waves her sister off. She can see where the canvas gaiter was punctured, and as she lowers it, she sees some of the fluid has oozed down into the sleeve. There's a smaller hole in the denim pant leg as well, a wet patch, and she's breathing quickly now.

There's no pain. No pain. You lucked out.

She pushes the pant leg up, rolls the heavy socks down to reveal the unblemished skin. She runs a hand over the leg, as if her eyes can't be trusted. Her joints are loosening with relief. She crooks her arms over her raised knee, rests her forehead on her arms. She closes her eyes, and wishes she hadn't, because she can see the strike again, the muscularity of it, how incomprehensibly fast, and then it feels as if a hive of bees has been loosed in her blood, a rapid thrumming of blood, but no pain. Adrenaline. *Excitement.*

"Sis?"

Nance looks up, sees Meredith standing over her.

"You okay?" Meredith sinks the shovel blade into the grass. "My God, you've been bitten, haven't you."

But Nance is already rising to her feet. She can still hear the low buzzing from the hillside.

Meredith's face is pale. She's staring at the gaiter lying on the ground. "You *have* been bitten." She raises the shovel, pivots on her heel, as if looking for the culprit. As if she plans to go after it.

Nance grabs her by the arm. "No. Stop." She hauls her sister back by the elbow, merely intending to hold her in place. Nothing more. But then she's shaking her sister, and it's more than adrenaline—the way her blood bolts through her. She's shaking her sister hard, her hand biting into flesh. Nance is leaning in now, and it's as if all the years of frustration have been compressed into a hard point behind her eyes, and she's seeing Meredith at ten at the dinner table, refusing plates of food, whittling her flesh down with starvation, or overdosed at fifteen. At eighteen, battered by her latest boyfriend, a whole string of boyfriends. Dad's phone call: "Meredith's gone to the apartment. . . . I'm not sure she should have done that." Then she's seeing Joe, on his way out of the house—"See ya, babe"—and then it's Ned, and he's saying, "*Ever since she came out*—" And she's feeling Ned's knee in her back, and his hand on the back of her neck, and she's shaking Meredith. She's got Meredith's shoulders in her hands now, and she's shaking her and yelling, "You never listen, do you? Not now. Not ever. It's always about you, and you still don't give a fuck who you hurt."

Meredith finally acts. She swings her arms up and breaks Nance's grip, stumbles back. They stare across the short space at each other.

Nance takes a series of deep breaths and looks at the long grasses waving down the slope of the hill. When she looks up again, she says, "Goddamn you."

Meredith doesn't move for a long moment. And then she rubs a hand down her arm where Nance's fingers have been. She stares at her sister, says, "Man oh man. When did you start to hate me so?"

The sisters hold their places, and the silence between them lingers. Nance is the first to break off her gaze. She looks at the sky, where the vultures still circle, at the clouds drifting on the far horizon, then down at her feet, as if she's forgotten something in the grass. She stoops over to buckle the gaiter back on. Her hands are still shaking.

When she finishes, she straightens up, saying, "Keep in my footsteps. Don't step outside of them, you hear?" She drills a finger into Meredith's chest. "I mean it."

She swings the hook through the grass ahead, sweeping a slow path, keeping her strides moderate so that Meredith can follow.

On the road, Nance stops. She looks up the dusty length of road to the drive where her vehicle is still parked. Wishes now that she'd driven the short quarter mile. She'd stow the gear, climb in, and drive off. Leave her sister in the dust.

Now all the whispering through the roadside grass has become sibilant with snake rustlings, and even though she knows it's mostly imagination, still some small part of her is turned to the leg that was struck, checking in. She glances at the hill they've just left, at the cut of stone and dirt where the snakes are denning, and it's as if she can feel the radiant heat of all those bodies, and smell the tunneled dirt. Below the road is a broad swath of wheat that the wind courses through like currents in a river.

At the truck, Johnson joins them. "Any problem?" he asks. "Did you find the snakes?"

Nance pitches the snake hook into the back of the truck, then lifts the shovel from Meredith and throws it in next to the hook. "Found them," she says.

"And a whole lot more," Meredith mumbles.

Nance gives her head a tight shake. She extends her hand to the man. "Thanks for letting me know about it."

"Glad I could help," he says.

"You'll want to keep clear of there until a good cold spell hits and they go to den." Nance is about to turn away, when she remembers. "Found a dog. Small, white and brown. Looks like it's been dead awhile."

"Wondered where he went." Mike shakes his head.

"Oh," Nance says, "I'm sorry."

He looks puzzled. "No," he says. "He wasn't mine. Just used to come around a lot. Belongs to a family up that way." He points a thumb over his shoulder. "I'll let them know," he says, and walks back up the drive toward the deck and his spotting scope.

When Nance turns to Meredith, her sister's looking down the hill. "We should get going," Nance says.

"Fine," Meredith says. She strides over to the passenger side of the truck, boosts herself up into the seat. She slams the door, looks out the open window.

Nance shuffles over to the driver's side and eases herself in. She backs out of the drive, deciding to take the bench road down to the Cherry Lane Bridge; it's a long, dusty, slow, and torturous route. She wants the time, the solitary lane winding in and out along the river. They swing by the new den site, but Nance hasn't much thought for it now. She'll gather those ideas later. Right now, she's got enough damage on her hands. "I don't hate you," she finally says.

Meredith raises a hand, cutting her off. She keeps on staring out the side window at the hill vaulting up from the road.

Nance pulls the visor down over her side window to cut the glare. The truck rocks over the gutted lane, skirting the hillside and hugging the hairpins turns. They bump down a short grade, pass over a cattle guard. In the hollow to their right is a set of corrals where a herd of horses bunched head-to-tail drowse in the shade of a cottonwood. Nance gears down for the abrupt climb on the other side of the turn. "Honest, Mer, I don't hate you."

Meredith blows out a breath. Shakes her head. "Well, that was a damn fine imitation."

"Christ Almighty. I'd just been bit by a snake. I was upset, okay? It's not something you ever really get comfortable with, you know."

Meredith turns toward her sister, lifts an eyebrow. "It was more than that."

Nance glances at the roadside, at the river winding next to them. She looks up at the rearview mirror, the plume of dust rising in the gravel behind them, the roadside weeds burdened with dirt.

"When you had hold of me . . ." Meredith says, turning away to look out the side window again. "I honest to God don't know what I did to deserve what I saw."

Nance pinches her lips together. She keeps her focus on the road. Her hands clench on the steering wheel, and when they begin to ache, she shifts them one hand at a time. Curls and uncurls her fingers. "I don't know what you're talking about," she finally says. "It can't have been that bad." The words are uncomfortably familiar.

Meredith nods. She slings her elbow across the window frame. The rest of the ride home is silent.

They park at the curb in front of Meredith's house, and the light's beginning to turn, the pitched roofs of houses waxing amber with late-afternoon sunlight. It's hot in the truck cab, and Nance shoves her sleeves up over elbows.

Meredith glances over. She leans back in the seat and closes her eyes. After a long moment, she says, "Smells like a change of weather."

Nance inhales, can't decipher what it is her sister senses. The air's hot and so dry, it's as if she can smell the musk of dust in it, the bitter bite of star thistle and wilting cheat grass. It's the last burst of heat before the autumn rains break the long, hot back of summer.

Neither of them move or speak, until Nance begins to believe the afternoon will wend on right into the early evening hours, and on past the supper hour, and on into the deep of the night, with them still sitting there, waiting it out—the change in one or the other. Or the weather. Hard to say which. Right now, she just wants to be shed of the day, and with it her sister's company, and the anger. Yes, anger. But hate? Surely not.

She leans her head against the door frame. "I can't deal with this right now. Give it a rest?"

Meredith nods. "Sure," she says. "No problem." She pops the handle, cracks the door open. "Tell you what: You figure out when you can deal with it, you give me a call. But you know what? I don't want to see or hear from you until then. And if that means never"—she shrugs—"so be it." She swings a leg out of the truck. " 'Cause this is like every bad relationship I've ever been in, and I'm not playing this game anymore. You get ready to talk? I'm ready to listen. As long as it's the truth." Meredith steps down, then leans back in the cab. She nods at Nance's wrist, at the ghost of a bruise. "You give me a call, and we could talk about that, too." Meredith steps away, closes the door, and heads for her house, arms swinging at her side.

Nance glances down at her hand, at the wrist with its telltale yellow cuff. She looks up and out the windshield, where waves of heat rise off the pavement, and the trees appear to shimmer in the swimming air. She's still startled by her sister's words. Her accurate way of seeing "like every bad relationship I've ever been in." She leans her head out the window, takes a deep breath, hopes her sister is right in thinking that a change is coming. She hopes it is rain, and that it drenches the hills and scrubs the pavement in great gully-washing troughs.

Meredith has gone in the house and Nance is still sitting at the corner, looking at the blank facade of the old Victorian. She shakes her head. She pulls away from the curb, and when she glances back in her rearview mirror, she sees a car parked kitty-corner from the house. Halfway down the block, she's musing how much the car looked like Ned's, and she's almost midway down the second block before she turns around. She can't imagine what he'd be doing parked there. Waiting. For her?

But when she gets back to where the car was, of course, it's gone.

Early afternoon, Ned's at his desk. The office door is closed, and he's staring past the stack of papers that has fallen into what appears to be a kind of benign chaos. His secretary has buzzed him three times in the last half hour, and he finds it annoying, is inclined to swat at the intercom, or snap at the woman who is now hovering outside the door. Wants to tell her, Leave me alone. Take a flying crap. But he won't do that. Not in so many words. Instead, he ignores the intermittent buzzing, sits with legs crossed, staring at the wall, at its mail-ordered diplomas and self-congratulatory awards.

It's not exactly that he's lost interest in work, just that it no longer appeases what constricts his spine, or eases the closeness in his head. Won't keep his legs from vibrating—standing or sitting—nor halt the sudden fears that bolt him to his solitary bed these nights. There's nothing and no one to decipher the fragments: this woman, that woman, a spot of dark in the dirt, and limbs, and always, as if seen from a distance, himself as a young boy with some *man? Woman?* Thinks all of this is nothing new, and nothing to save him those other times, either. Not the women, not Nance, or before her Marla, or Tina, or even his mother. Not the respectable lives with their carefully fabricated histories and change of names: Ned, Nick, Nate, Neil. Each time like a change of clothes that might finally make the man. He still believes one of these times it'll prove the charm.

This time, he wants to blame Turnbull, the incredible stinking corpse. Or Nance. Better yet, Meredith.

He uncrosses his legs, pulls closer to the desk, and eyes the crosshatch of papers. He settles his elbows on a stack, steeples his fingers under his chin. A couple of papers drift onto the floor. He waits for the others to avalanche after, but the desktop seems to have achieved a state of temporary stasis—that fine line between neglect and chaos. Before he leaves today, he will rearrange the surface yet again so that Cate will still believe in his devoted industry.

He swivels toward the view of the empty playground and the swings—their limp nooses dangling over ovals of dirt. At the far end of the swings is the cage of monkey bars, and at the farthest end of that a teeter-totter, cocked and ready. The sun has just now quartered the blue sky. He imagines the silence. Pictures himself under the soundless drift of clouds, amid the playground paraphernalia. Middle of a school day. All the children safely locked away, tooling their crafts at small desks: finger paints, crayons, and Playdoh tomfoolery. Reciting math tables, sounding out cue cards, or cramped over workbooks. He could go sit in on a few classes. Read a book to the kindergartners.

But he won't.

There's no longer a sense of mission here, though he *has tried* these last few weeks to recapture what it was that kept him on task. He should give a shit. Finds himself strangely past that.

Out on the street, a car speeds beneath the flashing yellow. Ned looks toward the vacant lot where cops perpetually lurk. No lights, no sirens. Lucky bastard.

And it is luck—so much so, that he's come to believe he's singularly blessed.

Tina was the best of it, he thinks. His first. His longest run. He was twenty-five, and she, at nineteen, knew how to keep things interesting. She was game, by God, at least for a while. Until what it took to keep him interested got *too intense,* or so she said. He thinks about her face, her red lips loose and slobbered, all floaty against that white shock of cheek, the straw of her hair. *Too intense.* He hasn't thought of her in weeks, and that surprises him. He used to dredge her up routinely.

He lets his focus go soft, past the playground and the fifteen-foot cyclone fencing, past the stand of trees and the cutout bungalows. He's staring past place and time, until he's standing at an open car door, looking into the backseat of their ancient Ford Fairlane. A real piece of work—that car. Banana yellow on the bottom and white on top, with a cream-colored vinyl interior that must have looked pretty good back when it was new.

The radio's turned down low, and the Stones are playing some old honky-tonk shit she just can't get enough of.

They're pulled over onto the side of a dirt forest service road in Washington. In the mountains. Tall timber all around. Through a narrow copse of firs, he sees a glint of blue that is a lake. He knows it's cold in that lake and that it never really warms up. Subalpine. One of any hundred or more in the area that are just small dots on forest service maps.

He leans into the car and over the backseat, where Tina's folded. No other way to say it. Knees tucked up, feet bundled under, arms bound beneath her rib cage, her head dropping to the side. A damned awkward angle. She's staring, as if to say, *Now look what you've gone and done.* That's

220   C l a i r e   D a v i s

what he remembers, the way her eyes fix on his, follow him no matter which way he stands, or where he goes. Glazy eyes, as if the blue is receding behind frosted glass.

He hadn't meant for it to happen. *Too intense indeed.* But he'd gotten caught up, couldn't foresee how that thing would quicken in him—call it pleasure. No. *Call it relief.* Yes. Just letting go. And truthfully, it was as if he weren't even there. Or if he were, it was only as an observer, perched way back, waiting for whatever it was to run its course.

Sometimes he believes he might have stopped it if he'd been better prepared. He might have yanked on its chain, or stifled the impulse. If only he'd been forewarned—as he is now.

But back then, how could he even suspect? Who'd believe himself capable of such things? Who in their right mind would dream it?

He tries to reconfigure the scene, put them in their appropriate places and play it out to some other conclusion. This time, she doesn't back away. Her face doesn't take on that look of reckoning, the inevitability just as clearly declared as blades of grass rising into the air before a lightning strike, the way fleas leap from the rabbit's body before the thresher hits. Her face announcing his intent. A kind of self-fulfilling prophecy.

This time, he doesn't form the fist. This time, he doesn't see that rabbitty look in her eyes, her bottom lip falling slack. The excitement doesn't become compulsion, like scratching an itch. Or a sneeze in bright light that you just do and do and do. Until her knees buckle and the right side of her face slumps like soft wax, and a bone has chipped in his knuckle, a small, bright bite of pain that he will not notice until much later while sitting in the empty car. Maybe he cried. He must have.

He's breathing heavily and shifting from foot to foot. So? It was a mistake, and there's no use crying over spilt milk all these years later. Instead, he's practical about it. Maybe that's what it took. Maybe it took Tina to straighten him out, to keep him from stepping into it that deeply again. Or too often. He has slipped a time or two since, say with Marla, some few others—a barn comes to mind. The stub of a shovel. He shakes his head. Thinks of the more fortunate couple over in north Lewiston.

The man? *Wee Willie Winkie* still alive, and functioning at some level. Hardly the brightest to begin with. And the woman? Checked out of the hospital and gone, it being such a great big disposable world out there. But overall? He's kept a pretty steady course. He's almost grateful for the lessons.

He'd weighted Tina carefully, dropped her off a cliff into what he could see was the deepest hole in the lake, the bluest eye in the green, green waters. He meant her to be food for the fish, or ground to pebbles against the sandy bottom. But he'd heard of another woman, the Lady of the Lake, found in just such conditions—Lake Crescent—back in the early thirties. He had, in fact, researched it, called up the old clippings of the infamous case. She'd been murdered by her husband. Her body, snagged by fishermen years later, was curiously preserved by the cold and deep, the flesh still plump, waxy, and intact.

So that of a late night in the half-dark between sleep and rising, or in the bright white of day and dreaming as he is now, Tina sheds rocks and muck. She rises effortless as a jellyfish, her arms and fingers, legs and feet trailing the belled torso, buoyant into the wavery shadows, to where the spindled light fractures in diamonds across her buttocks and the backs of her thighs; she ascends to pierce the lake's skin with no more noise than a carp rolling on the surface. In this way, she comes to Ned, whole and repaired and cleanly preserved, her skin translucent as cellophane, and the soft organ tissues, the muscle and larded flesh of her— breasts, buttocks, thighs, and arms, even the smallest of her pudgy toes—just like that Lady of the Lake—has gone to soap.

He finds her haunting a comfort. Unlike Turnbull: the artifact, a withering curiosity. Perhaps it's because she's his, his own undying love, a surrogate child, or sister, and maybe that's why it's always her he comes to, when he's with other women, when he's bringing himself to conclusion in the dark of his own room, in the shower, in the alley, the kitchen, the neighbor's side yard while watching this person or another dressing or fucking, or when he's in the car, the theater, or late at night, say, in the children's bathroom at school.

It's this last thought that chases him from the room finally, out the door, and past the exasperated Cate, who half-stands, as if she's about to follow him down the hallway. Except that she doesn't, and even she's not sure what it is that keeps her behind the desk. When he leaves, she sighs and rises and shuts the door to his office; she keeps her eyes on her hands, well away from the room with its unkempt desk, its blinds kinked above the windows like sleepy eyelids. Wonders what has changed. She used to enjoy work, looked forward to it. Mr. Able being so . . . so fatherly with the children and all. What is it that's different? She hears the minute hand drop into its ten-minute-till slot on the wall clock; the bells will ring soon, signaling recess and change of lessons.

She hurries back to her desk, even as any number of teachers in the classrooms are glancing at the clock as well, planning the next lesson, or handing children over to the playground monitors so the teachers may ease their aching feet out of tight shoes in the lounge. At least one of them glances up through the paned door in time to see the principal striding past, and is pleasantly relieved it's not his classroom the man's aimed at.

Ned's not aimed anywhere in particular. He's walking down the glossy hallways, past the classroom doors, behind which comes a sound like the mumbling of bees from deep in a hive. Past the *bop bop bop* of basketballs, the squeegee squeak of rubber-soled shoes on the gym floor, the exclamation of whistles.

He steps out of the school and into that back lot where the Dumpsters are clapped tight, but from within which a stink rises of spoiled milk and soured hash, sawdust and vomit. He hurries away, and fishing in his pocket, he pulls out his keys just as he reaches his car. Later on, he'll come back, or call in to say he suddenly took sick.

He even believes this story, feeling queasy, light-headed, and in need of some time off, but within a block or two of his street, he's fine and restless, and weary of that shambling brick house—its vacuumed rooms, its two-storied view of the valley. He winds down the grade toward downtown. Parks in one of the shaded parking lots. Gets out of the car and leans his hands on the hood to stretch his back.

He strolls Main, past Morgan's alley with its gallery of shops. Past the old bank that's been commandeered as an art museum by the small college up the hill. On the sides of it are murals painted by one of the local artists—bits and pieces of history, done trompe l'oeil—the native Nez Perce riding their spotted Appaloosa horses. He remembers seeing the woman paint these pictures, a longhaired redheaded woman. Irish, he'd guessed, a colleen for sure, though she would not say, and kept to her perch atop a ladder the entire time he'd spoken with her.

He walks the length of Main on the north side of the street and loops back on the south. He takes his time, peering in windows, studying his reflection in the tall glass, the trickle of pedestrian traffic behind him, the still-green trees. It's a warm September day, and he carries his suit coat draped over an arm. His shirt collar is unbuttoned, tie long gone— ruched up behind the sun visor in his car. He nods to the few women he passes, keeping an eye out for anyone he might know. A story in his head: a meeting with council members, the Rotary, or some other such everyday nonsense. He finds no need to use it, though. He is footloose. He laughs. Truant.

He stops in at an antique shop, finds his way to the back of the store and a small booth that favors old postcards, vintage photo albums. He fingers his way through a box of old photos, stopping to study a few: a young man swimming; a towheaded youngster on a tricycle, chubby knees smudged with dirt; a couple perched on the hood of an old De-Soto. These he sets aside. Finds photos from the turn of the century, from the twenties, and pre–World War II. He picks a dozen. He's partial to the photo of a bearded old man in religious garb. Thinks, *An uncle, perhaps? Father Sean, to be sure. And here—spinster Aunt Ellie.* He picks out one from the fifties with a portly woman sitting in a lawn chair, a plate of food balanced on her bumptious lap. He shies clear of group shots that might differ too widely from the singles. It's an amiable collection. He looks for something a bit more exotic, but this is Idaho, so how exotic can you get? He fingers deeper into the bin and comes up with the picture of a young cowboy standing next to a corral, a lariat dangling from a hand. Even in the shade of the cowboy hat, his eyes squint. Ned tries to imagine him in the family. As a father, say. Not a fussy thing about him—his jeans gusseted in dirt, shirt collar opened to the throat, an impudent grin. He studies the crafty hands, the slouch in the man's hip as he stands with a foot cocked on the corral rail. He looks at the photos that have found their way to a small pile on the counter. He picks them up, fans them like a deck of cards.

There's a moment of panic. *It doesn't necessarily mean anything. Just keeping the options open.* He waits a beat or two, then carries them to the counter. Pays in cash. The merchant glances up from the little TV he has set up behind the counter, and then gets to the business of making change.

No one ever questions these purchases, these photographic odds and ends—as if it's the most ordinary thing in the world to do. A world of men and women buying families wholesale out of secondhand stores and junk shops. He tucks the package into the inside pocket of his suit coat. It could all come to nothing, and over the years he might slip them into his family album. Say to Nance, Look what I found, or maybe he'd just drop them in the garbage, or hand them out to the kids at school.

He's walking the avenue with a new lift in his step. He ducks his head at two middle-aged women, says, "Afternoon, ladies." He flashes a smile, then pulls open a store door for them and holds it. Enjoys the blush that seeds their cheeks. He strikes off westward.

He passes a small coffee shop with a hip ambience—moody and a bit cerebral for Lewiston—with its stacks of books and magazines, its small lending library in back and espresso machine up front. A month or so ago, the doors closed for good when the owner threw her hands up in disgust and chased all the customers out in the middle of business hours because she'd run out of ice.

The final straw.

Ned understands completely. Sometimes that's all it takes: running out of ice one time too many. He works his way down the street and sidetracks into the far corner of a parking lot that's a block short of the YWCA's shelter for abused women. He steps up to a small plaque fixed into the brick and cement wall. It reads: MARY THE ELEPHANT. SHE ONLY WANTED A DRINK OF WATER.

He puts his hand on the plaque that marks the spot where, back in the late twenties, a circus animal was shot. It was a small Asian elephant, one of a troupe of elephants in a traveling circus unloaded from train cars down on Snake River Avenue. The animals had been without water long enough that at least one of them became frantic.

He'd read about it, sometimes likes to picture it. The smallest of the elephants, Mary, charging down Main Street, through the crowds that have gathered to see the circus. The handlers with their sticks and prods try to drive her back—at least one of them badly hurt—and the women in their long skirts, running. The kids in knickers beating a track ahead of the elephant, as if it's a game.

It charges down the street, breaking the great panes of windows, trailing a wake of glass that glitters like diamond chop. What a great hullabaloo that must have been. He thinks about the screams. The animal's. The women's. He'd have liked to have heard it.

Until Mary gets to this point, a garage where they'd been washing cars, and turns in, stampeding two young schoolteachers ahead of her, chasing them up onto a balcony and holding them hostage there while she takes her fill of water.

Ned smiles. Because this is the way it always happens. The Snake and Clearwater rivers—the confluence of the two, the thing she must have smelled, all that water, is still a short two blocks away, but her frenzy to get there has been abated by this small pool on the garage floor, by the scrub buckets, the trough of rinse water. He imagines her grunty pleasure, the massive body swaying from side to side, eyes glazing with relief as she dips her trunk in. The handlers are moving around the now-quiet animal. They must be sweaty, flushed with the heat, the chase, and wiping their foreheads with the tag ends of shirts. Laughing among themselves. Maybe dipping a hand or two alongside the elephant's trunk into the water and dousing their hot foreheads, their sweaty scalps. Knowing she'll be calm now. She'll be the good old Mary she's always been. Hears them talking to one another: *Not that much bother, really. Thinks herself a bit of a princess now and then, but who's to say she ain't? You see that woman running ahead of her? Bit o' an elephant herself.*

It's now then that the mayor comes on the scene—noted big-game hunter, rifle levered over his arm. Aiming to shoot himself a *damned elephant*. And he does. Walks up to the quiet animal, raises his rifle, sites in. Shoots it square behind the ear.

Mary goes down.

Down like a building collapsing on its foundation, crumpling pillars bowing out and toeing under, ribs billowing just before they snap like tent stakes, and all along the length of spine is an implosion of bone as the gravid mass sifts earthward, a slow shifting that quakes up the torso in fleshy waves, stops at the juncture where the head with its ridiculously small ears and otherworld's trunk folds back on its body to look one last time to where the handlers stand on locked knees, to where the mayor is already turning away. Looks back to where the garage door opens onto the wide blue of the sky and the overlapping hills with their splotched grasses and domed prominences appear gravid and elephantine themselves. These pachyderm hills that must have for some instant seemed like distant kin.

He ponders briefly what it feels like to be chased down the streets, to run for the bright smell of water and be shot just as your thirst is quenched. Was it hugely satisfying, he wonders, to be finished, finally and utterly. Not just with thirst but with all your appetites. Exonerated in the end. He can almost envy Mary. Even as he understands the impulse that killed her, a thirst all its own.

He turns from the plaque, still musing about the mayor and his request for a trophy—a leg to be hollowed out for an umbrella stand, say, or the tail as a whisk. Some small keepsake. A memento of his big-game hunt in downtown Lewiston, Idaho. So they sawed off the trunk. Gave it to him. And Mary's trunk, story has it, was stretched and mounted on a board, and it's still hanging in a house—belonging to a descendant of the mayor's—somewhere up in the quiet residential area of Normal Hill, along with his other trophy kills. Ned imagines the trunk, a sad, limp thing next to springbok and kudu, lion and bear.

He turns away, walks back to D Street, where he's parked, slips into the heated interior of his car, and opens the window for fresh air. A glorious day, after all. A fine day for hooky. He almost feels bad for Cate, for the mess he's left her. He sets his suit coat on the seat next to him, pats the jacket to hear the crinkle of bag inside, the compact package of photos. *Just an exercise. A diversion. Nothing more.* When he pulls out onto the street, he knows exactly where he needs to go. He drives back toward his sister-in-law's house by way of Main Street, past the parking lot with its sad little plaque, past the closed coffee shop and the ruin of fired buildings. Overall, a satisfactory little place, he thinks. He's already feeling nostalgic, though he doesn't understand why. It's not as if he's already gone.

Chapter Eleven

N ance can't explain it, for although there's been no tangible threat, for the last week she's felt on the edge of something and every corner's a potential drop-off. If asked to trace the feeling, she'd lay it down to being snake-bit. Her vulnerability. The way she'd let her defenses lapse, and the anger with which she went after Meredith. She blames the general state of confusion she finds herself in so much of the time.

Even walking downstairs to the smells of bacon and coffee, her steps shorten and she wishes she could do an about-face out the front door to find some quiet cafeteria where she could sit down, have a cup of coffee and a bite of toast, next to a *genuine* stranger.

It's no secret anymore that she and Ned are having trouble. Some mornings while passing their old room, she will see he's already gone, the bed so neatly made that she can't help but wonder how early he left. Or if he'd even been in it. It is, in some respects, like living with a ghost— or suddenly discovering she's become one herself.

When she enters the kitchen, he's seated at the table, a newspaper opened in his hands. He doesn't look up as she enters, or as she crosses the room to the coffeepot. The newspaper remains raised when she stands with a cup in hand across the table from him.

"Ned," she says. *There must be a better way?* "I thought maybe we could talk this morning?"

The paper doesn't stir. He's staring at the bottom of a page.

Nance clears her throat, repeats his name. She pulls her chair out, tips the paper down with a finger. "I thought—" she says, and is taken back by the startled expression on his face, as if he's surprised to see her there, her hand on the newspaper. She can see he's struggling to compose himself.

"Caught me daydreaming," he says.

Nance nods. "You do a lot of that these days."

"Do I?" He's staring past her shoulder. She could swear he's on the verge of drifting off again.

"We need to talk," she says, her voice rising, keeping him present.

He sets the paper down. Cocks his head. "Anytime. We can talk anytime." Then he's standing up, folding the paper under his arm as if he means to leave.

"Now, Ned. I want to talk now."

He seems uncertain what to do. He looks at the hallway behind her, and then back down at the table with its scraps of cold eggs, limp bacon. "Well, I've already finished," he says. "Maybe later?"

"I think we should separate, Ned. I could rent a room, or move in with Meredith. Give us some real distance to think this through."

The paper's neatly tucked up under his arm, but there's something loose about his face. As if he doesn't understand. As if he's genuinely surprised.

"Surely you've thought of this?" she says.

He takes a long moment. It's an almost pleasurable musing, and then there's a flicker deep in his eyes, and he fumbles with the paper, shifts it from under one arm to the other. He shakes his head. "No, I hadn't." He looks down at the breakfast setting he'd laid out for her: the bowl of cereal untouched, the sliced oranges. "More coffee?"

"No, Ned, I don't need more coffee."

The possibility of infidelity occurs to her, as it has any number of times these last few weeks. A thing she's been reluctant to entertain. "Is there another woman, Ned? Is that what's going on?"

His head snaps up, eyes widening. He laughs. "I can't believe you'd even think that. When have I ever given you reason to believe . . ."

He moves away from the table. "There are no other women, Nance.

None," he says, his gaze steady. "None." He crosses his heart with his fingers. "Hope to die."

She shakes her head. His look is so genuine, the gesture so childlike, she feels compelled to believe him. She sighs. "Then I don't know what to think. What's changed us."

He holds the newspaper in hand, turning it about, front and back. His mouth opens, closes. Then he says, "We've hit a bad patch, that's all. You don't get a divorce for a bad spot in the road. A pothole." He waits a moment, then walks out of the kitchen and into the hallway.

Nance is on her feet and following. "It's not that easy, Ned. This is not a bump in the road, a pothole. A sinkhole maybe. Come on, Ned, we live at opposite ends of the house." She reaches out, tugs on the back of his shirt. "We rarely speak to each other, let alone *talk*."

He stops. Turns. "Hey, we're *talking* now, aren't we?"

"Are we? So then tell me. Where is it you go to when you disappear for whole hours at a time?"

He shrugs, turns, and starts up the stairs. "Tell you what, Nance. Why don't you just insert a little chip in my back, too. Then you could track all my movements. Keep it in a little book along with your snakes."

He pivots on the step. "Maybe I like my privacy. Maybe I'm just beginning to appreciate how much I need some time to myself."

He climbs the stairs, speaking over his shoulder. "Ride it out, Nance. We just ride it out. All marriages go through this sort of thing." At the top of the stairs, he shrugs. "We'll be better for it."

"I don't know that I believe that, Ned." Nance reaches the top of the stairs, steps to his side. Wants to hold him back a moment but can't bring herself to take his hand.

He enters their old room, where he walks over to the bed and sits. His shoulders slump. "A few months from now, a year at the most, we'll look back at this time and wonder what it was all about. Trust me."

Trust. *Shouldn't that be easy?* She thinks about Joe. *Never an issue then, was it?*

He pulls his T-shirt over his head. Looks at her from under it. "I got to get ready for work. You want to watch?"

Hard to explain why the suggestion's so upsetting. Coming on the heels of an argument, it feels . . . brazen. Nance turns away.

By early afternoon, she's hauled out her bags, imagines what to put in each, though she is unwilling to pack them—to turn tail and run.

"Just ride it out," he said.

Can't do that either, though, can she.

All morning, it's felt as if a lid has been clamped over the valley, the air still and hot. But now, through the opened screens, she feels the first of a new wind stirring, the hint of a front moving in. *Just another dry storm?* She wonders. Whatever it is, it has her restless, as well. The walls of the house suddenly too close for comfort.

When she leaves, the bags are left empty and open on the bed. She steps out onto the porch, looks west to where the wind is riffling in, the leaves of the sycamores twitching like anxious hands. She drives to his school, intent on bringing this thing between them to a head. She'll talk him into a walk, where it might be easier for the both of them, outside the familiarity of the house.

She pulls up outside the school, glances at the far corner where she knows his office is. She enters through the wide front door. Inside are the usual smells of chalk dust and floor polish. Hamburger and a little backbite of tomato sauce. Spaghetti? From the cafeteria comes the high-pitched chatter of children, as if the weather brewing outside has sifted in under the doors and stirred them up, as well.

Ned's secretary's behind the counter, elbows braced on the tabletop, chin slumped on a palm. She sees Nance and straightens her back. She smiles. "Good to see you, Nance. Been awhile."

Nance nods, inquires after Cate's family, then asks to see Ned.

Cate glances over at the closed door. She laughs, a high, nervous whinny. "He's gone out."

"Well, if I could leave a message?"

Cate stands, crosses around the counter, and slings Nance's arm under her own. She pats her hand. "Why don't you come with me?"

It takes Nance a moment to orient in the half-light of his office. The blinds are drawn. There's a closeted smell, as in the room of a shut-in. Cate leads her to his desk. The top is crowded with three orderly stacks of papers. His pen is pigeonholed in the pen holder, which is squared off in a corner. She can't help but think of his dresser at home, the bundles of shirts, ordered in stacks by color and sleeve length.

She looks at the walls. No pictures. No knickknacks or memorabilia. *There isn't a personal thing here.* Even the awards and diplomas lining the walls have a uniform anonymity, with their identical dime-store frames— as if he'd bought a crate of them at a liquidation sale.

"I thought you should see," Cate says, pointing at the desk. "The only thing that changes is the order of what's on top."

"Yes?"

"Nothing's getting done. Not really." She fusses with one of the stacks. "I've taken care of what I can, but . . ." She waves her hand at one of the file drawers. "There's a backlog in there I can't begin to manage."

"I don't understand." Nance fingers through a few papers. "What's he do during the days?"

Cate shrugs. "I don't come in much when he's here." She points at the windows. "He spends a lot of time looking out—watching over the little ones on the playground." She smiles. "I've always thought that sweet, you know?"

Nance nods.

"But it's all he does now. That and monitor the computer. Scrolling Web sites. Says he needs to keep in touch with what the kids are exposed to out there."

Nance doesn't find that so alarming, is, in fact, relieved by what she's hearing. "So? He's not keeping up with the paperwork?"

Cate tugs on a file drawer, revealing files crosshatched and bulging inside. "I can't do this work. It needs *his* attention. I've filtered what I can to Rod, the vice principal. But people are starting to notice. I thought maybe you should know. You could talk to him?"

Quite a revelation.

After that, she drives home, but doesn't have to stop to know he's not there. She cruises past her street. Drives Main, turns up Thain. She's not sure what she's looking for, but her heart quickens each time she sees a car like his. The wind is blowing in fits and starts, and on the horizon she sees a boil of red clouds, a quick punch of lightning.

She drives over to her sister's house, parks at the curb. Meredith's on the steps, looking out over the western hills. Another crackle of light, and the wind rattles dust and paper down the street. Nance hurries out of the car and across the lawn, hugs her sister, and the two of them run for shelter.

It's a fast-moving front. A hard blow of wind, a crack of lightning, and then thunder cannonading down the range of hills. The sisters watch as the storm grinds down on them, the air red with dust from the farmlands of eastern Washington. A raft of newspapers tumbles down the street, and a young cat gives it a short humpbacked chase before streaking back into the sheltering shrubs.

They move inside, go into the kitchen, where they can look out at the darkening hills. Over a glass of ice water, Nance tells Meredith what has been going on. What she's discovered about Ned's work.

They sit silent a long while, and then the sky is already brightening, the storm having mostly passed. There's the distant sound of sirens. Nance looks at her watch; it's nearing four o'clock. He'd normally be coming home soon, another couple hours. But who's to say what's normal anymore?

She knows she needs to talk with him, but she dreads it. Inordinately. *And what kind of wife does that make you? He's still your husband, isn't he?* She believes herself competent, intelligent. A capable woman. Not a person she'd consider timid or fearful. But she admits to feeling . . . nervous. "He makes me feel anxious"—isn't that what Meredith's always said?

When she glances up, Meredith's looking at her. "You're thinkin' of going home, aren't you?"

Nance nods.

"Think he'll be there?"

"I think I need to find out."

Meredith looks out the window at the hills. "Damn. I knew you were going to say that. I'll get my jacket."

"That's not necessary," Nance says, but she has the sudden feeling it is, even knowing how Ned feels about Meredith. She's just as certain Meredith shouldn't be there. She sinks her head into her hands. When did she come to be so . . . uncertain? So wishy-washy?

"I'll just stay until I'm sure everything's cool, okay?"

Nance looks up. "Christ, what do you think? That he's going to hurt me?"

Meredith doesn't answer. She lifts a jacket from a hook on the back of the kitchen door. Nance rises to her feet, feels stiff in the joints, as if she's aged just sitting at the table.

Walking down the front steps, Nance hesitates. "Do you really think this is a good idea? You coming along?"

Meredith snugs an arm around her sister's shoulders. "It'll be fine, Sis. Just think of me as a little ballast in heavy waters."

Atop the hills, a column of smoke is rising into the sky. Nance watches it build a long moment. "Hill's on fire."

Meredith opens the truck door, pauses as she steps up onto the running board. She looks over her shoulder to where Nance points. There's the sound of fire engines in the distance. "Go figure . . . When it rains, it burns." Then she's settling into the passenger side of Nance's truck. "Giddyup," she says.

The house is dark. The hills above the valley are mantled in smoke. Nance can smell the sweet burning grass. She looks down the valley and then across the river and west to the range of hills where the fire is concentrated but moving easterly. She's glad for the broad swath of water between her house and the fire. She looks at the scattered ranches across the way, the small houses dotting the near hills and the road that winds among them—the old Spiral Highway, an unlikely escape route. She imagines the traffic creeping down the wider Lewiston grade, headlights on to pierce the veil of smoke. Wonders if Ned's somewhere on the prairie or down in the valley itself. If he's watching the burn even as she is.

They cross the street, and when they enter the house, Meredith's at Nance's heels. The house is cool, and Nance opens the drapes to let in the last of the afternoon's sunlight. Meredith's chirping along, mostly about plans for a late-fall trip upriver with Pete. She follows Nance into the study, where she picks up Ramone, looks him eye-to-eye before putting him back down. "You could come with us," she says. "Give your snakes a good-night kiss before bed."

"I'm sure they'd appreciate that," Nance says, then stands listening to the vaulting silence of the house. There's no message on the answering machine, but she hadn't really expected one.

"You hungry?" she asks.

Meredith nods. "What you got?"

Nance leads the way. The kitchen's clean, counters cleared. The pantry shelves are stocked, and the refrigerator is quietly humming. She's struck by the ordinariness of the place—feels again as if she's over-reacted. How could anything be wrong with everything so normal?

"Just a snack," Meredith says. "Cheese? Crackers? Nothing that's a lot of work." She looks at her hands. "I should wash up." And then she's gone, leaving Nance to peruse the fridge.

Nance sets out the cheese board, slices some cheddar and pops a left-over wedge of Brie into the microwave. Nukes it. She slices apple into thin strips. She's searching through the cabinet for crackers when she becomes aware that Meredith hasn't returned. She doesn't hear water running. Doesn't hear anything. "Hey, Sis?" she calls out. She walks into the living room, backtracks into the central hallway, calls up the stairs. "Sis? You up there?"

Nance stands at the foot of the stairs and the light through the hall window dims and then wavers toward bright. Dust drifts in motes down the staircase, and Nance notices the small puffs of fuzz that have been shepherded alongside the carpet. She hesitates, then climbs the stairs. Upstairs, her sister's not in the bathroom. Nance turns down the hallway to the guest bedroom—her room these past weeks—where her bags are still open, lying empty on the bed.

She finds Meredith in the master bedroom—Ned's room now—rummaging through his dresser.

"What are you doing?" Nance asks.

"Going through his things," she says.

"Well, stop it. Those are *his* things."

"So? You're his wife."

Nance walks into the room, lifts a manila envelope from her sister's hands. "But you're not."

"Right. Point taken. What's in it?" She reaches over to flip open the clasp.

Nance looks in, sees photographs. She pulls a few out. They're old, some of them gone to sepia and gritty with age and touch.

"Family album?"

"No, that's downstairs."

"Curiouser and curiouser," Meredith says.

Nance fingers through the pictures. Some have writing on the back. She walks them over to the window. She squints. "Can you read these?"

Meredith stands at her elbow, looking at the back of a picture. "'Abigail.' It says 'Abigail Turnbull, 1942.'"

Nance sorts through the others and finds another scribed in pencil. She studies the image: a young sailor on hands and knees, swabbing the deck of a ship, a gun turret at his back. His sleeves are rolled up, cap tipped back on his head. There's a sheepish smile on his face. It's a touching photo, and she finds it hard to reconcile this young navy man with the elderly recluse, the lover of cats, and, finally, the stinking corpse across the street. Remembers now that the police had thought someone else had discovered the body first.

Where was Ned when she walked back across the street? On the porch. And didn't he seem, at the time, strangely unsurprised. Asking, "So what did he look like? The old man?"

She drops the photos back in. "They're Turnbull's. The old guy across the street." She drops the envelope on the bed, walks over to the dresser and shoves aside Ned's sweaters, tosses a couple shirts onto the chair.

Meredith snatches at her hand. "What are you doing?"

"Finding out what else I don't know about my own husband."

"He'll know we've been in here."

Nance nods, her jaw set. "Your problem being?"

Meredith lets go of her hand and they stand that way a long moment, looking at each other.

"You said it yourself. *I'm his wife.*"

Meredith shrugs and says, "I'll check the closet and under the bed."

Nance remembers her dream—old man Turnbull stashed beneath—and nearly has to sit down. She's suddenly uncertain she wants to go any further with this. She braces herself, opens a second drawer, and starts in.

They make quick work of it, and Nance is the one who hears the rub of paper brushing against clothes when she closes the bottom drawer. She finds a second envelope tucked in the drawer slats.

Meredith looks at the chaos they've created and starts cramming things into open drawers, but Nance is walking out of the room with the two envelopes tucked under her arm, and so Meredith gives it over and follows.

In the kitchen, Nance slaps the envelopes onto the counter. On the butcher block, the snack of apples and crackers wait; the heated Brie has cooled into a stiff slump in the microwave. Neither sister touches the food. Instead, Nance retrieves the thin album from the living room and sets it on the counter, where they compare the new pool of pictures alongside Ned's family photos.

Amazing. No two people looking that much alike or unalike that any other two couldn't be substituted. A generic batch so scattered over time that any changes could be chalked up to aging, bad camera angles, lighting. Easy enough. Genus and species: *Homo sapiens,* of the family Anonymous; subspecies . . .

Meredith's shaking her head. "I don't get it."

Nance looks at the wall clock. It's half past five. She looks out the window over the kitchen sink. It's still light out, but that's starting to fade with the haze building on the hills, the sun cowled in smoke. It's going to be a big fire after all. She briefly wonders about the people whose homes are in the way of the fire. They're probably already packing up the kids and dogs, and if given a choice, most families would pack the family photos next.

But what about the ones who are gone, say, having left the house to run errands? A day trip to Spokane, or up into Moscow or Pullman. How could they imagine that by evening they'd arrive in time to see their lives have burned down around them. They'll want someone to blame. They'll start with the firemen and sheriffs, then the town council, and work their way up the ladder, even blaming God, for all the good it'll do. Last resort? They'll turn on themselves. They will blame themselves: for not having kept the green belt around the home; for spending the day away when there'd been plenty of work to do right here; for not having had some inkling of disaster—a kind of precognition, which some of them may even claim to have had, in some future place, on a better day than this one.

How could you know? There's a hitch in her breathing, like a dull probe beneath one of her own ribs. A lightning strike. Three teens in a park.

A baseball bat, of all things.

Something that benign. She looks down at the photos.

She's nervous about the second envelope: ordinary, letter-size, thin, the flap tucked in. There's a tiny crawling on her skin, the small hairs rising on her arms, the back of her neck. She opens the envelope to a bit of newsprint. It's a story and photo of a woman murdered back in the twenties. The photo's grainy and old, and while the newspaper reproduction doesn't do it much justice, she can see the woman's clothed and lying on a table. Obviously dead. Face turned away. The whole *thing* looking plumply sodden. There's a caption beneath: "Lady of the Lake, Lake Crescent, Washington." She scans the article: A woman, murdered by her husband, is pulled up by fishermen from the bottom of a lake ten years later. Her body's mummified by the cold. Adipocere. Nance knows about this: cool, moist, anaerobic, the perfect conditions for this kind of mummification.

She looks up at her sister. There's a grim set about Meredith's mouth. Nance holds her hand out, and Meredith hands over the other clippings that have dropped from the envelope. One of the more recent, from the *Lewiston Morning Tribune,* early summer of this year. A couple found badly beaten in a motel room: the man in critical condition, the woman stitched up and released from the hospital. In a side note: same motel—another man found a room away, dead of aspiration. The motel owner quoted as saying, "I don't know nothing about it. But they was all together earlier. Mighta been one more with 'em."

She picks up another column, her heart beginning to jump. This one, a rape and beating in Pullman. Another in Grangeville. One in Spokane. In Colfax, a missing person. Some older clippings. More missing persons. All women. The small clippings feel so slight in her hands, her fingers stiff and thick. She shakes her head, feels as if she's having trouble processing the information, fails to understand what it all amounts to. She backtracks, looks through the clippings and the descriptions of "men of interest" middle-aged, older, young, tall to medium height; blond hair, brown hair, wearing a cap.

Meredith's pacing the kitchen, stops to look out the window, glances back at the clock, and starts her pacing again. Nance wants to tell her to stop, to stand still for a moment. She wants the house to grow quiet once more, for it seems now to be full of minute rustlings: a draft through the window, a mouse scrabbling along the wood floor, the loose string wagging from the edge of the curtain. Nance is overwhelmed, trying to absorb what it is she already knows: that her husband is not who she thought he was, that her life is not what she believed, and that this home and everything in it is now somehow suspect.

Meredith's tugging on her arm. "Come on, Sis. Let's go."

"Where?"

"Anywhere. To my house. To the police."

"And tell them what? That my husband's turned odd. That he collects other people's family photos and calls them his own. That he keeps old newspaper clippings?"

"Fine. Then you tell me."

"Wait until he comes home."

"And?"

"Ask him about this." Nance spreads her hands over the counter's contents.

"Just like that."

"Just like that."

"And what do you think he'll do?"

"Tell me the truth."

Meredith slaps her forehead with the palm of her hand. It's surprisingly loud. "The truth," she says. "*Now* he's going to tell you the truth. And you"—she nails Nance's chest with a finger—"are going to recognize it?"

Nance raises her chin. "I have to believe I can."

"Christ Almighty, woman. What does it take?"

Nance sets the clippings down, drills them with a finger. "More than I've got here." And even as she's saying this, she knows she has more. It's the thing she hasn't told Meredith. She feels his hand around her wrist again, her arm cranked up against her back. *What more does it take?* More. *More than that?* Yes.

"Fine." Meredith slaps her hand down on the counter. "You got a gun?"

Nance shakes her head.

"Does he?"

"Not as far as I know." She looks at the scattered photos, the articles. She keeps seeing the sad smiles on the faces in his gallery. If he was going to collect a mute collection of strangers for family, why these? What is it about them? She's studying the women in particular for something in her own face reminiscent of those others. Studies the set of their eyes, the abstracted look—as if they'd already been removed from the picture, only the photographer has failed to notice.

"I'd take it out in public. You know? Leave a note saying where he can find us. A nice public place. Like a restaurant?"

"I don't know," Nance says. She's stopped sorting through pictures and is beginning to listen. *Pick your spot.* Study the lay of the land. You don't put yourself between a snake and a hard place. She has a moment of confusion, wondering what she's trying to redefine. Her home? Or her husband? As that nondescript man of variable age, hair color, and height. But what if this collection is just a closet interest? She looks up at her sister, sees a fierceness there—in the way she stands, in her face. Imagine that. Little Meredith.

And yes, she *should* leave, get the hell out. Head for the nearest bright spot. Someplace public, where the crowds will hold her up even if her legs won't. But she's unwilling to give fear that much room to maneuver. She's learned that one the hard way, after Joe's death. So you run? Where does it get you? Away from the violence of the big city. Out into the great open spaces of the West, where the violence is just as real, and often just as random—as close as a madman down the block. The guy next to you in church. The snake in the brush. So then what? Where do you go when the running runs out? What's left?

Be brave. That's been mostly a matter of locking her knees against the impulse to run. "I'm not leaving," she says. She needs to take this one on home turf.

Meredith's shaking her head. "Goddamn it. How you can be so dense? Don't you see?" Her voice rises.

"What I see"—Nance pushes a photo forward and another, another—"is this and this." She shoves the clippings forward. "I see *all* this speculation. Bits of paper. We're two girls again, in the dark and scaring each other with stories. Only this isn't a story, it's my goddamned life. So I have to *know.* Do you understand? *I have got to know*, and I don't know how else to go about it other than stay right here and face him."

"What do you want? Proof positive?

Nance shakes her head. "Proof *enough*."

Meredith is standing at the side of the counter, contemplating the floor. When she looks back up, she nods. "I should have guessed." She pauses, then says, "So, is it hot in here, or what?"

"A bit."

Meredith looks at the back door. "Then how about we go outside. We could do the porch, hey? That's still close enough to home, isn't it?

Nance smiles and slips her arm around her sister's waist. Gives her a hug. "Should we bring the food?"

But when the sisters look at the snacks, neither of them is hungry, and so they leave them.

Outside, the light has a smudged quality, and, as if viewed through a Vaseline-coated lens, the hills have softened, features blunted under a wrap of gray. Across the river and against the base of the as-yet-unburned hills, lights of fire trucks glitter red among the blue of police vehicles. Closer by, down the row of neighboring lawns, she sees her neighbors standing in yards, or on porches or decks, and leaning over fences for news. But it isn't until an hour later, when the people start making their way back into the houses and the lights switch on in kitchens, that she begins to understand the pace of this thing. The color to the west is strengthening as the sky deepens. A thin bleed of red spreads against the brown grasses, and the black smoke spools upward, expanding eastward in a lid over the valley.

Dry lightning. A zigzag of light, a crack of noise, and a small pillar of smoke rises on the hills across the river. A few head of cattle scatter and then gather again to drift upwind. It builds a spearhead on the lamb's ears, the cheat grass, and star thistle that flank the hills, and by the time the fire engines arrive, the fire has snaked its way through the hackberry and buck brush, gained momentum on the sun-crisped fescue, and is channeling the smoke up through a gulley, building like a landlocked thunderhead over the prairie. It is late afternoon, so there's just a hint of color—a blush on the underbelly of the smoke, an opalescent here-and-gone quality to it.

When the lightning strikes, Ned's sitting at Roosters Landing, a restaurant and marina on the Washington side of the confluence of the Snake and Clearwater rivers. He's seated outside on the deck. His boot heels are hooked over the iron railing, baseball cap pulled down over his brow. Below, the marina with its piers, gas pump, and bait shop. Coupled to the floating docks are two cabin cruisers with the names *Pier Pressure* and *Kiss My Wake*. There's one small wooden sailboat, an elegant little vessel, the *Skookum II,* looking out of place among the numerous jet boats and Jet Skis. There's a clanking and the squeegee sound of tires rubbing between boat and dock as the winds hike waves over the floating walkways. At the water's edge, a few ducks huddle in the shallows, and the school of carp—fattened on the bits of gristle, french fries, and biscuits that the diners throw down—rolls from side to side, rocked in cradles of sand.

He's the only one outside. The other customers have fled to tables inside. Even the waitresses have stopped asking about his needs and fret on the other side of the door. But Ned's enjoying the weather, the wind that skates the other plastic chairs onto the far side of the deck.

It's front-row seating on the approaching storm—the wadded ball of clouds that, in a year of drought such as this one, will expend itself in dry lightning and move on.

Horizontal rivers of light ford the cloud banks, quicksilver streams branching out over the hills, lifting the static grasses and prickling the hides of feeding cattle below. There's the frieze of light against dark sky, snap and gone. Then the puny streak of smoke like a snuffed wick, and the quiet that follows. In fact, he is one of the few who actually sees the fire's genesis, that first spark hopping from the crown of the hill, the instantaneous flash and crack that startles even the diners safely seated behind windows, so that they jostle water glasses, or drop forks, or bump knees on table braces.

Ned's squarely seated, giving no more indication of the strike across the water than a blink and a click of teeth. It's as if he's fused to the planks, and the planks to the ground, and the ground to the river. The river, he sees, is just a sad reflection of the hierarchy of light overhead, while the thunder firing down the range of hills and drumming in his chest confirms to him they are hollow. Drilled, and cored. He's a marsh reed. A snag of clothes on a stick. A fence of slats that won't keep out the wind. When he unfolds from the chair, unhooks his heels, and lifts himself, he feels comfortably removed, like a pilot steering a skiff that lists into the wind, and he plants his feet a long moment before stepping off. He walks through the door and into the restaurant, stops to pay his bar bill. He leaves a generous bit for the waitress, smiles his most charming way, and then heads out the front door.

The wind rocks the car and a scattering of large drops hit and run down the windshield in rusty tracks. He turns left onto the road that crosses the river at the Red Wolf crossing—the bridge an elegant concrete arc over the pewter river. Very pretty. He slows on the upgrade, wondering where it was that, years before Ned had ever come here, some other man stopped his car in the dead of night to drop a woman's body, piecemeal, into the current below.

There was more to its unlovely history of accidents and intent—the guy who toppled off, the car wrecks, the jumpers. There's no other traffic, so he idles. The clouds have bunkered over the hills, masking the place where he'd seen the strike. When he looks at the water rushing below, he senses what it is about bridges that attracts murderers and suicides. He gives the car gas and is rolling on the downside to where the road skirts the base of the hills. Perhaps it's in the nature of bridges, he thinks, an affinity with the desperate—their tenuous stance in the world, a foot on each shore, neither here nor there. The convenient abyss between.

He turns left onto the road paralleling the Snake. All the dead brewing in the current, the ones no one thinks to look for, the odd parts, or oddballs. He knows enough of its history to know that its usual calm is a slippery surface. The Snake.

He's traveling the same speed as the current, past the port of Wilma, with its double-decked pallets of milled lumber, and at the far end of the yard the shaggy-barked logs piled in high, wide mounds, waiting for shipment. Then there's the river, and the docks. The cranes with their cables and winches idle in the late-afternoon lull. The road follows the greater pool of Lower Granite Lake—the backwash from Lower Granite Dam hemmed in between the the steeply slanted canyon walls. Center river is a wedge of land, Chief Timothy Park, abandoned to a host of solitary gulls, fisher birds: cormorant, heron, and kingfisher.

The road he's on, Wawawai, follows the east fork of the slack water, and it's a two-lane road with little or no shoulder. Past the bend, where the railroad tracks switch from riverside to hillside, all that separates him from the ten-foot drop to water is a short metal guardrail—its fractious history recorded in dents and pleats.

The heart of the storm is beating on the far side, the rumbles distant from the streaky light, and periodically he glances up. The hills are sheer rock face, undercut by the forces of an ancient flooding. Here and there, a shallow cave is pocked into the rock. Then there are the long steep inclines of shale, the fragile balance between the angle of slope and slide as easily upset by too much rain as by a slow freeze, or fast thaw.

Trackside, just clear of the rabbitbrush that crowds a five-string barbwire fence: Here the land lurches away in sudden side canyons, and he passes a spread where a clutch of cattle stand, backs to the wind on the hillside. There's the Nisqually rest area, and a couple miles farther down, the Blyton recreation area, both of which are little wider than a pullout. He's within a couple miles of the Wawawai County Park when he comes upon the young woman biking into the wind. He imagines her caught by the sudden weather. A long way from home. And this being the only way out, for at the other end, there's nothing more than a thousand-foot climb up a twisting road through Steptoe Canyon before surfacing on top of the prairie.

Ned keeps going, travels the last five miles at a leisurely pace, turns left into the park, a small bit of green with an even smaller inlet off the main body of water. There is an outdoor pagoda, its roof stacked like a witch's hat, and a grouping of picnic tables. Willows line the shore, and a stand of black locust winds between the outbuildings and the road.

Ned parks the car, feels the buffeting wind. There's one other car, a Saab, and a lone figure in a hooded coat standing on the small isthmus of land between the main body of water and the pond. No one else. But why would there be? It's a weekday, a workday, and glancing at his watch, he notices that it's been an hour or more since the dependable Cate's locked up. There's a curious opaqueness settling into the canyon air, a thin brine of ozone and smoke. He backs the car out, heads past the grove of locusts, through the hairpin turn at the entrance, and back upriver.

When he sees the woman, he slows. He pulls alongside and lowers the window. "Do you need help?" he calls across the seat to her.

She's smaller than he'd thought. Her head's down, hair splitting in a wake around her face, ends tucked into a zippered jacket. He can see she's tired, and cold, and, yes, frightened.

"Do you need a lift?" he asks.

She gives her head a tight shake, keeps her eyes on the road ahead, but the bike's wobbling. He believes he can hear her breathing above the sounds of the wind and the noise of his engine.

He knows what she must be thinking: *It's the rock and a hard place.* She's thinking rock, determined to stay the long haul. He pulls ahead. In the side mirror, he sees her foot slide off the pedal and touch ground, the bike stops, and the woman's holding it there between her legs. She's looking up the road to where he's pulled away.

He stops, lets the car engine run. She's walking the bike up to the side of the car. She leans into the opened passenger window. She must feel the heat wafting up from the interior, because there's a welcoming sag to her posture.

"Change your mind?" He keeps his hands at ten and two on the steering wheel.

"My bike . . ." she says.

He pops the trunk, a roomy thing. He puts the car in park and steps out, leaving the door open and the car running. "Here," he says, taking the bike from her. She's a little thing, folded into her windbreaker, knees knobbed beneath tight jeans. Gutsy, biking this stretch alone. Reminds him of Nance. He rolls the bike around to the back and sets it against the bumper. The only things in the trunk are tire iron, crowbar, jack, pipe wrench, and rope. He tosses the tire iron and jack to the deepest hold,

lifts the pipe wrench out, and it follows the others with a clank. The girl
stands there, hands pocketed, body curled inside the wimpy jacket. He
slides the bike in, cocks the wheel upright, then fastens the trunk lid with
the rope. He's headed back to the driver's side when he notices she's still
standing at the back.

"What?" he asks.

"Maybe I shouldn't," she says. She's looking down the road. And
then he sees in the distance what might be a car—the Saab from the park,
he guesses. He walks back to his side of the trunk, and the closer he
comes, the farther she backs away.

He stops, spreads his hands. "Hey," he says, and shrugs. "It's all the
same to me. Tell you what." Feels the Saab coming on. He leans his hand
on the trunk lid. "I got to go. You can stay here and try to bike out. But
there's a fire up canyon. Smell it?"

She nods.

"Could get bad pretty quick. But I'm not going to force you." He
smiles, sees that's what wins her over. As it has so many others.

She nods.

He walks to his door, settles himself in. She settles in the other side.
Looking in his rearview mirror, he sees the Saab pulling up. A woman in
the driver's seat.

He lets the car roll forward a couple inches. "Buckle up now." The
Saab has stopped behind him, and the woman's getting out, but he's already pulling away, with the girl pressed against the far side of the car,
hands tucked between her knees.

"So where's it you're going?"

She's wrapping the seat belt over her lap. "Clarkston. I just need to
get to Clarkston." She sneaks a glance. "I can bike from there."

"We can do better than that . . . I'll take you where you need to go."

"Clarkston."

Ned's humming now. The car's hugging the center line. Just the
other side of the passenger side is the rail and beyond that the water.
Her hand is on the door handle, as if with the least startle she'll throw

open the door. *And do what? Roll right into the river?* He looks up at the rearview mirror as he banks into a turn, sees the Saab has fallen behind. He eases off the gas.

"Bad day to be out," he says. "You do this often? Bike all this way? By yourself." He's looking for a bench road, an access that might track up the hillside and out of sight of the main road, a ranch drive, say, though those are chained or gated, mostly.

They speed by the stretch of steep walls with their overhangs. The black rock daubed with mud swallows' nests, and here and there shallow caves, a few that are mildly deep, little better than a crawl space. He's over the center line, corrects the drift, and when he looks into the mirror again, the Saab's closing in.

He slows. *Let her pass,* he thinks.

She follows, thirty-five in a fifty-five zone. The girl's staring out the side window. Preoccupied with the water that is so close. At Blyton, he pulls into the parking lot, thinking the Saab will coast by, but the car follows.

He feels it now, the Saab like a vestigial limb, useless and annoying. He's at a crawl on the gravel lot. "You need to use the bathroom or anything?" he asks.

The girl shakes her head, so he keeps the car rolling, right out the far end and back onto the narrow road. He picks up speed, focusing on the road. The other car's headlights have come on now and they're jigging in the mirror.

He clears his throat, feels the scratch, and realizes it's smoke. The haze is thickening, and so he shuts the vents, turns on recycled air. The engine powers down as the air kicks in. "Smoky," he says. "Must be *some fire* up canyon. Good thing for you I came along."

The girl's nodding. "I saw lightning, and I didn't know if I should get off my bike or not. . . ."

The Saab's headlights bore into the trunk, through the bike and the rope and all the useless tools, through the upholstered seats, and drill him, center back. He thinks about the driver, wants to know what the hell she's after, but when he looks back, the artificial twilight has deep-ened, and what he sees instead is the halo of headlights, and behind that the blurred hills crowding into the dark.

His hands tighten on the wheel, and he picks up speed, ignoring the way the young girl grabs at her seat belt.

"Mister," she says, her voice rising.

His headlights are blunted by smoke, and the twists and turns rise up with a suddenness that dries his mouth. The next time he glances in the mirror, he sees the Saab has fallen well behind. Still, he pushes the gas pedal a bit longer.

"Mister," the girl says again. *"Please."*

He looks over at her, and then up into the darkened mirror, and when he looks at the road ahead, it is to see the guardrail jumping up on their right, and he swings the wheel hard, so that the car sluices to a side, drifts into the other lane. He lifts his foot, steers with the slide, then countersteers as the back end skitters and grips, then skitters again on loose grit before steadying out. He eases the car into the right lane.

When his heart has slowed, when he has time to think, he hears the girl crying and feels something like shame. It confounds him. He slows. "Well, that was exciting. Maybe a little too?"

It's then he understands that it's the pitch of her voice that bothers him. How readily her tears come. He looks over but can't see her clearly in the dashboard light. The road ahead is bedded with smoke. He puts on his blinkers and fog lamps. There's a luminous quality to the fabric of air behind him.

He means to distract the girl. "You go to the college?" he asks.

The crying quiets; there's a sniff. He sees her wipe her face with a sleeve. She shakes her head.

"High school, then?"

"Next year," she says.

He believes he hasn't heard her correctly. "So, you're in . . ."

"Eighth grade." She turns her face to him. She's wearing braces. It's clear she's pleased to be thought older.

There's a pink glow in the gloom ahead and the port buildings are reconstituting themselves out of the dark, and there's the burn of road flares, as well. As they near the port itself, a fleet of emergency vehicles lines the road. A sheriff waves him to a stop. Ned opens the window to look out and up the hillside, can barely see the shapes of men in yellow jackets working the lower slope, chopping out firebreaks to contain the fire that crowns the hill.

The cop leans in, says. "Take it nice and slow," and steps back while speaking into a walkie-talkie. The Saab has closed the distance. Ned negotiates the single open lane, with an eye to the car creeping along behind him.

They cross over the Red Wolf Bridge and Ned tries not to think of the long drop, or the indelicate thoughts of body parts. Not now. Not with this child seated next to him. She directs him: a right turn, a left, and another left onto a street named Maple. When they arrive at her house, the Saab's still in tow. Parks behind him.

He gets out, unties the bike. He doesn't even look at the other car. He keeps his face down, springs the bike loose.

The girl's father is a portly man with a walrus look about his face— bristling mustache, small eyes, and domed head. He's hugging his daughter and claps the seat of her pants, says, "Your mother's half-crazy with worry," and sends her at a run for the house. He takes the bike and thanks Ned. He shakes Ned's hand, and for that moment Ned feels a real affinity for the man, and why not? Didn't he bring the child home to her family? Safe. No telling what could have happened. Who she might have met up with. A young girl out there. Alone. And that's the way he sees it. The rest of it, after all, never having happened. Not really mattering. No more than a dream. Or any one of a thousand errant thoughts he can't be held accountable for.

When he turns away, the Saab's door opens and a woman steps out. Middle-aged and big-boned. A burly yet girlish walk. She covers the distance in a few strides, and when she looks Ned up and down, he's startled by the blue of her eyes, even in this light. Then she's snatching his hand and saying, "Good to meet a Good Samaritan." She drops his hand, then plumps her own into a jacket pocket. "I saw the young girl biking earlier on. Worried about her then, and when I saw you picking her up—well, I didn't mean to doubt," she says, "but these days . . ." She looks down the street into the dark and over the tops of the houses, where a corona of light fires the near horizon. "These days, you have to be so careful."

Neds waves it off. "No harm," he says. "How could you know?"

"True," she says, "too true."

She fishes her hand out of the pocket, catches his hand in hers again, and gives it another shake. "Well, still and all, it must be difficult being a decent man these days. All the suspicion." And then she's heading back to the Saab, and when she pulls away, she floats him a cheery wave over the roof of her car. He watches the taillights trail off into the dark.

He looks up over the rooftops to the hills, to the top third of the hill that is fully engaged. It's a spectacular, splendid sight. He stands watching it a long moment before he turns away, settles into his car, where he sits another few minutes. He doesn't know how to feel. Turned upside down and around—righteous and filthy. Wonders how such things are possible.

Chapter Twelve

When he arrives home, he sees the lights are on, and so he knows Nance is there. He feels stricken—that's the word for it, *stricken*—with relief, as he couldn't bear the thought of walking into an empty house. Not now. Not tonight. Though he'd half-expected her to be gone, up country with her snakes, or at her school office, or more likely at her sister's. A place he is not welcome.

But she is clearly home, and for that he feels grateful. He wants her with him tonight. He wants to celebrate. He wants to feel her breathing at his side in his bed once again. He wants to sleep and be dreamless. He wants Tina to keep to her own bed deep in the lake. He wants to rise in the morning and find the fire has burned the hill down, all the spindrift weeds and wooden fence posts, the log remnants of the old stagecoach route. He wants a clean burn, for he feels as if he's just come to the end of a long journey, as if he's been raked up from the ashes. He thinks of the young girl. Thinks it *significant*. He locks his hands in his lap. They are trembling. He finds himself on the verge of tears, and embarrassed for it. The shadows beneath the trees slip up over the curbs and back down. A breeze chases through the branches, and the air becomes momentarily dense with smoke, which then lifts, and in the clearing air he sees the tops of the roofs burnished with the light of the distant fire. He takes a deep breath, and another. He feels himself steadying. He looks in the rearview mirror, runs the back of a hand over his eyes, his fingers through his hair.

There's a kind of energy building, a resolve to pull this all together. To take another stab at the life he has. After all, it hasn't gone that far this time. Nothing irreparable.

He jogs the stairs of his home. He strides through the living room, and then he's in the central hallway, calling, "Nance" and "Nance, I'm home."

But there's no answer, and so he takes the stairs two at a time, and then he's at the door to the guest bedroom, but she's not here, either. "Nance?" he repeats. Heads toward his room, where lights are on, and when he enters, the commotion hits him. The dresser drawers, the shirts, sweaters, jeans, underwear, and socks, a jumble on the bed, the floor. He turns in a slow circle. He feels . . . betrayed. Foolish. He's standing there with his hands at his side, and then realizes his hands are fists, and the fists are as tight as the knot in his chest.

He moves over to the bed, sits on the end of it until he can breathe properly again. Until his hands stop knotting and shaking and he can let his jaw unclench. When he feels he can handle it, he steps over to the dresser. The photos are gone. He feels under the drawer for the news clippings, pulls the drawer out, turns it over, lets it fall, and when he looks up, he sees himself in the mirror. The plump reflection. The image of a healthy, well-to-do man. He fingers the sides of his forehead where that invisible vise is beginning to clamp down. Just another turn of the same old screw. Just another goddamned thing, like the headlights on his heels and the big blowsy woman acting as his self-appointed conscience.

He can smell smoke and understands it is the new flavor of his skin.

He abandons the bedroom, walks down the stairs with his hand steady on the railing. He steps into the empty study with its computer and its file cabinets. The taxidermied snake sprawls on the bookcase, glass eyes brightly polished. He considers a different ending, something fitting, something petty. Thinks of all the fire engines, the emergency vehicles, sheriff and police bottlenecked at the base of the fire. The stuffed snake seems as if it breathes. So *damned* lifelike. He never wanted the thing in his house. He flicks its side with his finger and the tail rattles. He startles backward, and then reaches over and pinches the rattle free, shakes it in the snake's face before slipping it into his pocket.

He leaves the room. "Hey, Nance," he calls softly, and walks into the kitchen, where his *family* photos have been spread out like a game of solitaire. They're a handsome batch, and far better-looking than the real thing: his father, the chubby little man he became, steeped in self-pity. His drunken bouts. His mother, another real piece of work. As blind and deaf and about as useful as a wailing wall. His family life, his childhood, fairly normal, except for that indistinct *Boy, don't you remember how*–half-remembered–*Mustn't tell*–pain.

"Nance?" He sorts through the photos, picks out the two, and pockets them. Leaves the replaceable others. There are snacks on the butcher block, but he can't bear to think of the tacky cheese, the flat crackers. He walks up to the fridge, pulls the door open. Another wife would have had dinner on the table. Hot out of the oven. *"Meat loaf, sweetie. Just like you like it."* Like Tina. It's true–the first one's are always the best.

The racks are crammed: jars half-full, condiment lids jelled tight. Sticks of butter on a plate. Milk, juice, a six-pack of beer. He rummages through the crisper drawer, as if it might hold a message. The lightbulb at the back of the fridge is uncomfortably bright, like lights in a rearview mirror, and he pictures the knobby knees. Small hands tucked between thighs. He's humming and running his hand over the food: oranges, a grapefruit, a head of bagged lettuce. An oily slick from some bottled dressing, and he can feel at his back that familiar jerk. As if someone's there pulling all the right strings. When he straightens and steps away, he stops to listen to the quiet of the house, and beneath that he hears the conversational patter. He turns to the window over the sink, overlooking the backyard. Two voices. Nance. Her sister.

He sees it now, the food on the butcher block: the sliced cheese, crackers, and apples. How nice. Company.

He steps out into the dark. They are sitting in lawn chairs, side by side. Two dark heads, so similarly shaped, inclined toward each other.

"Just a little while longer," Nance is saying, then checks her watch, the illuminated dial a bright coin in the dark.

"But no more than that," Meredith says. "At least let's go back to the front of the house. To the porch."

But Nance doesn't answer. She's sitting with her head cocked to one side, as if she's listening to some other conversation, and Ned realizes he's humming under his breath. He stops, and Nance sits forward in her chair, calls, "Ned?"

She swings her legs around, and he considers stepping out of the shadows, but he's interested in the way she's balanced, out there, on the edge of the chair and his patience. Wonders if she understands what a fine edge it is. *Tina didn't.* He pushes that thought away. Doesn't want to go there. And just as quickly, Marla comes to mind. And another. And another that he can't place. He's pressed with his back against the house. He runs his knuckles down the brick.

Meredith's standing. "You hear something?"

There's a sigh. "Imagining things, I guess."

In the quiet, Meredith steps away from the brick patio and stands at the farthest point of lawn, on the crest of the hill.

Nance joins her overlooking the slope, the black shapes of shrubs hunching all the way down to the valley floor. And there's the valley itself, a wide fertile belt with its broadcast seeding of lights startling up from the dark in bright blooms, while mowed down its center is the black patch that is the Clearwater River, and to the west the Snake.

The hills across the way are a hot orange. The flames are launching across the dry scrub with a sound like the long intake of a breath. Behind the flame is a backwash of bright embers, where the heart of the fire has already passed. Nance can see the distant pillars of flame that are updrafts and pools of red in the convection of gullies. The emergency vehicles, their lights like small sparks against the greater. They've turned the water cannons roadside and over the timber in the port yards. There's a chopping sound in the air overhead, and she looks up in time to see a bucket dragging in the air on its cable beneath the helicopter.

"Jesus," Meredith says, claps a hand around Nance's arm. "That thing about scared the shit out of me."

"Me, too." It's Ned's voice.

Nance turns, and he is standing behind them. He's looking over their heads at the fire on the far hills. The sound of the chopper fades to a distant *whop whop whop*.

"Ned," she says, takes a steadying breath. "We wondered when you might be coming. . . ."

He doesn't look at her, but at Meredith. "Didn't realize we were going to have company." Nance steps into that space between her sister and himself. Taking sides. He thinks about his earlier plans to win her back to his side and bed. Before he'd seen the room. Before there were all these . . . obstacles to negotiate. He feels immensely heavy. Weary. Wonders if he's up to the task.

He steps back, gives them room. Manages to keep his voice steady. "Thought we might have a talk. Just you and me." He shakes his head. "But then, she *is* your sister. One of the family."

He turns away, starts toward the house. He stops midlawn, looks to where the sisters stand outlined against the edge of the hill. "You coming?"

Two houses over, a couple neighbors are sitting around a picnic table, watching the hills burn, and the sounds from there are like something from an untimely Fourth of July celebration, all *oohs* and *aahs*.

He waves to them. "What ya think, Dave? Pretty exciting, hey?"

The man waves back. "Oh cripes. But ain't it something. I wouldn't live on them hills for nothing. Could of told you this was gonna happen. But they don't listen. Most natural thing in the world," he shouts, "fire."

Ned nods vigorously. "Next to death and taxes."

"You betcha."

And then Ned's aiming for the back door.

Nance is still at the edge of the lawn, and Meredith's tugging at her arm, but Nance pulls away, and then she's following in Ned's footsteps across the damp grass. Feels a line of sweat above her lip. The smell of burning grass is thickly sweet. They stop at the back door. Nance can hear Ned moving about in the kitchen.

"Go home," she says.

"I'm not leaving you here with him."

"Listen." Nance grabs her sister's arm and shakes it hard. "Go home."

"No." Meredith leans in with a hard whisper. "We both go in, or we both leave."

Nance looks over her shoulder and then back at Meredith. There's the sound of a drawer closing. He's humming some jolly little tune, as if he's just come back from the market, or preparing a fun dinner for two. It strikes her as absurd—everything about this whole evening. The photos. The articles. She and her sister concocting some trashy tabloid tale. Finds herself questioning it all, as if it's just some sad mistake.

Nance feels a hand on the side of her face. It's Meredith pressing a loose coil of hair back behind Nance's ear. *Such a serious look.* Nance wants to reassure her sister, tell her it's all right. Everything's just hunky-dory. *Hunky-dory*—another of their father's expressions. She sees something of him in her sister, around her eyes. A quiet that suggests a weight that's never been let go. Some private grief, or a reserve of calm that in Meredith might just be strength. She nods. "I'm going to go in and talk to my husband. You want to come along, that's up to you." She pulls the door open and steps through. She stands the other side of the threshold, while Meredith looks back down the sidewalk to the street where the truck is parked.

"Keys are in the truck. Feel free to take it. But it's now or never, kiddo," Nance says, and turns away.

She climbs the short five steps up to the kitchen and sees Ned's seated at the counter. He's about to slip an apple slice into his mouth.

"Your sister leave?" he asks.

Nance nods, but then Meredith's standing at her back.

Ned's teeth snick down on the apple. He chews, swallows, waves a finger toward the counter. "Have a seat. A little cheese. Some crackers." He's pouring himself a glass of wine.

Meredith settles herself onto a stool at the near end of the counter. "We found your pictures," she says.

Ned's eyebrows wing upward. "Any of them you fancy in particular?"

The photos are still scattered about the counter. Nance wonders if any of them are actually family. She sees right away which two are missing, the ones she's always been most drawn to. Clearly, the only photos he considers worth keeping—the others so obviously discardable. *Isn't that peculiar? That you'd sense the real him without, it turns out, even knowing him.*

She points at his shirt pocket, says, "Those."

He looks down, acts surprised to see them there. He lifts the photos out, places them side by side: the young man in the car; the toddler astride the pony, the young woman at his side. The woman's holding on, as if he might bolt. He holds the photo of his father to his face. "Any resemblance?" he asks. He sets it down and picks up the other photo. Studies it. When he looks up again, a quirky smile has shaped his lips, but his eyes are disconnected from the amusement. "Wouldn't you know it? The pony had lice. My goddamn luck. Always my luck. I crawled with them for days." He runs his fingers through his hair. "So she washed my head in gasoline—they did that back then, you know. Gasoline. It burned like hell, but she meant well. Fuck. She always meant well."

Nance pulls the envelope of newspaper clippings out of her jeans pocket. Draws out the one with the photo. "And this?" She lays the others down. "And these?"

He picks up the Lady of the Lake article. "I thought it was interesting. Creeps you out, doesn't it?"

"Just something of interest?" Meredith asks.

Ned nods. "Did you read it? It plumps them up, you know. The fat gets denser. According to the article." Ned flicks her an impatient look; then he pushes the article away. He looks over at Nance. "What do *you* think? That I'm some kind of monster?"

Nance feels as if she needs to sit down. Locks her knees against the impulse to fold. She picks out one of the articles about a missing person, pushes it over to him.

He scans the article, as if reading it for the first time. Shrugs. He looks up, then glances over her shoulder to the far end of the kitchen, where the refrigerator has kicked in with a drone. His hands move to his face, a familiar gesture, the fingers rubbing down the side of his face as if scratching an itch. The cheeks and lips beneath his fingers as malleable as clay.

And the truth. It hits her. *Just as malleable?*

"This is embarrassing," he says, and flashes a shy smile. "She was married to this guy. Neil. Not a nice man. You wouldn't have liked him." He leans back in the chair, stretches his hands overhead, and laces them behind his head. "We had an affair. I'm not so proud of it, all right? But it was a long time ago, and I was young." He brings his hands down. "I left, and shortly after I came across this. She disappeared." He settled his hands in his lap.

Nance sees it, the way his gaze breaks, the way his focus flickers, darts like a minnow in shallow water. "And these others?" she asks, knowing she shouldn't. *Don't rattle him.* She keeps her eyes on his, watches as he reaches for an answer that will make sense, that will provide an out. *Has he always been so transparent?* Has she been that dense? Or is it something more complex than either of those. The obligation of trust, with a measure of willful ignorance. For it seems clear to her now—all those times she's questioned him and turned it on herself—that she was only too happy to suspend doubt, to bear the burden of blame rather than upset the tenuous balance they'd achieved.

Even as she wants to deny it, *this is a mistake*, she's coming to accept her own flawed perception. Now everything becomes suspect: the late-night errands, the meetings, the gifts and flowers. His distraction and their fights. Her heart's lubbing, and the kitchen's constricting about her.

"These others," she says, and looks up.

There's a blankness about his face, an unreadability that holds for a long breath, as if readying to shift into another thing altogether. She watches it with the same fascination of watching a snake molting—the tiny tears in the fabric of skin, signaling the change. She tries to recognize the man she's lived next to, worked alongside. Slept with. She's trying to understand how so small a shift of features could render him unrecognizable.

Like a snake in molt, and that startlingly blue scale that colors its eye. It comes to her that perhaps his face has been there all along, only now it's she who's shed the scales from her eyes, and out of the blur resolves the deeper reality. The real face beneath.

The thing her sister has sensed all along.

Meredith leans across the counter. "We're waiting."

His face shifts from confusion to anger and then to despair, in a moment so fleeting and brutal that it has Nance wanting to provide some excuse that's plausible, to fix what's come undone.

"Nance," he says. He's got that wide-eyed lost-boy look about the eyes. For a moment, she sees the child he was. The one in the photograph—on a pony—the way he clutches the saddle horn, a tenuous smile breaking across his face even as the lice are secreting their way up his legs and into his clothes to nestle in the dark. She thinks of the mother in the photo, how curiously emptied she looks.

"You can't believe . . ." he says.

You can't believe. What she sees—this reasonable house with its leaky windows and old furnace. This neat man with his orderly wardrobe, his penchant for ice cream late at night. Her husband. Her reasonable, good life. She thinks about the articles, the missing women, and the full implication of those bits of paper hits her. She finds herself looking at his hands. Thinks of the soft pad of his palm, the square shape of his hands, the strength of his fingers. She veers away from this: the memory of those hands on her, the possibility of his hands on these others. She looks at the countertop. All those missing women. Scraps of papers. The aging photos of strangers.

Meredith stands. She sets her hands on the counter. "Well, I *know* who you are, you sorry son of a bitch."

"*You?* You don't know shit," he says. "You don't know fuck about me or what we have, me and Nance."

Nance snaps her head up. Wonders what it is he thinks they have that's any more real than these photos. "Lies," she says. She shakes her head. "All lies."

Ned's sinking his head into his hands, and he turns a bewildered face toward her. "Nance. Nance," he says, his voice breaking.

She feels the world shifting yet again, so that Ned is who he has always been. Tender. A man close to his emotions. And there it is, the warm, open face of her husband, a vulnerability in his eyes, and she can sense the fear that's alive behind them. She feels pushed to pity.

But Meredith will not be moved. She steps forward. "Goddamn but you're good," she says. "How many times has it worked for you." She moves her face closer. "How many women?"

He shakes his head. Looks over at Nance. "You don't think—"

But she does. For she sees something. Some chink in his face. A smile. Some inkling of . . . what? Pride.

In his accomplishments.

She rocks back. Feels the blood draining from her head, her limbs going thin. She moves back from the counter. Tries to speak. Tries again, says, "I'm calling the police."

She's stepping back when it happens. His hand latches on, swings her around, and leverages her over the counter. Her breath is expelled in a gust of air that scuttles the articles to one side. And then he's hauling her upright, and there's a calm about his face that belies the jerk he exacts on her arm, yanking it tight against her upper back. With his free hand, he grabs her by the hair.

She sees Meredith launching herself at him, throwing punches at his head. She hits him hard in the ear, and his grip loosens and Nance staggers free. Then he's got Meredith by the upper arm, and with his free hand, he palms the back of her head and shoves it against the counter, so that her face bounds off the surface. Meredith's face goes ashen, and her knees give out, and she's slumped, with her arm slung loosely from his hand.

Nance sees her sister slide to the floor. Sees the grip he still has on her, the fist he's raising over her sister's head, and then she's running at him, aiming for him, this new man in the skin of her husband, this new face she would not recognize but for that brief glimpse in the dark of her own bedroom. And then she's throwing herself into his side, hits him, and he's falling back against the chair.

Nance nearly hits the floor herself, landing hard on one knee before jumping up and running for the front door. She understands she has to take this into the open. She can hear the chair scraping, and then he's pounding down the hallway after her. She bolts out the front door, takes the steps two at a time, but he catches up at the sidewalk, snatches her shirt and hauls back on it, so that she's nearly tipped off her feet and choking.

Still, she has the presence to scream. And again. He's trying to clamp a hand over her mouth, shouting, "Shut up. What's the matter with you?" She's dangling by the back of the collar like a shamed child. His other hand is reaching for her arm, but she counterbalances. Twists free.

She hits the pavement at a run. Dashes around to the far side of the pickup, placing the truck bed between them. She reaches into the bed, and as he's cutting around the truck, she lifts the snake hook in both hands and swings hard. It hits his head with a solid *thwack*, the shock of the blow traveling up her arm. There's a stunned look to his face, and a black whip line of blood on his cheek, and then blood's flowing, pasty in his hair. His ear is strangely tilted. His hand rises, pushes at his hair. He's staring at his hand, at the blood black in the streetlight.

She double-grips the hook, wishing it had more heft. She backs toward the truck cab. *A blow to the temple.* And for a moment, it's Joe she sees, the side of his face concave—from where the kid hit him. She's breathing hard, tries to speak, though it feels as if something's lodged in there, and even if she could speak, she's not sure what it is she would say. Or scream? For all the good it would do? She feels her stomach rising, and swallows hard against it. She glances up the block with its long rows of houses, but it's dark and empty. Everyone gone? Watching the fire burn down the hills?

"Nance," he says, stepping forward.

Nance balances on the balls of her feet. *Careful.* She watches his body, because this she knows from field work: They always telegraph the strike.

His hands are turned up in a gesture of peace just before he shifts onto his nearer foot, swinging his weight in her direction. She meets his arm with the snake hook, midair, feels the rap of metal on bone, and then he's cursing and folding the arm against his belly.

He backs off. Another step. Nance keeps the hook raised in both hands. She sees the way he looks up at the house, remembers Meredith's still in there. Has a sudden recollection of Meredith, shovel held in front of her. Nance reaches into the truck bed with one hand, feels about, and finds the sturdy handle. She lifts the spade out, drops the snake hook behind her, and follows his retreat, the spade handle at an angle across her body.

He's wiping blood from his brow with the sleeve of his good arm. He backs up and finds himself blocked by his car. He leans against the hood. He shifts his weight, and his head ducks, and he winces. The arm radiates pain up into his shoulder and neck. He's feeling queasy. Nance is a short five feet away, the shovel held like a baton in both hands. He wonders if she's as adept with it as with the hook. He feels—what? Anger. Annoyance. All of this and pride, as well—she is his wife, after all.

"Isn't this a strange pass," he says; his tone is almost conversational. He takes a deep breath and steadies himself against the car. The house is quiet, and from outside appearances, with its solid brick edifice and lights bright in the windows, it's just another ordinary night. He's still not quite sure how he's come to this, bleeding on the hood of his car, his wife facing him off with a shovel. He wishes he could start over, play it out to some other ending. Walk up the front steps, pass through his living room and by his favorite lounge chair, check the mail on the side table. He and Nance would sit down to a meal. Go to bed early, with the next day's school plans already in mind. *School*. What will they do without me, he wonders. His children.

Her arms must be beginning to tire. He wants to tell her to put it down.

"This is ridiculous," he says. He laughs softly. "What do you think"—he nods toward the shovel—"that you're going to do me in with one stroke and bury me with the next? Damn this hurts." He lifts his arm with his other hand.

She catches herself almost apologizing. Takes a steadying breath. "I'm sure it does."

He nods. "Like a son of a bitch. Think maybe we should see about your sister? She might have hurt her head."

"No. *You* hurt her." She steadies the shovel. "And who else, Ned? Who else have you hurt?" She feels the knot rising in her throat, her voice a whisper. "My God, Ned, what have you *done*?"

He stares back at her. There's a flinch in the muscles around her eyes, a long intake of breath, a catch in his throat, and then he's blinking hard, struggling to compose himself. He lowers his face, looks at the arm held stiffly against his chest, says, "I don't know what you're thinking. Or why." He wants to wet his lips, but his tongue has gone thick and dry. "I've never hurt you."

"You make it sound as if I'm the exception," she says.

The street is still silent. Then from somewhere up in Turnbull's yard, a single cat sounds a low, pitchy cry, though there's no answer. Only the wind stirring in the trees.

"Tell you what," he says, flexing his hand. The worst of the pain is passing. Though he's badly bruised, bone-bruised for certain. He holds the arm against his chest. "I could use some help here. What say we get Meredith, and you drive us to the emergency room."

She can't believe she's hearing this, that he would even suggest it. "You're mad," she says.

He cocks his head to a side. "We've had a domestic dispute. Happens all the time. Hell, your sister's an old hand at this. Nance, Nance, Nance. This is me. Ned."

"Maybe," she says. "Maybe you are Ned." Nance backs up a step. "Or maybe that's a lie, too."

"Then what?" he asks. "What is it you're imagining? That I'm a rapist? A murderer? For God's sake, Nance, you're a mature, intelligent woman. Do you really think you could be married all this time to someone like that and not know?"

Nance shifts her hold on the shovel. Her arms ache, and the lock on her knees is feeling shaky. She looks at the man sitting against the hood of his car. A stranger who's dropped by for a chat. A button-down man with the crease still in his pants. Everything so normal that the shovel in her hands feels like a mistake, or a terrible dream. Her arms begin to tremble. She wishes some person, any one of a dozen neighbors, would come out on his front porch. Wonders if Dave and company are still oohing and aahing in the backyard. Would they hear her if she called for help? She imagines trying that, then thinks better of it. Doesn't want Ned to know how frightened she is, or to upset the odd standoff: his belief that he can win her over, her belief she can hold out long enough.

There's a movement up at the house, on the porch, and with a glance, Nance sees it is Meredith, with one hand on the porch rail—not steady yet, but there.

Meredith's at the head of the steps. "I've called the police. They're on their way."

Ned looks over at Nance and shakes his head. "Your sister makes a poor liar." He speaks louder so they both can hear. "There isn't a cop free in five miles. Not with that fire."

Meredith steps down to the lowest stair. "I told the dispatcher you had a gun," she says. "I told them you were outside threatening your wife with a gun. They'll be here."

He looks over the roof, shakes his head. "You were trouble," he says, "from the get-go." He looks up at Nance. "Didn't I tell you that? Didn't I warn you?" He slides off the hood and, reaching into his pocket, pulls out his car keys. He walks to the car door, opens it.

Nance understands he means to leave, and she steps forward. "You can't leave."

He looks up at her, surprised. He laughs.

She raises the shovel higher, takes a step closer. "I can't let you"—she shakes her head—"*loose* out there."

He settles into the car.

Nance steps in closer, brings the shovel up, swings it down onto the car, and the steel lands with a percussive *whang* as a headlight shatters. "I mean it, Ned."

She can see he's angry, half up and out of the car, as if he's intent on coming after her.

"Goddamn it," he says, "you can't just let it be. You got to push. *You just fucking got to push.*"

She moves to the far side and swings the shovel again, hard, and it skitters up over the hood, glances off the windshield.

Meredith's on the sidewalk now, yelling for help.

Across the street, a curtain's drawn to a side, and Lenore's head is silhouetted against the light. Ned pauses, halfway out of his car, then settles back in the seat, slams the door shut, and starts the engine. He cranks the wheel and guns from the curb even as the shovel is slamming against the front passenger window, shattering glass across the seat and his lap. Nance is yelling, but he can't make it out. He is leaving. Moving on. His hands wring the wheel and he turns down Eighth Street, past the small college. Time enough to examine what went wrong. All he needs is a bit of time. A new place—always one out there.

He thinks about driving by his school for one last look. His staff. The steady Cate. She'll miss him. His teachers: Pete Otto—second grade, excellent; Luke Baldwin, *the* man to keep eighth graders humble, might even make a decent principal himself one day. Ambitious, that one. He thinks of Suzy Long, sixth-grade teacher, whose quirky wit keeps lunch in the teacher's lounge bearable. And kindergarten—Wendy Cochrane, trying to balance teaching and a new baby. His people. He's hit with a wave of feeling—something akin to love and nostalgia, but he understands that, just like family photos, they are replaceable.

He turns down the short grade toward the river. The memorial bridge and traffic east out of the valley toward Missoula will be blocked with emergency vehicles. Maybe he'll go left, heading up Tammany Creek, and out to Lapwai, up the Winchester Grade to Grangeville, Riggins, McCall, Boise. Points south.

Or more to his taste, west through Clarkston and Pomeroy, Dayton, Walla Walla. Western Washington, the wet side. Seattle. Tacoma. Olympia, down through Oregon: Portland, Eugene. Or California. He's never tried California. Can't believe he's never tried California. Not the coast. Doesn't crave the standard fare of tourists. Nope. He'll try something different. Fresno maybe. Chico. Some place buried on the backside of the mountains.

He's at the bottom of Eleventh Avenue. The Snake River levee is across the street, and next to that are the grain towers of the Lewiston Grain Growers, the steel siding reflecting a furious pink against dark sky. It's semidusk in the valley, though, no pearly light here. Instead, it's a crimson glow. Across the river, on the glazed windows of shops and homes, is reflected fire, as if up and down the canyon and staggered in tiers above the river all the little homes have been kindled in a sympathetic torching, their aluminum sides glowing in shades of runny pink or a damp, sooty gray. Even the river below is capped with reflected flame. His eyes tear, but it's only the sweet grass smoke that drifts in through the shattered passenger window.

It's so goddamned inspiring. And all it took was a bolt from heaven and conflagration to make this place interesting. He laughs.

Next time, it'll go better. You learn from mistakes. Headlights are coming down the short grade behind him. He puts on his blinkers. Right. Then a left. Through Clarkston. Through Pomeroy and west, through Othello, Vantage, and the Yakima Valley, or maybe swing down through the Columbia River Gorge. Big country. Big enough to lose a multitude of Neds. He signals his turns. Tells himself he shouldn't feel bad; he's done a lot of things right this time. He didn't hurt Nance. Not really. And he's mostly kept it at a distance: *You don't shit in your own nest.*

He feels strong. Tells himself he's free in a way he hasn't been in years. This is always the best of it, when he's on the edge of something new, on the verge of becoming. Like reincarnation, but without the awkwardness of dying.

He drives the Snake River road, loops left and back onto the bridge, where traffic slows to a crawl. As with all emergencies, there's the usual flock of sightseers. The carloads driving up onto the heights for a clearer vantage of the fire, a made-to-order evening for bored teens. The sky is streaked with reds and orange, traces of blue, and here and there chutes of yellow rise in columns, spinning like the dust devils of summer. Smoke billows off the hills, a molten look about it, like embers seen through a cap of ash.

The vehicles are moving forward, and Ned crosses the bridge and keeps straight on through town, past the drive-in where he and Nance of a summer evening would go for shakes. He's heading downriver, west on Highway 12.

The canyon's hazy, darker here, the fire a backdrop illuminating the crest of the hills. He can catch glimpses of it from the side-view mirror. He's following the river, though at this point, it's a wide basin of slack water from Granite Dam. Across the river and above the port of Wilma's lights is where the fire company managed to hold the fire line, just above the road. Hard to believe that only hours before, he'd been driving that side of the river. *Was it really that recent?* Now the hillside is blacker than the river and he can smell the scorched earth, the smell of water and ash, a bitter stink that will last long after the burn.

He's traveling up the narrow canyon, the road straight in this stretch. Buoys mark the deep channel in the river. Along the roadside, the guardrails clip by, the metal rails looking strangely elastic where trucks have pressed too close. The car cuts a trim course through the turns, Ned's attention on the center line. On the near side is river, black, a glassy obsidian. In his rearview mirror, he sees the small stream of traffic behind, and beyond that the glow that is the burning hills. A fine exit line, he thinks. He's humming as he checks his speed. A modest sixty. *Wouldn't do to be caught speeding.* He glances into the mirror, aims it higher to see the fire breach the hilltop. He shifts in his seat, and when he looks at the road ahead, it is to see the headlights, two pair, side by side. For a moment, he's uncertain what it means. And then he understands: The headlights in his lane are truck lights, bearing down on him, and the lights will not swerve. Too late for the oncoming vehicle to do anything other than race toward some other, more hopeful conclusion. It's a squeeze play, for he sees now the two semis piggybacking next to the pickup and the rock wall next to the semis.

Ned's hitting his brakes, steering in the only direction left him, and hoping that tensile band of guardrail will be enough to keep him from the drop into the black. This deep stretch of river. He sees the pickup slewing to a side in front of him, the smoke of brakes and rubber, correcting, overcorrecting, the vehicle teetering a moment on two wheels. He sees the two tires folding into the concrete, the puffs of air as they blow. He sees the teens bunched like cordwood in the pickup cab, come to town, no doubt, to gawk at the hills on fire. In the white of his headlights, there is a pasty look about them, and a dawning comprehension of the incomprehensible. These young boys at the end of a long cruise, in a rattletrap Chevy painted with a dull primer, and an out-of-place white quarter panel on the near side that wavers as the truck threatens to pitch and hangs a moment in the air, almost settling back, the headlights falling full onto Ned just before it flips on its side. And the boys' hands rising up against the truck ceiling like a chorus of alleluias, and then there's the undercarriage, the slow revolution back over its wheels, though Ned sees little enough of this, just a glimpse of face, and hands and arms and the exhaust and a blown wheel, for he's distracted by the guard post that jumps up at his right, and the impact of the air bag that pins him against the seat, and the seat already breaking loose of the frame beneath him in a web of glass, then the bag slumping, and the scream of metal as the guardrail rubber-bands around his vehicle. He feels the car riding the air, aiming for the far shore, down the precipitous drop to that black slab of water that ratchets his teeth loose in his head and drives his belly down into his pelvis. He's rocked on the river's surface, the car tipping forward and back, and his hands are searching for the seat belt even as the river's rising up the fractured windshield and pouring in through the shattered passenger window with a surprising noise. How quickly it rises over his limbs, his torso, and, even more surprising, how it makes his mind brilliantly clear, the cold, so that he understands this might be simply another means of transformation, the past in ashes and himself cleansed in the river.

He has merely to survive it.

How curiously good it feels, and there's the sound of the river bubbling up out of hidden pockets from the interior of the car, and all the secret bits floating up, pencils and grocery receipts, a book of matches, a baseball cap, an empty soda can, a tennis shoe he does not recognize. About his head and neck, warm gulps of air are floating up from his clothes. Then, at long last, there's the slow fall through the black that the sole remaining headlight won't pierce. And he feels himself rising, hands pressed against the ceiling, his legs kicking, floating weightless in the confines, feeling the draught of the current, even as the car drifts down and down, like a leaf through the dense atmosphere, into the turbulent black, the small pieces, the odds and ends, the leftovers spilling out and upward, a twist of steel, glass, fabric, this and that, a bit of business to lodge in the clay, to bobble in the endless hydraulics, to drift down the patient current to where the river opens on a horizon of blue on blue, to a place where it's difficult to say where the water ends and the stars begin.

Chapter Thirteen

It's late, and Nance is packing the last of the household. She's sold the house. For a person alone, it's just too big. She's found a smaller place up in the Orchards, where her new neighbors keep a peck of chickens, and a Shetland pony that strips their fruit trees. She's surprised by how quickly her house has sold. Turnbull's has been vacant this whole time. Seems likely to remain so.

Pete and Meredith are across the kitchen from her. Meredith's wrapping glassware, while Pete settles them into thick-bodied cardboard boxes. Between odd bits of conversation, there's a companionable silence among the three of them. Nance is pleased to see Meredith so clearly happy, figures they will get married sooner or later, for when Nance hints at such, Meredith's not as quick to deny the possibility.

Nance yawns. She's had little enough sleep these last few nights, and truthfully, it's only been the last month or so when she's been able to sleep the entire night without being chased from sleep by dreams. Or, worse yet, roused for no understandable reason other than her pounding heart. But overall, in the five months since Ned's death, her life, if not content, is gaining normalcy again. For the most part. She has her work—in another month, she'll be traveling back upriver to the den for the counts. She has her sister.

She has the sympathy of the community. Sometimes she has trouble with that—a lack of patience with their kindness, a reaction that's clearly got most of them befuddled. "Such a loss," they said. Any number of people ready to stop her on the street or in the checkout at the grocery store to tell her how much Ned meant to them. The good administrator. The good principal—what care he took of their children. And even here, on the block, how they came to her and told her what a fine man he was—stories about fixing a flat or lending a hand when the kids moved out. Even old Leona from across the street: "I liked him better than some others hereabouts. It's gotta be hard on you. Not getting to put him to final rest."

For there was no body. The police, rescue crews, and divers located the car two days afterward, but the river was deep and fearsome, and the current had already done its work. "Does he swim? Your husband?"

She had to tell them he'd never claimed to be a strong swimmer. They kept doing the downriver checks for a while, but eventually those ended. There was, of course, always hope his body would surface, so that he might be laid to rest. But that could be years down the road, they'd said. What they did not say was that it could as likely be never.

Nance has learned to live with that. With that idea and the packet of photos, the small envelope of articles. When her sister mentioned them to the police, they'd looked at them, but with little interest. Just one man's peculiarity. When they left, they left the photos and articles, as well.

Nance is cross-legged on the kitchen floor, in stocking feet, rummaging in the junk drawer, going through the odd bits of paper, bundling pens and pencils, a couple of six-foot extension cords. She tosses out a handful of erasers that have gone to hard nubs. She finds herself looking at receipts, certificates of warrantee, trying to place them. It's not exactly as if she's suspicious. Though she's taken an inordinately long job of packing. Thorough beyond reason—no scooping things into boxes for her—an orderly picking through this and that. Room by room. A tedious scrutiny that she feels necessary.

"Collecting evidence," her sister says, and "You're getting morbid. Get rid of it. He's gone."

But that's not entirely true. There are the dreams. The hairs she finds in the bathroom sink. The smell of his cologne like an afterthought on her own clothes. His favorite foods in the pantry that she can't bring herself to swallow. She knows he'll be there until she finds a way to move beyond her own doubts.

What if . . . just what if they were wrong?

It's a thought she can't shake, can't dispose of, any more than she can the other possibility, with its packet of photos and articles already packed among her clothing.

And if they weren't wrong . . . She thinks of the missing women. Their families. The man beaten near to death. *What does she do with that?* What does she owe them? What explanations?

She's come to understand it's a two-edged thing—damned if you know; damned if you don't. But of the two options, yes, she'd rather know.

So she's struggling through, feeling in suit pockets and in the toes of shoes, sorting through the hundred odd notes in his school office, through computer files and E-mails. What's remarkable, finally, is how little there is to find that is definably him. Two pictures. The rest of it— the clothing, the things from his office, the awards and certificates—stuff of Internet diploma mills—as anonymous as the family photos.

She looks across the kitchen to where Pete's holding Ramone in hand. Ramone—complete with transplanted rattles—another mystery. She found him a month after Ned's death, the rattle torn off, cotton wadding trailing out the end. She took Ramone back to where she'd purchased him, to the taxidermist, who, appalled by the damage, made it apparent he was disappointed in her.

Pete's steering Ramone to Meredith's cheek with kissing noises. Nance smiles. Who'd have thought it of the weathered river man? This tender side. It gives her hope. For Meredith.

Nance believes she's done with love. She probably should have quit while she was ahead, having had Joe. If even for so short a time.

There's a kink working its way into her back. She looks at the emptied drawer. Interlocks the cardboard flaps on the top of the box and labels it with a thick, stinky black marker. She presses a hand into her back and then eases to her feet and stretches. She walks into the central hallway, from where she can see the emptied living room. Surprising how much larger the room looks without the sofa, the wing-back chair and ottoman. The TV and stereo. The bookcase. Most of the household's already been moved—those items that will fit the smaller square footage. What won't fit, or as in the case of the dressers she's never liked, or Ned's old lounger, has been sold or given to Goodwill. She'd offered some things to Meredith, but her sister declined, claimed she was already a furniture baron what with the stuff arriving from the family home they'd sold in Wisconsin.

Nance wishes she had it in her to do a clean sweep. Get rid of it all with one great lovely purge. But she won't. It's not in her practical nature, after all.

She crosses back into the kitchen, slips her shoes on. She walks past Meredith, who's settling Ramone into a box Pete has constructed out of two smaller ones.

"You okay, Sis?" Meredith asks.

Nance nods. "Fine. Just need a bit of fresh air."

"We're about done here. Want me to join you?"

Nance smiles, waves her off. "I'm okay. Quit worrying." But she can see it's done Meredith good to be placed on the other side of the sisterly equation: taking care of her older sister. Being there for her. Trusted. And Nance has to admit it's been a good thing for her, as well. Truthfully, she doesn't know what she would have done without Meredith's help arranging the memorial service. Or the everyday matters, cooking, cleaning. Staying evenings until Nance learned again how to sleep.

Isn't that the saving grace? To find again, after all these years, a sister. To discover she is liberated as well from the innumerable grudges she held against Meredith. It feels as if her breath is finally unconstricted. Sees it now for what it was—her own little hoard of bile, which was, in its own way, a satisfying means to punish someone for Joe's death. Someone besides herself. Curious, how it took this . . . this business of Ned, with his secrets, his private life, for Nance to come to an understanding of herself.

When she finally told Meredith about her grudge over Joe, it was the evening of Ned's memorial service, late at night, over a cup of tea in the kitchen, done quietly and without wounding Meredith, for Nance could tell it as it was. "I blamed you. As I blamed myself, for a thing over which neither of us had any control. No real part in. It *is*," Nance had said, "it simply *is*." She sees that for all the complexities we believe we understand, there are those that arise from a deeper well of possibilities: complexities we will never fully comprehend. Some essential mystery that in our half sight is both hope and despair. The horrific and miraculous.

Outside, the night is thick with the smell of damp soil. There's a tender bite of green just beneath. In another few weeks, the first daffodils will rear their lion heads in the March winds. She moves to the far end of the lawn, to the point overlooking the valley and the constellation of streetlights below. The swath of black that is the Clearwater River. The broader place in the dark that is the Snake. She stares at that belt of river a long while, that place where the cliffs rise highest and the river narrows into a deep keep. She thinks of the vehicle still down there, the water-filled husk. *You'd never know it.* For there's no hint that there's anything down there, certainly nothing extraordinary. Nothing to differentiate the presence of a car from the hulk of boulders, the waterlogged timbers. Nothing to indicate this new piece of the river bottom. Save a riffle, perhaps, rising up out of the depths, its responding ripples in the wider current.

Who would know? A river captain like Pete? Someone so finely attuned to the river, so in step with its pace as to notice this new hitch in its stride. Astute enough to see this dimple forged on the surface, and read of it the unseen complications of the deep. She stares long and hard at that distant place, as if it might come clearer—the canyon narrows that her eyes can barely make out, and the river, a thin silver line. A bead of light forever slipping between the hills.